THE
VERY REAL WORLD OF
EMILY ADAMS

SAMANTHA J ROSE

Immortal Works LLC
1505 Glenrose Drive
Salt Lake City, Utah 84104
Tel: (385) 202-0116

Cover Art by Paul Rose Cover Design

ISBN 978-1-7349046-2-8 (Paperback)
ASIN B088GPTC4K (Kindle Edition)

For the One who rushed to my rescue.

VOLUME 1

"YOU NEED THE DARK IN ORDER TO SHOW THE LIGHT." ~BOB ROSS

TRACK 1

THE BEGINNING IS THE END IS THE BEGINNING

I will never forget the first moment I met him. How could I? It was my darkest hour.

It was the night of the meteor shower, an event so extraordinary that it had been everywhere on the news—something about the meteors coming from out of nowhere, how there was no pattern to their existence, no known colliding orbit with the Earth, and how they left long tails of brilliant, bright light as they fell from the sky. It was a night of romantic proposals, and a crazy guy saying the end of the world was near.

Normally, I would have set up a chair in my backyard, surrounded by the fields of my small hometown, and watched the shower with an enthusiastic curiosity and naïve sense of wonder. Instead, I'd spent the evening dragging myself through the gloom of dimly lit city streets, far from home, where no one could even see the stupid stars for the streetlights and rainclouds.

I breathed in the smell of rain-soaked pavement and exhaust as I darted between buildings, cradling a broken arm. It was numb now, but only a few hours earlier it had burned like the bone had been set on fire.

Echoes of the scene resonated through me: the feeling of helplessness, losing all control of my body as it flew backward when my now-*officially*-ex-boyfriend shoved me. The feeling of weightlessness as I fell. The resounding crack when I tried to catch my fall. Lights had popped and fizzled in my vision as I tumbled down the stairs. My stomach had twisted with nausea and I couldn't breathe for the pain. Reliving it in my mind, my stomach lurched all over again, still unsettled, still threatening to climb up and out of my throat.

I looked down at the wet pavement, my hair sticking to the sides of my head in the rain as I watched the drops break against the ground. I could still see his face. I'd looked up at him from the bottom of the stairs and he had just stood there, his pale eyes looking but not seeing, his mouth half open. He had remained frozen like that long enough for me to pull myself together and run.

And I was still running, but it was without any direction. I had no destination. I was a confused and wounded mouse whose only thought was of escaping the monstrous cat who'd tormented me. I was scared to stop. I turned at every red light just so I could keep moving. If I stopped, he might find me. If I stopped, he'd dig his cruel claws deep into my soul and I'd have to go back. I could *never* go back.

But I couldn't return to my hometown, either, though I visited it in my mind. I could see it, cradled in the arms of the mighty mountains, where I could bust out a lawn chair at a whim and gaze in awe at the vast canopy of stars. The place was a broken memory, resting in jagged shards that I cut my heart on every time I thought about it. Tears burned my eyes as the beating of my heart grew heavy, as though it were bleeding and couldn't stop. That was when I'd usually try to think about something else, but not this time. I continued to cut myself against the memories, because all I wanted was to go *home*.

I wanted to see my dad again, to hear him play the piano and sing. I wanted him to tell me some crazy tale that couldn't possibly have happened then hear him end it with, "True story." I wanted to hear his advice, and I wanted to listen to it this time. How I wished I could go back and say, "You're right, Dad. That guy is *not* good for me."

But I couldn't go home. Not after what I'd done. I had no family. I had no friends. I had nothing but the shoes on my aching feet and the wet clothes clinging to my body. I was an outcast, one with the shadows. A stain on the pavement.

A stain on the pavement.

I'd lingered too long on the memories. A hole had opened up in my heart, black and dead, and my soul was being pulled in. The good memories were consumed by the horrors that had shattered them until the guilt, the shame, the helplessness and darkness were all that remained. I trembled, but not from the cold. I could feel the shadows dancing just under my skin. It hurt so much. I couldn't bear it. I couldn't.

Desperate to feel something else, I dug my fingers into the elbow of my broken arm and fresh pain shot through me—pain that hurt less than the hollowness that was growing inside me. My breathing came in ragged gasps like I was drowning. I stumbled into walls and people. People who pulled their coats up over their heads and turned away. I winced as I bumped into a tall woman, my fingers brushing against the back of her hand as she rose from adjusting her boot. She had a very deep, manly voice and asked if I needed help. Without really looking at her, I smiled and said I was fine. She moved on. They all moved on, which was for the best, really. This... me... what I had become... I was beyond repair.

No one could help me.

I let out a hopeless sob. How was I supposed to keep going? How was I supposed to keep carrying this? *How?*

I muttered under my breath, "A stain on the pavement... a stain on the pavement..."

For the first time in hours, I stopped. I listened to the rain spattering against the sidewalk and the laughter of a couple as they passed by, the sounds vivid to me in that moment. My thoughts drifted after them. I imagined the warmth of the home they must be going to, the smiles of the loved ones that probably waited for them there. I'd wanted to be them once. Still did. I longed for that kind of love. The real deal. To share a life with someone who actually loved me and have a family. To hold a child in my arms. My heart writhed in agony as I watched them walk away, as though I were a homeless kid with her nose pressed against the glass of a bakery window at Christmastime, peering at something I could see so clearly but had no hope of ever having.

A thought crept into my mind, and not for the first time that day. But this time, its presence seeped into the dark, lonely crevices like tendrils of fog, filling them with an eerie sense of comfort and peace.

I didn't have to keep going.

I didn't have to keep carrying the pain.

I'd been thinking about it for years. I'd researched the best ways to do it. And over the last few months, it had been the only thing to bring me any sense of peace—a calm in the eye of the storm. My breathing steadied, the whirlwind inside of me settled and faded. The shadows under my skin grew still, soothing and enveloping me like a comforting blanket. For the first time, the feeling of peace didn't go away. It was such a relief to the agony I felt that instead of shoving it aside, I clung to it.

I knew exactly what I needed to do. I'd known for months, maybe even years, but now, I was *ready*.

As I made the decision, the weight of my world lifted from my shoulders. I even laughed a little. I was done! I didn't have to do this anymore. No more worries about what I was going to do about my arm with no money or insurance to fix it. I didn't have to worry about that *guy* finding me, or about food or a place to live or about my broken soul and the black, rotting hole inside of it.

I was *done*.

I no longer walked aimlessly. Instead, my eyes searched for the right building. Just a little ways down the street to my right, a man hurried into an old apartment complex, his coat over his head, eager to get out of the rain. It was about ten stories or so, an appropriate height. It must've been undergoing renovations, as there was construction equipment parked nearby and scaffolding wrapped around one side. I darted toward the door as it closed and caught it with my shoe. I tried to pry the door the rest of the way open with my shoulder, but the stress of the movement shot fire through my arm again. Nausea swarmed, my vision spun and I thought I might faint until the guy who'd gone in before me doubled back and helped me with the door.

"Thanks," I managed to say without throwing up.

"Sure, no problem." He paused, his eyes widening a little as he noticed the shape I was in. I didn't look in the mirror much these days. It was always the same reflection—the gaunt specter of a twenty-three-year-old who'd been sealed in a tomb, alive. My green eyes were dull and sunken. My curly, blonde hair—which was now a wet, matted mess against my skull—was thin and broke like straw. My Deadpool T-shirt and jeans hung off my bones, being two sizes too big, though they hadn't started that way. He probably thought I was a banshee, coming to warn him of his imminent death.

"Hey, uh... you don't look—" he caught himself and changed his comment to a question, "Are you all right?"

I gave him a weak smile. "I just need to lay down."

I meandered down a hallway lined with peeling, peach wallpaper until I found the elevator. I stared at the worn arrow button and tried to press it with my mind, since my good arm was busy keeping the other one from dangling from my shoulder like a bag of rocks. When that didn't work, I mustered the courage to pry a finger away from my elbow and pushed it. The doors immediately opened. I stepped inside and pressed the button for the top floor, then leaned back against the wall as the doors closed, exhausted.

It was a long ride, listening to the elevator creak and groan like at any second a cable might snap. I inhaled the scent of a floral air freshener that tried in vain to mask the stench of moldy carpet and beer as the weight of my decision began to sink in, making my heart race. I instructed myself, *Make sure you dive head first.* My stomach fluttered.

I wasn't sure why I did it. Probably because my dad had been a preacher but even then, I'd felt sure that if there was a god, he'd given up on me long ago. Yet without really thinking, I cried silently from the depths of my soul out into the unknown, *Please... save me.*

A cheerful ding signaled the end of my ride and the doors rolled open.

I stood there for a moment, staring at the peach, oak-lined wall in front of me. As I willed myself to step through the elevator doors, they started to close, almost as if to try and stop me.

You can't stop me, I thought at the elevator as I darted out into the hall, the doors creaking back open as it sensed me pass through. I turned to it, stared it down, and said, "Give me one good reason why you think I shouldn't."

The doors rolled close.

I knew darn well the elevator never intended to say anything back, but still, my heart sank a little. "I thought so."

I wandered through the hallways, following signs that led to the stairs. Stumbling into the stairwell, which was lined with sheets of plastic that covered remnants of construction things, I saw the sign reading "Roof Access." The doorway appeared to have once been blocked for safety reasons but someone had broken through it, leaving the door unable to close properly. It felt like a sign. Everything had fallen into place. I took a deep breath to solidify my courage and as I did, peace returned with a sense of the rightness of what I was doing.

I pushed open the door to the roof with my shoulder and stepped out into the night. The rain had slowed till it had become a mere mist, though the sky remained as dark and starless as ever. I trudged over to the barrier of the roof and closed my eyes, drinking in the smell of rain. When I opened them again I saw that, far across the city, a nearly full moon was now peering out from beneath a fluffy blanket of clouds. I gazed down and wondered how I was going to climb up onto the barrier.

From the shadows behind me came a rich, deep voice, gentle yet all-encompassing, like thunder at the end of a storm, "Beautiful night tonight, isn't it?"

I whirled around, my long hair whipping me in the face. I winced as my arm throbbed with the sudden movement, buckling over as the agony consumed my body. My vision faded with stars and I was sure I was going to throw up. Anger and frustration rippled through the shadows under my skin.

He spoke again, his tone cheerful at first but growing concerned as I didn't move from my about-to-barf-everywhere position. "I'm sorry! I didn't mean to startle you, I, uh... are you okay? That's a stupid question, you're clearly *not* okay."

I tried to breathe, to steady myself and not faint into a puddle of vomit. I forced a polite smile without moving, saying in the strangled tone of someone who'd just been punched in the gut, "I'm fine."

"Oh! Well good," he said with upbeat sarcasm, "That's good. I'm glad we got that cleared up because for a moment there, I thought you might be in terrible pain. And then, of course, I'd want to do something about it, so, I'm relieved to get out of that. Of course, I *would* be happy to help, you know, if you needed help because you *were* in pain, but since you're not... but if you *were*..."

I didn't know what it was—maybe it was so he'd stop talking—but something about his words forced my surrender. Tears brimmed my eyes. "All right, I'm not." I sniffed, wishing I could wipe away all the snot and tears or even just brush away the strands of hair that were sticking to my face. "I'm not okay. But there's nothing anybody can do about it. Not unless you can work miracles. Maybe turn back time."

After a moment of silence, he said, "Well, unfortunately, I can't turn back time, but I have been told I am a miracle worker."

A small smile—one nearly nonexistent but genuine nonetheless, and the first in months that wasn't triggered by the thought of death—made its way to the corner of my lips. I willed my body to straighten itself enough for me to look up at him and, after a great deal of effort...

I still couldn't see him. My hair was plastered to my face and blocking my vision. I usually hid my ugly face behind my hair and should've felt relieved that he couldn't see me, but I was beyond caring now, and my curiosity outweighed my reservations. When jerking my head to the side didn't work, I tried blinking as a method of brushing it away, but it was only as effective as blinking-wet-hair-out-of-your-eyes could be. He had an accent. British, maybe? No... Portuguese? I didn't know what a Portuguese accent sounded like, but I thought his might be it. All I knew was that he sounded fancy, and I imagined him wearing a suit, making me uncomfortably aware of the shape I was in. But so far, the only evidence I could see to confirm my theory was that he appeared to be wearing a lot of black.

For all I knew, he could've been wearing a Snuggie.

He continued, "For example, right now, I am going to perform the miracle of restoring your sight."

My smile grew. "Oh, hallelujah!"

His shoes clicked against the pavement as he stepped toward me, his tone becoming that of a doctor about to perform surgery, "Now, this may feel a little bit awkward, since I'm just some strange *stranger* hanging out on a roof who actually hates touching people and being touched *by* people, and really, just, most people in general."

I smirked and nodded. "I get that."

"People are absolutely terrible, aren't they?"

He had no idea how true that statement was to me. "They really are."

"I'm glad we agree," he added thoughtfully. "I feel like we've developed a special bond over this and are strangers no more, but best friends."

"I think we need matching bracelets."

"Yes! We should go pick some out on Tuesday."

My smile grew a little more. "Sounds good."

"Perfect! Now, onto the miracle, then."

I closed my eyes, flinching a little as very calloused fingertips brushed across my forehead, pushing the strands of rain-soaked hair across my cheeks and eyelashes. It was only a moment, maybe two fleeting seconds before it passed, but in that mere flicker of time, a warm, soothing light spread throughout my body from his touch. And not "light" in a metaphorical sense, but in a very literal sense. There was no other way to describe it, it was *light,* warm and radiant, like basking in the sun on a summer morning. My shoulders relaxed, I hadn't realized how tense they were. My breathing steadied. My broken arm and heart grew pleasantly tingly and the pain in them diminished until I could hardly feel it. The heavy shadows were chased out of my skin and I stood upright, feeling lighter.

All in a mere two seconds.

His touch left, but in its place there was a little flame that had been ignited in my soul. A light that was all my own. It was barely a match-light in comparison to his sunlight—flickering, sputtering, and threatening to go out with a mild breeze—but it was there and alive, and certainly hadn't been before. I kept my eyes closed, basking in it. I let out a sigh, and the few lingering remnants of darkness drifted out of me into oblivion, replaced by something I'd forgotten. Something that hurt but in a good way, in the way wounds hurt as they heal. Something I hadn't felt in years.

It was hope.

Tears spilled down my cheeks, but they were a different kind this time. A kind that was welcome, that came from the small flame; a life inside of me that had been reignited with a single spark. And I realized, this... this was *real* peace.

I felt like I was waking up from a deep sleep. I didn't want to open my eyes. I was refreshed and happy and yet disoriented. I'd forgotten where I was. I was... on a roof? Why?

Then I remembered. The memories flooded back to me, but instead of drowning in them, they were held at a distance by this little light and the indescribable feeling of optimism that came with it. I was aware of my heart, broken but still beating; of the warmth of my pulse against the chill of the air, and of the mist of cool rain I breathed into my lungs. Traffic hummed below. Nothing else existed but this moment and in it, I was alive, and somehow, that now *meant* something. Somehow, that gave me room to hope. It was as though I had been seeing the world from deep under water and had been pulled from the murky depths and placed back on my feet where I could see it all more clearly, though I hadn't yet opened my eyes.

My mind raced. *But wait, only two seconds ago, I was... what just happened? None of this makes sense. It was just a moment, a touch. What did he do to me? And how... how did he do it?*

I was determined to ask him the second I opened my eyes—but I couldn't do it. What if this *feeling* was the dream? What if I opened my eyes or spoke and it all went away?

"There," he said. "Now, not only will you be able to see, but you also have a face!"

I laughed. Actually laughed, which made no sense. How was that possible? I could've sworn I'd forgotten how. Then, without thinking, I let go of my broken arm and quickly wiped my face with my sleeve, hoping the tears and snot had blended in with the rain. When I realized what I'd done, my eyes shot open and I looked up at him.

My jaw dropped.

He was, hands down, the most beautiful man I had ever seen. His bright blue eyes seemed to glow in the night against his dark skin like bottled lightning. The face they were set in was the commanding face of an angel, and not in a Nicholas Sparks novel way, but in a very literal sense that if I had pictured an angel—well, this man exceeded all of my expectations and was what I *should've* been picturing whenever I'd heard the word. It was as if each feature had been cut from stone and blended together so flawlessly that no piece was out of place, neither more prominent nor distinguishable above the rest.

And all of these features were expertly highlighted with eyeliner, black and silver eyeshadow, and dark red lipstick. A gorgeous mane of black curls framed his face, protected from the rain by a large, black umbrella. What I could see of his chest beneath his black cocktail dress and long black coat made it clear his body was that of a sculpted, muscular god. Though he wasn't feminine in the way he carried himself or in his physique, he wore that dress with an air of confidence that stated that not only was he perfectly comfortable wearing it, he knew he looked good in it.

I thought of the wrestler, Zangief, from "Wreck-It-Ralph" and how he could crush a man's skull between his thighs like an egg. This man could do the same, while wearing high heeled boots.

He furrowed his brow at me. "What?" He glanced down at himself. "Is there something on my dress?"

I picked up my jaw, feeling stupid and apologetic. "No, no, I just—"

He waved this away. "I'm just messing with you. I get that look all the time. When I'm *wearing* a dress, when I'm *not* wearing a dress. I'm in a band. Tonight was Ladies' Night at the club where we play and, as you can see, I take the responsibility very seriously. On '80s night, I wear a ruffled shirt and a suit jacket with blue sequins."

I busted up. "That sounds amazing. Do you do the big hair—?"

"Oh, absolutely. What is '80s night without big '80s hair?"

"I would love to see that. I bet you rock big hair and blue sequins, but probably not as well as you're rockin' that dress."

He tossed his hair back and posed with his hand on his hip. "You're right. That is simply impossible."

Laughing this time reminded me that, though my arm didn't hurt near as much anymore, it was still broken. I winced, cradling it again. I wanted to ask him how he'd taken so much of the pain away. I wanted to know if he was, in fact, an angel, and if the other members in his band enjoyed looking pretty. My mouth opened once or twice to make words, but my brain couldn't process any of it well enough to form them.

His expression grew concerned. "So, I can see that your arm is very broken, and I was wondering, what in the world are you doing on a roof when you so obviously belong in a hospital?"

I looked down at my beat-up Sketchers. "Well I... I can't go to a hospital because... I don't have..." I couldn't look at him. I couldn't say it. I didn't want charity and I didn't want to look like I was looking for charity. "I just can't go."

I could hear in his tone that he saw right through me. "I see." He pressed fingers to his lips thoughtfully. "Well, if you'd like, I am sort of a doctor. Not really, but sort of."

I raised an eyebrow. "Sort of, huh?"

"It's a long story—sure to bore you to tears. But the point is, I can help you, if you'll let me." His eyes brightened. "I know you have no reason to trust me. I'm just some stranger on a roof, but I won't be at peace until I know that I have done all I can to help you."

I shook my head, my heart pounding as I tried to wrap my mind around everything that was happening. I couldn't help but hope he was telling the truth, and I was terrified I'd see that hope shattered. I'd been let down so many times, if I was let down again, I knew I wouldn't survive it. "I don't want charity—"

He gave a small shrug. "Nah, this isn't charity. This is just a friend helping a friend. That's what friends are for, isn't it?"

My breath caught on a sob, those stupid tears returning to me. I masked it with a derisive snort and blurted, more angrily than I meant it to be, "We're not friends! I mean—*why?* Why do you want to help me? Nobody cares about me, why do you? You don't know me! You don't even know my name!"

He didn't miss a beat. "What is your name?"

I hadn't expected that. I hesitated. "It's Emily."

He repeated it with reverence. "Emily. Well, Emily, my name is Richard. My friends call me Rick—except when I'm in drag like this, then they call me Lipstick Rick. And I can tell that you are in pain—"

I snorted again. Of course I was in pain, my arm was broken.

He hurried on. "I can see it in your eyes, it's more than a broken arm. And I can see it because I've seen it in my own eyes before. And I know, I *know* what it feels like to be broken." He thought for a moment, smiling a little in a dark sort of way. "Indeed, I've actually felt a bit of a connection to that Humpty Dumpty character you hear about. To have a great fall, and to be so broken that no one, not even you—*especially* not you—has any idea how to put you back together again. And people go away, you know. They abandon you because it's too much work, and sometimes it's because they don't know what to do. And other times, you push them away..."

My eyes filled with more tears as I watched him, his expression growing distant, reliving some dark moment, before he continued, "Because who in the world could possibly help you? Who are you to be saved?" He looked down. "I get it, Emily. And I know how terrible it is to be alone through it, and right now, you don't have to be. Sometimes, you just need some help picking up the pieces, and I'm here to help you do just that. I enjoy puzzles."

I choked out a laugh to keep from sobbing. With his words, the sunlight he held radiated from him, comforting and kind, wonderful and strange. So strange. How did he do that?

He smiled. "And you know, I've found in my life, through these terrible storms, that what often seems like a tragic ending turns out to be the beginning of some... *fantastic* adventure. The beginning of a new chapter. But only if we keep going, you know. Keep *reading* to see what happens next. It's up to us to turn the page—just one page at a time. That's all you need to do. So what do you say? Are you ready to turn the page on this?" He thought for a moment before adding, "I realize that I'm quoting at least three different songs in saying that—that's the mind of a musician for you—but don't let it deter you from the very real idea."

I smiled, then frowned at my shoes. The darkness that had left me had returned, pressing upon me, reminding me it was still there. It made the little light within me flicker as I thought of what walking away from the edge of the building would mean. I'd still have to carry the burden of being broken. I'd still have to hurt. I'd still have to run. The weight of my world sat back down upon my shoulders, looming over me like a dark shadow. "What if it's too late?"

With a curt shake of his head, Lipstick Rick said with a matter-of-fact tone, "It's never too late."

At this, I seized the little thread of hope I now had and turned to him. "Then, yes. I am."

He smiled. "Follow me."

TRACK 2
TRUE FAITH

I couldn't help but see the elevator as very smug and quite pleased with itself, as if it had something to do with everything that had just happened. I decided it was allowed to believe that, and said a quiet "thank you" to it as we got on.

Lipstick Rick's lips squished into an amused line and, with a raised eyebrow, he glanced from the closing elevator doors and back to me. "Did you just thank the elevator?"

I stifled a laugh, feeling stupid. "Um... it's a long story."

A smile slowly curled the edge of his mouth. "Right... so, you and the elevator go way back, then?"

"Waaay back," I said, "to a whole like, fifteen or twenty minutes ago."

"Wow!" he said with mock surprise.

"Yeah."

"You go back that far, huh?"

"Yeah, I'm not as young as I look," I said, unable to pass up an opportunity to throw a totally obscure, Bing Crosby, David Bowie Christmas Special reference into the conversation, even though I was sure there was no way he'd catch it. "There's a real history there."

"Well, obviously." He gave a small shrug, then continued with a knowing smile, "And, really, no one is as young as they look these days."

That was the next line in the quote! *Wait a minute.* I wondered, *Did he just...? No, he couldn't have! There's no way anyone else on this planet has repeatedly listened to the entire skit leading up to David Bowie and Bing Crosby's 'Peace on Earth/Little Drummer Boy.'* Still, I pointed a finger at him and asked, "Wait. Did you just...?" I snorted a bashful laugh. It was such a dumb question, but it was too late now. "Did you just finish my quote from the David Bowie Christmas Special?"

He grinned. "So you *were* quoting the special! I honestly didn't think you were, but I saw the opportunity and couldn't help myself."

"No way! So did I!" I let out an exaggerated gasp, about floating away to the moon. "Be still my heart! I thought I was the only one! You've officially claimed the number one spot on my BFF list."

"Well, it's about time! You know, I think our BFF bracelets need to have Ziggy Stardust and Bing Crosby engraved on them."

Ziggy Stardust was David Bowie's alter ego and was way better than Bing Crosby. Even with our imaginary bracelets, someone would be coming up short. I grimaced. "Nah."

"Yeah, about halfway through saying that, I knew I'd made a mistake, but I was already committed."

I chewed my cheek. "What about Major Tom?" Major Tom was an astronaut created by David Bowie.

"Yes! That's fantastic! But I get the Ziggy Stardust one, of course."

"Why do you get Ziggy Stardust?"

"Well, he *is* a rock star, like unto myself. And you are a..." He searched for a word. "...person." He added with cheerful defensiveness, "You're the one who suggested Major Tom!"

"But that was back when I thought I'd get Ziggy Stardust and hadn't thought it through."

"What's wrong with Major Tom?"

"He gets sent up to space in a faulty ship! So see, by making me Major Tom, you just killed me. I just *died* alone in space! That's such a sad ending for me. You should feel bad."

"Wha—?" He seemed baffled yet he smiled just the same. I was surprised at myself. I couldn't remember the last time I had felt this comfortable around anyone, probably because I never had. I'd built about a million walls around myself in order to keep myself from ever *being* myself, as being *myself* had only ever gotten me into trouble. Yet somehow, there in the elevator, nearly all of the walls had fallen.

I was pretty sure the elevator would be taking credit for that as well.

I debated whether or not to confess that I was joking and apologize profusely for being stupid when Lipstick Rick said with a sigh, "Well, I suppose I do have some regret, but, it was either you or me. But hey, at least you get to *go* to space! I should think you'd enjoy that."

A grin spread across my face. "Well yeah, but I don't want to *die* in space! Have you seen *Gravity?*"

"Yes." He added smugly, "There were quite a few flaws in that film."

"Oh, psh!" I said with as much sarcasm in my voice as I could muster. "Like you would know."

"I'm Ziggy Stardust. Of course I know."

I laughed and leaned back against the elevator wall. It was so nice to laugh. This whole thing, it felt... I couldn't quite find a word for it. It was absurd yet wonderful. I couldn't believe how fast my whole existence had changed. There was something wrong with that, right? There was no way this was actually a good thing. There was a catch. There was always a catch.

With a jolt, the elevator moved. We'd been standing in it for so long without pressing a button that someone else had summoned it. It brought me back to reality. How had I forgotten—even for just a few minutes—that I had a broken arm? When I remembered it, I realized the pain was still nothing more than a distant, dull ache that only amounted to a mere annoyance. How was that possible?

Lipstick Rick said, "So, since this history between you and Mr. Elevator here goes all the way back to fifteen or twenty minutes ago, I'm going to assume that you probably don't live here."

I should've seen this coming. "No." Before he could follow up with any unwanted questions, I hurried and asked, "Do you?"

He studied me for a moment. "Nope." He pushed the button for the first floor, adding it to the queue.

Then what was *he* doing here?

The doors opened on floor seven for a stout, balding man in a thick, gray jacket that smelled like cats and soup. He raised his eyebrows at Lipstick Rick, who shot him a wide grin and winked. The man tentatively got on the elevator, glanced over his shoulder at Rick, then shook his head as he pressed the button for the second floor.

We rode in silence. My heart drummed away in my ears, one thought racing to another as I went over everything that had happened since Lipstick Rick had made an appearance. When the man left and the doors closed, I blurted, "What did you do to me?"

Lipstick Rick furrowed his brow. "I beg your pardon?"

"Up on the roof. When you... when you brushed my hair out of my face, m-my arm, it didn't hurt as bad after." *Among many other things,* I thought to myself but didn't dare say. "It was unbearable and then it wasn't. How did you do it?"

The elevator dinged and the doors opened. Lipstick Rick said to the elevator, "Thank you, Mr. Elevator," and strode elegantly toward the front door of the complex with me following at his heels. He held the door open for me, and when he spoke, his tone was gentle to the point where I felt like a small child who'd just asked if Santa was real. "That is something I'm afraid I cannot answer, Emily."

I didn't like that. "Why not?"

He wouldn't look at me. "I'm afraid it's not that simple, and really not something I desire to discuss."

I followed Rick down the street a ways before his words really sank in and as they did, the happiness I'd been feeling on the roof and in the elevator faded, leaving me like sunlight falling behind a dark cloud. My stomach turned into a heavy rock. I became very aware how cold I was and shivered. The dull ache in my arm increased ever so slightly with a fleeting pang.

He continued, "I'd rather focus on something else. Like getting you somewhere warm that has magical hot chocolate. This is definitely hot chocolate weather."

My mind grew foggy as it lingered on a painful thought. *Did I imagine it? Was everything that just happened, everything that I felt... my imagination running wild? Am I so desperate for help, so hopelessly longing for a savior, that I actually imagined a miracle? Am I that pathetic?*

Of course I was. Of course it was my imagination. I felt so stupid. My heart ached. The flame I'd felt burning within it, so fragile and small, flickered. The shadows around me grew stronger, eager to invade.

I didn't notice him staring at me. "Emily?"

"What? Oh." I hid my inner-meltdown with a small smile. "Uh, hot chocolate. Yeah. Sure." The thought of hot chocolate on my miserable gut sounded horrible. I bit my lip, lost in my head. *No. I couldn't have imagined it. Something happened. Something* had *to have.* I grew a little dizzy. *But it doesn't make any sense. It makes way more sense to assume I imagined it. Ugh! I'm so stupid.* I broke out the mental boxing gloves and started beating up my brain. *Stupid, stupid, stupid. He has to think I'm so crazy. I am crazy. Man, I really need help... ugh, what's the point?*

"Sooo," Lipstick Rick said, his voice a long, loud ring snapping me out of my downward spiral, "are you from around here?"

"Huh? Oh. Um, no. I..." I reviewed the day: me being shoved down the stairs, me running, then walking briskly and then deliriously, taking a bus and riding until I couldn't sit still, then walking some more and ultimately realizing that I had no idea where I was. "I'm just passing through."

"Oh! Okay. Well, where are you staying?"

Nowhere. "I uh, haven't decided yet. I just got here not very long ago."

"Is that right?" He considered this. "Huh. Unfortunate first impression of the area, you breaking your arm. How'd you do it?"

My insides seized up and with a knee-jerk reaction, I told him with a finality that I hoped he'd catch, "I fell."

To this, he simply said, "Oh."

Terrible, awkward silence followed. My shivering grew more intense, the movement making my arm ache. I thought about how much my feet hurt. I looked down at them, a bit surprised they were still there. I was expecting bloodied stumps. They hurt more than my arm.

He stopped us in front of a small, worn down gas station, the only thing within sight that was still open. I looked at it, puzzled. "We're stopping here?"

He smiled as he opened the door for me. "You might not think it, but they have totally... *drinkable* hot chocolate here."

I stepped inside, feeling the cold melt from my face as I was engulfed by the warmth of the store. To my right, there was a row of booths lined up against the front windows leading to what had once been a quaint sandwich shop but was now closed indefinitely. To my left, there was a burly gas station attendant with a shaved head, thick beard, and neck tattoo, sitting behind the counter and reading a newspaper. He glanced up at us, a smile sneaking into his expression as he returned his attention to his paper, all without saying a word.

Lipstick Rick told me to sit while he got the hot chocolate. I did, gladly, relief rushing over my feet. I laid my head on the table, wondering what in the world was with Lipstick Rick's obsession with gas station hot chocolate, and how he expected me to hold the cup when one arm was broken and the other was its brace. I bitterly wondered *when* he planned to fix my arm and then *if* he planned to fix it. Maybe he was the next Ted Bundy and planned to murder me instead.

That seemed likely, especially given my talent for trusting the wrong people. It was such a talent, in fact, that I was sure if it were allowed in the "Talent" portion of the competition, I could've easily won Miss America. But there was also a chance that he was a true saint who was sincerely trying to help.

I doubted it.

Despite all of this, the little flame that had been ignited refused to go out. I couldn't ignore it. Even when I told myself, *You should just go back to that apartment building and finish what you started,* I couldn't do it. I didn't even lift my head from the table. I justified this surrender to hope with a sigh, then thought ninety-five-percent-sarcastically, *Miracles need a leap of faith, right?*

Lipstick Rick returned. He had thought through my inability to hold a styrofoam cup and loaded mine with a small straw. He sat down across from me, pushing the drink toward me, saying, "Here. I promise that this fantastically mediocre hot chocolate works miracles."

I glared at it. "Is this how you plan to set my broken arm? With hot chocolate?"

"Fantastically *mediocre* hot chocolate," he corrected. "And no. It's not quite that magical. But I assure you, it is absolutely essential to the healing process." He pushed it toward me a little further.

Having decided that I had nothing to lose—I was the perfect serial killer victim—I pushed past my nausea and took a sip.

TRACK 3

SUPERHEROES

The hot chocolate wasn't actually hot. It was more like chocolate water put in the microwave for thirty seconds. It also had a funky, metallic aftertaste, like it'd been microwaved in a can and the can had caught fire and melted a little. But the whipped cream made it drinkable. And it was, somehow, magically soothing. My whole body relaxed as warmth spread throughout it from my stomach.

There was more to it than that. I felt... *better*. My stomach stopped hurting, and as the warmth spread to my aching feet, they didn't feel quite so achy. I sipped more of the hot chocolate. The warmth spread to my head. I was so rejuvenated! I could run a marathon! I started chugging it. It was so terribly delicious. I wasn't drinking it fast enough. The angle was all wrong. I let go of my bad arm and grabbed the cup, adjusting it so I could drink what was left at the bottom.

I couldn't believe how much better I felt. I wasn't tired anymore. I wanted to bounce and sing, then jump up on the table and summon birds to me through a musical chorus.

I stared sadly at my now empty, styrofoam cup. "Wow. That was so... gross and... fantastic."

Lipstick Rick smiled, setting down his own cup. "I told you."

"Yeah! I mean, what do they put in this stuff? Meth? I mean... woo! I just—I wanna go climb Everest. Wanna climb Everest with me?"

"No." He raised an eyebrow. "Have you seen those people that climb Everest? I look at them, on the edge of death, in all of their gear, covered in snow and trudging through more snow, and I can't help but wonder..." his face contorted into a confused grimace, *"Why?"*

"Normally I would agree with you, but I really think if we packed a couple cases of this stuff, we'd be up and down Everest in like, two hours. If that! Woo!" I bounced in the booth a little. "I'm the Flash! I'm the happy Flash!" I giggled. Actually giggled.

At that moment, words came tumbling out of me, quick and uncontrolled like an avalanche off of Everest. "Are you sure this isn't coffee? I don't drink coffee, so I don't know for sure. I like how coffee smells, though. We should go shopping. You're very stylish. I need you to help me pick out a whole new wardrobe because I don't have any clothes except for what I'm wearing. Or at least, that's what I would want to do if I had money. I don't have any money. Well, I have fifteen cents. A nickel and a dime. I spent the rest to take the bus over here. I don't even know where I am," I laughed at the absurdity. "I've just been running and running all day because I tried to leave my boyfriend and he pushed me down the stairs."

Lipstick Rick's eyebrows shot up. "Really?" His voice took on a sarcasm that had a dark, venomous tone to it. "Well, I can't imagine why you'd want to leave him. He sounds like a *prince*."

I shrugged. "Yeah. It happens, though, right?"

He shook his head. "It's not supposed to."

It was bizarrely painful to stop myself from saying more. The avalanche wasn't tumbling down Everest, it was coming from my mind, and I had to fight to keep myself from spitting it out. I frowned. "Why am I telling you all of this?"

Understanding me more than I did, Rick said, "It's part of the healing process. You needed to get it out. You started there because those are the most recent injuries. They're fresh on your mind. Really, you can't keep trauma like that locked inside of you. It'll eat away at you until it consumes you. Tomorrow morning, you'll wake up with an inexplicable urge to write down everything you've just kept yourself from telling me. Don't ignore it."

Lipstick Rick's expression softened, full of compassion, saying so much without any words. To my dismay, a warm, comforting feeling emanated from him, the same as I'd felt on the roof. I studied him. Was I imagining it? It was so warm, so real.

He held his hand out to me across the table. "Give me your hand."

I hesitated, then did as he asked.

At his touch, I felt warm light rush through my entire being—

comforting, healing. It lingered at my heart, as if it were cleansing and stitching up the dark, decaying wound that had opened up there, the relief from the pain stung my eyes with tears. It rushed to my head, bathing it in a light that consumed my vision so that, for a moment, the room disappeared into a flash of white, burning away every last lingering shadow. It spread to my feet, then to my broken arm. With a strange, unnerving jolt, the broken bone shifted back into place, which should've hurt like crazy but instead it was Lipstick Rick wincing in pain. My arm grew tingly, like it had fallen asleep, the warmth gathering at the break until it burned.

I looked up at him. His gaze was far away and his eyes... they were *glowing*. Bright blue, almost white, like he'd been plugged into something, the light and color in beautiful contrast against his dark skin.

He let go and slumped into the booth, his face pale, his eyes dim, looking weary.

I carefully touched my broken arm. Heat radiated from it, but there was no pain. I lifted it, and to my shock and with a flood of tears, I could move it with ease.

I was healed.

He'd *healed* me.

I should've realized how strange this was, that this was a miraculous event worthy of its own chapter in the Bible. I knew this. The tears soaking my cheeks spoke of how deeply I knew this. But there was a disconnect in my brain keeping that knowledge from getting to my conscious mind, and it couldn't sink in, having been overloaded and frozen with the information. With both of my trembling hands, I wiped my face—which also radiated heat—and said simply, "Uh... um... Wow. That..." I looked at the hand I hadn't been able to lift less than two minutes ago. I felt my arm, opened and closed my palm. "That doesn't h-happen. That, um... you don't see that every day. Th-thank you?" I said it as a question, wondering, *Is that what I should be saying? Yes, yes that seems right.* "Thank you. Thank you so much. There aren't... I don't have... words."

"You're welcome."

"H-how... did you... how did you do that?"

"It's a gift I have, I guess you could say. Something I can do. Although, I couldn't have done it without the hot chocolate."

"Wh-what are... are you an angel or something?"

He laughed. "Oh no. No, no, no. But that's kind of you for mistaking me for one. I'll take that as a tremendous compliment." He brushed back his hair proudly.

I shook my head, knowing I should be feeling something but was somehow unable to reach it. "But you... you made me think that what I felt on the roof was all in my head."

"Did I? I didn't mean to. I wonder if, perhaps, your brain has grown an eternal pessimist inside of it and that's why you took it that way, which I understand. I had an eternal pessimist living in my mind once. He was very easy to listen to. Life seemed," he grew thoughtful, "less risky—less disappointing—when I assumed the worst of everything.

"Let me give you some advice, though. Life is much more enjoyable if you can find the strength to murder that eternal pessimist and find hope in even the worst of times. Solutions to problems come much easier this way. You'll feel stronger, happier, and you'll even find that you're disappointed a lot less than you were when you were constantly seeing the worst in everything. Ironic, isn't it?" He looked back down at his cup, his face a tired sort of pale. "All I said before was that I couldn't answer your question. I'm still not answering it. Not really. I could tell you all the details, but I don't want to." He reached out and took a drink of his hot chocolate. I could somehow *feel* how much he didn't want to tell me. He was done with the topic.

All I could do was blink at him. Though something restless stirred deep down inside of me, wanting all of the answers, my numb brain couldn't give it a voice. A fog seeped into my mind, making my eyelids heavy. *Besides,* I told myself, *it would be rude to press him for answers, right? Sure! That seems... right. I mean, I totally understand not wanting to talk about things.* "Okay, then," I said, as if I'd been out shopping and he'd just handed me my bags. "Well, thank you for this!"

No, that definitely didn't feel right. I had enough vague sense to know that. I shook my head. "That seems so... *not* enough, just saying 'thank you.' I mean..." I rubbed my forehead with the hand I hadn't been able to lift only moments earlier and a feeling of elation burned in my gut through the numbness. I grinned. "Now I really *can* climb Mount Everest!" *What a dumb thing to say.*

With a deep sincerity that resonated from him, he said, "You really can, if you want to." He looked disapprovingly at his cup and added, "Though I can't recommend it." He readjusted himself, leaning toward me but still staring at the cup. I could smell his perfume, the light fragrance of orange blossoms, making me feel as though I wasn't sitting in a dirty gas station but in a beautiful garden in late spring. The look he wore became thoughtful, searching. Finally, he said, "You know... I understand just how difficult it is to reset your way of thinking after living in a dark place for so long. Though I've done my best to heal your mind, what you choose to do with it from here, well," he looked up at me, "that's up to you. But, if you want a different life, if you want a different mind, you have to start stepping away from the old one."

I nodded, trying desperately to reach through the fog that had gathered in my head and grasp things. One phrase seeped through. Healed my mind? What did he mean by that?

He sighed. "I just want you to know—and I hope one day you really will know—that, though we sometimes make mistakes... sometimes very big mistakes... and though people may break us and we find ourselves somewhere dark, wounded and bleeding," his expression turned heavy, weighed down with his memories. "Left alone, empty and certain that there is no way that you will ever feel whole or happy again," his gaze returned to mine, the light within them brightening a little, piercing through the numbness. "I promise you that those moments pass. To say this—to suggest that such pain is but a moment may seem like an attempt to trivialize it, but it isn't. I know those moments, Emily. Those moments are unbearable and very real, and seem to have no end in sight."

I looked at him, this person who held so much light, his words lingering at the edge of the fog just enough for me to see a little of their meaning. How did he know what I had been feeling?

My thoughts shifted. I ached on his behalf and wondered what memories haunted him.

He continued, "But there is a promise, woven in the very fabric of time—*every moment will pass.* You just have to hang on. And then, when the happy moments come, their beauty will be just as relevant, even more so. Even more intense and real, because though the darkness and pain has dug a deep hole, it has left behind the ability to fill it with *joy*. And when those joyful moments come, you will know to treasure them. Savor them like a good meal. Take lots of pictures and remember them. Because it all passes, which makes the good times so much more precious and beautiful. Those moments are unique to each person, made for us and us alone, and are something so worth hanging on for.

"You don't want to miss those moments, Emily. As someone who has felt that unbearable pain and ended up on their own roof—metaphorically speaking," he took my hand, his eyes now burning bright blue again, "please, hang on. When you wake up tomorrow, do everything you have to do in order to save your life. Kick out those who make you miserable. Make every change necessary to steer your life in the direction of your heart's fondest dreams. Change your thoughts, make those sacrifices. It's all worth it in the end."

Tears poured down my face, though the terrible disconnect in my mind kept me from truly understanding why. I could sense the hope he'd brought me, like the winter sun warming the glass of a window after a long, cold night, but I just couldn't break through to it. I shook my head, trying to chip away at the glass. "You make it sound so simple."

He furrowed his brow. "Of course it's not simple. Changing your life —it's painful, confusing, lonely, exhausting—all of those extremely difficult things. There's nothing simple about it. But," he held up a finger, as though what he was trying to say were hanging in front of him in the air and he was pointing it out, "it is *possible*."

"How do you know that? How do you know any of this? I didn't..." I balled a hand in my hair, trying to find the words for the question I really wanted to ask. "How do you know why...?" *Why I was on the roof.* After all that effort, I couldn't bring myself to say it.

Looking as though he hadn't slept in days, he grabbed his purse and umbrella and stood to leave. "I just do. C'mon. Let's go find you a place to sleep."

"What? But I—" I wiped away tears and tried to stand, only to fall back into the booth. My legs had given up on me. The fog poured through my mind, taking it over.

"Uh oh. Oh, dear."

"What?" I asked, knowing I should probably be worried, but wasn't at all. "What's happening?" My eyelids felt as though small weights had been hooked onto them. My brain had given up on trying to figure out anything and was now spinning in somersaults in my skull, squealing, *wheeeeee!*

Lipstick Rick sounded frustrated. "I'm never exactly sure when this is going to kick in. It affects everyone differently." He reached down and wrapped a massive arm of stone-like muscles around me, lifting me up onto my feet as though I were made of cotton. He helped me toward the door. "You know when you download updates onto your phone, or a computer—"

My head fell forward. The numbness was overtaken by delirious happiness. I forced my head upright again so I could say to him, "Wow! You are so strong. You just lifted me up out of the booth like I was nothin'!"

The gas station attendant looked up from his newspaper and hollered, "Good night, Lipstick Rick!"

I gasped and turned to the attendant. "That! That should be the title of a children's book. Don" you guys steal it. It was my idea first, people!"

Lipstick Rick laughed. "See you later, John."

I lit up. "First two pages right there."

John ignored me. "Ha! Lipstick Rick saves the day again."

I turned excitedly to John. "He saved my life! This guy is an..." I almost called him an angel but caught myself, "*not* an angel. He is a magic man." I sang the chorus of Heart's song, "Magic Man."

Lipstick Rick dragged me out the door. "This is precisely why I don't give anyone details."

The cool night air sent a chill through me, reminding me that my clothes were wet, but I got over it right away. I laid my head on his shoulder. "You smell so good. And I really like your hair." We stopped for a moment outside the gas station while he searched his purse for his phone. "And your face... I like... your face is..." I never finished telling him what I thought about his face.

"Thank you," Rick said, gently bumping my head off his shoulder and waking me from a two second doze. "Come on. We still have a bit of walking to do."

As we started down the street, Lipstick Rick continued, "As I was trying to say earlier, your body is behaving a bit like a computer after giving it an upgrade. In order for it to function properly, it has to power down and restart. You need to sleep. While you sleep, your body will finish applying the upgrades."

I furrowed my brow. "Upgrades? Wait... am I going to wake up a superhero or something?" I gasped. "Will I have superhuman strength? Will I be able to fly?"

"Uh, well, no. It's not that kind of an upgrade."

I frowned. "Oh."

"Well, really, the flying is up to you. You will be perfectly capable of eventually acquiring a pilot's license."

"So this isn't like being bitten by a radioactive spider?"

He sighed dramatically. "Alas, no. But nevertheless, when you wake up, I really don't think you will be disappointed."

We crossed the parking lot of a new-ish Hampton Inn hotel. A confused and concerned desk clerk checked us in as I fell asleep on Lipstick Rick's shoulder. He gave me another nudge and helped me down a hallway toward the elevators. I asked him, "Does your whole band dress up on Ladies' Night?"

He shook his head. "Just me. They're no fun."

After an elevator ride to the right floor, Lipstick Rick gave up on dragging me everywhere and carried me down the hall to the room in his arms. When he sat me back on my feet to open the door, I awoke enough to ask, "So..." I fought to remember what we'd been talking about, "Wha —what's the name of your band?"

He tried multiple times to get the key card to work. "Screaming Riot and the City of Warning."

"Wow. That's a lot of words. But I like the ones you've picked and the order that they're in."

He chuckled. It was deep and genuine. "Well, thank you. And thank the random word generator that Chuck-the-keyboardist found on the internet."

I thought of Charlie Brown. "Chuck?"

"Chuck."

"Chuck." I nodded. "Alright, I will." I addressed the empty hallway, "Thanks Chuck! To you, and your magical, random word generator."

He gave up on the key card and held out his hand a few inches over the lock on the door. I was sure I must've missed something, because right after that, I heard it unlatch. He helped me into the room and toward a bed, which I collapsed in. I couldn't recall in my life, not even during the worst of times, when I had been so tired. He peeled off my shoes and put the blankets over my gross body. I tried to look at him, but my eyes were too heavy and the pillow was too soft and the blankets too warm.

"Do you do this regularly? Are you some cross-dressing superhero, rushing in to fabulously save the day?"

"Well," he said with mock arrogance, "I guess you could call me a fabulously dressed superhero. Of course, I am far too humble to say that of myself."

I laughed as much as my tired body would allow. "You know, I haven't laughed this much in... I can't even remember when. Thanks for doing that... for reminding me how to laugh. For... for everything."

His voice was angelic and sincere. "You're welcome."

That was the last thing I heard.

TRACK 4

IN YOUR WILDEST DREAMS

I slipped into the most restful of slumbers, feeling an unfamiliar and wonderful level of peace. I dreamt that I was back at home, sitting in a lawn chair and curled up under a warm blanket. I breathed in the smell of rain-soaked grass on the cool, autumn breeze. The storm had passed and the night sky was clear and covered with stars. I heard the rickety back door of the house swing open then tap closed, and the sound of footsteps against the grass. I looked over my shoulder to see my dad approaching me with another blanket and two mugs of hot chocolate. His head was shaved, as it had been since I could remember. He was wearing a *Skillet* tour T-shirt and jeans.

"Can I join ya?" he asked.

I patted the ancient, yellowing lawn chair beside me. "That's why I busted out Old Faithful here."

He handed me a mug and sat in the chair. Though he wasn't a big guy, it creaked and groaned under his weight, sounding as though at any moment it would collapse and he'd fall right through to the ground. It had been like that since I was a tiny kid. One time, my cousin— Klondike, as he was known, due to his insatiable love of Klondike bars— sat in the chair, just to see if his six-foot-two, three-hundred-eighty-five pound frame would finally put it out of its misery. The chair screeched more than anyone had ever heard before, as if crying out in sheer agony. He sat in it through the entire family barbecue, which lasted at least three hours, shifting and waiting, sure the moment would come and yet miraculously, it never did. Klondike left with a great deal of respect for the chair, and from that moment on it was known as Old Faithful. It'd passed the Klondike test. It was a very special chair, now reserved only for special people.

My dad definitely fit the bill of special people.

Dad threw his blanket over himself and looked up at the sky, the moon reflecting in his brown eyes. "It should be starting any minute now."

We watched the stars, surrounded by a chorus of chirping crickets and frogs. It was around then that I felt another presence nearby, as though someone were watching *us*. I glanced over my shoulder at my house, expecting my sister or some-unknown-being to walk through the door, hoping for the some-unknown-being. My sister's sour attitude about everything tended to ruin, well, everything.

But no one ever came out of the house. Still, I just *knew* someone else was there.

Dad interrupted my paranoia. "What is it, Em?"

I looked over at him. "Oh, nothing. I was just wondering if Jane was going to join us, that's all."

Dad gave a yeah-right snort. "Old Faithful here will break before that'll ever happen." He bounced in the chair, trying to get it to collapse. It didn't. "Nope. Not tonight."

I laughed and nodded. "Okay."

"The *real* Old Faithful will dry up before Jane ever joins us outside. In the cold. With the uncool nerds and their boring stargazing."

"I believe you."

"The Leaning Tower of Pisa will fall over."

"Yep."

"They'll find Jimmy Hoffa's body, before—"

"I get it!" I laughed.

Dad folded his arms, clearly amused at himself, before his expression grew serious. He said all parental-like, "You know she loves you, right?"

I looked away, fiddling with the trim of my blanket. I wasn't sure how to answer that. My mom had named my sister after the author Jane Austen, but I personally felt that she'd turned into more of a mad Bertha-Mason-from-Jane-Eyre sort of person. If my bedroom were set on fire while I slept, she would've been the number one suspect. She had the magical ability to make me feel as small and miserable as possible, with cutting words that would've made Hitler surrender, ending World War II before it'd even begun. More than once, I'd thought to myself, *If only we had a time machine... we could sic her on Hitler.*

A star fell, leaving a gorgeous streak of light across the sky. I sat up. "It's starting!"

Dad sat up, too, both of us leaning forward as if we were watching an intense thriller in a movie theater. One by one, more stars fell from the sky. I'd never seen anything like it. Their tails were brighter than those of any meteor shower we'd ever seen before.

I looked over at Dad. His face full of wonder as he said, "Isn't that something?"

I smiled at him, no longer watching the sky. My heart felt all warm and fuzzy, but then an ache devoured it and I knew this was only a dream, a wish for what *should* have been.

I missed him so much.

That was when I heard footsteps to my left. I looked over as a tall figure in a long, black coat appeared with another lawn chair and sat down beside me. I didn't recognize him at first. He wasn't in make-up or wearing a dress, but the glowing blue eyes gave him away. He was wearing a dark purple, button up shirt with a few buttons undone near the neck, revealing his smooth, muscular chest. His black hair fell only to his ears, though it was still curly near the ends.

It was Lipstick Rick, only without the Lipstick. So just Rick.

My heart fluttered a little. I couldn't help it. He was such a beautiful man.

He cheerfully leaned against the armrest of the chair, his chin resting studiously in his fingertips as he watched the stars fall. I stared at him, confused. Something was different about him. I couldn't explain why, but though it was impossible, Rick felt... *real.*

He glanced over at me. "Hello."

"Hi."

"You don't mind if I join you, do you?"

"Um..." I turned to look at my dad. He leaned back against his chair, quite content. He gave a small wave of his hand that said without words, "don't mind me." I turned back to Rick. "Nope."

"Great!" He looked around. "So, where are we?"

"Oh, um, this is where I grew up." I sighed. "I guess you could call it my happy—slash—sad place," I chuckled mirthlessly. "This is how last night should've gone."

"Should've?" He pondered this. "I see."

Realizing how that might have sounded, I hurried and added, "Well, no—not like—I mean..." Feeling the need to clarify my statement to imaginary Rick, I scrambled to find adequate words. "Last night—it was *miraculous* and, I don't regret meeting you at *all*, and I'll never forget what you did and I'm super grateful—like *super* grateful—"

Mercifully, he held out a hand to stop me. "I knew what you meant." He pointed to my dad. "Who's this?"

I glanced over. "That's my dad."

Rick gave him a warm smile and then looked up at the sky. "You wanted to see the meteor shower last night."

I followed his gaze to the dozens of falling stars. "Yeah. Dad and I used to keep track of this stuff. We'd sit out here and talk about, ya know, scientific discoveries, the stars, space travel, stuff like that, though we're hillbillies and don't know what we're talking about." I laughed a little. "We'd go on about conspiracy theories, what we thought the Mothman was, and about aliens and what they might look like and where they came from."

"Really?"

I nodded, basking in the nostalgia. "Yeah. Last night, wandering around... I really wished I was home with him, watching this." I wanted to cry and it threatened to wake me. "Jane, my sister—she wasn't into that stuff. It hurt to think of him watching it alone or not at all."

I took a deep breath, waving this away. "Anyway, I saw a little bit about the meteor shower on the bus. Some guy was talking about it and I was nosy and looked over his shoulder to watch this video he had of it on his phone. But it's not *quite* the same."

Rick shook his head. "No, it's definitely not."

We watched the sky for a few seconds, listening to the frogs and crickets and my dad sipping on his cocoa.

Rick broke the serenity. "I honestly never would've pegged you for a conspiracy theorist."

I snorted and shrugged. "Well, we were never serious. I mean, it was just for fun, ya know? Something we liked to do on nights like this. We liked to kick around stupid, impossible ideas."

Rick raised an eyebrow. "Impossible, eh?"

"What's that saying? Something about being able to entertain an idea without accepting it?"

He nodded. "I believe it was Aristotle."

I pointed at him triumphantly. "Yeah! That guy! Look at me, sort-of quoting Aristotle. I feel so smart."

Rick looked genuinely amused. "You should. It's a well-known fact that only geniuses sort-of quote Aristotle."

"It sure is, Rick."

He gazed back up at the stars. "Well, perhaps you can go home now —go back to kicking around impossible ideas with your father."

"Ha!" I shook my head. "Yeah, no. That's not gonna happen. That's more impossible than our impossible ideas."

"Really? How so?"

I looked at the grass. "I can't go back home. Not after what I did." I said something to imaginary Rick that I'd never uttered out loud. "I broke his heart, Rick. I don't know how he could ever forgive me."

Rick's bright blue eyes grew sad. As silence passed between us, he became absorbed in thought, as though he were cooking up his own stupid, impossible idea.

He cleared his throat and readjusted himself to better face me. "You want to know what the best part about dreaming is?"

I found this to be a rather odd thing for someone in my dreams to say, as I couldn't recall ever having anyone in my dreams acknowledge that I was dreaming before. But I thought nothing more of it. "What would that be?"

He grinned. "In dreams, you can really have some fun."

"True." I eyed him suspiciously. "What did you have in mind?"

He leaned toward me. "I have an idea. This is what we're going to do. I'm going to just, hang out, let you fall back into a deep sleep, and we'll see what sort of nonsense your mind comes up with all on its own."

I stared at him, concerned. "Yeah, that idea kinda frightens me. My brain comes up with some pretty weird stuff."

His grin now matched the mischief in his eyes. "Even better!"
At this, I drifted away into the swirling voids of sleep.

TRACK 5
WOULD YOU GO WITH ME

I was with the dashing Sir Richard III, who had wavy locks of coal-black hair and warrior muscles, and a plump, straw-haired man named Gary. We were in camouflage, making our way through a hot, humid jungle full of gigantic dragonflies and mosquitoes that exploded into great, green messes when we shot them with our rifles.

All of a sudden, a fire-breathing monster appeared out of the immense foliage, standing on its hind legs. It had the ferocious body of a turtle and the head of a... well, a turtle, but with two horns sticking out of its temples pointing skyward and two more out of its jaw pointing to its nether region. It stood five stories tall and when it roared, we could see two rows of nasty, sharp teeth. It had massive hand-claws, which I decided to call *clands*, and a long tail with four vicious spikes coming out of the end that would've made the Stegosaurus proud. The three of us pointed our rifles and shot at its face and legs, even firing a couple of bullets at its armored chest for good measure, but it was useless.

"Its hide is too thick!" I said, taking a few uneasy steps backward.

Sir Richard shouted, "Run!"

We fled through the trees, fire burning at our backs. Every step the monster took shook the ground beneath our feet, causing us to stumble. Gary tripped over a vine and fell. I reached for him and cried, "Gary!"

Gary squealed and rolled out of the path of the monster, disappearing into the bushes. But instead of going after him, the monster's eyes fixed on me. Sir Richard grabbed my arm. "Come on!"

I sprinted away, thinking about following Gary's plan and hiding when Sir Richard took my hand and yanked me off course to the right, throwing us into a deep ravine. After tumbling several feet down into a stream, I rolled ungracefully onto my hands and knees and scolded, "You could've warned me!"

"Oh, I'm sorry!" Sir Richard said with a tone rich with sarcasm, "Next time we're being chased by a gigantic turtle I'll turn to you and say, 'I beg your pardon, ma'am, but we're going to make a hard right here and then we'll probably fall several feet down into a ravine. Best brace yourself.'"

"Yes," I said, standing up, pulling leaves and branches out of my hair and pointlessly trying to brush mud off my clothes. "That'll do just fine." I looked around. "Think we lost him?"

On cue, the monster burst through the trees with flames smoldering from its nostrils and teeth. It roared angrily into the sky, fire bursting from its wide open mouth.

"Nope!" Answered Sir Richard, a giddy grin spreading across his face. How he found any of this fun was beyond me. Panicked, I shot at the monster a couple of times, but this only brought its attention to me. My stomach sank, my brain cursing me for my stupidity. "Oh no..."

As if in slow motion, I watched as its jaws opened wide, a furnace burning at the back of its throat. I cursed as I made a run for it along the ravine. I dove into water that was just deep enough for me to lay safely under as flames burned mere inches above me. I broke the surface and turned to look as the beast stepped closer, towering over me. I crawled backward on my hands and feet.

Whatever was I to do?

The great Sir Richard III swung in on a vine, landing majestically onto the back of the creature's neck, busting out a long, metal whip and wrapping it around its throat in a very Indiana Jones-like fashion. The theme song played through the jungle around us, the trees holding speakers in their branches and swaying back and forth in time with the music. The monster clawed at Richard and roared. It reached behind its neck in an attempt to grab him, but Sir Richard was far too quick. He dropped down behind the creature's back and out of its reach. Fire burst into the sky as he dug his heels into the monster's shell and pulled the whip more securely around its throat. It dug at its own skin until its eyes rolled back into its head and, with a roll of thunder, collapsed onto the ground.

Sir Richard jumped down from the defeated foe, strutting up to me and offering me a hand. He helped me out of the water as I beamed at him like the damsels in old black and white movies. "My hero!"

Out of the air, he pulled out a 1940s gangster hat, which he placed on his head and tipped to me as he said with a fantastic Humphrey Bogart impression, "Here's staring at goats, kid."

I laughed, the hat and the Bogart voice giving away what he was trying to say. "Uh... do you mean, 'Here's looking at you—'"

He leapt on the cue, continuing with his impression, "'Here's looking at you, kid.'" Richard leaned against me, resting his arm on my shoulder. "Stewie, 'I think that this is the beginning of a beautiful friendship.'"

Of course, our celebration was far too early, for there came a deep rumble that shook the earth.

The beast wasn't dead.

Slowly, it rose from the ground. A tree handed Sir Richard a gigantic, double bladed axe, the blade carved and shaped to look like flowing waves that were highlighted by metallic blue veins. It was unlike anything I'd ever seen before. A sly smile crossed his features as he spun it, then tipped his hat down so it shadowed his glowing, blue eyes.

As the thing bellowed fire at the sky, Richard moved to attack.

I grabbed his arm, stopping him as I realized what the beast wanted, the answer resounding within my very bones. "You don't have to kill it!" I announced. "I know what it wants!"

Richard turned toward me, looking like he was waiting for me to say something profound such as, "It wants the answer to the meaning of life." I returned his gaze and said longingly, "It wants... french fries!"

Richard's expression changed into a baffled and amused stare. "*What?*"

That was when Gary appeared from behind the monster, calling to us with exaggerated enthusiasm, "*I have french fries!*"

He rummaged through his backpack and dramatically displayed a colossal sized container of fries.

Richard raised his eyebrows. "Oh! Wow, I... wow."

The spiky tortoise saw the package of fries and happily clapped its clands together, shaking the earth again as it plopped down beside Gary.

Gary and I looked at each other and laughed cheesy, elaborate laughs. The pair of us sat with the monster and we all ate french fries while Richard just stood there, bewildered, axe at his side, looking like he'd just walked off the battlefields and onto the set of a McDonald's commercial.

The container of fries magically multiplied and I held one up to Richard, asking, "Would you like some fries?"

That was the breaking point for him. He doubled over with from-the-gut laughter. I didn't understand why at first. I was almost insulted. French fries were not a laughing matter. But then I remembered I was dreaming, and the conversation from my previous dream flooded into my mind. Everything around me took on a whole new perspective and I couldn't help but join in with his laughter. I looked down at my imaginary fries. "I, uh... I think I want some fries."

"Really? *No...*" He walked over to me, still chuckling.

I thought of how absurd the whole situation was and shook my head. "Oh man. I warned you. My brain comes up with some really weird stuff."

His face was alight with glee. "And I love it. This was fun." He heaved a sigh. "Alright. I guess it's my turn." He dropped the axe and took my hand, pulling me up from the ground. "C'mon."

He led me through the tall grass and trees until we entered a clearing. The strange feeling crossed my mind again—that Rick was somehow far more real than the french fries were. I did my best to brush this off as he said, "Tell me, what is your favorite thing to do in dreams?"

That was a no-brainer. "Fly."

He smiled wryly. "I thought so."

"And almost every time I do, I tell myself 'oh, this is so easy! I'm going to totally remember how to do this when I wake up!' But I never do."

He nodded, a look lingering in his eyes as though he were recalling his own moments of flight. "Yes, flying is amazing. When it comes to real life, though, having wings really helps out a lot."

I pouted like a grumpy kid, annoyed that I didn't have wings. "Yeah. Unless you're a penguin."

Rick frowned. "That's true. Poor, unfortunate souls." He cheerfully moved on. "Anyway, you're going to fly tonight."

"Really?"

"It's the only way to get there at the moment." He looked over at me, his eyes full of a warmth that made my stomach do a happy sort of somersault. That was when he blurted, "Ready—set—go!" and took off running, pulling me awkwardly along with him. We ran across the clearing and through a group of trees that spat us out right at the edge of a cliff. My heart bounced up into my throat. My instincts wanted me to throw on the brakes, but Rick yelled, "Jump!"

So, I tossed my fears aside and jumped, officially answering the age old question, "*If Rick told you to jump off a cliff, would you?*"

Yes, apparently so.

Rick whooped and hollered as we fell, but I couldn't find my voice to make a sound. My gut leapt inside of me in a delightful way, my blood rushing through my veins as the feeling of weightlessness took over. There was something so different about the sensation, something I couldn't quite put my finger on, but I knew it didn't feel like a dream.

Rick and I soared up into the sky at an astonishing speed, the wind rushing past us as the world fell away. I clung to him, amazed at how vividly I could see the Earth below from that height. I realized the elusive feeling was that of a distant memory, like I was recalling all of these experiences for the first time in years. The rivers, the lakes, and the mountains were clear and majestic, and the air we soared through was crisp and fresh, like a rainstorm had just passed.

The dream feeling returned, the realness slipping away as we kept climbing, pushing beyond the clouds. We soared past the planets, beyond the sun. In an instant, the stars zoomed by us as if we'd turned into the Millennium Falcon and had entered light speed. A thrill consumed me and a smile spread across my face that refused to leave.

We slowed down as we entered a new solar system, passing planets I'd never seen before. One was massive and covered with swirling white clouds, its surface below glistening in the sunlight as though it were made of diamonds. The sun in the distance was a brilliant, pale yellow, so much so that it was almost white, its shimmer making me want to label it as a *happy* star—though I had no idea if it was actually happy, or if a star could even *be* happy, it just seemed happy to me. We turned toward it, soaring past a red planet full of lightning before descending upon a world that appeared to be around the size of Earth. It was covered in white clouds, not unlike the planet we encountered as we entered the solar system, but there was a clear difference with this one. Beneath the thick clouds were oceans that were violet and blue. There were few surfaces of land, but what was there was a rich, dark green toward the north and south. Along the middle was a large, barren wasteland full of red and brown dirt.

We sailed down through the clouds toward the green land near the very top of the planet, right along the seashore, the smell of mud and the salty ocean air pleasantly overwhelming my senses. The feeling returned to me as we landed on a ridge covered in tall green and yellow grass, nagging at me that this was somehow more than just a dream, though I couldn't imagine how it could be anything else. The plants that grew up through the grass had large, dark green leaves with swirling, red veins. In fact, as I looked around, even the leaves of the trees in the forest behind us had red accents amid all the green. I looked over at the ocean, hypnotized by the violet waters mirroring the dark end of the setting sky.

A hushed, "Wow," escaped my lips as I moved away from Rick, staring in awe at my surroundings. Out in the distance, on opposite ends of the sky, were two moons. "Two!" I exclaimed, pointing up at the sky. "Two moons! I've always wanted there to be two moons." One was red and brown in color, the other one was farther away and white like Earth's moon.

Grinning like a child at Disneyland, I turned my attention to the forest. I tromped through the grass toward it, entering a spot of land that had been mowed. That was when I noticed, tucked away in the trees, was a little cabin. Though it was small, it was well kept and built with care, the design of it deliberately and artistically matching the forest so it blended in with the trees. It had a pointy roof and a tiny chimney. The roof had grooves carved into it in fancy designs lined with something shiny. These grooves led to elegant rain gutters, cut and carved to look like clouds. They lined the entire roof, dumping out onto a thin wheel that rotated over a small pool of water. It was like... well, a watermill.

I pointed at it. "What's that?"

Rick approached me. "I can't be sure, but I believe some people would call that a 'house.'"

"*No*, the wheel-thing on the house."

"Oh, that. Well, it's kind of like a watermill, but much more efficient. It rains a lot here—like, a *lot*—so they found a way to turn that into an excellent source of clean power. That wheel powers electricity to the house. Wealthy people have smaller, more efficient machines that can be put in more convenient places. But, you know, you do what you can with what you've got."

I froze. I turned to him, my heart pounding, about to ask him a very important question before being distracted by the fact that he had changed back into his black pants and long sleeved, purple shirt, though he wasn't wearing his coat anymore. "You changed!"

He glanced down at himself. "I did! I hate camo. And the wonderful thing about dreams is that you can change your outfit in the blink of an eye."

I'm still in camo. This self-conscious thought was devoured by the realization that he'd, yet again, referred to this as a dream. I narrowed my gaze suspiciously. How many times had he done this now? I hadn't been counting, but I was sure it had to be three, at least. How could someone imaginary, who lived only in my mind, be less convinced of this being reality than me?

I gave a curt shake of my head and forced myself to focus. "Okay. So, anyway—what is this place? Where are we?"

He didn't answer right away. I watched Rick intently as he looked from the house to the ocean, his expression pulling painfully at my heart. He carried a small smile, but his eyes were full of pain. I followed him as he strode closer to the house before sitting on the short grass, his elbow resting on his knee, facing the ocean. I sat beside him. He told me, his deep voice somber, "This is my happy—slash—sad place."

TRACK 6

SPACEMAN

Wait... My thoughts picked up speed at they swirled around in my brain, *My happy-slash-sad place was my backyard. Does that mean that this is... his...?*

My eyes widened as all the pieces fell into their proper places, like punching a code into my brain and setting off a bomb.

I tried to keep cool, to not let the excitement get to me, to not freak out, but... but...

He raised an eyebrow as if he somehow knew the inner struggle I was having. "It's okay. Let it out. It's not like I was expecting this to *not* come as a shock."

I let out a long, slow breath. "Hooooooooooly crap! You're an alien!"

He winced. "Oh c'mon, don't say it like that. '*Alien,*' that's just so—"

I tried to find another word. "SPACEMAN! You're a spaceman!"

He looked relieved, like someone had just removed a thorn from his toe. "Yes, that's much better."

I put a hand to my forehead, as if doing so would keep it from exploding. "Of course. Of course you are! This makes so much sense!"

But then again, I thought, *this is a dream. I can't know for sure that the real Rick is actually from outer space.*

I asked him, "Are you really a spaceman from outer space?"

He nodded. "Yep."

"Of course you are! Are you really?"

He chuckled. "Yes, I am, indeed."

His answer wasn't changing. *Wouldn't his answer change if he were imaginary? A part of my own mind?* I couldn't say for sure. I couldn't remember ever having these kinds of conversations with any other characters in my dreams. As I studied him, the feeling kept nagging at me. He *felt* real. But how could that possibly be?

Either way, my excitement at the idea of him being from outer space took over, draining away all care as to whether or not this version of him was actually real. I giggled as my inner nine-year-old self was unleashed and blurted really fast so my words were almost unintelligible, "Ohmygosh, you'rereallyfromouterspace! You'reaspacemanfromouterspace! OUTER SPACE! You have to tell me everything! What's your favorite food? What do the animals look like? Are they different? Of course they're different! I wanna see one. Can I see one?"

"A-all right," he held out a hand to stop me, though I thought I detected a bit of happy relief in his expression. "Just, calm down."

"This is your planet!" I looked over at the cabin. "That's your house!" Maybe it wasn't. "Is that your house?"

"Uh, yes. This is my childhood home."

I slapped my hands to my face. "That's so cool! I don't know what I was expecting of-of other worldly houses but, I guess I wasn't expecting them to be so similar to Earth-houses."

He shrugged. "Four or more walls and a roof. Pretty universal shelter."

I rolled my eyes at myself and threw up my hands. "Of course! That makes so much sense! This *all* makes so much sense!" I wasn't sure it would still make sense when I woke up, but at the moment...

He was smiling now. He stood up and reached down to help me to my feet. He gestured to the grass with both hands. "My brother and I used to sit here... well," he studied the grounds. "It was closer to the house, actually, under the shade of the trees. We'd sit there and watch the stars come out. See, we played at night instead of during the day, so watching for the stars was like watching a clock count down. And the moment it was dark enough, we'd run out onto the beach and play in the sea." As he spoke, the sun sank a little farther in the distance, littering the sky with stars. It was incredible and humbling to look out over the night sky and not recognize a single constellation.

I caught Rick watching me with an affectionate look in his eyes that made my heart tumble around in my chest in a stupid way. "I have to say, I love your enthusiasm. It's not quite the reaction I expected."

I turned to him. "Are you kidding me? This is like, the coolest thing ever! I feel like I'm nine-years-old again. I mean, I always knew there had to be life on other worlds, our planet's not *that* special, but the odds of life coming in contact with ours..." I chuckled. "Basically, I used to be kinda like Mulder from the X-Files, but he held on to his beliefs a lot more stubbornly than I did... which begs the question, how *did* you end up on Earth?" I answered the question for myself, tossing up a hand. "A spaceship, obviously."

He shook his head, looking up at the sky. "Nope. I didn't travel that way."

My brain blew up again and the sound of the explosion slipped out of my mouth in a slow whisper, "*Whaaat?* Then how did you—?"

"It was a portal. I found it quite by accident."

"*Oh-ho-ho-ho!* A portal! That's so cool!" I tried to wrap my mind around this information. "So... so... like... is it still there on Earth? I mean, can you go back home?" I gasped, my hands flying to my face again. "Can people from your planet come and go as they please and we, the people of Earth, are just dumb and clueless and have no idea?"

He looked at me, that affection still in his eyes. "No. I'm certain that no one on Thera knew about it except for my friend and me. It wasn't opened by anyone here. And then shortly thereafter, it was destroyed."

So much... sooo much information. So many mixed emotions. I tried to pick a place to begin. "Thera? Is that—"

"The name of my planet? Yes."

I looked over at his little house with sadness. "So you can't go home? Is that why this is your happy—slash—sad place?"

His gaze followed mine toward his house, the pain returning to his eyes. "No. This isn't my home anymore." After a moment's pause, he said with a finality that was laced with bitter, angry sorrow, "I never want to come back here." He turned to me. "But it's nice to visit it in memory sometimes."

I could understand that. Returning home would definitely not be easy for me. Part of me wanted to ask him why he didn't want to come back, to compare battle scars, but I knew it wasn't my place to pry. "So...

if the portal wasn't opened by anyone *here*," I gestured to the ground, "who opened it? Was it someone..." I was having a hard time bringing myself to say the thought out loud, "Someone from *another* world?"

He nodded, his cheeriness returning. "Yes."

My stomach sank to the dark underbelly of the planet. "Not Earth or Thera?"

"There are lots of worlds out there, Emily."

This thought freaked me out in a very bad way, but I tried to remain cool. "Mmmkay. Cool, cool. And did this person come to Earth?"

"Yes. Basically what this portal was, was this massive bridge —*massive*—built between several different planets, bending the fabric of space and time through an alternate dimension. It was extremely impressive. But the guy who built it, his intentions were not good. He was basically like a super villain straight out of a comic book, believing that he could cure the universe of violence through violence." He shook his head. "Really, people's logic sometimes." His actions grew more animated, shrugging and throwing out his arms in frustration. "I mean, here we have a clearly intelligent being, who's built this *extraordinary* thing, but his views on obtaining universal peace are completely skewed and irrational! Although, looking back on it, we should've let him hit Thera.

"Anyway, naturally the portal had to be destroyed. My friend and I ended up on Earth with no way back to Thera and quite happy about it."

"Your friend?" I grinned. "So there's more than one of you?"

His eyes darted uncomfortably to the side, like he'd just let a secret slip. "Yes. Well, anyway... I've always assumed that when we destroyed the portal that this madman died in the process, but since he was left *in* the portal and his remains ended up who-knows-where, we may never know for sure."

That wasn't very comforting. "Huh. Okay."

He reassured me, "Most likely he is very dead."

I nodded. "Well, that's-that's good." I sat on the grass, looking out over the ocean, the moonlight glistening over the waves. Rick sat beside me, closer to me than I expected. I shook my head, questions whirling around in my mind like numbers in a Bingo machine, waiting for one to pop out randomly—*B12!* "Why did you guys only play at night? Is it too hot in the day or something? I noticed that like, half of your planet is a desert."

"Thera is certainly warmer. It almost never snows, so it was a bit of a shock to move to Earth—but no, that's not why. My family, we were... we were in hiding."

The words echoed in my head. *In hiding?* I looked at him, my heart sinking for him. Before I could even think of how to respond, he said, "Anyway!" He cleared his throat. "My, an interesting dream this has been."

There he went again, talking about the dream. Still, I simply couldn't pass up the opportunity to say in my best Yoda voice, "But a good dream it has been, also. Mmm, yes." It was a terrible impression. I sounded more like a wizened old cat lady struggling to clear her throat of a hairball. Not even dream-me could do a good Yoda impression.

He suppressed a laugh. "Was that... was that supposed to be Yoda?"

I cracked and started laughing, hiding my embarrassed face in my hands. "No! Don't look at me!"

Then of course, Rick spoke in a perfect Yoda voice, "More practice, you need, young Padawan."

How he got his deep voice to bend to that level of exactness was beyond my understanding. "Ugh! Seriously? First Humphrey Bogart and now a perfect Yoda?" I shook my head. "It's just not even fair."

His eyes glowed with mischief. "Oh, you have no idea how good I am at impressions."

I shook my head. "Honestly, is there anything you can't do?"

He looked out over the ocean and sighed, almost sad. "I am completely incapable of being anything other than what I am."

I smiled at him. "Well thank goodness for that."

He returned my smile, his gaze full of warmth. "You know, I like who you are—this person that you are in your subconscious mind, unrestrained."

My stomach twisted in a nervous, giddy way. "Thanks. You're probably the only person that does."

"But are you happy? I mean—here, now, having let yourself just *be* for a moment, even though it is only in your mind—have you felt happy?"

I looked over at him. "Yeah. Happier than I've been in... I don't even remember when."

"Then it doesn't matter. Other people's approval is never going to make you happy, Emily. Approval may seem nice, but in reality, it is a cage that is constantly changing shape. It has limits and restrictions, and what was a hit yesterday is forgotten tomorrow. Besides, there is only one face that you're guaranteed to wake up to every day for the rest of your life, and that's yours. So live according to your conscience. Love the things that bring you joy, fight for the deeper things in your heart, the things that fill your soul with *fire*, because those are the things that make you who you are." He nodded at the sky. "Then one day, you'll find your people. People who appreciate who you really are, that you don't have to hide around. They're out there."

He looked at me intently. "Will you do that for me? When you wake and the dreams are gone, promise me that you will try to let this person out and let yourself *be*?"

His words pierced me, filling me with a strange, burning hope and a desire for something I couldn't quite explain. My heart pounded, sure that I couldn't have dreamed up such a speech. He had to be there. He had to be real.

But how was it possible?

"I promise."

He nodded. "Good."

I smiled bashfully and shook my head. "How do you come up with these speeches? Are you like, some kind of cross-dressing-spaceman-motivational-speaker-preacher?"

He grinned. "Well, I don't know how motivational I actually am, but the rest is more accurate than not. Although I will admit, I do quite enjoy the sound of my own voice."

"Ah, that explains it," I teased. "Well, you do have a great voice."

"I do, don't I?"

I laughed. "You really do." I looked away from him, overwhelmed with a profound longing as I prayed in my heart, *Please be real.*

Rick pointed to the far east, saying quickly, *"Watch-watch-watch! You're going to love this."*

I looked over to where he was pointing just as a huge ball of purplish-white light sailed across the sky. Tendrils of light rippled behind it in great threads, looking almost like water, as though some heavenly being were trailing their finger across the surface of the sky. I watched it in amazement before I could find enough of my brain to utter, "Whoa..." I leapt to my feet, wanting to get as close to it as possible.

Rick followed and stood beside me. "I never did learn what it is. I've theorized that it's a comet that's caught in our planet's gravitational pull. While the moons have a nearly spherical orbit, this comet would orbit in a huge, narrow oval at an incredible speed with our planet on the very edge of it. I'm probably wrong, but, whatever it is, every ten hours or so it passes by, and quite uncomfortably close to the surface. It's a terrible hazard. Still incredibly beautiful to look at, though."

Even if everything in my life had been set right—if my past were erased and I knew I could wake up with a clean slate and go home—I still couldn't have been more content than I was in that very moment. I was sure of it. I swallowed happy tears as I watched it disappear in the west. "I had no idea any of this existed."

"Makes the world seem so small, doesn't it? Knowing there is so much more out there."

I nodded. "Yeah, it does."

"But doesn't it also make life so much more meaningful? Here we are, on this floating rock amidst the vast chasm of space, weaving our own footprints among the stars, living our own adventures. You have to ask yourself—what footprints do you wish to leave behind, you know? What story, what adventure, will they tell?"

I looked over at him, watching his eyes begin to glow more brightly as he stared up at the stars, his face alight with a joyful passion as he spoke. He was more enchanting than the sky.

"There's so much out there and so little time, we can't allow ourselves to lose our light to dark moments, not when all we have is *now*. Though the years of our lives are like a mere grain of sand in the tapestry of space and time, there is nothing in existence that is more precious. It is the adventure of life—being faced with dark moments—moments where we discover our own light as we fight to burn that darkness away, growing stronger through them, brighter, better, more compassionate, till we find our place among the stars in the night sky. It's all part of it. And it's *ours*. Our gem that no one can truly take away. It's our own small, priceless treasure—the gift of adventure."

He ran a hand through his hair. "I'm rambling. I just..." He shifted his feet, then looked at me steadily. "I brought you here for a reason. I was hoping to help you put your sorrow into perspective. The universe is so big, there's so much out there, so much to live for. I..." He ran a hand through his hair again.

My heart beat against my chest, sure to wake me. I could almost feel my slumbering form and the warm sheets covering my still-damp clothes. "What do you mean, you 'brought me here?'"

"Well, not *literally* brought you. I'm not capable of that. It's more like..." He scrunched his face, thinking. "*Shared* with you. You see, these are my memories."

I blinked. It was all I was capable of doing.

He continued, "I hoped that, by showing you a piece of my world, perhaps you might see that impossible things might be more possible than you thought. If something as impossible as me is possible, then it's possible for you to rise above your circumstances, your past, your demons—whatever they may be—and accomplish the impossible, achieving a good life—the one of your impossible dreams, and thereby make the impossible, possible." He laughed uncomfortably. "How many more 'possibles' do you think I can squeeze in here? Do you think it's possible to stop me?"

I would've laughed. I wanted to laugh. But all I did was blink some more. "But... but this is a dream. I'm dreaming. It's not real. *You're* not real."

He rubbed his wrist, looking guilty. "I can't say that I've ever really done this before, at least not like this. It's a bit of an invasion of privacy."

"*Yeah*, a bit."

"But I've noticed with dreams, the subconscious mind has a far greater ability to speak the truth than the conscious in its own, absurd way. And I had to be sure you were alright. As I said earlier, I won't be able to live with myself unless I know that I have done all I can to help you. After our chat in the elevator, I knew right then and there— this girl has to make it."

"But how is any of this even possible?"

"With the same energy I used to heal your arm." The lost look I gave him prompted him to continue, "All living creatures have energy—even the grass, the flowers, and the trees. Some people would call this energy a 'life-force' or 'soul'. The lower the life form, the less energy it has but it's still there. Humans have a great amount of it. You can feel it when you walk into a room. You can sometimes *feel* whether a person is happy or sad, or if something terrible has happened. But for humans, the energy is only powerful enough to really move your own body and only lightly manipulate the world around you. But, creatures like myself have... more."

I shook my head. "How did you know why I was on the roof?"

He hesitated. "I felt it. As I told you, the energy I have is much more powerful than that of humans. One of the side effects is that I can feel intense emotions through touch. Sometimes when I'm just near a person, if their feelings are strong enough and unrestrained. When I'm in a crowd, it's not always obvious who is feeling what, but when you bumped into me on the street, your hand touched mine."

I remembered bumping into a tall woman with a manly voice, the one person on the street who'd asked me if I was okay. It was so obvious now.

She had been Lipstick Rick.

He went on. "I recognized those feelings, having felt them myself before. I knew it was only a matter of time. So I followed you."

Tears burned my eyes. All the care he'd taken, all that he had done, just to help me. "Why? Why are you doing all of this? Why would you risk so much? I mean, for all you know, I'm a total jerk who'd sell you out."

He smiled and shook his head as if I'd just told him I'd once seen a penguin on stilts. "No you wouldn't. I'd have felt it." He added, "Also, if you were to sell me out, no one would believe you, but," that brilliant affection lit up his eyes, making my heart outright dance, something I had thought it would never do again, "I know you wouldn't."

Well, he wasn't wrong about any of it, especially the part where I would never, *ever* do that, but still. "Why? Why are you trying so hard to save me?"

His gaze softened. "I can tell you're someone worth saving."

The little fire that had been ignited within me at the beginning of the night had officially grown two sizes. I could feel tears spilling from my eyes, not just in my dream, but onto the pillow I was resting on. For someone to say that to *me*...

He glanced over his shoulder, as if seeing something there that I couldn't. A distant song played. It grew louder and louder until the melody and lyrics were clear. It was "Lady Marmalade." Rick looked back at me, taking a deep breath, his expression growing sad though he wore a smile. "I have to go. I wouldn't if I wasn't absolutely convinced that you'd be alright, but I can see that you're a strong person, far stronger than you think." He nodded. "You're going to make it."

I wanted to stop him, to ask him to stay just a moment longer, but instead I forced myself to say, "Okay. Yeah, of course. You do what you've got to do."

His smile faded. He looked torn. He placed his hand on my shoulder. "It's going to be all right. It will get better."

"Okay." I hurried and added, "Thank you, Rick, for everything."

He chewed his cheek for a moment, "Lady Marmalade'"now blaring in the background. "My real name is Rain."

I brightened. "Rain?"

"Yeah. Well," he gave the "R" a heavy roll, then pronounced each following letter, "*Rhaenmeinnah*, but I can't expect anyone to be able to pronounce that so, just Rain."

I smiled. "I like Rain better than Rick."

The beautiful world around me faded as his presence left me. Comfort and warmth flooded through me as darkness enveloped me, the only thing remaining of him being "Lady Marmalade." Just before I slipped back into a deep sleep, where no other dream was to be remembered, I thought I heard the music abruptly stop, followed by a very annoyed, "*What*, Nothe?"

TRACK 7

new

I drifted to consciousness, feeling warm and wonderful though I had no recollection as to why. My eyes blinked open to late afternoon sunlight and white curtains. I felt well rested for the first time in... I couldn't remember when. My brain was swept up in a pleasant delirium where I didn't recognize the curtains, I couldn't remember where I was or how I'd gotten there, and for a few blissful seconds, I didn't care.

I rolled onto my back, staring up at a white ceiling. Moving made me realize that my hair was gross and I smelled like B.O. and mud. That's when I finally became concerned and wondered, *Okay... where am I?*

All the memories rushed back.

I bolted upright, then laid my head against my knees as blood rushed to my brain. I rubbed my face, which was grainy and disgusting. My clothes felt like paper towels that had been origami-ed onto my body. I studied my surroundings. The room was simple—two queen-sized beds, a desk, TV, and obscure paintings of flowers hanging on the walls.

My gaze froze on the object on the bed next to mine. It was a black duffle bag with what appeared to be a note.

A whirlwind of emotions swept over me—all the feelings that I should've felt the night before when I had been numb: panic, terror, excitement, happiness, hopefulness, holy-CRAP, what-the-CRAP-is-happening, I'm-going-crazy, is-this-real-ness. These emotions wanted to erupt from me in a scream, but instead I just sat there, staring at the bag.

The whirlwind shifted as I realized it was real. Last night *had* happened. No one would ever believe me—not that I would ever tell anyone or had anyone *to* tell, but if I did, they would institutionalize me. But it was real. *He* was real.

Bad things had happened. I distinctly remembered being pushed down the stairs, snapping my arm and all that had led up to it, but then...

I reached over and felt the arm that had been broken. I looked down at it and moved it around. Sure enough, it was still fixed. It was as good as new. There wasn't a single bruise or scar.

Wait. There were *no* scars at all. Not on either of my arms.

There had been scars up and down my arms from where I'd taken a knife and cut myself just to feel something else, and because my unseen wounds didn't bleed. There'd been a scar on my left wrist from when I was a little girl and had gone to war with a cat and lost. There'd been a scar on my right palm from when I was a teenager and had tried to flip a light switch I couldn't reach using a sharp pencil and had accidentally stabbed myself with it in the process. Not my brightest moment.

All of them. All of the scars were gone.

With a very swift yet stiff and mechanical rising from the bed, I marched toward the bathroom and stared at my reflection.

My blonde hair looked like rope that'd been used to tie a muddy dog outside. My face was streaked with dried tears and dirt, but my eyes... The last time I'd seen them, they'd been sunken, like the eyeballs in the skulls of Halloween decorations, lifeless and dim. And now, they were bright and clear. They were healthy. They almost glowed.

I fumbled for the faucet with trembling fingers. I used the complimentary bar of soap to scrub off all the dirt and grime and see if the miracles washed away with it. I grabbed a towel and patted it dry, bracing myself for disappointment.

But I wasn't disappointed. Without the mud and dried tears, my cheeks had a pleasant, rosy hue. My skin was like smooth porcelain and held the glow of youth—not that I was old, but yesterday I'd looked like a corpse. I leaned over the sink, trying to get a better look. The few scars and wrinkles I'd had were gone. I couldn't believe it. I looked...

I looked like the years that had been stolen from me had been given back. I'd been given another chance. My bone structure was still that of a girl in her early twenties, but my skin... I could've been sixteen.

I had to touch my face and stretch my skin around just to be sure this wasn't some sort of illusion, but the new face wasn't going anywhere.

I emitted noises that were somewhere between excited laughter and sobbing. My brain couldn't quite decide which to do.

I pried myself away from the mirror and stumbled back into the bedroom, pulling on my hair like a confused mental patient as I meandered toward the duffle bag. My stomach did a gleeful somersault as I gently picked up the note, which had been written on the complimentary hotel notepad, and read:

I, Sir Richard III...

The room spun and I had to sit down. I read that line seven or eight more times before I continued:

I, Sir Richard III, hereby bestow upon you, Emily, the START OVER kit. This should have everything you will need to give yourself the new beginning you deserve and chase the adventure your heart desires. I know you will use it for good.

First things first—throw out those old clothes and those old shoes. The sun has risen on a new day! Leave the ruins of the past behind you.

It was an absolute pleasure meeting you, Emily. I'm grateful for the opportunity I had to steal time with you for one day (David Bowie 'Heroes' reference there, aren't I clever?). I wish for you and your life nothing but the best and purest happiness.

My heart cracked. A cold sensation rippled through my limbs, leaving them feeling numb and my body out of place. I read the note again, and then again, each time hoping for the words to change, and each time more and more joy ebbed from me.

He was telling me goodbye.

I shook my head and stood, setting down the note. *No*, I told myself. *He wouldn't do that. He wouldn't do all of that and then just leave!*

I unzipped the duffle bag, not sure what I would find but hoping for some sort of clue, some semblance of "Just kidding! It's not goodbye! You didn't think I'd up and disappear on you, did you?"

The first thing I found immediately distracted me from the note. It was a darling, silky soft, knee-length dress. It was black and backless with a strap wrapping behind the neck and a graceful V in the front. It was love at first sight. I would've put it on immediately, but I was on a mission, and in desperate need of a shower.

I gently laid the dress on the bed and dove back into the bag. I found another, more casual dress, two pairs of jeans, shirts, socks, a hairbrush and three different pairs of shoes. It was like raiding Santa's bag of toys on Christmas morning.

As I reached the bottom, I discovered a rather strange sight. At first, I thought maybe it was a ridiculous bag design, something meant to be a funny gag. Underneath a clear layer of plastic, were what appeared to be rows of $100 bills. I poked one and was surprised to feel texture. I poked each of them as I counted how many Ben Franklin faces I saw. I counted them twice. There were twenty of them. They felt lumpy under the plastic as if there were really $100 bills underneath it.

I fumbled along the corners of the bottom of the bag until I found the edge of the plastic and pulled it out. Sure enough, it was a plastic bag that had been zipped shut and vacuumed sealed, with twenty Ben Franklins staring sternly out at me.

I had to sit down again.

My brain tried to do the math. Twenty $100 bills. That was... two-thousand dollars.

My shaking hands nearly dropped the plastic bag as I unzipped it. I reached for the first Ben Franklin...

That was when I realized that what looked like *one* Ben Franklin wasn't just one, it was a small pile.

I took it out and started counting. Then I counted again. And again. Then one more time, just to be sure. There were ten. Twenty rows of ten Ben Franklins. *Real* Ben Franklins. My vision spun as the number jumped from two-thousand dollars to twenty-thousand.

I had to lie down.

Just last night, I'd had nothing. *Nothing.*

How? Just... what? Was he the world's richest man? To just be able to give some random person twenty-thousand dollars and say, "Okay! Here you go! Now be good! Don't spend it all in one place! Ha-ha-ha."

Once the hysteria subsided and my brain was able to settle, I decided I couldn't take it. I couldn't take any of it. There was no way!

What kind of person did he think I was? I didn't care that he'd disappeared, I was determined to find him and give all of this stuff *back*.

I threw the money into the plastic bag and slammed that back into the duffle bag. I carefully repacked the shoes and the clothes—feeling a small twinge of pain when I reached the black dress—and marveled, after several attempts, at how Rick or Rain or whatever his name was, had managed to fit all of that crap into one bag.

I had the decency to shower. I used the hotel's crappy shampoo and the entire, tiny bottle of conditioner in a sad attempt to untangle the rat's nest on my head and return it to curly, blonde hair. I paused to begrudgingly admire the condition I found my body in. I had been so thin from trying to fade away, but now my skin was pleasantly plump and smooth. Not only this, but I noticed my brain was clear. For years, I'd been fighting a thick fog that deprived my mind of any light. It had been heavy, weighing me down so my shoulders slumped and I always felt exhausted. But now, the fog was gone. I could stand up straight. I could see sunlight clear as morning in my head, because there were no clouds in sight. While I was irritated at my situation and ready to give that stupid spaceman a piece of my mind, there was no desire to fade away over it. I just knew, somehow, someway, I was going to figure everything out.

I had health. I had my mind.

Man, it was such a weird feeling.

This left me muttering bitterly to myself, "Rick—or Rain..." my train of thought derailed as I said his name. "He said his real name was Rain, but does he *want* to be called Rain? Some people are like, 'My real name is Daria' but it's like, a special secret and they would rather be called by the name everybody else knows them by..." My voice gradually rose, echoing off the shower walls. "He did not clarify this at *all*. No! He just said, 'My name is Rain' and he disappeared. Poof! Just like that. *Why*? Why did he do that? What? Am I supposed to look in the mirror and say his *real* name three times to summon him and he'll magically appear? Ugh!"

I scrubbed my face with vigor. Then, calming down and setting my thoughts back on track, I continued, "Well, whatever. He was right." I looked over my body and had to admit, "I am not disappointed with these upgrades."

After drying off, I practically drank the complimentary mouth wash, hoping it'd help my rancid, I-don't-remember-the-last-time-I-ate breath. I forced myself back into my gross clothes, grabbed the duffle bag, and set off to find Rick.

TRACK 8
CRITICAL MISTAKES

I started with the guy at the front desk of the hotel. He was tall and a bit lanky, with a crisp haircut and bow tie. I let my hair fall into my face, trying to hide as I said to him, "Excuse me, sir. Hi. Sorry to bother you. Um. I'm looking for the person who, um, who rented the room I'm staying in..." I winced. "Uh, *rented* is probably the wrong... term. But you know." *This is going badly. Get to the point, Emily!* "I was wondering if he like, left a message for me or something... anything."

He scrutinized me with suspicion and concern. "Yes, I remember you two from last night."

I was taken aback. "Wow. Really? You poor thing. We got here really late last night. Wait—what time is it?" I looked down at my imaginary watch.

"It's..." He looked at the clock behind him that had been clearly visible to me, "8:15. I work from eight to four."

"8:15?" I turned toward the entrance. It was dark outside. In my haste to get out of the room, I hadn't realized that it'd taken me over two hours to hyperventilate and shower. "Man, that sucks. I'm sorry."

"It's not so bad," said the guy with a small shrug. "I'm a night owl."

I readjusted the bag on my shoulder. "I hear you there. I swear I sleep better during the day." I considered what time it was and added, "Obviously."

He let out a weird grunt of acknowledgement and turned his attention to his computer. "Remind me which room you're staying in?"

"One-sixty-seven. I remember it really easily, because it's how many times Beetlejuice saw *The Exorcist*."

He was unamused. I chewed my lips, feeling stupid for saying stupid things as he did some very serious searching. "Let's see... paid in cash for a seven-day stay..."

My eyes widened. "What? Really?"

He gave me a curious look. "Yep. And there are no messages."

My heart sank. "Okay. Thanks for checking."

"Are you okay?" His voice lowered to almost a whisper. "Did he hurt you in any way?"

"No! Gosh no, not at all. He saved my life. I, um..." I heaved a sigh. I glanced up at the guy's brown eyes, going through a brief debate in my head. I had an almost uncontrollable urge to tell the man everything, every mistake I'd made that'd brought me to that hotel counter. The muscles in my jaw twitched. My tongue was anxious—anxious! I'd never felt such a thing. It took all I had to fight it, the effort bringing tears to my eyes.

Finally, I said, "I, uh... I was a mess last night. I was passing through and I was injured and had nowhere to stay, then I met Rick and he brought me here. He paid for the room so I could have a place to sleep and then he disappeared and he... *he left his stuff.*" My annoyance at the situation seeped into my words and a few tears slipped through as I held up the duffle bag. I tried to mask it with a shrug and smile, saying, "Dang it! And, um, I thought that the least I could do to repay him—because I can't—I can't repay him for saving my life, for anything he did. And I mean," I threw up an arm, losing control of my tongue, "what do you do with that? Being in someone's debt like that forever. I just..." I cleared my throat, feeling embarrassed. I'd already said way too much. I was burdening this poor guy with things he couldn't possibly care less about. "Anyway, I'm so sorry for going off. I'm kind of a mess. I just, I thought the least I could do was return his stuff."

"Wow." To my surprise, he gave me a kind smile. "He sounds like he's a real Good Samaritan."

The story of The Good Samaritan ran through my mind. I knew it well. It had been one of my dad's favorites and he used to tell it all the time. It'd been told by Jesus, about a man traveling to Jericho who'd had the misfortune of falling into the hands of thieves, who then left him for dead. Not a priest, nor Levite, nor baker nor candlestick maker (though the latter two were probably just in the version my father had told me) would rescue the man. Only the Samaritan, someone who'd been despised by all the rest, stopped to help. He tended to the man's wounds to the best of his ability, took him to an inn to be cared for, paying for the care in advance, and left the next day.

I thought over my own life—every step, every wrong turn—and had to bite my lips to fight another urge to tell it all.

●

I HAD GROWN up in a small community. My dad was a banker and a preacher. He was well respected and had accidentally become a therapist to many people due to his compassionate nature. He had a kindness that people could just *feel*. It happened all the time. He'd be sitting on a bench at Wal-Mart and some stranger would sit beside him and tell him their whole life story. My dad would have a wise answer to whatever dilemma they might've had and leave them with renewed faith in humanity. My mom passed away when I was young—*very* young. But I could still remember her smelling like cookies, since her favorite thing to do was invent new desserts. I remembered how she'd hum as she put on her make-up and how I felt safe in her arms. I remembered her smile. Though she'd often said the words, she really didn't have to tell me how much she loved me, because her smile said it all.

But then she died. And of course, Dad had to work, which left me in the care of my older sister, Jane, who resented having to babysit me. I supposed I understood. She wanted a normal teenage life. She didn't want to raise me.

As I grew older, I preferred clothes that advertised my favorite bands and had cartoon characters on them, not the girly, trendy things. Everything I did was terribly awkward. After being bullied relentlessly, I taught myself how to be invisible. There was a consequence to that, though. I ended up so very alone. Loneliness is a strange and terrible motivator. It can get people to do very stupid things, like, begin to believe that they, indeed, don't really matter, and then do anything to feel like they do. That was what happened to me, anyway.

When I was sixteen, someone noticed me. He was cute and funny. And manipulative and awful, playing on my fears and insecurities the way artists manipulate clay, but I couldn't see that yet. There was just something in my gut told me dating him was a bad idea.

However, one night as we washed dishes, Jane was quick to point out how I was being thoughtless and rude. With her sweet, serious tone, she said, "I'm not saying this to be mean, but… I mean, I guess you *are* pretty, but more like a pretty *boy*. You know what I'm saying? And *clearly* your personality isn't winning you any friends. So," she gave a hesitant shrug, "do you really think you can do better than him?" Before I could scoff at her, she continued with a frown, "And seriously, what about *his* feelings?" She shook her head disapprovingly, her perfect, brown curls brushing against her rosy cheeks. "If you keep it up, you're going to lose him and probably die alone. Just sayin'."

Her words both depressed and terrified me. And I *was* being selfish, wasn't I? I just wanted to be friends, but he wanted more. What right did I have to put him through that? I soon abandoned all of my boundaries, desperate not to push away my only friend, to cure my loneliness.

I slept with him long before I was ready. Sure, I was curious, as most teenagers are, but I really didn't feel like I had a say. It got out of hand, and then I just really wanted it to be over. And if I went through with it, it would be. Right? I couldn't stop him and say no. It would've made him feel stupid. What right did I have to do that to him?

Rumors spread about me and, as I looked back on it, I knew they were most likely spread by him. They were things no one else should've known. My peers treated me like I was a *thing* and no longer human. A guy at school had looked me over as though I were something disgusting and yet to be pitied, like a bloodied and dying animal on the side of the road. When I was home, Jane acted like I didn't exist.

Things quickly deteriorated from there. I felt horrible and vile, desperate for help but unable to find my voice. I was too naive to fully understand exactly what was happening to me and didn't know just how badly I *needed* to reach out to my dad for help, but I couldn't even look him in the eye anymore. Whenever I was home, I locked myself in my room and refused to emerge.

I was more alone than ever.

My boyfriend used this against me. He showed me that he was the only one who cared about me, the only one who truly accepted me. Thus, when I confronted him on how my dad was pressuring me to break up with him, he insisted on us running away together instead. I had no choice. What was I without him?

My dad had money that he kept hidden for a rainy day, adding to it every so often. It amounted to $3,733. I knew where he hid it. It was under a loose floorboard, beneath the rug in his bedroom. My boyfriend convinced me we would need money for a fresh start, to keep us on our feet until he found a job. He promised we would pay my dad back eventually.

What choice did I have? *What was I without him?*

I stole the money and we ran away. After that, I knew I could never go home.

The abuse went on for years. It wasn't really the kind that left visible scars, just the ones I put on myself and the time he pushed me down the stairs. Instead, it was my soul that was dying, with people just passing by. I knew it was what I deserved.

Until I met that cross-dresser on the roof. The spaceman. My Good Samaritan.

THIS REALIZATION HIT me like a wave. My eyes filled with tears and I fought to hold them back. My voice trembled as I said to the man at the desk, "Yeah. He literally is."

And I have to find him, I thought desperately. *I have to.*

The man's smile grew. "And I can tell you're better. You look much better than you did last night. I almost didn't recognize you."

I laughed a little, swallowing tears. "Yeah, I almost didn't recognize myself! And I *feel* a lot better. Thank you." I sighed. "But now I don't have any idea where he went."

"Well, I will keep an eye out for him."

I was grateful, beyond any possible words, for his kindness. "Thank you."

TRACK 9

WALKING IN THE AIR

M y next stop was the gas station across the street. The attendant had addressed Rick by name. I was certain this guy would know where I could find him and prayed he was there.

As I threw open the gas station door, I found the burly man with the neck tattoo sitting behind the counter with his newspaper. It was a miracle! I rushed inside, made sure the store was empty, and approached him. I drummed my fingers on the counter, letting my hair fall to hide my face again. "Um... e-excuse me?"

He looked up from the newspaper, not saying a word.

"Hi!" I smiled. "S-sorry to bother you, but um... so, I was here last night with someone—"

He returned his attention to the newspaper and said with a bored drawl, "Ya don't say."

"Uh, yep. I... I do say," I let out an awkward, very-fake chuckle.

He stared at me, expressionless. If I had been nervous before, it was nothing compared to how that deadpan look made me feel.

I moved on. "Um... so, anyway. So..." I cleared my throat, aware of how very sweaty my palms were, "I'm here because... the guy I was with —who-who was dressed like a girl, because he's awesome, um. He, um..." I lifted up the duffle bag with a smile, trying to look as though this entire situation wasn't bothering me. "He left this. And, um, I have to give it back. But I don't know where he is."

He looked back at his paper, saying in the monotonous tone of one who clearly doesn't care, "That's a shame."

I knew what he was doing. I'd seen the move before. My heart pounded violently in my chest, trying to break free and run away screaming from the confrontation that was sure to arise, one that I was terrified I'd lose. My voice grew unnaturally pleasant, "Um... I was hoping you could help me. I'm-I'm sorry, but, this is really important. I-I heard you say his name. I know you know who he is. And I just need you to please help me find him, so I can give this back."

He turned a page in the paper. "I don't know what you're talking about."

My stomach lurched as if in a speeding car that'd hit a barrier. "I... I'm pretty sure you *do* know."

"Well, you're pretty wrong."

The new little fire in my soul flared up in anger and words snapped out of me before I could stop them. "Well, I heard you call him by name, so I'm *pretty* sure I'm *not*." I was surprised at myself. I pointed a mental finger of chastisement at me, *What's the matter with you? That was rude. Don't be so rude!*

He continued reading, unfazed, as if my mortal form had turned into nothing more than a heavy wind rattling the door.

I had an urge to throw stuff at him. The display of chips was beginning to look like a magnificent arsenal of weapons. But instead, I shifted my feet, saying, "Look, I'm... I'm *really* sorry for that outburst. I didn't mean—I just—this is really important to me. Can't you just point me in a general direction? Please?"

He grunted his next couple of phrases a little more loudly. "I told you, I don't know what you're talkin' about. I wasn't here last night."

My stomach twisted with anxiety, begging me to give up and leave, but this guy was my last hope. The little light kept my feet firmly planted on the floor and words forced their way out yet again. "But you *were* here. I remember you. I remember that neck tattoo!"

"Lots of people have neck tattoos."

"No they don't!"

He looked up from his paper and fixed me with a murderous glare that I was sure, had his goatee been made of snakes, would've turned me to stone. He slowly rose from his chair, set down the paper, and approached the counter, towering over me so I had to tilt my head back to look up at him. I shuffled a couple of steps backward, sure this man had just grown several feet in every direction. Each word he uttered dripped with venom. "Here's what you're gonna do. You're gonna *keep* that bag, and you're gonna leave, and never set foot in this store again. You're gonna stop putting your pretty little nose where it don't belong and MOVE. ON. Understand?"

My heart lodged itself in my throat in an effort to flee. My vision spun. I could hear my pulse in my ears and my tongue had swollen. Tears stung my eyes as I stared back at him with trembling fingers. For a brief moment, I lost all courage. I was determined to do exactly as he said—pick up the bag and run.

But then I heard my sister's voice in my mind, *"What about his feelings? ...Do you really think you can do better?"* I thought about my ex, how he'd made me feel stupid for everything I was. How he'd made me feel powerless. How he'd used me, tricked me, violated me. I thought about how I'd been treated like a ripped up candy wrapper, robbed of anything of value and discarded, blown around by everyone else's wants. Not even needs, just *wants*, because I didn't matter. I'd been pushed around until I was finally pushed down the stairs. That was how I'd spent my life—like a doormat. I'd been stepped on, torn up, and covered in mud.

Then I thought of Rick, and how he had made me feel. I thought of the kindness and beautiful affection that had been in his eyes when he looked at me. The sincerity in his voice when he spoke to me. He'd completely accepted me. He'd healed me. He'd risked *everything* in order to convince me that I mattered.

My feelings mattered. What I wanted, *mattered*. This was *my* life.

I'd had enough.

The fire consumed my soul. I balled my hands into fists until my fingernails dug into my palms. I wouldn't back down. Not this time. Tears threatened to spill down my cheeks as I stared up at this giant. My vision gave a violent spin and my voice shook, but my tone was rich with resolve. "You don't understand. I just want to give this back. It's too much. I can't take it. I can't. He saved my life." My voice rose in volume. "He didn't just save my life, he *gave it back*. I destroyed it. *I* did! *Me!* By my stupid choices! And then he swoops in, he saves my life, he heals my arm and not just my arm, but my whole body. My body was sick because I *made* it sick and he fixed it! And then he—he leaves all this stuff! *Who does that?"* I couldn't look at him anymore. I was losing control of my words and in spite of my best efforts, I started to cry. "Who just fixes a person—who just sets everything right and then says, 'Oh by the way, here's some gorgeous new clothes and a ton of money' and then just disappears? Not asking for anything—just disappears like nothing happened!" I was practically screaming now, "*WHO DOES THAT?*" I took shallow breaths, my voice fading to a near whisper, "I don't deserve it. I don't."

I threw the bag onto the counter. "Take it. You take it and give it back to him."

I finally glanced up at him and was surprised to see his expression had softened. Understanding showed in his eyes. Still, he didn't back down. He pushed the bag over to me, saying softly, "He don't help people unless he thinks they deserve it." When I didn't take it, he nodded at the bag. "Take it and go."

"No."

He shook his head. "You need it. He wouldn't have given it to you if you didn't."

I studied him. He was a mountain, unmoving and unflinching. My muscles deflated and my shoulders slumped, all power leaving me as if the silence between us had sucker punched me in the gut. He had no intention of helping me. No matter how much I screamed and pled my case, I would never get him to bend. And he was right. I had nothing. I needed it. I really did.

It was the first battle I'd shown up to on my behalf, and I'd lost.

Wiping snot and tears on my already gross shirt, I grabbed the bag. As I hoisted it back onto my shoulder, my knees gave out on me and I stumbled into the chip rack, knocking several bags onto the floor. I yelled, "I'm *not* picking those up!" I swung open the door and marched out... only to immediately feel guilty, run back in, and quickly stack them back onto the shelves. I scurried out as fast as my trembling limbs could carry me.

Just the night before, I had been walking in the air, in a world full of wonder and magic as pieces of my shattered life were stitched back together with careful hands. Now, as I walked away from the gas station sobbing, I felt as though I'd been knocked out of the sky. Rick had been an answer to a hopeless prayer, and so much more than I could've ever hoped for. And now, with the rising of the sun, he was gone. He was really gone. How could someone I had just met leave behind such a massive, empty space?

That night, I sat on my hotel bed, watching Seinfeld reruns while drinking a Dr. Pepper, eating two large fries and a chicken enchilada the size of a plate. It was a nice escape while it lasted, but the second the M*A*S*H theme song started, reality crashed back down. I shut off the TV and went back to staring at the bag on the bed beside me.

I wanted to know why he'd left, but then again, maybe I didn't. Maybe it'd hurt too much. I kept going over everything I'd said and done. *I had to have done something wrong*, I thought. *I scared him away.*

Still, despite all I'd put him through, he had done everything he could to help me. I would never forget that. I thought of that night before, how my world had come to an ugly end. And now, one day later, I had everything I needed to start again. He had set me free. There was no way I was going to take that for granted. I was determined to start my life over and somehow, this time, I was going to get it right.

With this in mind, I took a pen and the complimentary notepad and wrote down every bottled up wound that wanted to spill out, including the new one where Rick had left me. It took up every free space of every last square sheet of paper. I stared at the end results for several minutes before ripping them up and flushing them down the toilet. A weight lifted off my chest as I watched the pieces wash away into the sewers where they belonged.

The next morning, I threw away my old clothes and my old shoes and I put on a new outfit. I hoisted the duffle bag onto my shoulder and left the hotel for good, more than ready to move on.

VOLUME 2

"YOU DON'T HAVE TO BE CRAZY TO DO THIS, BUT IT SINCERELY HELPS."
~BOB ROSS

TRACK 1
DAYS GO BY

I sat on the bed in my new apartment, holding a brand new music box in my hands. My heart bled with nostalgia and regret as I traced the carvings, thinking of the old one that had sat on my mother's dresser back home. This one was about the size of a child's shoe box and made of dark mahogany. The carvings consisted of scenes from Star Wars: A New Hope, and cheerfully sang the theme song when wound and opened. My mother's had been tiny, delicate, and old. The wood had been chipped, the dark finish worn and patchy, but the delicate carvings of flowers and waves declared that it had once been beautiful.

My mom didn't have any reason to keep it. It hadn't held any sentimental value to her. She'd found it in an antique shop somewhere and had bought it for the song. It was a melody she'd never heard before and one I hadn't heard since. She'd wind the battered little box, open the lid, and hum along as she put on her make-up. That was why my father had kept it after she died. He told me it reminded him to see the world as she had seen the music box. "She could see that the box was so much more than its scars," he'd told me, "that the beauty was still there in its song."

He'd said this to me when I was around eight-years-old. He'd caught me listening to it in his bedroom after a particularly bad day at school. After cutting candy and gum out of my hair, I'd laid on my parents' bed with the music box. I'd focused on the music, trying to pry fading memories of her from the crevices of my mind and piece them together. Memories of her hugs. Of the sound of her voice. I thought if I could see her loving smile again, everything would be made right.

Dad sat beside me. I could tell he didn't know what to say, but that had never stopped him from trying before, so it wasn't about to now.

"Sometimes, when things get tough for me," he'd said, "When I start to think that people are a bunch of..." he tried to think of an appropriate phrase for an eight-year-old, "evil slimy, worms that eat poop."

I giggled. "You said 'poop.'"

"I did! I did, because that's what they are. Poopy worms that eat poop."

That made me outright laugh.

He continued. "But when I start to think that way, and start to think that things ain't ever gonna change, that's about when I hear your mom's voice in my head sayin', 'Just listen closely, Eli. You're gonna hear the world sing.' And you know what? When I listen to her, I always do." He smiled warmly. "Always do. True story."

I smiled at the memory of those words. I remembered thinking at the time that it was a weird thing to say and wondered why I'd never heard Mom's voice in my head. But after meeting Rick, I thought I was starting to understand what my dad had meant. The world was battered and broken. But listening closely, I was beginning to hear the melody. It was sweet, subtle, and beautiful, buried underneath all the madness. I could hear it in the compassion and healing kindness given by others. It was there and just as real as the rest of the mess. And, as Rick had shown me, it wasn't too late to become a part of the song.

Over the last three weeks, I had tried to. The new thing I asked myself at least once a day was, "What would Lipstick Rick do?" This question had led to some very interesting situations. Like, when I decided to find an apartment in the city, which I had learned was a very small city compared to the others surrounding it along the West Coast. It was called New Haven. The name was rather fitting, at least to me. I found an apartment five blocks from the beach. I offered the landlady six-thousand dollars up front to let me move in without a background check or references. To my surprise, she started crying. Instead of looking for a quick way out of the situation as I normally would've done, I tried to do what I thought Lipstick Rick would do, only without any of the grace or charisma.

I swallowed my anxiety and patted her on the shoulder the way someone would try to console a hungry lion and asked her what was wrong. She ended up telling me about how her young son had been diagnosed with some rare disease, how the hospital bills were piling up, and how she had no idea what they were going to do. I sat and listened to her for at least an hour, just letting her cry and get everything out. I felt so bad for her that I ended up giving her three-thousand dollars more. She tried to give it back, but I wouldn't take it. She hugged me more tightly than I was comfortable with, but I did my best to return it.

In one day, I had given almost half of the money away, but I didn't think Rick would've disagreed with my decision since she clearly needed it more. And for a few shining seconds, I felt a sense of purpose and direction. I knew I wouldn't be able to give away thousands of dollars to every person suffering from misfortune that crossed my path, but I was sure that in each situation, I could think of someway to help.

Once I had a place to live, I started looking for a job. It wasn't easy, but I managed to find one as a waitress at a greasy spoon restaurant down the road, where the manager—Marie—took pity on me and had little issue with my list of issues, so long as I was willing to work for crappy pay. Marie was a thin woman in her early thirties with long, black hair, extremely pale skin, an intimidating stare, and a very scary, dry sense of humor that always left me wondering if she was really joking. But she was an excellent cook, with very unique recipes—which she claimed she had gotten from a book that had been handed down to her through several generations, dating back to the Salem Witch Trials. Her great, great, great (etc) grandmother had been accused of witchcraft because she wouldn't share the secret ingredient to her potato basil soup (it was basil).

Thanks to whatever Rick had done to fix my brain, I was able to manage my anxieties rather than hide in the bathroom, afraid of everyone and overwhelmed by the craze of the restaurant business, which I was certain I would've done had I been working there only a few weeks before. Marie was happy enough with my work that she gave me plenty of hours, so I knew I wouldn't starve to death. I'd be able to pay my rent and hopefully save some of the money I had left over from Rick. What I was saving for, I didn't know. Just... something.

As I left the restaurant for home after my first day, I found an old man sleeping in a nest he'd made underneath a cardboard box in an alley. His blankets were dirty and torn, and though I was several feet away, I could smell sickly sweet body odor and rotting fabric. I couldn't breathe as I tried to adjust to the sudden stench. My initial reaction was disgust and fear since he was probably crazy and who knew what he'd do to me. But I asked myself, "What would Lipstick Rick do?" I was sure that, whatever he'd do, he'd be smart about it, but I also knew there was something that could be done.

The next day, I bought a fluffy blanket and, wrestling my feelings of trepidation, took it to the old man on my way to work. He accepted it with a gleam in his eye. "Would you look at this! It's brand new! It smells so nice." He sniffed it. "*You're* so nice. Thank you, thank you."

I was starving by the end of the day, so I made a sandwich at the restaurant to take home with me. On my way up the street, I found him still sitting there on the sidewalk. I sat with him and gave him half of my sandwich. I learned his name was John. He had dark, freckled skin, brown eyes, and salt and pepper hair. He had a rich, soulful voice that easily rivaled Barry White's. Hanging out with him soon became routine. Every day I worked, I'd brave the smells and split my sandwich and just let him talk. He told me how he'd fought in a war a long time ago. It had been a very big deal at the time. He'd warned the people how their selfishness, greed, and lust for power would cause the world to end, and he insisted with elaborate nods, "It hasn't happened yet, but one day, they'll see... they'll see."

He told me how he had lost his wife, children, and all of his friends during that war. After that, he'd spent a lot of time traveling and ended up here. Now he was on the lookout for monsters. The bad ones and the good ones, and the one monster that was somewhere in between. "Especially that one," he'd said. "He could really make a mess of things." He said the bad ones had fallen from the sky. They stuck to the shadows mostly, so he encouraged me to not walk in them because these things were very, *very* bad. I assured him I'd do my best.

After a couple of weeks, he told me how much he looked forward to seeing me. I was very happy to hear it, as I'd spent a lot of time worrying that I wasn't doing enough for him, wondering, *Shouldn't I help him get some anti-psychotics or something? Or at least find him a good psychiatrist? Or an apartment?*

As if perceiving my thoughts, John said to me, "You know, it does a lot of good to just have another person *hear* you. It's been a long while since I had someone to talk to and I forgot how nice it is." He looked at me thoughtfully. "You need someone to hear *you*." Before I could say a word in response, he looked up and pointed at the sky with a knowing smile, as if the sky had spoken to him and had made an excellent point. He patted me on the shoulder. "You'll find him—no, *actually*," he listened again, then nodded, "he'll find *you*, and *then* you'll find him." He chuckled, like this was a very clever joke. "Life is so strange." He sat back, taking another bite out of his sandwich.

I stared at him, puzzled. Deep down, a part of me was really hoping he was making a real prediction and that it was about Rick, but I knew better. Still, I knew he meant well so I went along with it, as I always did with the weird things he said. "Well, great! That's great."

"Well..." He looked back up at the sky. "Hmm." He shook his head. "That's what's most likely to happen. It depends on what you choose to do."

"Oh... kay..."

John took another bite. "Now what I want to know is, are you finally going to buy your dad that music box?"

I had told John about my tradition of buying my dad a music box every year for his birthday since I'd left home. What I hadn't told him was how I'd actually *run away* from home, stolen his money, and would therefore send the music boxes without a return address and from a different post office each time. I always sent the music box with a birthday card containing whatever money I'd been able to scrounge up, and a letter that would consist of me pouring out my heart in a hopeless apology. I would tell him how I wished I'd listened to him. Once or twice I told him how I wanted to come home. But mostly I just wanted him to know that I missed him and thought about him all the time. I would say how I knew I could never make up for what I'd done and that no apology was enough.

Yeah, I left all of that out when talking to John.

I told him, "You know, I think I'm gonna. It's a pretty awesome box."

"If you want to save yourself a whole lot of grief, you know what I think you should do? *Before* you send the box?"

"What's that?"

"I think you should call him."

My whole body seized up in terror at the thought. "I don't have a phone that works." It was the truth. I had bought a phone with plans to get a landline, but conveniently, in that very moment, I decided I didn't need it after all.

"Ever heard of a pay phone? They still exist, ya know. They're rare, but they exist. I'm telling you, your dad would love it if you called him to wish him a happy birthday this year. I know I would, anyway. There is nothing I wouldn't give to hear my daughter's voice again." He paused, listening to the sky. "Now, if your sister answers—"

My eyebrows shot up. My brain scoured through all of its memory files in an attempt to recollect whether or not I had ever—even once—mentioned Jane. My brain came back to me with, *I can't find anything!*

I stammered, "M-my sister?"

He nodded, like this wasn't weird at all, as if we talked about her and her silly shenanigans on a daily basis. "Yes, your sister. If she answers—"

"H-have I ever told you about my sister?"

He paused, his eyes darting to the side. "How else would I know about her?"

It was hard to argue with that. I made a mental note to be more careful about how much I blabbed to John.

He went on, "Anyway, if she answers, just hang up and call back later. Don't try to talk to her. You only want to talk to your dad."

My heart thumped against my chest, sending blood racing through my veins so fast, it actually stung. Because, as much as I hated to admit it, he made sense. I needed to talk to my dad. I wanted to hear his voice. I wanted to go home.

But what if he didn't want me to? What if he hated me? What if that was all he had to say to me? But even if all of those terrible possibilities were true, didn't I need to know for sure? Because, even though I didn't believe the odds were in my favor, there was a chance—a small, ant-sized chance—that I was wrong.

I did my best to hide how much John's words affected me and muttered, "That's good advice."

"I know."

TRACK 2

TELEPHONE

That conversation echoed in my head as my fingers gripped the music box I was holding. I fought to find a way around John's logic, finally landing on the question that now dictated my life:

What would Lipstick Rick do?

Honestly, in this case, I wasn't sure right away. Rick had vehemently declared he would never return to Thera. Still, I was quite sure that if he had wronged his parents the way I had wronged my dad, he would be brave. He would face the consequences and make it right.

"Curse you, John," I whispered.

But it would take a miracle to find a working pay phone—which gave me an idea. I told myself, "You know what? If I see a pay phone, I will call him."

I did my usual routine when it came to the music boxes. I poured my heart into a letter, letting him know that I had left my ex, how I could see more clearly *why* I had done the stupid things I did and better understood what had happened to me, and tried to explain it. I told him I was okay now. I didn't know why I put that, I wasn't sure he'd care, I just felt like I needed to. I talked to him about the meteor shower, how I had dreamt that I'd watched it with him. I let him know how much I loved him, and again, with tears stinging my eyes, I told him how I was so very sorry. I put the letter in a goofy birthday card and stuffed five-thousand dollars into the envelope. It tore a little—flimsy thing.

As I approached the post office, I saw it.

A pay phone. I actually saw a pay phone.

It was like finding a unicorn, only I wasn't at all excited about it (though part of me wished I had a camera). My stomach dropped and my palms became sweaty. I forced myself to look at my shoes in order to resist its silent, siren-like call and pass it, telling myself in an out loud, angry whisper, "I can't take what John said so freaking seriously. He's crazy! Nothing will happen if I send it before I call. I need it to get there *on his birthday!*"

I successfully made it beyond the pay phone and sent the music box, but passing it again on my way back proved to be even more difficult. I tried to keep walking, but my shoes now weighed a thousand pounds. My steps slowed to a stop and I found myself, very much against my will, turning around to stare at it.

I felt a horrible pull in my gut, calling me toward the phone. I shuffled in its direction, my stomach in horrible knots as I bounced on my heels, glaring at the black receiver and the rusty cord. I rubbed my neck and looked up and down the block, hoping someone would swoop in and say, "Noooo! Don't touch that phone! It's covered in anthrax!"

Maybe it *was* covered in anthrax. Just because nobody was coming up the street and saying so, didn't mean it wasn't so.

That's a good point, me, I continued thinking. *Really, it's for my own safety that I don't make this call.*

I backed away.

Then I leapt at the phone, grabbed the receiver, and dug in my purse for change, only to discover that all I had were pennies and a couple of dimes. It wasn't enough.

I let out a sigh of relief and hung up the phone. Still, as I stared at it, I was startled to find myself feeling a twinge of disappointment.

When I returned to my apartment, I laid on my mattress—one of the few pieces of furniture I had—and, to my alarm, wept. I asked myself, *What am I doing, running away from my mistakes? What am I doing with this second chance? With this life Rick so graciously saved? What am I? A... waitress? I should be doing more... but what?*

I fell asleep, puzzling over the question and praying for direction. My prayer had so miraculously been answered before, I was really hoping the route would work again.

TRACK 3

PEOPLE ARE STRANGE

It was a slow evening at the restaurant. Marie, Chef Alejandro, and I were gathered around the bar, watching the news. Alejandro was in his early thirties with big brown eyes, sleeve tattoos and a large, jagged scar over his left eye that I just knew held a fascinating story but didn't dare ask him what it was.

Some celebrity on the news was claiming that he had twice been robbed of millions of dollars by a doppelgänger that looked and acted so much like him, he had been able to simply walk into the bank, go through all the protocols to withdraw the money, and walk back out. I had to read his name on the TV before I remembered it, which was ridiculous. How could I have forgotten?

It was Harold Grossman. He was one of those slimy businessmen that had his tentacles in everything—Hollywood, big corporations, even the government somehow. He'd seemed like a really *gross* man and had become an inside joke that my dad and I shared when we saw him on TV. We'd watch whatever show he was on and play a game we'd called, *Who's Grosser?* Harold usually won.

We watched Harold Grossman rant about finding whoever kept stealing his money, while the security cameras clearly showed him going into the bank and leaving. We all had a good laugh about that.

"You can't blame somebody else for what you don't remember doin' when you were high," chuckled Alejandro. "'*It wasn't me! I swear!*'"

"'But sir,'" I said all detectively. "'We have several witnesses and surveillance footage of you walking into the bank and making the withdrawal—'"

"'Well they're wrong! *You're* wrong! This is a conspiracy against me!'"

Marie added, "'Tom Cruise is a lizard man and the president's a vampire!'"

Alejandro furrowed his brow.

She folded her arms defensively. "What? He feasts on the blood of his enemies by night. Tom Cruise joins him on Mondays. They drink blood and watch football." I wanted to laugh but I wasn't sure if I should, so it came out in a weird, hesitant snort. She stared at me, which was really unnerving. After a moment of silence, she walked away, shouting, "That's the real conspiracy!"

Alejandro leaned into me and muttered, "That's why you're the waitress that talks to people, and she stays in the back—far, far away from people."

I felt a sense of triumph at those words. "I never, *ever* thought the day would come where somebody would actually tell me that I'm not terrible at talking to people."

"No, no, no, no. I didn't say you weren't terrible at talking to people, I just said you're better at it than Marie. The bar is not very high."

My lips thinned into an unamused line. "I'm glad you cleared that up."

The bell hanging over the door of the restaurant chimed as a group of men entered, laughing so on cue that they could've been the laugh track to the sitcom I imagined myself in. Alejandro ushered me toward them, but before I could say hello, Marie popped out of the back and handed them menus with a robotic cheerfulness and over-exaggerated smile that made her seem a little insane. "Sit wherever you want. No one's here, so it doesn't matter."

Alejandro groaned and disappeared into the kitchen. I peered around the corner at him and said in a hushed tone, "That wasn't *that* bad. At least she didn't bring up Tom Cruise."

Though their laughter *did* die off in awkward little bursts, followed by awkward little rounds of "um" and "okay" and an awkward exchange of glances where they seemed to be wondering if they'd just stepped into The Twilight Zone. The three gentlemen wandered through the restaurant before one of them—a man who looked to be in his thirties and reminded me of the Brawny Paper Towels lumberjack—motioned to a booth by the window.

Feeling pressure to be as charming as possible, I fought an onslaught of anxiety as I headed for their table. "Hey, y'all! My name is Emily, I'll be taking care of you folks tonight." My hillbilly accent had slipped into overdrive mode, as it tended to do lately when I was trying to show off my new confidence while scared to death. I bit my tongue and cursed at myself, telling my brain to *get it together* as they ordered their drinks. I said as blandly as I could, "I'll be back with those drinks in a jiffy."

I berated myself as I walked away. *In a jiffy? Who says that?*

The gentlemen in the booth eventually relaxed, getting back to their conversation and laughing. Once they got their food, one of them told me to pass his compliments on to the chef for his steak. He had an olive complexion, almond eyes, and shoulder length, black hair that had a shimmer to it worthy of a shampoo commercial. The third guy—a well-dressed man with short, blond hair and blue eyes—responded to this with, "See? I *told* you the food was good here! I usually try to avoid food cooked in this much grease, but on my off-days, I just get craving this place."

Several more groups came in, turning the restaurant into an unusually packed circus. As I grabbed dishes to take to an older couple sitting in the back, I heard the group of men erupt with laughter, followed by the lumberjack exclaiming something that nearly made me drop the plates. "Nothing like a night out with Lipstick Rick!"

The world around me faded into a void, back into my dreams where I stood on his world and once again, I'd forgotten how to breathe.

Nothing else mattered.

I was sure Rick didn't want to see me again. He had disappeared, after all. I knew I should leave it alone. *I really should,* I told myself. *I shouldn't say a word.*

I drifted toward the old couple in the back with their food. I saw them trade dishes from the corner of my eye when I walked away. Someone tried to hail me as I made my way to the kitchen and I promised I'd be right with them. I just had to think, to breathe. Alejandro didn't look up from his cooking as I darted to the far corner by the freezer. I rubbed my temples, my face, taking deep breaths.

My gut twisted and knotted up in a feeling that consumed me, reaching to my fingertips. I thought about how the worst mistakes I had ever made had happened when I hadn't listened to this powerful feeling —not running when it had told me to run, not turning when it had told me to turn. It grabbed me by the heart and screamed, *What are you doing hiding by the freezer?! Get out there and FIND HIM!*

Really, it couldn't hurt to just find him and say thank you, again, right? And let him know that his efforts weren't totally wasted?

My limbs shook as I made my way to the lumberjack's table. I cursed the fact that my hair was tied up in a messy bun and that I didn't have more loose strands to hide my face behind. I tried to make my voice sound as normal as possible, though it trembled, "Hey, y'all! How is everything? S-still good?"

They nodded politely and happily. The one with pretty hair said in a very kind tone, "Yeah, we're doing great! But can I get a refill on this Mountain Dew? And to go, please?"

"Sure! Yeah. Absolutely, darlin'!" *Stop it!*

My brain told my legs to move, but they didn't. The guys exchanged why-isn't-she-leaving looks before looking back at me.

My body seized up, caught between my brain wanting to go get his stupid drink and my gut screaming at me, *Just ASK THEM!*

My mouth started talking without my brain's permission, my anxiety peaking to a level that made the whole scene feel like an out-of-body experience. "So... I, uh, heard one of you guys say the name, 'Lipstick Rick.'"

All three pairs of eyes shot wide open. An "Uh, oh" escaped the lumberjack's lips.

The guy with pretty hair straightened, his demeanor uneasy but kind. "Oh! Uh, how do you know Lipstick Rick? Have you been to one of our shows?"

Feeling minutely better about things, I pressed on. "I uh—actually, Lipstick Rick helped me a while back. He literally saved my life."

The blond guy glared at the lumberjack and said in an undertone, exaggerating his name as if it were a very bad word, "Way to go, *Charlie.*"

My heart picked up the pace again. "I don't mean to pry or anything. I just, I really wanted to thank him again, for saving me. He did so much—"

The blond guy whisper-shouted to the lumberjack—Charlie—so I heard him perfectly, "She's probably crazy! You've brought the crazies upon us!"

I tried to lighten the situation by laughing at myself a little bit. "Uh, well, I am a little crazy, but—"

He turned to Charlie again. "She just admitted it! She's crazy!"

That backfired. "No, no, I mean, I just—"

"She just denied it! That means she IS crazy!"

The guy with pretty-hair sighed. "Bill..."

Charlie frowned at blond-haired Bill. "Seriously, why even bother whispering? We can all hear you." He leaned away from Bill in an I-don't-know-him sort of way and glanced up at me. "Sorry about that guy. He's crazy. Like, *really* crazy."

Bill responded with a marrow-melting glare.

My heart was pounding now. This was starting to feel like that night at the gas station all over again. "Look, I don't mean him any harm, okay? I just—"

Charlie held out a hand to stop me. "Look, kid. We get it."

I didn't feel like they did. Bill was looking up at me with a very suspicious stare, one blue eye narrowed and the other wide open.

The pretty-haired guy added, "We really do. We all owe Rick so much. Maybe, if you could bring me that Mountain Dew and our check, I can give you an address where you can find him."

Bill and I had the same reaction, only Bill looked like he might explode. *"What?"*

Pretty-hair guy ignored Bill. "Yeah, of course."

Charlie placed a calming hand on Bill's shoulder, as if to restrain him from strangling the pretty-hair guy.

I tried to ignore them. "That would be so great! Thank you! Thank you so much!"

"Sure! No problem!"

I asked if it was all going to be on one check and promptly excused myself from their table. I couldn't believe my luck! I was elated. I tried to remind myself not to get my hopes up. There was a very good chance any info he gave me would be bogus, but I couldn't help it. Before this, I had been certain I would never see Rick again. Sure, I'd stayed in New

Haven with a tiny thread of hope that I might bump into him someday. And every time the bell to the restaurant rang, I looked to see if it was him walking through the door, but I knew it was all a long shot.

Until now.

Then there was a commotion and Bill whisper-yelling, "Go! Go! Go! Go!"

I looked over just in time to watch all three guys bolt out of the restaurant. I sat down the Mountain Dew and chased after them. "Wait!"

I ran out onto the sidewalk. They were running way too fast for me to even have a chance to catch up to them with my short little legs. I shouted at them, "No! Wait! Stop!" I balled my hands into fists and bounced a little as I ended with, *"I'M NOT CRAZY!"*

At that, a voice with a weird accent said from behind me, "Shout it at them a little louder. That'll make it more convincing."

TRACK 4

TIME AFTER TIME

I took a deep breath and sighed. My shoulders slumped forward as all the oomph and hope vanished from me. I rubbed my face, feeling stupid, as I turned to look at the man who had spoken.

I froze.

He appeared to be in his late twenties or early thirties, leaning against the outside of the restaurant and holding a walking stick. He had messy red hair and angular, handsome features and wore a white, button up shirt with buttons undone near the neck, revealing a very pale chest and a strange, sunburst-like scar over his heart. But it didn't have the same texture as any scar I'd ever seen. It was perfectly smooth. It almost looked as though someone had taken a photograph of the noon-day sun and I was looking at the negative. This was all fine. What was unnerving about him were his eyes. One was bright blue while the other was unmistakably red. Not naturally-red-with-a-little-pink-in-it, but evil-robot-from-the-future-sent-to-kill-me kind of red. I felt like I'd entered *Wayne's World* 2 and had to resist the urge to point and say, *Why would I want to look at your eye? Is there something wrong with that weird eye?*

He smiled, his expression that of someone who'd found a dear friend who had been lost. His eyes even watered a little, as if he were holding back tears. But I was certain I had never seen him before. I would've vividly remembered that terrifying eye.

Forcing a sheepish smile and thinking about crying, I admitted, "Yeah, that didn't go very well."

He chuckled. "No, it did not."

I stepped toward the restaurant. He spoke again, a tone of reverence in his voice, "Emily Grace Adams."

I stopped. He knew my name. My full name. Only about three

people knew that. Slowly, I turned to face him. "How do you know my name?"

His weird eyes lit up with affection—an expression I'd only ever seen on Rick's face. Another pang of loss hit me. Why was this guy looking at me like that? I had an urge to demand an answer, but my heart was hammering too fast. I was too unnerved. Too shocked. I couldn't find my voice. My words squeaked out instead of speaking with any authority, "People don't know my name. My full name. How do you know my name? D-do you know my dad or something?"

"That's a secret."

I didn't like that at all. The little fire inside of me sparked and words slipped out. "That's creepy."

That was rude. My mind chided. Then I argued, *But that's creepy! He's being creepy! He should be called out on that, right?*

He went on. "I want to tell you how I know. I wish I could. You have no idea how much I wish I could tell you." He looked to be swallowing tears. "But I don't want to risk changing too much."

I shifted my feet. What was that supposed to mean? *I should leave*, I thought. *I really, really should leave...*

"I have been waiting for this very moment for so long... so very long."

I didn't care for that, either. Was this where he went all Terminator on me? Had I become Sarah Connor? No, I wasn't that important.

He straightened, moving his walking stick to his left hand, leaning on it instead of the wall. "I'm here to remedy a mistake that was made out of fear."

I furrowed my brow, part of me wanting to bolt back into the restaurant and hide under a table, and the other part insatiably curious and unable to move my feet.

"See, next Tuesday, Steve—the man with the magnificent hair—will crack under his guilt and finally give you a flyer for Bob's Club Festivus, like I'm about to do now." He reached into the breast pocket of his shirt and pulled out a folded sheet of paper. "After that, it'll take two more Tuesdays for you to work up the courage to actually *go* to the club, and then you'll spend the rest of the week fretting over everything and won't actually show up until the following Monday, which is Ladies' Night. Which means, it'll be three weeks and five days from now before you finally see Rain at the club, and I just can't have that, because..." His expression grew far away, the sorrow that had been buried underneath it rising to the surface. "All I ever wanted was more time... more time..." He looked down at the pavement and sighed, saying in a sing-song voice, "More time, more time. And so..." He straightened up again, his gaze piercing mine. The world stopped for a moment. "I'm *giving* you more time."

He stepped towards me, flattening out the paper and handing it to me. "If I fail at everything else, at least I can steal more time."

A wave of butterflies fluttered through me at those words, reminding me in a most unsettling way of the letter Rick had left me. Hesitantly, I took the paper from him. Sure enough, it was a cheap advertisement for "Bob's Club Festivus: A Club For The Rest Of Us," the "Hufflepuff House of Real Life," and "If you're a normal person, go to a normal person's club. If you're afraid to go out on Friday night because normal people scare you, come join us! We feel the same way." It advertised live music on weekends and Mondays, with Ladies' Night on Monday. I smiled.

Wait. What the crap was happening? Who was this guy? Did he just predict the future and then make it all irrelevant by changing it? And *why*? I looked up at him and it hit me. That blue eye didn't simply *look* like it was glowing—it *was* glowing. Just like Rick's eyes had done.

And then I realized, when he referred to Rick, he hadn't said 'Rick', he had said 'Rain.' He had called him by his secret-code, real name, which could only mean he knew Rain—the *real* Rain. Because... because...

Because he was *like* Rain.

I stared at him for way too long. "Um, w-who are you? Are you... are you Rain's friend?"

"Not the friend you're thinking of. It's a long story." He pointed to the flyer. "Rain will tell you. You should go back inside. You're going to get in *biiig* trouble if you stay out here talking to me."

So, there's three of them? I looked back down at the flyer. "Okay..."

As I mechanically turned toward the restaurant door, a soulful voice hollered, "Thipka!"

The man perked up and turned around, as did I. John emerged from the shadows into the glow of the restaurant lights. "I've been waiting for you."

My mind was blown. Had I just entered a parallel universe where Scooby-Doo was reality? If so, did that make me Velma? No, Velma was smart. I must've been some side character that was on only one episode —apparently *this* episode. Jinkies! "John?"

John ignored me and continued staring at the strange man. "Come to make a mess of things?"

The strange man didn't reply.

John continued, "I need to remind you that you can't stop it. No matter what you do." His expression grew very somber. "You can't change it. You can warn. You can help me build cities underground—"

Build cities underground?

"—and warn some more, but you can't stop them from coming."

My body felt abnormally cold. "W-who's coming?"

They both ignored me. The strange-eye-man's demeanor fell, but he said with a firm resolve, "I have to try. You *know* I have to try."

John nodded patiently. "I know."

"And I think I'd have a better chance if you were willing to help me. I know you won't, but—"

John gave a sad, gentle smile. "Why do you think I'm here?"

I was frustrated now. The little fire in my soul was throwing little fits. I could see my brain with its hands on its hips, worked up with a new attitude and saying, *You know what? I've about had it with this.*

Right? I said to my brain. *I should totally, like, say something. Right? Yes? No. Yes? Yes! I should!*

The strange man grinned. He said conversationally, "You know, I read about you in the paper recently."

John chuckled. "Yeah, I did, too."

"HEY!" I shouted. The little fire in my soul had exploded, my brain now taking whatever files it could find and throwing them at them. "*Excuse* me! What is going on? How did I end up on this week's episode of... of... I can't think of a show, but I'm sure there's one out there that's fitting!"

John looked at me as if he hadn't seen me there and asked, "Did you call your dad?"

That caught me off guard. "No."

He responded with a shake of his head. I would've felt better if he'd screamed at me.

At that precise moment, Marie opened the door. "Um, Emily?" I whirled on her, hoping my face was hiding my sudden panic. She looked annoyed. "While you're out here yelling at homeless people, there are some very angry customers yelling at me because they haven't seen their waitress in a while."

I felt terrible. Poor Marie. "I'm so sorry, Marie, I—" I turned to look back at the strange man and John only to find that they had disappeared. My gaze searched the shadows. I turned back to Marie to ask if she'd seen them, but she'd gone back inside the restaurant.

I rubbed my forehead, where I was now feeling the beginnings of a horrible migraine. I meandered toward the door, looking again at the flyer. I flipped the flyer over, hoping to find the answers to every single question wreaking havoc on my mind. Instead, I found something else, something that made my stomach sink into my spine. All over the back of the flyer, written in different sizes of letters and in red ink, were the same two words—

"SAVE THEM."

TRACK 5

HEART'S A MESS

I couldn't sleep. I went from staring at the ceiling to tossing onto my side and staring at the wall. I tried to close my eyes, but all I saw were the words "SAVE THEM" in bright red letters. If I dozed off, the letters bled.

I rehearsed the strange conversations in my mind, seeing that gleeful red eye stare into my soul. *"I'm here to remedy a mistake made out of fear... All I ever wanted was more time... I'm giving you more time."* And then John—John! Whom I'd trusted! *"You can't stop them from coming."* John was crazy, right? But then again—and the thought kept nagging at me—what if he *wasn't* crazy?

I did eventually fall into a fitful sleep where I dreamt of shadows that followed me down a dark hallway, whispering things to me as they stole my strength. As I reached the end of the hall, I crumbled into a heap on an old, familiar bed—my ex's old bed—weak and powerless.

I woke up sobbing, knotting my hands in my hair and pulling on it until it hurt, wanting that pain to outweigh what I felt inside. A hole had opened back up inside of me at the dream and I was being dragged in. I felt like I was back inside his room. Helplessness and shame swirled around inside me like a huge wave, vivid and real, and full of so much pain, gripping my stomach with heavy nausea. My thoughts ran wild. *I'm a monster. I'm horrible. I did this to me. It's my fault. It's all my fault.*

I let go of my hair and grabbed my blankets, holding them close to my chest as I struggled to breathe. I searched my mind for comfort, *any* comfort.

With warmth and light, I thought I heard my mother's voice for the first time since she'd passed away, distant and gentle. *"You're not there anymore, Emily."*

I clung to that thought like a life preserver thrown out to me in a storm-tossed sea. This wasn't real. It wasn't really happening again. I was alone, safe and sound, in my own room, in my own apartment. I focused on the cool fabric of my blanket, the shadows on the walls and the beating of my heart until the wave of horrible feelings receded.

I gave up on sleep after that. I wrapped myself in the blankets from my bed and planted myself in a nest of other blankets I'd made on the floor in front of my TV. I had a TV but no furniture—because I had my priorities straight. I drowned my thoughts and nightmares in infomercials and a documentary on World War II, since my landlady had helped me get free cable. I was grateful for it, as I only owned five movies and had already watched all of them at least eight times.

That Friday turned into one of the longest, most nervewracking days of my entire life. My mind chased back and forth, trying to decide between going to Bob's Club Festivus or burning the flyer and keeping a safe distance. I'd seen enough movies and had encountered enough terrible people to wonder: What if it was all a trap for Rick? Obviously, everyone who knew him was extremely protective of him and for good reason.

But then, if that Thipka-guy were setting a trap for Rick, why even bother giving me the flyer in the first place? Why not just go there himself? Why use me?

I thought of the haunting "SAVE THEMs" written all over the back of the flyer. Of how John had said, *"You can't stop them from coming."* No. I was convinced Thipka wanted me to deliver a warning.

But again, *why me?* I was sure Rick had forgotten all about me a long time ago. Probably forgot the second he left the hotel room. What did I have to do with anything? It was just dumb.

Work was awful that evening. I had indeed, as Thipka predicted, gotten into big trouble with Marie the night before. She stared at me mirthlessly as I explained to her and Alejandro how I had chased those guys because I thought they hadn't paid—which was partially true. It'd been in the back of my mind. But they had paid. They'd left money on the table. No good excuse had come to mind for my extended absence. Alejandro told me, "I like you. You're alright. But we need better from you." I took this as, "I don't want to fire you, but I will," and that made things weird for a while.

With all the cleaning and closing up, I didn't get back to my apartment to change until after midnight. My stomach twisted as I debated on what to wear. I was so nervous. I knew I needed to do this, to let Rick know he might be in danger, but as much as I wanted to deny it, as much as I wanted to believe that I was now Miss Independent and fine on my own, there was this gnawing hope that this time, he wouldn't go away. I knew I didn't deserve it, but I wanted him in my life. I wanted him to stay.

In a speed that impressed myself, I showered and tamed my hair so it hung in shiny, loose curls instead of a big bush on my head. I put on more make-up than I could remember wearing in years while trying to make it look as natural as possible, topping it off with a bit of pink lip gloss. Honestly, once I'd put on the black dress Rain had given me, I was quite pleased with the results. Even *I* thought I was good-lookin'. Though, when it came down to choosing shoes, I ultimately chose the sneakers over the fancy ones. With all the odd things going on, I thought I should be prepared, just in case I needed to run.

But I didn't wear socks. I thought that'd make it a little more acceptable.

I threw on a black coat, keeping my mace in the deceptively massive pockets, just in case, and grabbed my purse, praying I'd get to the club before it closed. I'd never been to a club before, so I had no idea when they closed. TV had told me that it was super late, so I had hope.

On the taxi ride there, I grew increasingly nervous. I wasn't sure they'd even let me in without an ID, or if there would be a huge line to get in like in the movie *The Mask*. I wondered if I'd need to bribe someone and imagined myself throwing money at people. Even if I could just throw money at people, would it actually work? Knowing my luck, the bouncer would just be like, "Nope. Still not getting in."

When I arrived at the address, I was surprised to find that Bob's Club Festivus was actually terrifying. It didn't look like a club, or *any* sort of functional building for that matter. It looked like a dilapidated bowling alley that was used as a haunted house attraction during the Halloween season. The words "Club Festivus" were in glowing, blood red letters that looked more like a threat than an invitation and reminded me of my nightmares from the night before. The "C" and the middle "s" flickered, and the "s" at the end of "Festivus" dangled precariously, like at any second it would fall off and shatter on the pavement. The windows were boarded up, the roof to my left appeared to be caved in, and the doors leading into the building were set at an odd angle, like they'd been broken down and haphazardly set back up. It looked as though its existence violated every safety code, and some part of me was sure that if I went in, the whole thing would burn down and I'd die in the flames.

Needless to say, there wasn't a line to get in. Sure, there was a velvet rope set up—a moldy, dust encrusted, velvet rope, as if one hundred years ago they thought that *maybe* there'd be a line—but there certainly wasn't one now.

As I stared up at the building, the taxi driver laughed maniacally and sped away, like he thought I was the most naive and stupid person on the planet and he relished the idea of me getting a lesson in real life.

Nevertheless, I was determined. I walked across the broken concrete toward the entrance, the rumbling of bass and drums growing louder and louder with each step. *Well, that means they're still open,* I thought. *Thank goodness.*

As I reached the door, something moved in the shadows next to it. I jumped and let out a startled cry, expecting a monster to leap out and eat me, but it was just a person. Apparently, they *did* have a bouncer.

I couldn't see his face at all. He was pretty much just a shape, like a shadow *in* the shadows. But based on his shape, he was massive and maybe wearing a suit. "Membership, please?"

I was a little scared to admit, "I-I don't have a membership."

"You can get one online."

"I don't have a computer."

"The library has computers."

I slapped a frustrated hand to my face, letting it slowly slide down my cheek until it fell lifeless at my side—a bit more dramatic of a reaction than necessary. I was so tired. "Um..." I shifted my feet. My nerves rushed to my head and I let my hair fall into my face, hiding it. "I just moved here so, I'm not sure where the library is. And I'm *here* now, so is there any way I can just, get a membership, like, *now?* Please?"

There was a long pause. I had no idea what was happening. Finally, he said, "Of course," and opened the door for me, which creaked and screamed like the movement was really painful for it. "The man at the desk will help you."

I stared into the doorway. Though the drums and bass had grown louder with the opening of the door, it looked as though it opened up to nothing. There was just a dark, black void.

I was missing the joke. "What desk?"

"Just go straight, and you'll see it on your left. Watch your step."

I peered back through the doorway. How in the world was I supposed to "watch my step" when I couldn't see anything? I raised an eyebrow and looked up at this shadow man who I couldn't help but picture as Lurch from *The Addams Family*. He chuckled.

I laughed a little back. "Ha-ha, okay, you *are* joking. I just wasn't sure, because I can't see your face—because obviously, there is no way for me to "watch my step," because it's pitch black, and I can't see, heh."

"Yeah." He chuckled some more.

"That's funny!"

"Thank you."

I paused. The things John had said about shadow monsters tumbled into my mind and I had an urge to warn this shadow man about them. But it was so crazy and so stupid... yet, after meeting Rick, and the strange encounter last night and all the "SAVE THEMs"...

I decided that, just in case, I'd rather take a chance and sound crazy than have something terrible happen to this guy that I could've prevented. Forcing myself to be courageous, I said, "So sorry, um... this is going to sound weird, but... I was told recently that..." I was having an out-of-body-level anxiety attack again. I knew if I said "I was told that there were monsters that live in the shadows" he'd probably ask me to leave, and definitely wouldn't listen to me. I tried to think of something equivalent, but believable. "There's a crazy, um... serial killer? On the loose? I just think, maybe, you should um... *not* stand in the shadows." I knew that made no sense, so I quickly added, "Because he hides in shadows. He's a shadow killer-person. Shadow hunter. He hunts in the shadows. It's really creepy. Honestly, you should just come inside." I offered a timid, dorky smile.

There was a long pause of silence. I had no idea what look he was giving me. Finally, he said, "I think I'll be okay."

I didn't like that. I *wanted* to like it and move on, but a gut-wrenching pull in my stomach was telling me I had to try harder. "No, really. I really think you should—"

He raised a hand to stop me. "I appreciate that." He gestured to the door.

I nodded and stepped forward, painfully aware of how insane that had all sounded and thinking, *I mean really, what do I know? John is totally crazy. I'm crazy for even thinking he's not crazy.*

Ugh, but what if he isn't? I couldn't shake the possibility. Seizing what little remained of my courage, I turned abruptly and said, "Just— don't stand in the shadows." I then walked as carefully as I could through the door and down the dark passageway until I bumped into a wall of thick curtains. I parted them and stepped through into light.

TRACK 6
THE EDGE OF GLORY

The inside looked nothing like the outside. Everything was elegant and full of color, resembling the inside of an opera house or a chapel, with large, wooden pillars lining the entryway and down into the rest of the building. The entryway was wide and overcast with pinkish-purple light. To the left, I found the large desk the bouncer had talked about. It was made of dark stained wood and had lovely, vine-like designs carved into the corners and around the edges. The floor at my feet was polished wood and covered with a fancy black rug, which stretched across the entryway platform and down a few steps into the rest of the establishment.

As I looked everything over, it was clear the building looked like an old bowling alley because it *had* been a bowling alley. Directly in front of me was a large, well lit, U-shaped bar that separated one half of the building from the other. The half to my right was still a bowling alley. It was lit with black lights and the far wall was covered in a gorgeous, neon version of the mural in the Sistine Chapel. To my surprise, four of the five lanes had groups of people on them, and I was sure I'd never seen so many different kinds of people all in one spot. One group was made up of gorgeous drag queens while the other consisted of people dressed up as unicorns, and judging by the eruption of cheers I observed from the drag queens and taunts they gave to the unicorns, they were playing against each other. I officially decided, *I have found my people.*

To the left was the actual "club" part. There were small tables set up near the bar and the rest was a dance floor, which wasn't full by any means, but had far more people than I'd expected and was just as diverse. It led to a stage that was just out of my view.

My stomach fluttered stupidly again and a thrill rushed through me, knowing Rick was on that stage. The band played the final chords of whatever the song had been as the guy at the desk hollered at me, "Can I see your membership, please?"

The crowd roared with cheers. A gruff, gravelly voice I didn't recognize muttered "Thank you" into the microphone. "We have about twenty minutes before the club closes and we're all forced to leave—" There was a lamentation from the crowd at these words. "I know, I know."

My knees shook as I ran up to the man at the desk. "Um, the guy outside said I could sign up here."

The desk-guy said something, but I wasn't listening. I was straining to hear the band.

Then I heard the voice I was searching for—deep, melodic, and sweet, setting my soul on fire, "Parting is such sweet sorrow."

Rick.

My brain flipped out. *Ohmygosh, that's him! That's him! Thatishisvoice! That is HIS voice! He's here! Heisonthestage!*

The desk-guy handed me a form to fill out. My fingers were trembling so much that my handwriting was more illegible than normal.

The gruff voice continued, "Anything else you guys would like to hear from us tonight?"

Some guy shouted, "'Sweet Home Alabama!'"

Another voice from the stage let out an annoyed groan. It was the blond guy from the restaurant, Bill. I frowned. I didn't like Bill.

Rick said politely, "No, Ted."

Bill added, "We already sang it tonight!"

The guy in the audience shouted, "Sing it again!"

Gruff voice chimed, "*Anything* else?"

I signed the bottom of the form. It was then that I received the dreaded question, "Do you have an ID?"

I winced. "Uh... no...?"

"Hold out your hand."

I gave the guy my hand and he stamped it with a cartoon baby wearing a diaper. He explained, "It just means you can't drink."

I paid my fee and left my coat with the desk-guy when the next song started. I didn't recognize it right away, as the band had added an impossible bass line to the introduction. But then I heard Rick's voice and it became clear: it was Lady Gaga's "Born This Way."

Their twist on it had turned the song from pop to heavy metal and it was amazing. Rick's voice... my insides did all sorts of stupid somersaults and dance moves at the sound of his voice. It was pure and majestic. I'd never heard a voice like it. His rich tone was full of enthusiasm, like he was pouring his soul into every note and the music poured that onto the crowd. As I broke away from the entrance and stepped onto the dance floor, I could feel it. The energy in the room was full of positivity. It was a happier place than Disneyland, but the happiness was coming from the music—from Rick.

With the stage finally in view, I saw him, and the world around me faded away.

He looked the way he had in my dreams, wearing dark jeans and a black, long sleeved, button up shirt with the top buttons undone and the sleeves rolled halfway up his forearms. His black hair curled at his ears. He was totally in his element on that stage, bouncing back and forth across it, engaging the audience and holding the microphone in one hand. He threw in Lady Gaga dance moves at the chorus, stomping his feet in time with the song. It was a while before I broke my gaze away and noticed the other members of the band. The guitarist was crazy-blond-guy Bill, and I hated to admit it, but he was an expert. The keyboardist was Charlie the lumberjack. And the drummer, who was lost in his drumming—his magnificent hair all over the place—was Steve.

The bassist, however, was someone I didn't recognize. He had short, dark blond hair and was a little taller than Rick, though just as muscular, and wore a short sleeved, button up shirt and jeans. He had sharp facial features and a very strong jaw line, and a face that, though ridiculously gorgeous, was inexplicably hardened—the face of someone who carried a heavy burden with them everywhere they went. Despite this, he looked to be enjoying himself as much or more than the others. When "Born This Way" bled into Lady Gaga's "Telephone," the band continuing with their heavy metal twist, the bassist took over lead vocals. His voice had a raspy, Bryan Adams quality to it that made me absolutely love it. I couldn't believe how good they were. I sincerely wondered how they weren't famous. The whole thing was done with such musical precision that I wished the lyrics to the song held a deeper meaning.

The joy that pervaded the room seeped into my soul, fueling the glee that was already in there. My nerves disappeared, and before long I was dancing with everyone else. While I knew my moves were awkward and terrible, I was so elated that I didn't care.

Once the song was over, I was pretty sure I cheered louder than anyone, blabbing to the guy standing next to me with the big, green and blue mohawk, "That was amazing!"

Cheerfully and without hesitation—which probably wasn't a natural reaction for him—he said, "Right? They made me *like* Lady Gaga!"

Rick crossed the stage and grabbed an acoustic guitar. He said something to his band and approached the microphone. "You know, I've been thinking..."

"Oh, no," said the bassist with a grin.

"Get comfortable, Rick's about to give a speech," added Bill. People laughed. I didn't, because I hated Bill and I thought it was a rude thing to say. *And just as I was starting to hate you a little less, Bill,* I thought, my eyes narrowed at him, hoping he could feel my very narrowed gaze of dislike.

Rick smiled and held up his hands in defense. "A *short* speech! Just a short one..." He gave a small shrug and muttered, "But yeah, get comfortable."

There was another ripple of laughter. He adjusted the microphone stand. "They say that, at the very beginning of the universe, darkness existed first. Now, I don't know for sure because I wasn't there. I'm also not a scientist. But, from what I understand, there could not have been light, because there were no particles in existence that *made* light—which makes sense. So, for thousands and thousands of years, there was only darkness. No life, no light, just energy, atoms... and darkness. But then, after thousands and thousands of years, atoms grouped together, and with a great deal of heat and pressure, they began to transform into these *new* atoms and all of a sudden, there was light and stars were born.

"Now, many of you—if not all of you—are out there thinking, 'Why, that's just *fascinating*, Rick, but what has that got to do with anything?' Well, I'll tell you, young Padawans. Think about it this way. All there was, was darkness, and then—through this small, transformation of particles, particles so tiny that we can't even see them, undergoing a great deal of stress—was born this brilliant, bright, life-giving light.

"*Light*, was the first rebellion.

"I believe it's the same now, in life every day. Darkness is everywhere and that's because it's natural. It's easy. People everywhere are full of it. I am quite certain there isn't a single person here that hasn't suffered at the hand of someone else's darkness. It's easy, then, to allow that darkness to consume yourself. Again, it's natural. It came first! The anger, the pain, the fear, the desire to give in to greed and lust, the need for vengeance. The desire to give up hope, to become bitter and lazy, or to just stop caring altogether. The pull is so strong, because frankly," he shrugged, "it's darkness.

"I see a lot of people thinking rebellion means to give in to that darkness—but isn't *giving in* the opposite of what it means to rebel? When the world is egging you on, taunting you to hit it back, what's so rebellious about clobbering it? When the world is telling you to give up, that it's hopeless, this is just the way things are, what good is it to lie down and surrender? You might not think clobbering the world and lying down are the same thing, but they're actually very parallel because neither of these things change the world... but they *do* change you. It turns you into darkness, officially making you a part of the world you hated.

"The thing is, it's easy to give in and be horrible—to become darkness. It's natural. What's much harder is *rebelling*: taking all of that heat and pressure and *pain,* and transforming it into light.

"If you really want to rebel against the darkness and horribleness that seems to pervade this world, become *light*. In the face of despair, when the whole world seems to have turned against you, don't give up hope—*become* hope. When you feel yourself pressed upon and overwhelmed by fear, *create* courage and *become* bravery. When anger and heartbreak consume you, and you feel that love simply cannot really exist, *become* love. When you're tempted to give into greed, become generosity. When you're tempted to give into hate or apathy, become compassion. When you're consumed by a desire for vengeance, become forgiveness and let it go. Become the light the universe lacks but needs so desperately in order to *live*. Ignite a spark in your soul. You cannot—absolutely cannot—dispel darkness by becoming darkness, you *have* to become light. This is the only way to truly rebel.

"So be a rebel. In a world of darkness, become light."

Whoops and cheers broke out all around me. A man to my right shouted, "PREACH!" I glanced over at the guy with the mohawk as he discreetly wiped tears from his face.

Rick's words filled my soul with fire. The little spark within me grew, fueling me with a desire to do... something. I didn't know what, but *something*, and something good. To find some way to change and be better—not out of a sense of condemnation, but out of a hope that I actually *could*. Perhaps I could overcome the past and leave it behind me. Perhaps everything could be made right somehow. I just needed to find a way.

I'd only felt that hope once before, on the night Rick saved me.

But as I looked up at the spaceman on the stage, the little spark also flickered with a deep and profound longing, twisting my heart with an ache that threatened to tear me in two. My brain then felt compelled to remind me that this longing was ridiculous, that I was unworthy of the affection of such a person, and quickly put me in my place, making me a little sick.

Rick turned his attention to his guitar, saying, "Anyway, those are my thoughts. The end."

I laughed. More people cheered. Charlie leaned into his microphone. "I thought you said it was going to be a *short* speech, Rick."

"Well, honestly, I don't know how to give short speeches. But if I'd have said that at the beginning, everybody would've left."

The band laughed, as did most everyone else. Somebody from the back of the audience shouted, "Sing 'Sweet Home Alabama!'"

Rick spoke again, "Anyway, on that note, I feel this is the perfect song to end the night on."

It only took a few notes for me to recognize the song and start screaming with glee. It definitely wasn't something heard on the radio every day. It was one of The Cure's few genuinely happy songs called, "Doing the Unstuck." The music filled the room with a wave of euphoria that forced every worry and care from my mind.

When it was over and people started to leave, I wandered over to a table and sat down. While the happy feeling still lingered in the air, it seemed to fade without the music, like someone opening the door to the bathroom after a hot shower. A chill brought worry into my mind. *Rick's going to think I'm stalking him.*

I overheard a group of young girls say as they made their way to the exit, "I don't want to go home."

"I know, this is the only place where life doesn't suck."

"Right? I feel like I can be myself here and no one will like, judge me, ya know?"

"Right? And I just feel so much better! Like, I can't even explain it... it's like..."

"Healing?"

"Yeah!"

"I know, right? I told you it was awesome."

Then one of the girls added with a melancholy tone, silencing the rest, "It's the only place I feel safe."

A pang of sadness struck me at what the last girl had said. My worries were stupid. This was about saving Rick, not about anything else. Whatever he thought of me or this encounter, he needed to know he might be in danger. He needed to be safe. Because the world needed him in it.

I sat there for several minutes, reciting what I planned to say when I saw him again. My line was going to be, "Hey, you promised we'd get friendship bracelets on Tuesday." I thought it was a very good line. I muttered it over and over again as though I were about to give a State of the Union address in front of millions of people. If I said it enough times to myself, there would be no way I could mess it up when my nerves punched me in the gut.

Most of the people had gone when the band started packing up their instruments. As I summoned the courage to go over there and find Rick, I heard a voice—that deep, majestic, beautiful voice—behind me.

"Emily?"

TRACK 7

DOG DAYS ARE OVER

My dumb heart fluttered like the floor had opened up beneath me and I was falling through. I turned toward him and rose to my feet.

There he was. My beautiful Good Samaritan.

His jaw dropped slightly as he looked me over in a whoa-you-look-so-different sort of way, making my nerves unbearable. But then, to my relief, his eyes lit up and a smile spread across his face. "Holy... wow! It's really you!"

I didn't know what to say to that. I tried to remember my line, but my brain was far more overwhelmed than I had anticipated and had thrown up its hands in surrender, screaming, *I can't take this kind of pressure!* I didn't get past the word, "Hey."

Man, that smile. That smile wasn't helping my brain at all, neither did his next few words, "You look stunning. Absolutely stunning."

Aww, geez, I thought, feeling my face go red. "Thank you. It's this dress, I tell ya. Does wonders for my boobs." I hated myself the second I said it and yelled at my brain, *Why did you say that?!* And then my brain cried.

He laughed, a genuine and surprised laugh. "Well, I uh... I do remember the dress. That's how I recognized you. I saw the dress and thought, 'I know that dress!'" He chuckled, but then added, "And I'm saying 'dress' a lot but, it's not the dress. It's the girl in the dress that's stunning—this person you were hiding. I'm very glad to see her again."

He sounded like he meant it. I smiled, brushing my hair behind my ear, my nerves beginning to calm. I remembered my awesome line and almost said it, but I noticed he was fidgeting with his fingers and chewing on his lips. I even thought I could feel it in the air around him.

He was *nervous*. Why was he nervous? Did Bill talk to him about me? Did he think it was creepy that I'd found him? My guts twisted and my head spun, but I did my very best to shove it all aside. I just needed to show him the flyer and tell him what the weird-eye-guy had said, and then I could go home and cry into a carton of cookie dough ice cream for the rest of my life.

When I looked back up at him, his expression had changed. His eyes were studying me, but the rest I couldn't read. I cleared my throat. "I, um... I'm so sorry for being creepy, just showing up here. I promise I'm not stalking you or anything."

He gave a curt shake of his head. "The thought hadn't crossed my mind."

That confused me. Then why was he nervous? I went on, unable to look him in the eye and speaking instead to to his shiny, black shoes. "I just... I had a very um, *interesting* encounter yester—"

"Hey, Rick!" The bassist showed up at Rick's side, clapping a hand on his shoulder. Everything about him—the way he moved, the way he stood, even the way he put his hand on Rick's shoulder—was extremely manly. I could just picture him on a horse in an old western movie shooting anything and everything and blowing up trains. Behind him, the rest of the band chatted away with each other, taking their stuff out through a back entrance. I had a sudden urge to just shove the flyer in Rick's hand and run.

The bassist glanced at me before saying, "I took your guitars out for you. Just remember that the next time I need help moving a body."

Rick smiled. "He's joking."

He gave a small shrug. "Yeah, he's right. I don't need any help moving bodies." After I let out a nervous laugh, he turned to Rick, "Ready to go?"

I was shocked to hear Rick say, "Actually, no." Rick gestured to me. "Robert, this is Emily."

Robert's eyebrows shot up. "Emily? *The* Emily?"

The Emily? I'm the Emily? So they had talked about me. I wanted to shrink into a tiny ball and disappear under a table as I thought of all the bad things that probably meant.

Rick chose to ignore Robert's remark. "Emily, this is my very old friend, Bob."

I smiled politely and reached out to shake Bob's hand, determined to give him a firm handshake since my dad had taught me that a handshake says a lot about a person. Bob hesitated. He glanced over at Rick before grasping my outstretched hand.

There was a very strange sensation at his touch that I could only describe as *searching*. It flooded through my hand, up my arm and into my head. It lingered there, making me feel as though I were a car and my brain was the engine, and he was doing a routine inspection. Looking into his honey-gold eyes, I saw that they were glowing, bright like the setting sun.

Bob wasn't human.

It was a very quick handshake. He dropped my hand like it was a hot pan he'd pulled out of the oven without a mitt. He wiped his palm on his shirt and gave a look that said the inspection had gone well. He told me, sounding genuine, "Good to meet you, Emily."

I didn't like it. I felt... weird. He'd just been in my head. What had he seen?

My mouth tried to form words but all I could do was point and mutter, "Uh... so y-you... wha-just..."

Rick glared at him. "What did you do?"

Bob told him matter-of-factly, "I didn't do anything."

"You *clearly* did something."

"I just shook her hand!"

"This is why I can never introduce you to people."

Bob folded his arms, saying with mock bitterness, "You never introduce me to people."

"I know! And *this* is why!" He turned to me. "What did he do?"

"I just, um... so..." I was light headed and had to sit back down. "I just... I could feel him... in my head, and I was just wondering..."

I didn't get to say what I was wondering, because Rick turned angrily to Bob and they began arguing in a very weird language that sounded like a mix of French, Spanish, and Japanese with the occasional clicking of the tongue.

Bob sighed and blurted, "FINE!" He said it so loud, it caught the attention of the rest of the band. He turned to me, arms still folded. "I'm sorry. I didn't *read* your mind." He glanced at Rick, whose hands were now on his hips, like a parent overseeing their child's apology. "We *can't* read minds on a whim, it takes a lot of effort. I was just, sort of, *feeling* for bad intentions." He nodded his head and shot me a look that said I should take the following statement as a compliment. "I didn't find any."

Rick glared at him and said dryly, "Well that's a relief. I was so very worried."

"Well, *someone* has to worry."

"HEY!" Someone shouted. It was Bill. My stomach sank, *Oh no...*

The rest of the band approached, their gazes all on me. Rick took notice of my discomfort and stepped closer to me, his presence radiating calm and soothing me.

Bill studied me with his crazy eyes. "You're that waitress from the restaurant! How did you find this place?" Both he and Charlie the lumberjack looked over at Steve.

Steve threw up his hands defensively. "It wasn't me!"

Rick asked, "What are you guys talking about?"

My insides began to eat themselves. *Oh no... oh no oh no...*

Bill pointed an accusing finger at me like I was on trial for witchcraft. "She was our crazy waitress. She wanted to know how to find you and when we wouldn't tell her, she chased us down the street!"

Rick raised an eyebrow and looked at me with a surprised, yet amused, grin. "Really?"

I wanted to die. I wanted to stab Bill and then die. The only thing keeping me from crying was the strange calm that came from Rick. I stammered, "It-it wasn't like that! I just—I—*and it wasn't down the street!*"

Before Bill could say anything else, I stood back up, deciding to end this nightmare *now*. I reached into my purse, pulled out the flyer, and handed it to Rick. "Here. Some weird guy gave this to me. He said a bunch of crazy stuff, and it scared the crap out of me, so I just, I wanted to give it to you. I thought maybe it was a warning or something."

Rick took the flyer and studied it. Bob gazed down at it from over his shoulder. They both raised their eyebrows at all the "SAVE THEMs" scribbled on the back. Rick flipped it over and, seeing nothing of interest on the other side, returned his attention to the "SAVE THEMs." Quite unexpectedly, he became... annoyed. He looked at Bob and spoke in the dark tone of someone describing their day at the DMV. "Thipka."

Bill reached over and took the flyer out of his hand. "Thipka? What's a Thipka?"

Bob said, "Not a *what*, but a *who*."

I wanted to say, "Cindy Lou who?" but kept myself under control. Thanks to Bill, it was easy to do.

Charlie, Bill, and Steve reacted to the flyer the way I had expected Rick to react. Their faces were full of panic. Steve asked, "Is he an... enemy?"

Rick folded his arms, his annoyance growing more severe, like it'd been two hours and he was still in line at the DMV. "No, it's Thipka."

Charlie asked, a tone of hope in his voice, "So... not an enemy?"

Rick told him in the exact same tone as before, "No, it's Thipka."

Bob, who had been lost in thought, finally explained what Rick was apparently too annoyed to find words for. "Thipka is like us," he gestured between Rick and himself, "just the sugar-free version. We have no idea where he came from. We found him in the portal." At this, Bill, Steve, and Charlie looked over at me, as if they were talking about something sacred that I shouldn't be hearing. I returned the look, surprised they knew about the portal while at the same time shocked that Bob was talking about it so comfortably in front of *me*, the crazy lady. Bob noticed everyone's reaction and turned to Rick, "She knows about the portal, right?"

Rick nodded.

"Good, good. I thought I remembered something about you sharing a whole bunch of top-secret information with a total stranger."

Rick fired a glare at him and opened his mouth to defend himself when Bob cut him off. "Okay. So, we found him in the portal, in a cavern on this one planet—can't remember the name... it had lots of trees..."

Rick turned to me. "It was beautiful. Kind of like that planet at the end of *Return of the Jedi*, the one with all the little bear-people?" He snapped his fingers to summon the noun, then declared, "Ewoks!"

The fact that he said this *Star Wars* reference to me made me feel a fraction-of-a-tiny-bit better about everything. I jumped all over the reference. "Yes! Ewoks! That's so cool! Though, it wasn't a planet in the movie. It was a moon." I wondered why I'd felt the need to say that.

He did a far-too-perfect Alec Guinness impression, "'*That's no moon...*'"

I laughed a nervous-but-genuine laugh, my spirits rising.

Bob's eyes narrowed ever so slightly at Rick before moving on. "*Anyway...* he was completely mangled. His wings had been torn off, half of his face had been replaced by this metal shell, his left eye was robotic, and so was his left leg and arm. He had shrapnel sticking out of him everywhere. Half of his tail was missing." Rick's body seized up at this description and all the calm feelings that had been emanating from him vanished. One moment I had been basking in comforting sunlight and the next, the sun had been blocked by thick, dark clouds. I even felt cold.

Inside my brain, Bob's words triggered the thought, "What? A tail?" and then my mouth blurted it out loud without my permission. I felt every gaze fall on me. My voice came out small and at a near whisper, "S-sorry. I... I'm just wondering if we're talking about the same guy, because I didn't see any of that when I talked to him, except maybe the eye... and a scar on his chest." I wanted to add but didn't, *And you also said he was like you, and you guys look nothing like that, so...*

I glanced over at the others, expecting them to have similar concerns, but they didn't seem to think any of these anomalies were odd at all.

Bob smiled, and I thought I saw the smallest hint of wryness on the edge of his lips. He said simply, "Well, you wouldn't have, would you?"

That made no sense. I looked over at Rick for help, but he wouldn't look at me. He just rubbed his wrists. He muttered something to Bob in their language and Bob said, "Oh. Oops."

Steve got everyone's attention by raising his hand. "But wait. You guys can completely heal! You have those super regenerative abilities and..." he glanced over at me, clearly second guessing bringing this up, "...*stuff*. If this guy is like you, why is he all"—he had a hard time saying it, like the idea really creeped him out—"*messed up* like that?"

Wait, what? I wanted to say, but managed to hold my tongue this time. *Is he talking about the kind of cellular regeneration that's in comic books? Like Wolverine and Deadpool?* Man, I had so many questions.

Rick answered, "With a great deal of effort, we can actually stop ourselves from healing or change how we heal so we force our bodies to scar. So it's because he chooses it. When we asked him why, all he said was, 'Why would I want to forget what they did to me?'"

The room grew heavy with silence.

Bob broke it. "Anyway, the creatures named him Thipka, which, roughly translated, means 'mangled.' He's never told us his real name."

I was really hoping someone would ask if the "creatures" spoken of were actual Ewoks, but no one did.

Rick added in his thoughts about Thipka. "And he's annoying."

Bob smirked. "He gets under Rain's skin."

"He left us for dead."

"Well, he *did* say he knew we wouldn't die."

"Not before he left us for *dead!* There was no, 'Oh, it's okay! Don't worry! You'll make it!'"

"Well, maybe if he'd said that, we wouldn't have fought so hard, and died."

I watched Rick search his mind for a comeback to that and when it appeared he couldn't find one, he chose to end the argument triumphantly with, "Shut up, Nothe."

Nothe? That was the name Rick had said when he'd answered the phone back at the hotel. It was Bob's *real* name. Of course! Nothe/Bob was Rick/Rain's best friend, the one with whom he'd discovered the portal.

Obviously. *Duh, Emily.*

I knew there was an incredible story here that I hoped they'd share.

Rick added bitterly, "I can't believe you're defending him."

Charlie the lumberjack cut in and asked, "Hang on, what do you mean when you say he *knew* you wouldn't die?"

Bill looked at Charlie as though he'd just said he preferred country music over rock n' roll. "What? *That's* your question? What about the part where he *left them for dead?* How did that even happen?" He looked over at Rick and Bob. "What were you guys doing?"

I agreed with Bill, though I would never say it out loud. Well, never mind. Actually, they were both very good questions.

Bob—Nothe—shook his head. "It's a long story, Bill. It'd be like sitting through *Gone with the Wind*."

Rick nodded, like they were discussing a medical procedure. "Yes. You'd totally need an intermission."

"Absolutely." Nothe turned to Rick. "You want to know what I think your problem really is? You hate Thipka because you're jealous."

Rick was outraged. "Jealous? Of *what?*"

Bob was alight with amusement. "You're jealous because he knew all of the songs from *The Greatest Showman* before you did."

"No, I hate the man for it! It was creepy! I'm not *jealous*," he said it as if the very thought was more abhorrent than finding a fingernail in your sundae after eating a few bites. He turned to me and explained, "He taught the people on the Ewok planet the entire musical. Not only was this a century before its production, it was on an entirely different planet."

Nothe corrected, "It was more than a century."

I needed a very important answer to a very important question. "Uh, hang on. Just—wait. Hang on... okay. How is that even possible? How the crap did he do that?"

Rick said something that silenced the room, "Thipka can see the future."

Every one of the band members gazed back down at the "SAVE THEMs" on the flyer, mortified.

Rick waved away the sudden panic like a bothersome fly. "Don't worry about that. That's just his signature. He carves or draws that into anything and everything. You leave him alone long enough to get bored and you'll find it somewhere."

The feeling of relief in the air was comparable to a fog lifting to unveil a clear, summer sky. It was very brief for me, however, as I recalled John and Thipka's conversation:

"You can't stop them from coming."

"I have to try."

Bob—or Nothe, whatever his name was—added, "Yep. When we found him in that cave, "SAVE THEM" had been carved into the walls, written in blood on rocks..."

Rick frowned, his eyes darkened. "Carved into his skin. All over every visible part. It was very unsettling."

"Anyway, when we found him, he told us that he'd been there for years, waiting for us to show up. He also said that he'd gotten into the portal a different way than we did." Bob shot Rick a quizzical look. "He never explained what he meant by that, did he?"

Rick shook his head. "Nope."

"And then, at the end," there was a look of regret in Bob's eyes, "he was left behind in the portal when it was destroyed."

"That he was."

They looked at each other, the same question written in their expressions.

Charlie asked the question for everyone, though clearly terrified of the answer. "So, how did he get here? Does that mean the portal is open again?"

There was only silence.

Bill concluded, "Well, that's it. Our days are numbered. The world is ending." He turned to Charlie, putting his hands on his shoulders. "Chuck, hug your family a little tighter tonight when you get home, will ya? And since Steve and I have nobody—"

Steve looked insulted. "I *do* have a girlfriend—"

Bill went on like he hadn't heard him, "—we're going to get drunk at my house and play Space Invaders."

Steve was baffled. "No we're not."

"What? Did you have other big plans for tonight?"

"Uh, sleeping. Sleeping was my big plan."

"There'll be plenty of time to sleep when we're all dead, Steven!"

"It won't be the same!"

Rick turned to me. "I need you to tell me everything Thipka said."

This ended the argument and all attention was fixed on me. An ominous feeling spread through my gut. I dug through my little purse and found the napkin where I'd written down every word Thipka had said to the best of my memory. "Um, he said, 'I'm here to remedy a mistake that was made out of fear.'"

When I said this, Rick's bright blue eyes widened. I had a feeling that, unlike me, he knew exactly what Thipka had meant.

When I got to the part about Steve giving me the flyer, everyone looked at him. Bill said with a glare, "*Steve...*"

Rick paled when I got to the part about wanting more time. He paced, running a hand through his hair. The air around him turned very cold.

Though I was terrified to say anything more in front of everyone without a script, I forced myself to tell him, "There's more."

I told him about John, the homeless man, and rehearsed the strange conversation that had been haunting my memories. Bob asked for a description of John, so I gave him one. They both knew who he was.

Bob explained, "We don't know his real name either. He just goes by 'The Prophet.' He'll show up at random and leave ominous messages about the future."

I was really starting to freak out now. "So, he can *also* see the future?"

Rick said, "No. Well, sort of. Not like Thipka."

Bob said, "The Prophet has... sources. He has visions and is told things from an unseen dimension. Ya know, as prophets do. Well, at least according to the legends back home."

Rick looked outright sick. "But Thipka..."

"He just *knows*. And he tends to mess with time, creating alternate pathways through it." Bob looked at me. "Like he did with you and the flyer. The Prophet isn't a very big fan of his. Apparently, you're not supposed to mess with time like Thipka does."

Bill shook his head. "What are we supposed to do, Rick?"

Rick rubbed his forehead. "I don't know. Honestly, the portal may not be open. It's possible Thipka got here another way, but we can't know until we find him."

Bob added, "If the portal *is* open, the entrance could be anywhere."

Charlie asked, his expression full of determination, "How do we track him down, then?"

Rick opened his mouth to answer but then shrugged, shaking his head and throwing up a hand. "It's Thipka."

Steve suggested, "Well, what about The Prophet? Can we track him down?"

Bob shook his head. "No. He comes to you." He sighed, looking at

Rick. Whatever he'd been about to say next was interrupted by the very tired-looking bartender, who I later learned was also named Bob. He was the Bob from the title of the club—Bob's Club Festivus. He'd been closing up the building while we'd been talking, shutting out lights and whatever else with a staff member. He appeared behind us, annoyed, and clearly hadn't been listening to a word we'd said. "Don't you guys sleep? 'Cause I'd like to."

TRACK 8
STAY

Everyone made their way toward the exit, except for me. I stayed put in order to keep my distance well behind the rest. Rick waited with me and matched my slow, meandering pace toward the entryway steps. Calm radiated from him again. I even thought I could *feel* that he didn't want me to leave. I couldn't explain it and was sure I was imagining it. Wishful thinking, most likely.

He offered to retrieve my coat for me and, like a perfect gentlemen, he helped me put it on. There was a brief, awkward pause before he said, "Before we go, I would just like to say something to you." He fidgeted with his fingers again.

I braced myself, expecting the worst. *Oh boy, here we go. Just don't cry in front of him.*

He took a deep breath. "I honestly don't understand the mind games humans play on each other and would rather express my intentions openly. I've observed that most painful misunderstandings are avoided this way."

I braced myself even more, *You think I'm creepy and want me to go away. Just hurry up and say it.*

"This might sound strange, as we don't know each other very well, but I would very much like us to be friends."

All the bad feelings vanished. My stunned brain stopped working. "What?"

He shifted his weight. "I would like to be friends. Is that... okay?"

"Yes!" I said, a little too enthusiastically. I quickly got ahold of myself. "I—just—that doesn't ever happen to me. Ever. Usually people want me to go away. *Far* away."

I couldn't read his expression, but there was a growing light in his eyes. "Well, I don't."

"Why not?" I gestured to myself. "Is it the dress?"

He looked baffled. "No, it's not the dress. If that were the case, I'd just go *buy* that dress and have tea with it every afternoon. No, it's because I think you're fun, and a very good person. And I feel like I understand you. I don't understand most everyone else, but I understand you, and..." He hesitated, glancing nervously at the floor like he was walking onto a shaky bridge. "You seem compassionate enough that, well, maybe you could understand me. So, that's why."

I couldn't believe what I was hearing. It was more than I ever could've hoped for. "But you left. At the hotel, you left."

Regret flashed in his eyes. "I went back."

My heart tripped over those words. "You did?"

"Yes. You can imagine my disappointment when I knocked on your door and found a very racist old woman there instead."

We both chuckled at that. I put a hand to my face, feeling a level of happiness that threatened to make me cry. "Oh no! I'm so sorry."

"It was awful, for so many reasons." He stared down at his feet. "So what do you say?" He looked back up at me. "Friends?"

I smiled. "Yeah. Yeah, I'd like that."

A genuine grin spread across his face, making my stupid heart flutter. I cursed at it, *It's not like that!* But even with the cursing, nothing could ruin the elation I felt in that moment.

Nothe marched back toward us. "Seriously, guys. What are you doing? You can talk outside!"

As we slowly resumed our exit, I decided that Rain and I needed to get one thing out of the way immediately. "Should I call you Rick or Rain?"

"Well, Rain is a nickname for my *actual* name, so I prefer it from friends. I use Rick with everyone else because it makes life easier for me. And besides, you never see 'Rain' on a personalized keychain."

I laughed. "Yeah, I get that."

Of all the questions rattling my brain, I found myself asking, "So, Bob is Nothe...?"

"Yes. Nothe decided on the name 'Bob' after we'd watched the movie *What About Bob?* He'd been trying to decide on a new, more modern-English name for himself and when he saw that movie, he thought, 'Hey... what about Bob?'"

I laughed. I'd seen *What About Bob?* as a kid and thought it was hilarious. I began to wonder how long he and Nothe had been on Earth. "That movie isn't very old."

Nothe, having been eavesdropping on our conversation, turned at the entryway curtain and stopped us. "That movie's older than you."

Rain gave a skeptical frown. "No..."

Nothe looked a bit smug. "I bet it is. How old are you, Emily? Seventeen?"

I shook my head. "I'm twenty-three."

Rain winced. Nothe seemed very entertained. "And that movie came out in... 1991? Let's look it up." He pulled out his phone and a few seconds later, announced with a triumphant grin, "Yep, 1991."

"Oh! I guess it is older than me."

I could feel the amusement pouring from Nothe as he looked at Rain, from whom I could now feel nothing. "Sheesh. And I'm nearly six months younger than you, Rain, which would make you... how many years old now? Gotta be—"

Rain's lips scrunched into an unamused line, his gaze narrowed at Nothe. "I stopped counting."

Nothe didn't relent. He continued with a mischievous look in his eyes, "Well let's see... Thera revolves around her sun at approximately 1.3—"

Rain clapped him on the shoulder near the neck, his fingers finding bare skin as he said smoothly, "You also stopped counting."

Nothe ended his calculations and gave a stiff nod, though his expression remained full of glee. "Yes. I also stopped counting."

A commotion rang out and someone—it sounded like Chuck—shouted, "Get Rain and Nothe!"

Steve burst through the entryway curtain, sickly pale, his eyes wild, and his clothes smelling like vomit. "H-help! There's—" He hid his face with the back of his hand and heaved.

Rain and Nothe didn't need any more information. Rain turned to me and said, "Stay here," before he and Nothe ran outside.

Steve nodded and pointed at me. "You don't wanna see."

A pit opened up in my stomach, draining all the warmth out of my body. My mind went numb as a horrible feeling of dread swept over me.

Steve fell to his knees, heaving again. Bob of Bob's Club grabbed a small trash can from behind the desk and placed it by him. "What's going on?"

Steve shook his head, rubbing his face. Sweat lined his brow. "I... I'm so sorry, Bob." He looked like he wanted to cry, but instead he vomited into the garbage can. When he stopped, his whole body was shaking. His voice trembled as he spoke, "I've never seen anything like it."

Bob glanced at the doorway, not looking so tired anymore. He asked patiently, "Steve, what happened?"

He looked up at Bob, his eyes full of sorrow. "Devon's dead."

TRACK 9
SAY IT AIN'T SO

Devon. I knew a kid named Devon when I was in fourth grade. He stole my very-small Millennium Falcon action figure. He claimed it fell into the vent on the bus, but the bus driver took the vent apart to look for it and it wasn't there. So where did it go, Devon? *Where did it go?*

Bob stared down at Steve, his face wrought with disbelief. "What?"

Steve held his head in his hands and didn't answer. Bob made for the door when Steve grabbed the hem of his shirt. "Don't! Don't. You don't want to see."

Bob whirled on him, his impatience rising with his voice, "See *what?* What is going on, Steven?"

Tears welled up in Steve's eyes. He opened and closed his mouth several times, trying to find the words, but all he managed to say was, "He... he had no face." He fought to hold himself together. His voice came out in hysterical, dry snorts as he tried to keep himself from sobbing. "His face is *gone.*"

I now understood what people meant when they said they felt like they'd been doused in ice water. It wasn't about the cold, though I felt frozen and my coat wasn't enough to warm me. It was the disoriented feeling—the wonder and disbelief of what had just happened and how it could possibly be happening. It was the shock, the difficulty of finding your breath, and the numbness that followed. Yes, I felt as though I'd been thrown into a pool of soul sucking ice water.

Bob's face reflected how I felt. In a shivering voice, he asked, "Then how can you know for sure if it's him?"

Tears stung my eyes for Bob at those words. I didn't know Bob and I didn't know Devon, but I knew at those words that Bob desperately didn't want the dead man outside with no face to be Devon.

But Steve didn't answer. His hands were knotted in his hair. He had become lost in his own head.

I wanted to ask them who this Devon was, but knew it wasn't a good time. The sick feeling in my gut gave me suspicions that I didn't want to be true. The story of the monsters in the shadows spun in my head. I thought of how the bouncer had been encompassed by shadow.

Seeing Steve in a heap on the floor with Bob just standing there staring at him, snapped me out of my thoughts. Steve was the only one of the group who had ever been remotely nice to me and it hurt me to see him such a mess with nobody reaching out to him. Tentatively, I went over to Steve and knelt beside him. I didn't know what I was doing, but I recalled how people comforted the distressed in movies and TV with a blanket. As I didn't have one of those, I took my coat off and wrapped it around him instead. In the way someone would try to soothe a wounded velociraptor, I put an arm around his shoulders and patted his back in a "there-there" fashion.

Steve glanced up at me, embarrassment emerging from underneath the whirlwind of other horrible emotions that showed on his face. I didn't want him to feel embarrassed—like he needed *that* wretched feeling on top of everything else—but I didn't know what to do to fix it except say, "It's okay. It's going to be okay." And then, pushing past my instinct that all humans were velociraptors, I hugged him as tightly as I could, trying to hug every awful feeling right out of him.

It appeared to help. He didn't seem to be embarrassed anymore, at least. Instead, he tried to talk, having a clear need to force the scene out of his mind, "We didn't see him right away, he was in the, um..." He furrowed his brow. "...in the shadows. I'd just assumed he'd gone home." He rubbed his eyes. "But there was this *smell*... and then we saw his shoe." His gaze fell, transfixed on the floor as though what he was describing were right there in front of him. "I've never seen anything like it. Not in real life. His... his..." He gestured to his stomach as he tried to form the words. With a great deal of effort, the words erupted from him like soda out of a shaken bottle. "His guts were everywhere." He took a deep breath. "Like in a horror movie. It didn't seem real, but it was... it was. And I just," he laughed a little, "I just stood there staring at it. I just... stood there. I couldn't..." His voice trailed off as he briefly disappeared back inside his head. He sniffed and wiped his face on his sleeve. "And the *smell*..." His body gave another lurch.

I wanted to throw up now, but I swallowed the urge and made myself hug him again. I couldn't believe it. I really couldn't. Everything Steve had said was... there wasn't an adequate word for it. It was the stuff of nightmares. I couldn't believe a scene like that was just outside the door. Something black and cold spread through me, like the ice of a silent river in the dead of night. Underneath this, I felt so bad for Steve. How could anyone ever recover from something like this?

As Steve took several deep breaths to end his hysteria, I watched Bob robotically make his way to the steps of the entryway and sit, his eyes glazed over, staring at nothing. Steve wiped his face, fighting to calm down, though nothing he did could stop his body from shaking.

The curtain parted behind me. I turned to see an extra pale Bill standing there, his expression stone faced. He announced to everyone, "The police have been called. They're on their way." He walked towards Steve and me. "I always knew something like this would happen someday." Bill looked down at me. "I'll take it from here, Florence."

I looked at him curiously and he explained, "Florence? Florence Nightingale? I was trying to give you a compliment. You ruined it. Now go away." He shooed me away with his hands.

"Fine," I patted Steve on the back one last time.

As I stood, he muttered with sincerity, "Thanks, Emily."

I left my coat with Steve and wandered down the entryway steps, at a complete loss of what to do with myself. I turned and watched Bill take my place at Steve's side, putting an arm around his shoulders. Steve looked a lot more comfortable with Bill than he had with me.

I looked over at Bob, whose gaze had fallen to the floor, his eyes red and tired. I thought about going over to him, but I knew him way less than Steve. I didn't have any idea what to say or do. I felt so helpless. I asked myself the standard *What would Lipstick Rick do?* question, but this time I was far too lost for that to do me much good. Rain seemed to have an ability to magically know *exactly* what people needed, and with this being such a sensitive situation, me *pretending* to know just didn't feel like enough. I didn't know who Devon was to Bob. He could've been anything from a simple, hard-working employee to a son. What was I supposed to do?

I hesitated, then finally made myself walk up to Bob and ask, "Is there anything I can get you? Anything you need?"

This brought him out of his staring contest with the floor. He forced a smile. "No. Thanks, though. Devon was a... a good friend. Good man. Kind. I just really hope it isn't him. 'Course, it's not right to pawn this stuff onto anybody else, either, so... hopefully it's not real at all."

Tears brimmed my eyes. I blinked them away, asking, because I needed to know, "Was he the... the bouncer? Outside?"

Bob nodded. "Yeah. He kept a lot of awful people out of this place. Threw quite a few of them out, too." He chuckled.

I hesitated again before asking, "Do you need a hug?"

He smiled a little, this one looking a bit less forced. "Not yet. I'll keep you posted, though."

I nodded and wandered away, my thoughts gaining traction like a locomotive leaving a station. *He was the bouncer...*

I turned away from the dance floor toward the darkness of the bowling-alley-area-thing, the train in my head speeding up. *He was the bouncer...*

I had to remind myself that I didn't actually *know* if it was a monster that had got Devon. I had no *idea* what had happened to Devon. It could've been a very sick, twisted person. That was usually the case. *Yes,* I told myself, *because people are horrible. Like velociraptors.*

As I turned back toward the dance floor, Rain appeared in the entryway. There was blood on his jeans and hands.

Seeing the blood, my whole reality shifted. Up until that moment, none of it had truly felt real. But seeing the blood... I knew.

The bouncer was dead. The guy who'd stood at the door, who'd let me in, who cracked a dumb joke—he was dead. And I...

I should've done more.

Rain's gaze had been focused on Steve and Bob, his face full of sympathy, but when his eyes met mine, he grew alarmed. He said to me, "Just, give me a moment. I'll be right back," and dashed to the back of the club toward the bathrooms.

I sat on the steps a good distance from Bob, who'd gone back to staring at the floor. My insides twisted with guilt. Was this my fault? This was my fault. *I should've done more.*

At that, I cried.

Shortly after this, Nothe came in and announced, "The police are here."

From there, time moved in a blur. Everyone was interviewed. I answered all of the questions from the young, dark-haired Detective Stanley Reece, sure that I was unhelpful, as I hadn't seen much and didn't know Devon. When my guilt consumed me, I decided that *everyone* needed to know about the monsters. As I rambled on about them, Officer Reece's interest in my testimony waned from his face.

So I talked louder, because in my delusional mind, I was sure I could hold his attention that way. "And-and I told the guy—Devon—I tried to make it sound less crazy and I told him it was a serial killer. I told him *not* to stand in the shadows. I told him he needed to move, but of course he didn't believe me. I should've insisted! I should've dragged him in or something. I should've done more!" I sobbed. Man, I was a mess. "I should've told him the truth!"

Officer Reece rubbed his forehead and sighed. "You really told him that?"

I nodded. "I just—I wasn't sure. I should've done more."

"And you say you were told about these... shadow monsters... from a homeless guy?"

"Yes. He said his name was John. He's gone now, though. I don't know where he went."

As Officer Reece wrote this down, his eyebrows curled up into his forehead in such a way that I imagined him thinking with sarcasm, *Maybe he got eaten.* "Well..." he cleared his throat. "For the record, I don't think telling him the, uh, *truth*"—he said "truth" with a questioning tone, like he very much doubted this was the best term for what was being described—"would've made any difference. You did what you could, okay? This isn't your fault."

Rain's voice said from behind me, "Thank you, Officer Reece." It startled me and he apologized. I hadn't heard him approach. It hit me how very drained he looked.

Officer Reece nodded to Rain and said, as if he knew Rain fairly well, "Make sure she gets home okay, will you, Rick? And," he added in a quick undertone, "ya know, gets some sleep, takes her meds."

"Of course, Stan."

Officer Reece patted Rain on the shoulder. "You're a good man, Rick." He walked away.

TRACK 10

MONSTER

R ain led me down the entryway steps toward the dance floor and out of earshot of anybody else. "He's right, you know. None of this is your fault."

I looked up at him, surprised. "How much did you hear?"

"Everything. I didn't get a chance to speak to you before the police arrived and I wanted to know why you were so upset—you know, aside from the mutilated stranger outside. So, after my interview, I came over and hovered around yours. I was mostly just waiting until you were done so I could speak to you, but I was also doing a lot of eavesdropping."

I sniffed and wiped my gross nose on the tissue Officer Reece had given me and shook my head. "The cop thinks I'm crazy."

"Which is precisely why what happened to Devon isn't your fault. Being as protective as he was of this place, if you had gone on about monsters in the shadows, he never would've let you in tonight. He would've thought you were absolutely loony. He had a much greater chance at living with the story you told him than the truth. You tried, Emily." He placed a hand on my shoulder and warmth flooded through me, calming my heart and filling it with peace. "You did the best you could. And I'm sure he really wished he'd listened to you in his final moments."

A wave of sickness pushed against the warmth. "That doesn't make me feel better."

Rain winced. "Right. Sorry." He let go of my shoulder. "Though it is true."

I worked up the courage to ask, "So... he was for sure, um, e-e..."

Rain caught where I was trying to go. Reluctantly, he confirmed,

"He was eaten. The investigators are calling it an animal attack, and from what I'm feeling and overhearing from them, he's not the first. They are a bit baffled by it. And frightened, though they'd never admit it." He glanced at the floor. "You didn't mention the shadow monsters when you were talking with us earlier."

My weariness was catching up to me. I could barely think at all. "I know. I'm sorry. It didn't seem like it was super important at the time, you know, compared to everything else. I actually forgot about it."

"I'm assuming the homeless man who told you about them was The Prophet?"

I nodded. "Yeah. I'd split my sandwich with him on my way home from work sometimes. One time, he warned me not to walk in the shadows because of," I sniffed, "of these monsters that had fallen from the sky. He told me they stayed in the shadows." I shook my head. "I just..." I rolled my eyes at the irony as I wiped away more tears, "I thought he was crazy."

Rain repeated the words to himself. "Fallen from the sky..." His eyes widened. "The meteor shower." He looked at me. "From the night we met. Remember?"

Through the whirlwind of shock and confusion, I felt a happy flutter as I confessed, "I'll never forget."

He smiled warmly at me before continuing, "That must've been what they were. It was said that the shower was abnormal."

Nothe walked over to us, bringing me my coat and looking exhausted. I thanked him and made sure Steve didn't need it anymore before gladly putting it back on.

Rain asked, "How's he holding up?"

Nothe sighed. "I healed his mind as best as I could, but it's just one of those things. It's going to take some time."

It occurred to me that they'd also been out there with the very-dead-Devon and I felt like a self-absorbed jerk for not asking sooner, "How are *you* guys holding up?"

They looked at each other and Nothe shrugged. "We'll miss Devon. He was one of the good guys."

I was surprised by this. How were they so... *fine* with it? Rain had blood on his jeans! Noticing my wordless reaction, Rain explained,

"We've seen... well, lots of horrible things. I wouldn't say you get used to it—you never really get *used* to it—but it gets to a point where it isn't *shocking* anymore. We will miss Devon, and finding him that way was... well, horrible. You never want to find your friends that way. But he's happier where he is. His suffering is over."

Nothe said to Rain, "Steve kept asking for us to call him back."

I furrowed my brow. "Call who back?"

Nothe told me matter-of-factly, "Devon."

"But... Devon's dead."

Nothe glanced sideways. "Yes, exactly."

Rain explained, "We can do, what you would call, *raise the dead*. But we call it *calling back the dead*. It's far from a simple process. It requires two or more *Hassune*, which are—"

Nothe jumped in. "That's what our species is called." His voice had a hint of venom to it as he said, "It means *'Terrible One.'* 'Has'—terrible, and 'sune'—one. It's the name the Therans gave us. Thank you, humans."

Wait, what do humans have to do with Therans? I wanted to ask this and started to, but Rain hurried on, "Yes, well, as I was saying, it's complicated. It's—" He stopped, appearing to not like that start. "Well, first you—" He stopped again, apparently not liking that one either. "So... there are a few known alternate dimensions to this one. In our philosophy, we call this dimension that we live in the Dimension of the Dying, or Shadow Dimension. There are bits of light and darkness, bits of life and death. As our life-energy travels through this dimension, it gains a charge toward light or darkness, life or death. So when our bodies die and our energy passes on, the charge we've gained will either carry us through to the Dimension of Light or the Dimension of the Dead. We don't really know what goes on in either. The Hassune religion has its say, but all we know for sure is that they're there, and those who end up in the Dimension of Light tend to want to stay there. Well, sometimes they don't, but they usually do. However, those who end up in the Dimension of the Dead desperately want back out, which makes *calling back the dead* a rather dangerous process, because you really don't want those from the Dimension of the Dead to get back out."

Rain studied me to make sure I was following. All I could really do was blink and say, "Okay."

It was enough. He went on, "But the whole process starts with fixing what killed the body in the first place—"

"Which," Nothe cut in, "in Devon's case, would mean re-growing a face, limbs, several organs... and seriously, that much work is *beyond* what we can do on our own."

"And once that is done, one Hassune has to trigger the heartbeat, while the other holds open the doorway into the Dimension of Light, which is something every living creature has inside of them. It's kind of like one of those gigantic cathedral doorways with two big doors—you know what I mean? Where one door—one side—is in the brain and the other is in the heart, and you need to push both of them open for it to work."

"Yes. For example, Bill!"

Rain pointed at Nothe's good example. "Yes, Bill. See, Bill used to be haunted by voices and see things beyond this dimension because the side in his mind was ajar."

"When Rain found him, he was homeless. When Bill came out to his parents, they kicked him out of their house. He was just a teenager. He didn't have any access to the medicine or therapy that humans use to help them cope with these sort of things, and the voices made it impossible for him to hold a job." A dark, angry look appeared in Nothe's eyes at this. "I guess they thought this would motivate him to come home and *not* be gay. He would spend his time yelling at the whir of traffic and throwing cans at cars. He had a whole pile of cans in a shopping cart."

"It was very tragic," Rain said, his eyes heavy with the memory. "So I closed the door."

Nothe brightened. "Problem solved. But that's why he's so weird."

"He's still a bit paranoid. I closed the door, but I can't change anyone's way of thinking."

Bill made so much more sense to me now. I felt a great swell of empathy toward him, something I'd thought was impossible just a couple of hours ago.

Rain added, "And when you call someone back, once that energy returns to the body, it leaves a scar. One that can never go away under any circumstances." He gestured to his chest. "Right over the heart. That's where they tend to enter. The longer the body has been dead, the bigger the scar."

A lightbulb went off in my head. "So, that scar on Thipka's chest..."

Rain gave a grim nod. Nothe elaborated. "Thipka can hide all of his other... issues... but he can't hide that. No one who has returned from the dead can. It's like a constant reminder of what's been given back to you."

"Right," said Rain, "and as I was saying earlier, while these doors are open, the Hassune then issues a call into that dimension—a call for the energy of the deceased to return to their body. But the thing is, they don't *have* to return. They can choose to remain in the Dimension of Light."

"And most of the time," added Nothe, "they do."

"You can only hold the doors open for so long, because opening the doorways to the Dimension of Light weakens the seal of the doorways to the Dimension of the Dead—which is also a door every living creature has inside their brain and heart, as Nothe mentioned."

Nothe grimaced as though they'd begun talking about a kid who'd thrown up on the Ferris wheel. "It's like those gross, tar-like energies can just *feel* those doors are open, so they'll push against their doors with everything they've got."

Rain was pulling a similar face, like he'd been standing in line for the Ferris wheel and had witnessed the whole thing. "Not just that, but it's like they're *listening*. They hear the call and *know* that a body is vacant—"

"And they want it."

"So not only does the Hassune have to open the doors and call to the deceased with their own energy, they have to press against the doors to the Dimension of the Dead and keep those energies *dead*. It's very exhausting. So, if you hold the door open for too long—too desperate for that individual to return—and your own energy weakens, a door to the Dimension of the Dead can slip open."

Nothe said darkly, "And something *else* can get in."

Rain's expression turned somber. "So the body becomes alive again, but the person in it isn't the person who left." He looked at me. "We've seen it happen before. It's... it's not good. When those dark energies come back, they tend to come back with a vengeance."

"Which is why we don't like calling anyone back from the dead."

Rain said brightly, clapping Nothe on the shoulder, "Luckily, Nothe here is rather sensitive to energies that have passed on. He can sense if they're happy where they are and if they'd return. So he knows whether or not it's worth the risk to try."

"In Devon's case," announced Nothe, "he doesn't want to come back. He died a horrible death and is not interested in doing it again, which I had to explain to Steve several times."

Rain shook his head. "I honestly don't know why anyone would want to come back."

I was surprised to hear him say that, after he'd spent so much time teaching me how important it is to live.

Nothe gave Rain a look he didn't see. There was profound sadness in his eyes. "Death is so much harder on the living."

Rain nodded thoughtfully, and when he looked back at Nothe, the sadness had disappeared. "Indeed, you're right."

Everything they'd just told me was so overwhelming and I was so tired, all I could do was focus on the one thing they'd said that had given me any sense of peace: Devon was content, and he didn't want to come back. I really liked that thought.

I glanced up at Rain. He was looking at me with concern. "This must all be so much for you to process."

I rubbed my eyes as I forced myself to say, "Yeah. Honestly, I'm really surprised you guys are telling me all of this. I mean, your secrets are all safe with me, but..." I didn't have the brain to finish that thought. Instead, I looked at Nothe. "Especially you. I just met you."

Nothe shrugged. "I'm just hoping to freak you out so you'll go away." He shot me a wide grin. "After all, we all know that if you were to go out and blab about any of this, no one would believe you."

This was as true now as it was when Rain had said it. And as for the rest of his statement, I could somehow feel that he wasn't joking.

After shooting Nothe an annoyed look, Rain said to me, his tone rich and sincere, "Whatever Nothe's reasons, mine is simply that I feel like I can trust you. It's a rare thing for me to trust people as I trust you. It's hard to explain why I trust you, I just... do. And I just said 'trust' a lot. I think I need some sleep."

I chuckled. I deeply appreciated what he'd said, but I couldn't think well enough to say so right then or find any of the questions that were hovering around my consciousness. I did manage to nod. I hoped it looked like a grateful nod.

Rain pulled out his phone. "Well, it's nearly 4:30 in the morning." He looked at Nothe. "If we're going to—well—" He glanced over at me. I was too stupid-tired to think much of his weird pause. "How about you give the guys a lift to their homes and explain to them what's going on and I'll uh—"

Nothe asked, "What *is* going on? That's why I came over here. I can't tell them what I don't know, now, can I?"

Rain winced. "Oh that's right! I didn't tell you." He then rehearsed all I'd said about the shadow monsters—*shamonsters*, I decided to call them.

When he'd finished, I remembered more of what The Prophet had said and told them, "He also said there were two good monsters and a monster with his own agenda."

Nothe looked like he'd been slapped in the face. "Oh, well, that's nice! I guess we know what The Prophet *really* thinks about us."

Rain also seemed hurt. Nothe started pacing. I could feel a gentle wave of upset-ness radiating from him like heat from a lamp.

I asked, "What do you mean by that?"

Nothe turned to me. "Isn't it obvious? He's talking about us! We're the"—he made subtle quotation marks with his fingers—"*good* monsters."

Rain added, "And Thipka is the one with his own agenda."

I couldn't believe what I was hearing. "You guys aren't monsters!"

Rain turned to Nothe. "It's probably safe to assume that everything The Prophet says is some sort of clue." Nothe stopped pacing and his expression grew wary. Rain went on, "Perhaps the offense is intended, in order to lead us down the path he wants us on."

Nothe's eyes narrowed. "I hate riddles. *Why* does he do that? It's dumb. Doesn't he realize it's more efficient to just tell us what he wants us to know? Of course he does! He just likes the game, I tell you!"

"'If you look at the numbers on my face, you won't find thirteen anyplace.'"

"Oh, stop it," Nothe snapped. *"Batman Forever* can't make this better."

"Fine." Rain looked at me. "Is that everything he said? Is there anything else we should know?"

My sluggish, dying brain rummaged through the memory files. "I can't think of anything. He did tell me to call my dad before I sent him his birthday present."

Rain waited, expecting me to continue. When I didn't, he asked, "Did you?"

"No."

They both reacted as though I'd just missed a touchdown pass at the Super Bowl. Rain lamented, "You should've called him!"

I threw up my arm. "I didn't have enough change for the pay phone!"

Rain laughed. "The *pay* phone? Who still uses a pay phone?"

Nothe shook his head. "That's going to come back to haunt you later."

I felt defensive now. "You guys were mad at him like, two seconds ago!"

Rain also shook his head in a very 'tut-tut' sort of way. "Doesn't change the accuracy of his warnings."

I was too tired to deal with this. I looked down at the hardwood floor and had a sudden, inexplicable urge to lie down on it.

Rain caught my shoulder. "All right, all right. You're exhausted. You've been through enough tonight. I'm taking you home. Nothe," he looked over at him, "the guys—"

Nothe turned away. "Yeah, yeah. I'm going."

"I'll, uh, meet up with you later."

They exchanged a nod and parted ways.

Rain led me through a back door near the stage to a gorgeous, dark blue Infiniti. He opened the passenger door for me, and as I sat, I realized how much I was dreading him leaving. Despite the deep pain that was now growing in my forehead just above my right eye and how my brain was drowning in a swamp of information and questions, and even though all I wanted to do was sleep, I didn't want to go home and be stuck in my apartment all alone, in the dark. And I just outright didn't want him to go. I tried to think of something to put off the inevitable and was surprised to find, underneath my near inability to keep my eyelids open, that I was hungry. I hadn't eaten since lunch. My breath was probably rancid.

I knew that after the evening we'd just had, what I was about to ask was going to sound bizarre, but as Rain got in the car beside me, I did it anyway. "Do you know if there's a twenty-four-hour drive-thru around here somewhere? And do you have any gum?"

Rain smiled. "I do—to both of your questions. If I didn't have something I needed to do, I'd take you to Denny's."

I smiled at that, and said tentatively, "Well, maybe you can take me to Denny's tomorrow."

He grinned. "It's a date."

TRACK 11

MY HERO

"Well, not *date*, date," Rain stammered. "I mean—like—I meant that more as a figure of speech—"

"Right. Of course." I waved this away. "You're fine. I knew what you meant." Although I couldn't remember ever feeling such dizzying euphoria and bone crushing disappointment in such a short period of time.

"Unless, of course..."

I caught myself holding my breath. "Yeah?"

He looked away. "Nothing. Never mind." He ran a hand through his hair. "Sorry, I'm tired. Let's get you home."

As we drove through dark, empty streets, a few of my many questions floated to the surface of my exhausted mind, but I wasn't sure what was polite to ask and what wasn't. Could I ask about his Deadpool powers? I also really wanted to know more about Thipka's wings, shrapnel, missing tail, and all the insane things Nothe had talked about.

My thoughts were derailed by a song on the radio. It was "I'm Gonna Be (I Would Walk 500 Miles)" by The Proclaimers. I brightened. "Aw, man! I love this song!"

Rain turned up the volume. "It is a classic."

"When I was fifteen, I wrote in my journal that I would know who my future husband was..." I had to think of how to phrase the sentence, because I couldn't remember how words worked, "because he would sing this to me."

Rain looked over at me, thoroughly amused. "So... whoever sang this song to you, was the one destined to be your future husband?"

I pointed at him. "Yes!"

"*This* song?"

"Yes."

His listened for a moment. "And it was very much *this* song? Of all the love songs known to man, *this* was the song upon which the fate of your future happiness would rely—the one that would determine who you would spend the rest of eternity with?"

I narrowed my gaze at him. "Don't you judge fifteen-year-old me!"

He laughed. "Oh, I am judging. And I am judging harshly."

"I'll have you know, sir, that this is one of the greatest love songs of all time! Right up there with 'Rhythm Divine' by Enrique Iglesias."

Rain dramatically put a hand to his forehead as if he'd gotten a severe headache. "Oh dear heavens, no. Take it back! Take it back!"

I began to sing the chorus to "Rhythm Divine." Rain cranked up the volume on the radio, trying to drown me out.

I busted up laughing and turned the volume back down. "I'm just messing with you—well, about the 'Rhythm Divine' part. The rest is all true. But I do like that song!"

"I am so making you listen to 'Journey from A to B' by Badly Drawn Boy. Now *that* is a love song—"

Our conversation was cut short by the crunch of metal and glass as a large, soft body collided with the car with a sickening thud and rolled off to the side. I was thrown into the seatbelt as the scream of breaks ripped through the silent streets. Once the car had stopped, we exchanged wide-eyed glances before I finally exclaimed, "What the crap was that?"

Rain's expression reflected my question. He hadn't seen any more of the thing than I had. It had happened so fast, just a blur of leathery skin and very dark fur, almost violet in color. Maybe it was a... big dog? Had we hit Clifford the Big, Violet, Leathery Dog?

We took off our seatbelts and got out of the car, searching the street behind us, expecting whatever-the-thing-was to be lying in the middle of the road, illuminated by streetlights.

But there was nothing there.

The blood in my veins turned very cold. I had a terrible feeling in the pit of my stomach. Something wasn't right. Something was very, very *not* right.

For a moment, neither of us moved. Rain spoke in a near whisper, his voice unnaturally calm, "I fear that we have been followed."

I blinked. "W-what?" I thought I knew what he meant, but I didn't want to be right. I was hoping he'd follow that statement up with, 'By that practical joker, Officer Reece. He must've used one of his many Halloween props to give us a scare. He's such a character.'

But instead, Rain said, "Stay in the car." His eyes glowed ever so slightly.

He didn't have to tell me twice. "Okay." I stepped backward and opened the car door.

A loud pop and the shatter of glass sent the world to my right into shadow as the streetlight next to me exploded. I cried out and jumped inside, slamming the door shut. I looked out my window, growing sick with dread as I watched the streetlights around us go out, one by one, shrouding us in darkness.

I sat there, frozen, my heart pounding violently in my ears. I covered my face with my hands. I couldn't breathe. My face and my fingers were numb. I chanted in my mind, as if they were the words to a spell that would make it all go away, *This isn't happening... this isn't happening...*

Lights popped and fizzled in my vision. My brain couldn't process anything, it was too much.

My eyes widened as I watched a big, violet *thing* with gigantic wings drop onto the hood of the car. I couldn't find my voice to scream as it reared its round head back and shattered the windshield with it. I scrambled for the door handle. I couldn't find it. Where was it? *Where was it?*

The door flew open. Rain pulled me out of the seat as a violet claw tore at my leg. Pain shot through me as we tumbled out onto the cold asphalt. We scrambled to our feet and stumbled away from the car, my right leg giving out on me as blood poured down my calf. Rain held me close as we searched the darkness for the thing, but once again, it had vanished from sight.

The thought flashed across my mind, *It just wanted us out of the car.*

We were sitting ducks. Fish in a barrel.

I couldn't breathe... I couldn't breathe...

Rain grabbed my hand as he guided us back toward the Infiniti, a wave of serenity rushed through me at his touch. My vision returned to normal, my breathing steadied. His blue eyes pierced mine. "Listen to me." he added gentle emphasis to each following word, "everything is going to be alright."

I nodded vigorously, my mind clearing. "Okay." I wanted to believe him. I really did. I just kept nodding to myself as I repeated the word a few more times, "Okay. Okay. Okay."

"Okay?"

"Okay."

He let me go. "Stay close to me."

I nodded. "Okay!" 'Okay' was the only word I could remember.

Rain reached toward the shredded hood of the car.

It looked as though the hood and the engine were melting. Pools of metal swirled through the air toward Rain's outstretched palm, molding into what at first looked like a large staff. But as more metal flowed, it became clear that what was forming was a massive, double-bladed axe. In the moonlight, I could see that the blades were shaped and etched to look like flowing waves, highlighted by metallic blue.

It was the axe he'd had in my dream.

I blinked a lot. I couldn't feel the ground beneath my feet. I'd almost forgotten I was bleeding and that we were about to die.

It wasn't exactly what I'd pictured all those times I'd imagined my dreams coming true.

He spun it expertly, as if it weighed nothing, and turned toward the four-story building behind us, examining the top.

He grabbed my arm and pulled me behind him. The air all around us had changed. I breathed in fear like a fog, filling my lungs and draining my soul of light. Mixed in with the fog, like dew drops, were feelings of emptiness and desperation that brought tears to my eyes and made the hairs on my arms stand up. And a *hunger,* ravenous and merciless, as though my stomach had been ripped out of me, leaving nothing but a black pit that could never be filled.

I fought to separate these feelings from myself, to push them away from me. They weren't *my* feelings, but they had engulfed my mind.

I looked up at Rain and saw that his eyes had become watery and red. "This is much worse than I imagined."

Rain stepped slowly across the street toward an alleyway, his gaze never leaving the roof. We reached the sidewalk and stopped. He pointed at the top of the building. "There it is. Do you see it?"

I looked up. I didn't see it right away. It took me a moment to realize what I was looking at, because all I could see were two big, round, yellow lights hanging off the side of the building. Then I realized, they weren't lights. They were eyes.

I was having an out-of-body experience again.

Rain put a hand on my shoulder. "Stay right here and don't move. No matter what happens, *stay here.*"

He swung the axe into both hands. With every step he took, the eyes dropped down the side of the building in spastic leaps of several feet, eagerly making their way toward him.

A scream echoed through the streets. It was unlike anything I had ever heard, shrill and off tone, not quite human. It made the blood in my veins bubble and sent a wave of terror running through me, as though I were trapped in a nightmare with a demon and I couldn't wake. I limped several steps backward, away from the alley, fighting tears, my legs begging me to run.

It leapt at Rain from the shadows. Its mouth opened abnormally wide for its face, like the emptiness that had filled the air had taken form. Its skin was a deep violet, almost black, its wings boney and bat-like, its hind legs short with massive claw-like feet and a long tail that fanned out near the end. But its face... its face was the most disturbing of all. It had tall, bat-like ears and an upturned, bat-like snout, and its lipless mouth was full of teeth—but its eyes, the shape of its face, the cheekbones and skull... it was so *human.*

Rain swung his axe, hitting it across the chest in a splatter of blood and knocking it into the shadows. It let out another soul-piercing scream and flopped around before scurrying off.

I told myself that the blow had killed it. It was going to wander off and die.

I took several small, stiff steps toward the alley, searching the shadows, looking up and down the sides of the buildings for the eyes. I couldn't see them. I forced myself to take a few more steps forward, as did Rain, listening to the sounds of cans being thrown around and bottles breaking deep within the alley.

Out of the darkness, a leathery mass dropped onto Rain's back. The creature's mouth opened, its jaw detaching and clamping down onto Rain's shoulder, pulling and tearing at the muscle, the little knife-like claws of its wings digging into his arms and chest. Blood pooled down his back as he cried out in pain.

It was eating him. *It was eating him.*

Rain dropped his axe and fell to one knee as he grabbed the monster by its wings and attempted to rip it off of him, but the creature had driven its hind claws into his ribs. Blood poured out of the wounds as it held onto his ribs like tree branches. As Rain pulled, there was a snap.

He was going to die. Rain was going to die.

I started screaming and tearing at my hair. I paced helplessly, my blood feeling as though it'd been set on fire. "HELP! SOMEBODY, HELP!"

The streets were empty. There was nobody. Nobody was coming to save us.

I couldn't let him die. Getting eaten was sure to be terrible, but I couldn't let him die. I'd rather get eaten than let him die.

I charged at the monster, screaming, "NOOO!" My brain started yelling at me, *Go for the eyes! Go for the eyes!*

I grabbed the monster by its head. Deep, horrible hunger, desperation, *emptiness* burned my skin at its touch. My fingers dug into its yellow eyes without mercy, like I was smashing boiled eggs. I tried to convince myself that was all they were. They weren't eyes. They were boiled eggs.

The creature let out a scream and I felt its pain. Anger and terror consumed me like a violent storm from where its skin touched mine, but I refused to let go. It threw back its head and elbowed me in the ribs with its wing, throwing me on my back and knocking the air out of me. I tried to expand my lungs, to get air, to *move...*

I couldn't move.

The thing turned its bleeding eyes onto me, letting out weird, pig-like snorts as it sniffed the air, its head twitching from side to side as the popped eyes regained their shape. It scurried toward me in sporadic steps. I forced myself to sit up, desperately digging into my pockets, my breathless brain screaming at me, *Move! Move! Pepper spray! Pepper spray!*

The monster jumped on top of me, pushing me to the ground. Intense pressure drove my hip into the concrete as it held me in place, its mouth opening wide, its breath wreaking of blood and rotting flesh.

I unleashed the pepper spray, spraying its bleeding eyes and its open mouth with a steady stream of pain. It let out its loudest cry yet as it fell backward, covering its face with its wings and writhing on the ground. It took off into the safety of the dark alley.

My eyes burned, drying out like I'd just chopped a particularly vengeful onion. Man, that pepper spray was brutal.

"Rain," I gasped, crawling over to him. I gagged at the sight of his shoulder and my vision spun. A large chunk was missing from it, pieces of flesh hung out of the wound in threads. He was soaked in blood.

Adrenaline pushed me past the nausea. I gently put my arms around him and coaxed him onto his feet. With his good arm, he grabbed his axe and hobbled onto the sidewalk.

It was about then that I noticed the sensation of hot fluid now pouring down my lower abdomen and leg. *Oh crap.* My brain yelled at me, *Don't look at it! You'll faint! Don't look at it!*

Rain stopped abruptly. A dark, sickening rage flowed from the shadows of the alley and an off-pitch growl rent the air.

Rain turned just as the monster leapt back out of the shadows, hitting it again with his axe. It fell to the ground, nearly cut in two. I watched in horror as strings of muscle and sinew threaded through the wound, pulling the severed parts of the creature back together and sealing shut as if nothing had happened.

The creature pushed itself back up from the ground. Rain's eyes glowed brighter than I'd ever seen them, piercing the darkness like sudden sunlight, his gaze fixed on the creature. He lifted his injured arm. As the monster reached for him, he flicked his thumb against his forefinger as though he were tossing a coin, and the beast exploded. Its legs stumbled backward without its upper half and collapsed, blood pooling all around it.

I stood there, frozen. My brain was spinning, swimming in a fog. I needed to sit down. I really, really needed to sit down. But even more, I needed to know it was dead. I had to know it was dead and never, *ever* coming back. Rain and I hobbled toward the remains, my nausea now significantly worse but my curiosity overpowering it. I studied it, stammering, "Is it c-coming back?" That was all I could say without puking.

"No," Rain said, his voice weary yet his words full of venom. His face was ashen and he looked like he was fighting to stay upright. "It can't come back from that."

It was as if someone had flipped a switch. Every muscle in my body relaxed and a weight lifted from my chest. I told myself to get away from the guts before I collapsed and the second I had, I threw up. I hobbled a few steps away from that mess before I fell to my knees on the sidewalk. My whole body shook and my hip hurt really, *really* bad, making me think, *That stupid shamonster better not have ripped my dress.*

The lights in my vision grew steadily worse until they were all I could see. As if from deep under water, I could hear Rain call my name. "Emily? *Emily?*" The next thought I had was, *The sidewalk is nice and cold against my face...* Where The Sidewalk Ends *is a great name for a book.*

TRACK 12

BLISS

That was the last thought I had for a while, until I heard Rain's voice again.

"Nothe, I have some news," I heard him say. His voice trembled and growled with exhaustion as he spoke. I could hear another voice talking as though through a tin can. Nothe's voice. Rain was on the phone.

"What?" said tin-can-Nothe with alarm. "What happened?"

"Well, we don't have to meet up to kill the monster anymore, because it's dead."

"*What?*"

"Yeah, it didn't go very well." Rain sniffed. "Well, except that, now it's dead. So at least there's that."

Nothe's tin can voice was annoyed, "Why didn't you call me?"

"Well I'm calling you now, aren't I?"

I was soon aware that I wasn't lying on the sidewalk anymore. I was in Rain's arms. He was holding me as though he'd been carrying me and had decided to sit down. My head rested against his chest and I could hear the drumming of his heart. A stupid, giddy thrill ran through me. I went to curse myself for it and found that I was too tired. Besides, we'd nearly died. I'd let myself have this one.

I tried to open my eyes to see where we were, but I had apparently gained one thousand pounds in my eyelids and it was now impossible. I could feel that it was chilly. Rain's body was propped up against something, probably a wall. I could smell garbage and exhaust under the stench of blood and sweat.

After some incoherent, angry grumblings from Nothe, Rain went on, his tone defensive, "I didn't intentionally *not* call you—there wasn't time!" There was another, more hopeful growl from Nothe and Rain erupted, "*Yes*, of course she's..." he caught himself mid-sentence and made his voice drop to a softer tone so as not to wake me, "She's still alive!"

Tin-can-Nothe said, clear as a bell, "That's a shame."

Rain's whole body tensed, anger rising to the surface. Nothe added playfully, "I'm kidding! I'm kidding... mostly."

Rain was quietly indignant, "I'll have you know, she saved my life, actually, and with..." He chuckled, "With fingernails and pepper spray, of all things. She was... she was very brave."

There was more grumbling from Nothe. Rain went on, "Look, we're not doing so well. She's unconscious and I can't take another step. I need you to come and get us. Quickly. Please. There's still about forty minutes before the sun is sufficiently bright." His voice was growing weak as though he were fighting sleep, but he pressed on. "I'm honestly a bit nervous being out here. We're soaked in blood. If there are more of them, they'll be drawn right to us and, well, we might as well be lying on a dinner plate with a bit of garnish."

"You get so dramatic when you nearly die."

"I also called the police with my Jerry Lewis impression and they're searching the area. Although, I think someone may have called them before I did." He let out an airy, ah-ha sort of laugh. "Now they'll know Emily's not crazy."

There was more grumbling from Nothe and then, "I'm in the car, on my way."

Rain didn't hang up. He sat there for a moment, then his tone grew somber, "Nothe... it was Theran."

Nothe sounded stunned. "What?"

"The monster. It was from Thera. One of the failed experiments. That's what The Prophet's insulting riddle meant. Same lab, same planet... we're all monsters."

"Oh, wow. Here I thought knowing the answer would make me feel better."

"It's a pretty vicious insult, indeed. It was probably stuck in some dark, decrepit pod for who knows how many years, floating through space. Probably ate itself to survive—you know how they are. It was starving and miserable. I got a good look at the remains, it's... it's bad."

"How bad?"

"Very, very bad. Just, get here."

"I'm on the road, driving."

"Thank you," Rain added quickly, "We're on Canon Avenue, by the arcade."

He hung up shortly after. I considered worrying about what he'd said, but I was somewhere between dreaming and awake and couldn't remember why. In my mind, I was trying to stitch up my dress and was mortified to discover that I'd patched it up with polka dot fabric. This pulled me a bit more out of my subconscious just in time to feel a small cloud of a very delightful emotion rise from Rain, a feeling that was very bright and kind. It took my sleepy brain a moment to put a word to it, but I soon recognized it as *fondness*. A very strong fondness. With it, Rain's calloused fingertips caressed my face as he brushed hair behind my ear. He spoke with an air of disbelief in his tone, "You risked your life for me." As he said it, I thought I felt the fondness grow brighter.

My stomach fluttered, and instead of kicking myself and listing all the obvious reasons why this feeling was irrational and misguided, or attempting to convince myself that it didn't exist at all, I decided I was going to cherish it for the moment. All of those reasons on that list would still be there when I woke, but in this moment they didn't matter. Though everything was horrible, though the world around us was collapsing and Rain and I were covered in blood, in *this* moment, my life was perfect, and I was actually happy somehow. I let this happy feeling follow me into my dreams, right into a vintage dress shop where I hoped to find a cute, little black dress. I searched through racks of clothing while trying to ignore the yellow eyes that were hungrily watching me through the window.

TRACK 13
AWAKE AND ALIVE

Somewhere between my dream of shopping at a dress shop and waking, I found myself in a field, laying on a blanket, alone, admiring the stars. It hit me how much I missed them. Being constantly surrounded by artificial light, I couldn't remember the last time I'd seen the sky covered in stars. Some of those stars had planets revolving around them and others were twinkling galaxies. And there I was, a single, tiny person on a tiny rock floating through space around a tiny star—well, tiny in comparison to other stars. I thought of how, perhaps, somewhere out there, there was another small, sentient life form, living across the vast chasm of space, looking out over the same universe, seeing our galaxy or our glittering little star, and thinking the same things... and what a marvelous idea that was.

I could feel myself waking up, which made me realize I was dreaming. It felt as though someone were blatantly touching my face with their hand. Not my dream face but my *actual* face. Not two seconds later, clouds appeared above me in the sky, shifting together to form a giant Nothe, wearing loose-fitting jeans and a Talking Heads T-shirt. I felt like I was in *The Lion King,* at least until Nothe declared, "I need you to get off my couch."

I furrowed my brow, terribly confused. "What?"

"At least sit up! You're completely hogging the couch."

I stared at him. I had no idea what he was talking about. "Am I on your couch?"

Then I heard a very loud whisper in my very real ear, *"Wake up!"*

I jumped awake. Nothe was sitting beside me on the arm of the couch, his hand a few inches from my face—which wasn't far enough away, so I gave it a shove.

I sat up and Nothe slid onto the cushion next to me with an exasperated, "FINALLY!" He was holding a plate of steak and potatoes, which smelled amazing and made my stomach grumble with hunger.

I was wrapped in the most ridiculously soft comforter I'd ever had the pleasure of meeting. It was dark blue, fluffy, and super poofy. I felt terrible guilt for using it. I'd probably gotten blood all over it. I looked.

"Oh, man," I said, feeling sick. "I got blood all over this awesome blanket. I'm so sorry."

"You should be sorry," Nothe said as he picked up the remote and turned on the TV, flipping over to a saved recording of Dr. Phil. "How *dare* you bleed."

I laughed a little, but it was nervous and half-hearted since Nothe didn't even crack a smile, so I couldn't tell if he was joking.

Rain appeared from the hallway, wearing a long-sleeved, button-up shirt and jeans. His shoulder was back to normal, though his eyes had dark, tired rings underneath them. "Nothe, I told you to let her sleep!"

"She was totally hogging the couch. Other people have needs, too, Rain. Like me! I need to eat lunch and watch Dr. Phil."

"So sit in the chair!"

There was a recliner adjacent to the soft, brown couch. A perfectly good chair.

Nothe said in a don't-you-know sort of way, "The chair isn't my comfy spot."

Rain glared at him, then rubbed his forehead in a surrendering-manner that clearly stated there was no point in arguing with the man. Instead, he apologized on Nothe's behalf.

I looked around at the living room. It was almost twice the size of my apartment, though that didn't necessarily mean it was spacious. It just meant I lived in a shoebox. It was a nice change of surroundings. The walls were a warm yellow. Various guitars hung along the wall on one side of the TV while a gorgeous, baby grand piano sat beside the other. The room led into the kitchen to my right, where I could see through a sliding glass door to swaying palm trees in the backyard.

I blinked and rubbed my eyes repeatedly as I studied the scene, because every time I looked at Rain and Nothe, they were surrounded by light. No matter what I did, I couldn't shake it. After the night I'd had, though, seeing lights wasn't a terrible side effect. It could've been way worse. Honestly, I'd expected to feel horrible, but I could sit upright without any pain. My mind was clear, my hip didn't hurt. The only discomfort I had came from the crustiness of the dried blood on my leg and the sensation of my dress sticking to my body like it'd been glued there.

Yet, in spite of seeing Rain get partially eaten and nearly being eaten myself, and in spite of the knowledge that there were more monsters out there and a mysterious portal to multiple worlds that had possibly been opened, I felt upbeat and cheerful. Had Rain and I almost died a gruesome death? Sure, but we were alive now. Was it possible that we were all totally doomed? Absolutely. But we'd figure out a way around it somehow. Did Nothe like me? Probably not, but I didn't have to live with him, so it was okay.

Did Rain blow up a monster with his mind powers?

Yes. He had... and he'd made an axe out of the remains of his car somehow... yes...

He'd blown up a monster... with a flick of his fingers.

And he'd nearly been eaten. *I'd* nearly been eaten. I could still smell the shamonster's breath, see those empty eyes...

I jumped a little when Rain touched my arm, half expecting to explode. "Emily? Are you alright?"

I noticed then that I was breathing like I'd just walked up a flight of stairs. "I'm—I'm fine. I think I just need to walk around a bit. Or something. Can I use your bathroom?"

This led to a very quick tour. The house wasn't a mansion by any means. It was a single story home with a short hallway that led from the living room to the bathroom, with doorways to two bedrooms on either side at the end and a closet on the left that opened up to a washer and dryer. Each room was well kept and cozy. And it had a good sized yard and a pool with a fancy little waterfall.

As I reached the bathroom, Rain offered, "You know, if you want, I have some clothes you could change into. I happen to have a fabulous selection of dresses." He grinned.

I laughed a little. As much as I wanted an excuse to stay with Rain longer, I felt the need to leave right away, especially since Nothe had made it clear he wanted me gone. I glanced over in Nothe's direction, though I couldn't see him through the wall. "That's okay. Thanks, though. But I could really use a ride home—" I remembered what had become of Rain's car. "Oh. Wait."

He shrugged. "We'll take Nothe's truck."

Nothe overheard this and hollered, "No."

I felt obnoxious and guilty. Rain gave me a reassuring nod and at that, he turned and walked back into the living room.

My trip to the bathroom led to the discovery that my dress was, in fact, torn. I was devastated. Underneath was a particularly nasty scab embedded with fabric threads. I imagined it was where the monster had dug into my hip bone with its hind claw. I carefully touched it. It didn't hurt. The skin wasn't broken. My leg was as good as new.

How in the world did Rain do that?

And how had he blown up a monster with his mind?

I washed my hands and my face a little. My vision was still a bit off, but it seemed to be improving. All around my reflection, I could see a faint, small light, like a fine mist, but it wasn't as bright as what I'd seen around Rain and Nothe earlier. I rubbed my eyes some more but it did nothing to help it.

I leaned against the sink, my thoughts wandering. *Rain.* I sighed and held my head in my hands. I was awake now. My magical moment with him had passed and reality was settling in. The time had come for me to confront it.

Emily, my brain said to me. *Listen, let's take a good look at these feelings that keep popping up here. We can't ignore them any longer. Let's just be honest—it's understandable! You've been through a lot. And now you've met a guy that's beautiful, and kind and smart and funny, and goes way out of his way to make you feel good about yourself, and yet—and here's the kicker, the real kicker—I* actually snorted out loud to myself, *he asks for* nothing *in return. Nothing! Who does that?!*

Rain. Rain does that. I rubbed my face, forcing away the sudden urge to cry as my brain went on, *But it's unrealistic and you've got to let it go.*

I sighed again. My brain was right. Reality was crashing down on me like Thor's hammer and it was really depressing. I was sure there wasn't another soul alive who was as amazing and wonderful as Rain. Which meant I was going to be single forever.

I thought about the night before, about lying in his arms. Already the memory had faded a little. Why couldn't good memories stay? Why couldn't they be frozen in perfect images, vacuum sealed with the beautiful emotions and magic? The very worst of memories never seemed to fade. They haunted my dreams and lived in the crevices of my mind. Why couldn't the very best ones receive the same treatment? Instead, they ebbed away, little by little, like sandcastles in the waves.

I'd write down every detail I could remember when I got home—about his fondness, his touch. It was as close as I could get to taking a photograph of that sacred moment. I needed some way to look back on it and remember it forever.

My brain tried to cheer me up, *Well, hey. Cats are funny! You might end up alone with a bunch of sad notes, but at least you'll have cats! That'll eat you... when you die in your apartment... alone...*

That was it. I'd had it with this conversation.

I didn't make it far down the hallway before I stopped. Rain was speaking in a very threatening tone, "Nothe, if you don't put an end to this, so help me, I am going to take this remote and throw it into the pool, and you will be forced to watch Nick Jr. *all day* unless you get off the couch and change the channel MANUALLY!"

Nothe hissed, "You wouldn't dare."

Dr. Phil's drawling voice was replaced by Dora the Explorer's headache-inducing shouting, "CAN YOU SAY, 'BACKPACK?'" and another character, "SAY 'BACKPACK!' SAY 'BACKPACK!'"

Nothe sounded downright villain-esque. "Rain... give me the remote..."

Rain's voice did not waver in its dark intensity. "Without this, there will be no more access to your recordings of Dr. Phil."

Nothe's plate clicked against the coffee table as he set it down. "It doesn't have to be this way."

"Unfortunately, you've given me no other choice."

For a moment, all I could hear was the singing of Dora's backpack. Then there was a scuffle. The remote flew across the living room and into the kitchen. Nothe went after it, but didn't make it very far before

Rain grabbed his legs and dropped him to the floor. Rain leapt from the ground, made a mad dash into the kitchen and seized the remote, with Nothe at his heels. Rain stood next to the sliding glass door, both men breathless. Nothe dared him, "Fine! Do it! Go ahead. See if I care. I'll just *fix* it!"

"No, you won't. Not after I crush it first. All of that water, corroding those tiny, microscopic little pieces... *warping* them. It takes so much care—so much detail—to find all of those pieces, cleanse them of corrosion, fix each one, and then put them back together again. It'll be much easier and less exhausting to simply... *purchase another one.* At the store. With all of those *people.*"

Nothe was losing it. "I *hate* people!"

Rain stepped toward the door. Though he tried to maintain his commanding tone, Nothe's voice had a hint of pleading to it. "No. Don't."

"Say you'll be nice."

"I hate you so much right now."

"That's not very nice."

"Well, *you're* not being very nice."

"You started it!"

I decided that maybe this was a good time to intervene. I did my best to hide my amusement as I traipsed out of the hallway toward the kitchen. Rain hid the remote behind his back when he saw me, trying to look innocent.

I rubbed my eyes again. I had been mistaken. My vision was *not* better. The lights around them were as bright as ever.

Nothe smiled at me. "Hey! Why, look at you, uh..." He tried to think of a word to call me. "Gorgeous!" He put a hand on his hip. "My, you've just emerged out of that bathroom like an angel out of a church on Sunday morning. Glorious and radiant, like the, uh... like the Angel of Death! After slaying the wicked, what with all of the blood on your face."

I wanted a shower even more now. I hadn't thought that possible.

He turned to Rain, beaming. "That was nice of me, wasn't it?"

Rain glared at him. "No."

"C'mon, Angel of Death? That's a good thing!" Nothe's shoulders slumped. "Whatever. I can't do this. I don't know how to be nice. I think it's a disease. Are you really going to torture me for something I can't help?" He added, throwing his arms out dramatically, "*Have you no compassion?*"

Rain sighed and put his hand to his eyes. "You're such a child."

"*You're* a child!"

He handed Nothe the remote, saying, "This isn't over."

Nothe smiled. There was a look in his eyes that I couldn't read. "I wouldn't have it any other way."

TRACK 14

LIGHTS

With great reluctance, Nothe agreed to let Rain borrow his orange Toyota Tundra to take me home, though he insisted I sit on a towel. I supposed it was fair, even though all of the blood on me was dry.

The second we drove away, I jumped to my first question. "So, how did you blow up a shamonster with your mind?"

He raised an eyebrow. "Shamonster?"

I felt like a dork, but it was too late now. "Yeah. You know, a monster that lives in the shadows? Shadow-monster... shamonster..." Why was I still talking?

He nodded, amused. "I see it. A shamonster."

"Yep. Shamonster. How did you blow it up? And make an axe out of your car? I mean, what was *that*?"

"Yeeeah, I was kind of secretly hoping you'd forget that."

"Oh, I'll never forget that."

He hummed in an of-course-not sort of way. He rubbed his lips. "Well, as I believe I told you once, briefly, I am... well..." He ran a hand through his hair. "I am made up of a more powerful energy than most living things—or life force or chi or spirit or whatever you wish to call it —and one of the abilities that comes with this is, I can manipulate matter that comes within the reach of my energy. Like, how you can manipulate your body. You use your brain to send signals to your limbs and they move as you wish. What my energy does is similar, only on a much greater scale. My reach is farther, and more *inclusive,* I guess you could say. And it's not something that comes easily. It's not even something that really comes naturally. It's something I've had to train myself to be able to do and quite frankly, it's exhausting. But I can create connections to the world outside of myself, to matter within about a three-foot radius around me, and get it to move as others would move an arm or a leg.

"So what I did there with the shamonster, see," a giddy, little thrill went through me at his casual use of my dumb word, "I, er... well, it really came down to timing. I had to wait until the monster was within reach. Then I used my energy to see the particles it was made up of and sent out a signal to tell them to separate. And then they did. And then it died."

I stared at him. "Mmmkay. And the axe?"

He gave a small shrug. "Same thing. I simply reorganized the particles of the car into an axe." He gave me a cheerful, and-that-is-that sort of look, as though he were discussing how he preferred to separate his laundry.

I stared some more. "Right, but see, the brain... it has these things called neurons and-and nerves, and *that's* how it sends signals to the body, very *physically*. Through... through nerves..." I tried to remember Mr. Staker's human biology class in high school. "I think sodium is involved..."

He furrowed his brow. "Right. It's not *quite* the same."

I shook my head. "No."

"But it's similar!"

"Sure, sure."

"It's still a very physical thing."

"Of course."

"Just, instead of nerves, it's energy that's manipulating particles on a level that simply cannot be seen. Well, except by me and Nothe," he added begrudgingly, "and *Thipka*, I guess, because of the level of our energy. Of course humans don't tend to see this energy, but that's simply because their energy is very small. It takes a great amount of energy to be able to see the small, seemingly invisible things." He rubbed his neck, looking nervous. "I'm rambling."

"Is that... is that also how you healed me?"

He hesitated. "Well... mostly. But I really couldn't have done it without the hot chocolate."

I shook my head in awe and told him with all sincerity, "That's truly awesome, Rain."

He smiled, looking slightly relieved, though I was sure I could see a sadness in his eyes. I wondered where it was coming from, but then all the recent events scrolled through my mind like a list of side-effects in a prescription drug commercial. I decided to move on to my next pressing question. "Also, last night, when you were talking to Nothe on the phone..."

"Oh. You heard that, did you? I thought you were asleep. Your pulse was so low."

"Well, I mostly was. I went dress shopping right after, so," I laughed a little. "Anyway, you said the monster was from Thera and that things were bad."

Rain grew somber. "It is bad. When examining the corpse, I discovered something lining what was left of the spinal column. It was basically a computer, wired into the creature, which appeared to be specifically connected to its digestive system. I took what was left of the computer in hopes of figuring out why it was there, but honestly, I'm not tech savvy and neither is Nothe. We haven't been able to figure out how it works yet. All we have are guesses. But, seeing as several of these things were dropped on Earth, it's pretty safe to assume that the Therans sent them here on purpose. That, whatever the monsters consume, the information is gathered somewhere."

That made no sense to me. "What? Wha-why? Why would they do that? I mean, I get gathering information, but why like *that?*"

He responded with a dark smile. "The Queen would think it was funny. The destruction and terror they cause—she would find that very amusing, indeed. Plus, it's cost-effective, since they're totally expendable to them."

I was disgusted. It hit me right then just how little I knew about him and his world. This revelation came out in a less-than-politely-worded question. "What kind of planet do you come from?"

He shook his head. "You really don't want to know."

My mind fought to make sense of all of this. "So, is it because they're... they're failed experiments? Is that why they're expendable?"

He grew visibly uncomfortable. "You heard that part, too, eh?"

"I did, yeah."

He chewed on his lips for a few silent seconds before finally saying,

"Yes, it is. Perhaps we can save that story for another time." He hurried on, "Anyway, I can't imagine that the computers inside the shamonsters are powerful enough to transmit a signal through space. The information must be sent elsewhere, to something local, something *bigger*, and then that thing will be what sends the information to Thera. If they discover just how rich this planet is with organic life, that they could inhabit it..." Rain's expression was grim. "Well, it won't be good. These people aren't simple scientists and explorers."

"They're basically the white man taking over the Americas."

He considered this, then agreed. "Precisely."

Silence as loud as thunder filled the car as my thoughts spun in the wind. My brain wanted to run away and binge-watch *Seinfeld* and pretend none of this was happening. Finally, I muttered, "Maybe it can be stopped somehow. If we can find the big computer-thing—"

"Assuming there is a big computer-thing—"

"Maybe there's a chance it hasn't sent any information yet. Maybe we can set it on fire, blow it up into a thousand little pieces before it sends the signal."

"Perhaps. But we would have to find it first."

My stomach tangled up into one gigantic, horrible knot. I felt so helpless. I looked back over at Rain, who looked defeated. I remembered what The Prophet had said to Thipka and my blood froze over like the Ohio River in the dead of winter, *"You can't stop them from coming."*

I decided this was as good a time as any to ask, "What did Nothe mean when he said I 'wouldn't have seen' Thipka's half a tail or whatever?"

Rain shifted as though I'd just asked him if he'd pooped yet today. He kept glancing out the driver's side window like he was ready to excuse himself from the moving car. I didn't know why he was being so weird about it and I didn't know how to make it better, though I tried to sound soothing as I added, "And, I mean, he said he's like you, but you don't have, like, *wings*," I laughed a little, "and a tail, so, like, what does he—"

He pointed at the oncoming traffic. "Oh my stars! Look! Look at that car!"

I straightened, confused as my gaze darted over to what I saw as very ordinary cars. "What? Where?"

"Shoot, it's gone. I don't know how you missed it. It had the most massive, hideous spoiler I have ever seen."

I smiled and joked, "Well, maybe they needed that spoiler."

"Only if they're flying to the moon."

I laughed. "I'm so sad I missed it."

"I'm sad for you. It was a real treasure. And what made it better, was that it was a neon green Dodge Neon. Absolutely fantastic."

I laughed a little more before we fell into silence. I was quite sure the whole car-thing had been Rain's not-so-subtle-attempt to get out of answering the question. It was so strange to me. He'd been so honest with everything else, what made this so difficult to answer?

I stared out the window as my exhausted mind pondered over this, watching the trees, buildings, and people as we drove by. I rubbed my eyes again. I kept seeing those lights, and they were downright obnoxious. The trees, grass, flowers, birds, people and their dogs—they all had lights around them. But they weren't the same. Some were dimmer than others, even among the people. A select few had dark shadows around them instead. Even Rain. When I looked at him closely, I could see that, though the light around him was brightest of all, there were parts of it that were like thin little shadows, like cracks in a lightbulb. Though they were small, they were very dark and deep.

Rain glanced sideways at me as I stared at him. "What?"

I rubbed my face, feeling stupid. "Nothing. Sorry. I'm just seeing these like," I struggled to describe it, "*lights*, around everything, everywhere."

"Lights?"

"Yeah. Ever since I woke up. Like, all around you, there's a light. And around Nothe, and around me. Though around me and like, trees and stuff, it's not very bright, but around you and Nothe..."

Rain smiled as he understood. "Oh! I know what that is. When I healed you, I also healed what I could of your energy—as being attacked by a monster leaves more than just physical wounds. I can't heal everything, some things just take time, but I did what I could. And in doing so, I *charged* it, making it more powerful and vibrant, and now you're seeing things sort of as we see them. Things on a different level, that are made of a finer matter."

I sat forward. "So, I'm seeing..."

"You're seeing living energy—living light. Your light is more powerful for the moment and so you can actually see, through your energy, the *lights* of living creatures." His expression was cheerful as he pondered this. "I imagine you can't see these lights as clearly as I can, but—"

I put a hand out to stop him, my heart pounding with excitement as I considered what he was saying. "Wait. Dude... does that mean I can move stuff with my mind right now?"

He appeared to have never thought of this before and to be nearly as curious as I was. "I honestly don't know."

I was outright giddy. "Oh, man. I can't wait to get home and try!" Then I wondered, "But, why didn't I go through this last time?"

He shrugged. "It takes a little time to fully kick in, and then I imagine you slept it off. You only slept for a few hours last night. The effects don't last very long, it's not a permanent change."

"Then we have no time to lose!"

Rain sped up, running a couple of yellow lights as we made our way to my street. I eagerly guided him into the parking lot of my apartment building, which I was sure had been a Motel 6 at one time. I led him up the stairs, warning with, "Sorry, it's kind of a mess." I ran into the apartment with the enthusiasm of a chihuahua, wondering what to test my possible magical powers on.

I was too caught up in this to notice that Rain was just standing in the doorway, looking around my apartment in shock. His gaze kept going back and forth between the "couch"—which I'd made out of blankets on the floor—to the TV. "Mess?" He said, "What mess? There is nothing here to *make* a mess."

I ignored him and darted into my tiny kitchen, grabbing a spoon from a drawer and setting it on the counter. Rain closed the door and meandered in. I focused on the spoon as he told me in a tone that suggested I might not have noticed, "You don't have a table."

"Nope," I said, concentrating very hard and telling myself, *Feel the spoon, Emily. It is an extension of yourself, like an arm, or a toe.*

He picked up the phone that was sitting on the counter nearby. "You have a rotary phone."

I broke my concentration to cheerfully exclaim, "I do! I love rotary phones. They make me all nostalgic."

He picked up the receiver and placed it against his ear. "There's no dial tone."

"I haven't set up the service yet."

He hung up the receiver and returned the phone to its spot on the counter. "But, you *do* have a cell phone, right?" He looked skeptical.

He was right to be. "Uh... no..."

He glowered at me in disbelief. I might as well have offered to show him the time machine I'd used to jump to the future from 1985. "Then how is anyone supposed to reach you?"

I shrugged. "I guess they just come over."

"What if you're not home?"

It was hard for me to imagine that kind of situation, but I did my best. "If they wanted to reach me that bad, then I guess they'd go to my work. That's the only other place I'd ever be."

"Well, I believe it, as you clearly never go to the store. But wait—how do you have a job? You don't have a phone for them to call and say, 'Hey, Emily, you got the job.'"

I shrugged yet again. "I told Marie my situation and she just said, 'Be here Monday at six.' So that's what I did."

I could tell he was deeply annoyed but was doing his best to keep it under control. "Didn't I leave you with enough money to at least buy a *couch?* Please tell me the reason you didn't buy a couch or phone service is because you invested in a pilot's license."

I felt a small flutter at just how much he remembered of the night we'd met. I'd actually forgotten about the pilot's license.

His concern was fair. "Well, you did give me enough for all that. You definitely did. It's just that..." I hesitated. His eyes didn't leave mine as he patiently waited for my answer. I sighed. It was his money. He had a right to know what I'd done with it. "My landlady, she told me her kid was sick and the bills were piling up, so I gave her nine-thousand dollars. And I gave a bunch more to my dad. I owed him. And then I decided to save the rest. It's hidden under my mattress."

Rain studied me, then his expression softened. He said in a tone of honest observation, "You're telling the truth."

"Of course I am. I wouldn't lie to you."

That wonderful affection lit his eyes as he smiled, making my heart dance. My brain yelled at it and told it to *Settle down! Stupid thing.*

Rain shook his head. "Of course that's what you did with it. I am constantly surprised by you. You're so very unique. With all that has happened, all that you've been through, if anyone had any right to keep all of that money for themselves, it was you. And yet you chose to live like this in order to give nearly half of it away to someone you felt needed it more." He held a hand out, like he was trying to physically grasp the words. "I'm just in awe."

My stomach high-fived my heart. My brain had about had it with both of them.

I looked away bashfully. I hated that Rain was so nice to me. It made me uncomfortable. Why did he have to be so nice to me? So of course, I had to say something stupid to make up for it, "Well, I did splurge on a comfy mattress and a TV."

His smile turned into a grin. "Well, someone has their priorities straight."

"Sure do, Rain." That was when I remembered the line I had planned to use back at the club, "Hey, you promised we would get friendship bracelets on Tuesday."

His eyes lit up. "I did promise that, didn't I? Well, I guess I know what we're doing this Tuesday."

I laughed. The movement reminded me that I was disgusting, which reminded me of the spoon on the counter. "But today, you're going to teach me how to move this spoon with my mind, and then I'm going to shower."

Rain spent a half an hour trying to teach me how to be a living poltergeist, but my energy lost its charge before I even came close to figuring it out. At one point I really thought I could feel the spoon, but it was gone before I could do anything about it. On the bright side, I got to see Rain move the spoon several times with his powers.

Later, after I emerged from an unintentionally long shower and put on pajamas—even though it was only three in the afternoon—I found that Rain had brought me a late lunch and a black leather couch, and black TV stand, explaining that if we were to watch a movie, we'd need a couch, because he wasn't about to sit on the floor. We agreed on beginning the original Star Wars trilogy and sat on the new couch, eating lunch, being boring, laughing and forgetting just how much trouble we were in for a little while. There, in the midst of our storms, everything was perfect.

HIDDEN TRACK:
TIME WILL TELL

Meanwhile, just across the ocean

Thipka was silent as they cut through the dark green jungle foliage. Well, near silent, except for the occasional line sung from *The Greatest Showman* and all the *Save Them*s muttered under his breath. This had become such a part of his mind that it was as natural to him as blinking and he'd grown just as oblivious to it. He was leaning more and more against his walking stick with every step as the stub attached to his robotic leg throbbed with pain, but he hardly noticed. His focus was on finding a group of trees tangled together. They'd reminded him of friends mourning at a gravesite, with their arms draped over each other's shoulders. They'd stood at the edge of a large clearing that held a deep crater that cradled a big, black box. He waited for the air to change—a sign they were close. He anticipated growing dark and heavy, as if the whole Earth were in mourning, like the planet itself knew the devastation the box was about to bring.

But the feeling never came.

When he found the trees, he was unnerved by how cheerful they all seemed. They were no longer weeping over a grave, but friends at a party. He was also unhappy with how easy it had been to get there. He'd expected to find shamonsters swarming the place, just as he had last time. But now, they were eerily absent.

He didn't like it.

For the first time in their two hour hike up the mountain, Thipka turned to see if The Prophet had kept up. He hadn't only kept up, he was chatting away to himself—or rather, to the unseen companions he had around him. Well, unseen to everyone else. Thipka could vaguely see them as balls of light. He counted three of them today. Sometimes there were fewer, sometimes there were more.

He interrupted The Prophet's jabbering. "We're here. Are you ready for this?"

The Prophet's eyes twinkled. He gave Thipka a knowing smile, as if he knew some sort of secret. Thipka didn't like that. The Prophet glanced to his right at one of the lights, then asked Thipka, "The question is, are *you* ready?"

Thipka's stomach gave a nasty twist. He didn't bother answering. Instead, he pushed through the trees, hoping to walk into a battle— actually *hoping* for it—but instead, he found...

Nothing.

No crater. No box. The clearing was empty.

Thipka's hands moved to his hair, pulling at it. "No..." He proceeded through the clearing, his eyes searching for the broken trees that once led to the large crater, but finding only peaceful wildlife. "NO!" He whirled on The Prophet. "*Where is it?*"

The Prophet was unfazed. "If you'd have been listening, you would've heard me mention a time or two that it's not here."

"I *know* it's not here! It is very clear that it is NOT HERE! *Why* is it not here? It was here! I remember it! It's *supposed* to be here!"

The Prophet shook his head. "You are trying to rewrite the fabric of Time. Did you really think Time would just let that happen? That it wouldn't right itself?"

"*What?* Time has no mind!"

"Time moved the box." The Prophet grew serene, his eyes glazing over, listening to something Thipka couldn't hear. Then he blinked, returning to the present. "I don't know exactly where it is, but I sense the box is where Time knew you wouldn't look. It's closer to home."

Thipka responded with a panicked, baffled stare. The Prophet continued, "The box isn't here, is it? How else can you explain it? Time moved it. As I said before, Thipka," The Prophet stepped toward Thipka, his eyes full of sorrow and truth, "you cannot stop them from coming."

Thipka flexed his fingers as if fighting the urge to strangle him. "Why didn't you tell me this *earlier?*"

He shrugged. "I didn't know earlier."

"What's even the point of you? I thought you came here to help me!"

The Prophet brightened. "I am helping. I'm here to let you know that you can't win this one. That way, when you lose, you won't feel so bad."

Thipka snarled, "I've stolen moments—"

"No, you've been *given* moments. You can't rob Time, Thipka."

Thipka loomed over The Prophet, his eyes glowing as if set on fire. "I *will* save them."

The Prophet looked at him with deep empathy, as though he could see all of his pain as if it were painted on a canvas in front of him. He put a calming hand on Thipka's shoulder. "Yes. You will save them." His eyes filled with tears. "But you can't save all."

VOLUME 3

"THERE'S NOTHING WRONG
WITH HAVING A TREE
AS A FRIEND."
~BOB ROSS

TRACK 1

STANDING OUTSIDE A BROKEN PHONE BOOTH WITH MONEY IN MY HAND

There I stood, my feet planted on the pavement as I stared down my old enemy: the disgusting, rusty payphone by the post office. I glared at the globs of gum lining the inside of the booth and the graffiti that decorated the outside. I fidgeted with the coins in my pocket. I had the correct amount I needed to get the thing to work, I'd made sure of it this time. My heart hammered against my ribs, desperate to change my mind, but it changed nothing. It had been a little over a week since my brush with death, I could officially face anything. Even this, which was more terrifying than the prospect of being eaten alive.

There was no turning back this time.

"Today," I said out loud to myself, "Emily is phoning home." Out of the corner of my eye, I glimpsed a confused woman passing by who looked around to see who I was talking to.

I dragged my legs forward. I reached out and picked up the sunbaked receiver that smelled like alcohol and rotten sushi. With trembling fingers, I deposited the coins and dialed the number.

It's been five years, I thought with a warring mixture of hope and despair, *Maybe Dad's changed his number.*

The whirring dial tone turned into a ring. Each ring was like a scream, making my heart leap into my throat and my head spin with stars. After three rings, I debated hanging up. Then someone answered.

There was a pause, followed by a woman's voice. "Hello?"

All of the blood rushed from my brain and limbs, turning into a lump in my gut.

The woman repeated, annoyed, "Hello?"

Her annoyed voice gave her away.

It was Jane. My sister.

The Prophet's words flashed through my mind, "*If your sister answers, hang up and call back later.*"

I should've hung up.

But I had come so far. It had taken everything I had just to pick up the receiver. And despite our differences, hearing Jane's voice struck something within me that I'd fought to bury—a deep longing for home. I realized that, I *missed* her. I missed how she used to make me spaghetti when I was little. I missed the nights from our childhood where we'd sleep in a tent in the living room. I missed her dumb—and often very smelly—fart jokes, making me laugh until I couldn't breathe. Her voice had reawakened an ache I'd felt so many times, for things to go back to the way they used to be.

Still, the fact remained that things had changed. At some point, my sister decided she did not approve of the weirdo I'd turned into. She also hated me for my mistakes, and I was sure that running away had made things much worse. Yet a part of me clung to some sad hope that she'd missed me.

But I knew better. I knew The Prophet's counsel was solid.

But then again, I hadn't called my dad when The Prophet had told me to. How much longer could I afford to wait? Besides, she didn't have to know it was me.

All of these thoughts scrambled through my head very quickly, but took long enough to warrant an even more annoyed "*Hello?*" from my sister.

With a tremor in my voice, I asked, "Is Eli there?"

Jane took a moment to reply. When she did, her tone was cold. "That depends on who's calling."

I tried to think fast. "My name is..." I thought of the last movie I'd watched. It'd been *Beetlejuice*. I'd mentioned to Rain how I wanted to see it again, so he'd bought it for me and we'd watched it together. "Barbara."

Her voice did not warm up at all. "Barbara?"

"Yes. Barbara. My friends call me Barb."

"Barbara, what?"

I didn't get the question right away. "Huh?"

"What's your last name, *Barb?*"

"Oh. It's, um..." I thought of a *Weezer* song. "Jonas. I'm Barbara Jonas. I'm an old friend of Eli's. From school." I added—and quite bravely, I felt, as I wouldn't have dared to say it to her only a few months ago. "And I don't care for your tone, missy."

Silence followed. For a moment, I thought she'd hung up on me. But then she said, "Emily?"

My stomach froze over. I couldn't speak.

I couldn't read her tone. "Emily, is that... is that you?"

The light that flickered in my chest started screaming at my brain, *Hang up! Hang up! Hang up!*

But my brain argued, *No wait. Maybe she'll be nice. Maybe she misses me.*

I took a deep breath and confessed, "Yeah."

There was more silence. Then she started. "Do you have any idea..."

I had hope. Hope for the words, *How much we've missed you?* And, *You need to come home.*

"...how much you've put us through?"

I realized then that the tone I couldn't read was red hot anger.

She went on, each word laced with venom. "Who do you think you are?"

My frozen insides shattered. Just those words. That was all it took.

I should've hung up.

She continued, "After everything you've done, you..." She snorted. "You really have some nerve. After everything you've put Dad through. How *dare* you call here? Like, how can you even *imagine* looking him in the face again? What makes you think a little *whore* like you can ever set foot in this house again? Do you have any idea how much he's cried over you? Because of what you did? You seriously disgust me—"

I hung up. I could only stare at the receiver. I wasn't crying. I wanted to cry, but I couldn't. I struggled to process what had happened. Everything I had feared, all the reasons I'd never wanted to call... I'd had hope, but it had just been crushed into a thousand pieces.

I knew it now. I knew it for sure.

I could never go home.

As I turned away from the pay phone, taking steps in the direction of my apartment, the reality began to sink in. My breathing came in labored gasps and tears spurted to my eyes. Old wounds that had been healing over the last couple of months were ripped back open again. I stumbled as I sobbed, hunched over with my arms cradled around me, gripping the unseen wounds in my chest. I was distantly aware of people staring at me, but I didn't care.

As I approached my apartment, I saw a figure sitting on the steps, wearing a suit jacket and jeans. He raised his head in curious alarm and stood up.

It was Rain.

His voice was rich with concern. "Emily?"

Everything inside of me wanted to run to him, but I felt disgusting. Not just because of the snot and tears streaming down my face, but because of all the stupid things I'd done. I didn't deserve him. I didn't deserve his friendship. I didn't deserve anything good.

His expression fell into one of sorrow and disbelief, as though I'd spoken all of these feelings out loud. I knew he'd felt everything. My emotions had consumed me. He strode toward me and held me tightly in his arms as he told me, "Don't believe it, Emily." A wave of immense comfort and warmth swept over me, soothing every wound, and I gave in, pressing my head into his chest and clinging to his clothes, holding him as close as I could.

After a moment, he guided me up the steps and into my apartment, the sunlight of his comfort radiating from him, calming me so I could gain control over my crying. Once we were inside, he sat me down and brought me a box of tissues from my bathroom, asking, "What happened? Who do I need to beat into a bloody pulp?"

I let out a half-hearted, airy chuckle as I emptied nearly half the box of tissues and covered my face. How could I tell him? He would wonder why Jane would say those things and I couldn't tell him why. What would he think of me? He'd see I'd brought all of this on myself. He'd see that I deserve it. *I* was the one who should be beaten into a bloody pulp. He would regret saving me. He would hate me, just like everyone else hated me. More tears to spilled down my cheeks. I couldn't do it. I couldn't tell him.

I shook my head. "I don't want to talk about it."

He studied me for a moment. It made me wonder what emotions of mine he was able to feel and what he was thinking. He sat down beside me and wrapped an arm around my shoulders. "Then you don't have to."

I could feel his comfort trying to chase away the storm within me. I pushed it away, telling myself I didn't deserve it. I didn't deserve his kindness. If he knew what I was, he'd hate me.

At these thoughts, he embraced me. He said, "I know what you're feeling. I've felt that way before."

I looked up at him, shocked. How could he have ever felt this badly about himself? It wasn't that I didn't believe him, it was that it made no sense. He was amazing.

He glanced away. "You don't have to explain why you're feeling this way. All I ask is that you don't push me away. Let me care. Let me be the judge of whether or not you deserve my help."

I shook my head. "You don't know what I've done."

"No, I don't. You don't know my past, either. Yet here we are. I know the person you are now. I know you have a good heart. I know that, whatever your past is, it's led to who you've become. And for right now, that's all I need to know."

I fought to hold back another flood of tears, his words meaning more to me than I knew how to express.

He smiled a little. "So. Will you please let me help you?"

I sniffed and rubbed my face with the gigantic ball of tissues, then nodded.

His smile broadened. "Good. Well then, I propose we eat the chocolate ice cream that you've been hiding in the back of the freezer—from whom, I'm not entirely sure—and watch *Happy Gilmore*."

"But I don't have—" *Happy Gilmore*, I was about to say, but he pulled it from his inside jacket pocket. "Ah."

"I remembered that you said you liked it. I found it in a bin for five dollars and decided you had to have it."

"Aww!" I sniffled again, my spirits already lifting a little. "That's so thoughtful of you. So *very* sweet of the guy I have to hide my chocolate ice cream from."

He looked away in mock-bafflement. "I don't know what you're talking about."

"Every time you come over, it mysteriously disappears."

He stood up and walked into the kitchen as he said with sarcasm, "Psh, whatever. I find your unfounded accusations insulting." He returned with two bowls full, saying, "I gave you the most. It was a tremendous sacrifice on my part but, I figured," he sighed an elaborate sigh, "you need it more than I do."

I let Rain's healing light wash over me as he sat beside me. We spent the evening laughing at the movie and before long, I found myself forgetting my pain. Though my hurt and regret were still there, more sore and vivid than when the day had started, Rain had given me hope and laughter, and this made it bearable.

At least, so long as I was able to ignore the nagging thoughts of, *If he knew what you did... If he knew who you were...*

TRACK 2

LADIES' NIGHT

The lights went out, shrouding everyone on the dance floor in darkness. Panic rushed through me, filling me with an urge to set the place on fire and scream, "LET THERE BE LIGHT!" I told my brain, *Calm down, calm down. This is all part of the show.*

There was a rumble of drums and a single chord elaborately played on a keyboard and guitar, followed by a shout and then silence. A spotlight fell on a tall figure wearing a shimmering white dress and high heeled boots, standing on the top of a platform at the back of the stage.

It was Lipstick Rick. His back was turned to the audience with one hand on his hip and the other in the air. He dropped the hand and did a dramatic turn toward the crowd, tossing back his gleaming, black curls and raising his shoulder in a very flirtatious, Jessica Rabbit fashion. His makeup and glamorous dress highlighted his naturally perfect features, making him the living embodiment of the word *fabulous*.

A dark bass riff followed the silence as another spotlight fell on Nothe, who was in a boring, button up shirt and jeans. Rick, with his hands on his hips, elegantly made his way down the platform steps toward the microphone and began to sing Meghan Trainor's, "Me Too," remade with a rich, metal flare. Lipstick Rick's voice was deep and majestic, every note sung with perfect pitch. He strutted across the stage, his confidence filling the room, spreading to every soul in the audience. By the end of the song, everyone was dancing and singing, even if they were terrible and didn't quite know the words, like me. Every care and fear of what had been and what could be, melted away. The only thing that mattered was that moment, and it was a happy one.

There hadn't been a show since the first time I'd seen them perform, which had been over three weeks ago. After Devon the bouncer had been eaten by a "wild animal," Bob, in his grief, had closed the club indefinitely. It was only through the persuasions of *Screaming Riot and The City of Warning* that he'd agreed to open again, and there was no better night for a grand reopening than Ladies' Night—which I'd nearly missed thanks to my poor sleep and merciless work schedule. The only highlight of my day thus far had been seeing an adorable baby boy in a high chair, with big blue eyes, big cheeks and a single curl of hair that stuck out from the side of his head. His gummy smile had filled my soul with sunshine, making me feel like Superwoman for the rest of the day. Yet it also left me pining for my own little bundle of sunshine. I told myself that maybe one day I could adopt—maybe—and spent the rest of my shift planning, in the back of my mind, for this impossible future endeavor.

I was so exhausted by the time I got home that I'd told myself, "Just a fifteen-minute nap before I leave. That's all I need," and then woke up at 9:32 PM. I tamed my curly hair and touched up my makeup in record time, throwing on a 1950s-looking teal green dress that I'd bought just for this night. I then rushed out the door and counted my lucky stars when I got to the club in time for the opening number.

Even without the club, I had managed to see Rain quite a lot. He would come by my apartment or visit me at work. When he'd visit my apartment on my days off, he would stay much later than I ever anticipated. He bought me my very first cell phone, so on the days he couldn't visit, he'd call and we'd talk until my ears were melting. Of course, I didn't mind. I never noticed how late he was hanging around until he was leaving, or how long we'd been talking on the phone until we hung up. Time had a way of disappearing when I was with him, as did the rest of the world in general, just as it was doing as I watched him sing.

Not that the world was forgotten. Rain had told me that he and Nothe were working on locating the possible big-computer-thing that would transmit information about Earth to Thera. Beyond that, we would often get into great philosophical discussions where we would solve all of the remaining problems of the world, curing hunger, hatred, and war. In our small corner of the planet, world peace was right in the palms of our hands.

The moment he would leave, reality would return from its hiding place, but it suddenly didn't seem so bad. The light in my soul would burn brightly, holding the darkness of my insecurities and despair at bay. It burned even brighter as I fell asleep, reflecting on our conversations and the dumb, fun things we did throughout the day. Yes, Rain was a very good friend and I was sure glad to have him around.

The song ended and the crowd erupted with cheers. Lipstick Rick took a gracious bow before the music started up again. Lights illuminated the rest of the band as they began to play Shakira. Chuck ditched his keyboard for an accordion and Nothe's raspy voice became Lipstick Rick's duet partner. Of course, Lipstick Rick fully embraced the role of Shakira, even going so far as to belly dance to the whistles and hollers of the audience.

As it ended, Lipstick Rick took another bow to thunderous applause. He brushed his black curls over his shoulder and grinned. "Oh, my goodness, thank you! You know, we wouldn't be standing here on this stage without you good people. You bring us back here. You bring us joy. We thank you for being who you are. I feel we also, all, need to thank the great Robert King for opening these doors to us, and for giving us a sanctuary to run to at the end of—what can sometimes be—a very long and difficult day."

The people applauded and cheered, as did the band. I could see Lipstick Rick looking beyond the crowd to the bar behind us, but I turned only in time to watch an uncomfortable Bob give a brief wave of acknowledgement before darting out of sight.

Sadness filled Lipstick Rick's eyes at this. I knew it wasn't because Bob was dodging the attention, but because of the wounds that were hidden behind the dodging. With a glance to the stage floor, the look faded into one of thoughtfulness.

"You know," said Lipstick Rick, resting his hand on the microphone stand, "I've been thinking..."

The band emitted an "oh, no" sort of sigh, all except for Nothe, who smiled at his shoes with a very amused, raised eyebrow.

Lipstick Rick continued as if he'd heard an encouraging "Woo!" instead. "About death and that sort of thing. And I've realized that, I have absolutely no words of comfort to give. As my dear friend Bob once said not too long ago, death is much harder on the living. And there are simply no words I can say that can take that sting away. Words cannot replace a soul—the warmth that your loved one once gave. Nothing can heal those wounds completely. I've lost"—his gaze returned to the stage floor, growing heavy and distant—"too many... too many." He shook his head. "So I know how completely pointless words are."

He straightened as he took a deep breath. "There is only one thing that I know to do when such tragedy strikes, and that is: Give the pain a purpose.

"That's right. Give it a purpose.

"But perhaps you say to this, 'Lipstick Rick, that is the most ridiculous thing I have ever heard.' And then I would counter this thought with, 'Well... that depends on what you do with it.'"

A smile fused to my face as I watched him approach the front of the stage. He shifted his dress in a very unladylike manner as he sat down on the edge, looking over listening faces until his eyes met mine. My stomach did a happy somersault as he returned my smile.

He squared his shoulders, his words filled with determination as he addressed the audience. "Now, let me tell you why—why you need to find the strength to carry on. Let me tell you why you need to give purpose to your pain."

His bright blue eyes fell back on mine. "Because you don't know what good things lay just beyond the horizon." His focus returned to the crowd. "You don't know how desperately the world needs your strength, your wisdom—needs *you*—to teach it the truths you've gained from your unique experiences. Truths that others have yet to find, but are searching for. You may not realize it now, but the world needs your voice, your empathy, your compassion. If you search the world around you, you will see it. You will see that you're not alone. Not really. And you will see that—we *need* you, my friends. We need your vision. Your example of courage through extreme difficulty, because others will see your courage and find their own. We need you to refuse to give up and surrender. We need you to give your pain a purpose, because as you find the strength to stand, you will lift others around you who have fallen. And I promise you that as you carry on, you will never regret it. Why?"

He looked back at me. "Because of the beautiful things that are on the horizon." Something about the light that reflected in his eyes as he said "beautiful" swept my soul right off its feet, and for a moment, there was no one else in room. "Those things are there," he said, "just beyond the storm."

He stood back up. "So, my friends, when you feel broken, carry on. When the pain is too much to bear, take one step forward, and then another. Because your future matters, and you are needed. Set the pain on fire. Become a light in the midst of darkness, and carry on.

"Anyway. The end."

Applause broke out among the crowd and things were shouted, but I didn't notice. I was too lost in my focus on Lipstick Rick. My heart felt full and wonderful, renewed with hope. This was something he always seemed to do—with his friendship and comfort, and again with these words. He got me to look at myself differently. Maybe I actually *did* have something to offer. And maybe, in spite of everything, I had a chance at having the things I wanted so deeply, like my own little family that watched meteor showers together. Maybe I had a chance at happiness.

A very hairy man wearing smeared lipstick and a dress a bit too big for him, shouted, "Sing 'Sweet Home Alabama!'" Jumping out of my trance, I couldn't help but notice that Nothe was no longer amused. His jaw was flexed, and he appeared to be having a wordless argument with the toe of his shoe. My heart sank into a pit of despair as he fixed his glare on me, as if the toe of his shoe had silently said, "It wasn't me! It was *her!*"

I really wanted to ask the toe of his shoe exactly what it had accused me of doing and why it was determined to make Nothe hate me more than he already did.

I now dreaded the end of the show. I even debated leaving at the last song. Lipstick Rick had seen me. He knew I cared and had shown up. And maybe he'd stop by after, without Nothe and his vengeful shoe.

However, my concerns with Nothe faded as Beyonce's "Single Ladies" filled the air. And as the evening wore on, I forgot them completely until the very last song. As I danced with a gorgeous drag queen named Mamma Mia—she was a big fan of Meryl Streep and Queen—I vaguely recalled that there was something I should probably be doing instead. I shrugged the thought away with an unsaid *Oh, well* and continued dancing.

Then the song ended. As Lipstick Rick bid a fond farewell to the crowd, I was gripped with a cold dread and the words, "Oh crap!" mindlessly escaped my lips.

Mamma Mia put a hand on my shoulder. "What is it, honey?"

I tried to smile. "Oh, I just remembered that I've got to go."

"Aww, so soon?"

"Yeah. There's this person that I'm avoiding and I'm worried that they'll find me and it'll be awkward and um, yeah. So I've got to bail."

I was about to say goodbye when she asked, concerned, "Is this person giving you trouble, sweetie?"

"Sort of."

"Well, you just tell me who it is, 'cause they'll be picking pieces of themselves off the floor when Mamma Mia's done with them."

I hesitated, seriously considering her offer before waving it away and stepping toward the exit. "That's so sweet of you, but it's okay. I'll..." I sighed. "I should deal with it myself, I just don't want to today."

"Well, who is it anyway? Now I'm wondering if its someone I know."

I anxiously shifted my feet. "It's, um..." I tried to remember the name everybody else knew him by. "It's Bob. From *Screaming Riot*."

"Oh! Well, yeah, I'm not touching that. What happened? He's usually so sweet."

"I have no idea. He just *hates* me, and I don't know why."

Before I could discuss it further or run away, Lipstick Rick appeared at my side. To my great disappointment, Nothe was right behind him.

The words *Oh, crap!* went through my mind, but I had the self-control to not blurt them out loud this time. "Hey!"

Lipstick Rick wrapped an arm around my shoulders in a hug. Mamma Mia nodded at me with a very knowing grin and wiggle of the eyebrows, as if to say, *Oh, I think I know why.*

What? Nothe hated me because Rain hugged me sometimes? I glanced over at Nothe. The very smallest hint of a narrow gaze was aimed at me.

I supposed it was possible.

But I was probably reading too much into Mamma Mia's very obvious, wordlessly-giving-me-messages grin.

Mamma Mia looked at Rain with a perfectly normal smile. "Look at you. You clean up nicely."

Lipstick Rick didn't remove his arm from around me. "Ah, Mamma Mia—you're looking stunning this evening, as usual."

She glanced away bashfully. "Oh, why thank you." A small version of that wry grin crossed her face. "My, you two have become good friends real quick, haven't you?"

Lipstick Rick's smile widened. "Well, when you bond over David Bowie—"

Mamma Mia gave a wave of her hand. "Oh, say no more."

"We had an instant connection."

I nodded, my heart ridiculously happy in spite of Nothe's presence. "We did."

"We have a great chemistry together. I feel like we should..." He grew thoughtful. Time stopped as I anticipated what he might say next, though my brain was working far too slow to make any hopeful guesses. At the same time, I swore I felt the tiniest wave of anger rush from the other side of him—from Nothe. It was so small that I wondered if my over-thinking mind was simply looking for things.

Finally, Rain concluded, "I think we should be in a play together. Or better yet, we should *write* a play!"

I didn't know what I'd been expecting him to say, but I knew that wasn't it.

"NO!" The word seemed to bounce off the ceiling. All eyes fell on the source—Nothe. "Don't let him write a play. It'll be nothing but monologues."

Mamma Mia laughed. "Oh, but they'd be such beautiful monologues."

Lipstick Rick looked at her with gratitude. "Why, thank you, Mamma Mia."

"Well, I suppose it's getting late," she said, glancing around. "It was wonderful seeing all of you." She shot me that smile again before disappearing into the crowd.

I tried to manage my anxiety and ignore Nothe as Lipstick Rick turned to me. "So, did you have fun?"

I grinned at him. "I did! I had a blast. You guys were amazing." I glanced over at Nothe when I said 'you guys.' "And I loved your speech," I pointed at Lipstick Rick. "*You're* amazing."

He shrugged with clearly-fake-modesty. "Oh, why thank you."

I was about to compliment his belly dancing when a group of people surrounded Lipstick Rick and Nothe, gushing over their show. The two of them graciously smiled and gave their thanks, but Lipstick Rick did not do so with near the ease or humor he'd had only moments earlier. In fact, he seemed a little overwhelmed, but he handled it with perfect kindness and charm.

I found myself pushed out of the way by these folks and standing awkwardly off to the side. Lipstick Rick was trying his best to keep an eye on me, but he could only do that for so long with that kind of attention. I saw this as an excellent opportunity to escape and meandered toward the exit. I picked up my coat from the desk and had almost made it to the door when a raspy voice called from behind me, "Where are you going in such a hurry?"

I froze. My guts wrapped themselves into horrible, unpleasant knots, and every muscle in my back went into a spasm. I forced myself to turn and smile politely. "Heyyy, Nothe."

Nothe stood there with his arms folded, wearing a smile that suggested he'd taken up a part-time job as the Grim Reaper and I was next on his list. We stood there in silence for a moment before I forced a yawn. "Well, I'm tired. I guess I'd better hit the hay. Goodbye!"

I turned to leave and he grabbed my shoulder. "Not so fast, there." He snorted. "Sheesh. Seriously. You must be really eager to hit that hay."

"Oh, I am."

"It must be fun."

"It is! You should try it sometime."

"Nah. It can't be that fun."

I furrowed my brow. "You just said it sounded fun."

"I changed my mind. Honestly, I'm not even sure what we're talking about anymore. No, I'm thinking—if I didn't know any better—I'd say you were just, trying to avoid me." He grinned that creepy, Grim Reaper grin again.

I made an unconvincing of-course-not face. "No! Psh, wha-why would I be trying to do that? Ol' buddy, ol' pal." I punched his shoulder so lightly that I barely touched him. He frowned at the spot.

I was ready to run for the door, but then his Grim Reaper face reappeared. "Well that's good. Because I'm hoping we can be friends."

I'd never been so terrified of the thought of friendship. "Oh! Really?" I couldn't stop the next word from escaping my brain. "Why?"

"Because you seem like such a fun," his eye twitched a little, "interesting person. Let's go do something fun. Just the two of us. To get to know each other better."

My eyes widened. "Like, right now?"

"Yeah. Why not?"

I didn't want to. I really, really didn't want to. *I should've left at the last song.* "Ohhh... I don't know. You know, it's so late..."

"Technically," he looked at his watch. "Two-thirtheen in the morning is early."

Where was Rain? My eyes darted around, looking for him. "And you know, the hay... it needs to be hit."

"Nah, the hay can wait. C'mon," he wrapped an arm around my shoulders and guided me toward the door, saying in a cheerful, growly tone that sent a cold shiver through my bones and made me think, *I'm gonna die,* "let's go have some fun."

TRACK 3

FRIENDS

As Nothe led me through the darkness of the parking lot to his truck, I managed to ask, "So, uh, wha-what's your plan, Nothe?"

"It's a surprise."

I didn't like that at all.

He opened the door for me and I asked a follow up question. "Did you and Rain er," I couldn't think of the word right away, "carpool?"

"Psh, you kidding?" Nothe said as I climbed in. "I can't get him out of his new Infiniti." He slammed the door shut, and I couldn't help but picture it as a casket closing over me. I thought about making a run for it as he made his way to the driver's side door, but I hesitated too long, and then it was too late.

He Grim-Reaper-grinned at me again as he backed out of the parking space, his golden-sunset eyes glowing with mischief. He said with his unnerving cheerfulness, "I hope you're ready for a morning you won't forget!"

I hugged myself and forced a smile, trying to mirror his enthusiasm. "Oh, I really don't think I am!"

He laughed, but it sounded forced and weird. I forced a laugh as well, but then I realized I was being stupid and wondered how I'd let myself get in the truck. I dropped my act and asked without the least bit of humor, "Seriously, Nothe, where are we going?"

The charade melted from his face. Mostly. "Well, I'm assuming that you're planning on hanging around us until you die—"

I didn't care much for that phrasing.

He went on. "And that there's very little chance you'll be changing your mind and, ya know, go away... far, far, *far* away, like to another planet, or a distant galaxy or even the jungles of Africa. I'd settle for

Africa. Or Spain! That's better, right? You're less likely to die there and it's absolutely lovely this time of year. There's great architecture over in Barcelona, it's one of Rain's favorite places—"

I glared at him. "Nope. I'm not going anywhere." Then I thought, *Maybe I should've lied.*

Nothe sighed, disappointed. "Yeah, I figured. If nearly getting eaten wasn't going to do it, then..." He straightened himself. "Well, anyway—so, *I* was thinking, that, if you're going to be a part of this team, maybe you should get a *really* good look at exactly what you're getting into here and help me out with something."

I didn't know what to think of that. "Oh?"

"Yes. I thought it could be a great *bonding* experience for us."

"Okay. So, what am I helping you with?"

He grinned again. There was something about this grin that was more unsettling than any that had crossed his face before. "I think I know where the box is."

My eyebrows shot skyward. "Oh!"

He nodded. "And I thought it would be really fun for us to go scout out the site. I could use your help taking notes, keeping a look-out, and whatnot. There's a notebook and a pen in the glove compartment there."

I opened the glove compartment and, sure enough, there was a small notebook with a pen stuck in the binding. I flipped through the pages. It'd been used to keep track of gas mileage and oil changes, but most of it was empty.

He asked me, "Did you bring your pepper spray?"

"I never leave home without it anymore."

"Good."

None of this was making me feel better. "Do you think I'm going to need it?"

He shrugged. "Better to be safe than sorry, right?" He looked very satisfied with this answer.

I wasn't satisfied. "Why would I need my pepper spray?"

"Oh, I don't know. Why do you refuse to leave the house without it?"

"Uh, I don't know. Maybe because I was almost eaten by a shamonster?"

He cringed at my use of the word "shamonster" but quickly recovered, saying with a defensive shrug and a matter-of-fact expression, "Look, I'm just saying, you never know what you might encounter out there in the big, bad world. Especially on an old farmer's private property. They're very protective of their land, you know. It'd be great if you could blind them before they shoot us."

"It's on a *farm?*" I was outraged, not over the location nor the idea of being caught trespassing on private property, but at the thought of how long we were about to be trapped in the truck together. The coastal cities stretched on for eternity, so to get to the farmlands, we'd have to be stuck together in a confined space for eternity. "That's gotta be a million miles away from here!"

"Nah. It's just a hop, skip, and a drive to the North, right there by the state line."

"The state line is like, three hours away!"

He was unphased, and as pleasant as ever. "It's quality bonding time."

I took a deep breath and closed my eyes, trying to calm myself down. I was so tired. I really didn't want to deal with an anxiety-riddled, forever-drive to some random farm to scout out something that was clearly outside of my level to handle. I just wanted to go to bed. That was all I wanted.

Once I'd reached a good level of composure, I smiled and said calmly, "Nothe, this..." I tried to choose my words carefully. I didn't want to hurt his feelings, just in case he was telling the truth about wanting to "bond" and not actually out to torture me. "This seems like something that Rain would be better at. You know? More... more *qualified* to handle. You and I can bond over something more normal. Like a movie, or—"

"Nah, you get kicked out of theaters for talking through movies—learned that the hard way. Besides, we should scout this out right away. It really can't wait any longer. We scouted a location about a week ago, but it didn't pan out. Then Thipka found me just before the show."

"Thipka?" As far as I knew, no one had heard from him at all.

"Yep. He was as cryptic as ever. He told me in his Vincent-Price-from-Thriller way that the box is closer to home, and this site immediately came to mind. It's one I've been researching. It seems mostly promising."

"Well, why didn't you guys go before the show?"

"It was literally *right* before we were supposed to go on stage. So I didn't tell him."

"Why not?"

"Because it was Ladies' Night." He said this as if it was a perfectly obvious and "Of course! Duh!" sort of explanation.

I said nothing to this, but apparently my thoughts were vivid in my expression.

He rolled his eyes, as if explaining this was something he shouldn't have to do. "Listen, I said it was *mostly* promising, not totally promising. There's no guarantee that my info is going to save the world. But Rain being at that show was guaranteed to save some small part of it, okay? We promised we would be there. That was the only way Bob would reopen the club. That club is a bigger sanctuary to lots of people than a cathedral is to a... you know, people who like cathedrals. So, I felt like I could sacrifice a few hours of checking out an iffy site in order to guarantee the survival of... ya know... *that* one."

I was surprised. I hadn't realized Nothe cared so much about, well, anything, except for Rain and Dr. Phil. I could actually understand his reasoning. All they were basing the threat of the world on were eerie ramblings and theories, but people walking away from the club feeling better about the cruel world they were stuck in, this was an actual fact. I nodded. "Okay. Fine. That makes sense. But I still don't understand why you wanted to bring me."

He sighed. "Bonding, I said! Bonding! I'm also trying to do you a favor here. You want to be a part of the group, right? But you don't feel like you fit in?"

I was offended by this assumption. "I've never said that."

"Oh, please. Maybe you've never said it out loud, but you say it in the way you slump your shoulders and talk like you're always in trouble."

I folded my arms and looked out the window with a frown. Did I really do that? I kinda did.

He continued, "So, I thought, if you and I were to take off on this little adventure and find the box, you could prove that you belong—bring something to the crew. You'll be able to relay information to everybody and they'll hang on your every word, and finally give you a chance. That's all you want, right? Just a chance?"

I responded with a sigh and thought, *You watch way too much Dr. Phil.* But unfortunately, he wasn't wrong. The only person in Rain's group that I felt comfortable with was Rain. Things were still really weird with everybody else.

The thought crossed my mind, *Could Nothe actually be trying to help me? Why would he do that?* It was so hard to believe, given everything I'd overheard him say and the things he'd said to my face, not to mention the very scary look he'd given me during the show.

But what else made any sense? Maybe, just maybe, he was honestly trying to get past whatever bad feelings he had toward me.

Geez, why was I being such a jerk? Didn't he deserve a chance, just as I wanted one?

I rubbed my eyes. "Yeah, I guess you're right. That's actually really thoughtful of you, Nothe. I just... I can't believe you'd be willing to help me."

He gave a small, mock-humble shrug. "Well, ya know. I am a saint, after all."

I let out a laugh that was more of an audible smile. "I mean, it really means a lot to me that..." I searched my muddled brain for the right words, "that you're willing to give me a chance." I looked down at my hands. "I don't have anybody anymore. Rain's really it. And I know how important you are to him, so, it just, it means a lot. I'm really sorry that I'm so cranky. I'm..." I hesitated. The old-me wouldn't say it, but the new-me decided it needed to be said. "I'm just not good with big, surprise drives in the middle of the night." *I don't know who would be.* "So maybe next time you could, you know, somehow let me know in advance that you're planning some really crazy expedition. If you can."

"It was a bit of a spontaneous decision," he admitted.

"Well, anyway. I do appreciate the gesture. I'd... I'd really like it if we could be friends." As I said it, I realized how much I meant it.

He cast me a sideways glance that I couldn't read.

Hoping for the best, I declared, "So let's do this thing! Let's find this box."

"Well, we're just checking out the site—"

I raised an imaginary glass as a toast. "Let's check out this site!"

Nothe smiled. "Alright, yeah! That's the spirit."

"Yeah!"

"Yeah!"

The cabin of the truck fell silent and remained that way for far too long. Eventually, I said, "It would be interesting if the box did end up so close to home. I'd be surprised."

"Why?"

"I don't know. There's a whole planet for it to fall on. I just wonder what the odds are that it's so close to..." *the only known extraterrestrials on Earth—well, the only ones I know of, anyway.* I almost said this but thought better of it. Instead, I ended more wisely on, "Home."

"Nothing really surprises me anymore."

Silence filled the cabin again. I thought about trying to sleep, but was worried it would be impolite. So I said, "I didn't know you and Rain checked out a site."

He flashed an in-your-face sort of smile. "I know this might come as a shock, but Rain doesn't actually tell you everything. You don't know that much about him. You don't know his history. You don't even know *what* he is." He bit his lips as if he'd caught himself saying too much.

I knew he was right, but I thought he could've been a little nicer about it. *Well,* I thought, *I guess I can't expect him to miraculously and immediately be 100% nicer. This stuff takes time.* I decided to be patient with him.

I said, "Well, I'd like to get to know you guys better. Um... how did you and Rain meet?"

"I wasn't inviting you to ask questions."

That strained my patience. "I thought we were supposed to be 'bonding' and 'getting to know each other better.'"

He twisted his mouth in an oh-yeah-I-did-say-that-didn't-I sort of way. "Right."

Again, I tried to be understanding. I understood not wanting to share any deep dark secrets with people, especially someone you weren't particularly fond of. There were things about myself I certainly didn't want to tell Nothe. "Look. You don't have to answer any questions you don't want to. No pressure, okay? And I'm sorry if that last question was too prying. I'm not good at small talk. But if you really want to try to be friends, or whatever, you've got to work with me a little bit."

He glanced over at me, a studious look in his golden eyes. "I'm not good at small talk, either. I don't know if you've noticed, but, I'm not much of a people person."

I feigned shock. "No!"

"No, no, it's true. Rain usually does all the small talk for me—all that little stuff you're socially obligated to do in too many places on this planet. Anytime I'm left alone, I almost always end up offending someone. I don't know if you know this, but, apparently saying, 'So, you're fat, huh? Have you always been that way?' isn't a great way to start a conversation."

I laughed. "Please tell me you didn't—"

"Yeah, I did."

I laughed harder.

With a smile, he defended, "Hey, there's usually a story behind weight gain! A lot of times it's a really uncomfortable one, but that just makes it more interesting. But I guess that also makes the question worse."

I shook my head. "Oh, Nothe. That's terrible."

"So I've been told. But usually, in hearing the story, you can find the thing that needs healing."

Once again, I was surprised. I had totally misjudged him, hadn't I?

He raised an eyebrow at me and opened his mouth as if to add to this, but changed his mind.

I said, "Well, I don't think I'm quite *that* bad, but small talk is something I don't totally get. I'm really awkward, which is why my tips at work are so bad." We both had a little laugh at this. I continued, "But, asking how you guys met—I really am curious. I bet it's a great story."

He smiled mirthlessly. "You know, I really wish it was. I wish it was something stupid like, we were fighting over the same album at that store —Dexter's Records. Or that we shared the same cab on our way to a

Duran Duran concert. But, it's not like that at all." He paused. "Are you sure you want to know the truth to that question?"

I shrugged, though a little wary. "Yeah."

"The whole truth and nothing but the truth?"

I remembered the pain and bitterness Rain felt toward his home planet and hesitated. "I think so. Unless it'll make you uncomfortable to tell me."

"It'll make *you* uncomfortable to hear it."

Now I was stuck on the bridge between plaguing curiosity and thinking it might be best to remain ignorant.

Amused, Nothe said matter-of-factly, "We were sold at the same market and bought by the same horrible person."

My brain went numb. "Sold?"

"Rain never told you, huh?" He smirked. "Imagine that. Yeah, we were slaves. We met when we were thrown into the same cage on a transport ship. Not like a boat-ship but like a hovercraft, plane-like ship."

"A spaceship?"

He gave a curt shake of his head. "No. Spaceships go into space. That's why they're called *space*ships." I glared at him as he continued, "These things would fly just high enough to soar right over bad traffic. Only super rich people had them, which makes sense, since only super rich people could afford Rain. Rain was this wild animal—strong, not obedient and scrawny and raised in captivity, like me. He'd never been owned, so he hadn't been broken yet. A super rare find for super rich people. He cost a fortune."

My heart broke. Not just broke, but shattered, leaving shrapnel throughout my chest. All I could say was, "Oh."

The darkness of the past surfaced in his eyes. Emotion poured out of them, like a mist bleeding from a lake and into the surrounding trees. "Those people, they really liked to break things. You weren't worth as much if you were already broken. They only bought me because they needed a Hassune to bleed."

What did he mean by that? "Bleed?"

He nodded. "Bleed." That was all he said, and I didn't dare press for more.

My brain couldn't fathom what I'd heard. There weren't any stored files for it to flip through that could contribute to an adequate response.

There was bitter amusement in his expression. "I was right, wasn't I? The answer made you uncomfortable."

I didn't know what to say. "It just... it makes me so sad. I can't even imagine..." I shook my head, unable to finish the sentence. Tears filled my eyes. I couldn't get the image out of my mind—of them in that incomprehensible situation—or even begin to imagine how terrifying and awful that must have been. No wonder Nothe was the way he was. How could anyone overcome those kind of scars?

Nothe's expression softened a little as he glanced over at me, but quickly returned to stone. "No, you can't."

Tears escaped me and I quickly wiped them away. I became lost in my head. Slavery was something that was so distant and foreign to me. It was something that happened in the past. Not now. Not to anyone I knew and cared about. No wonder Rain had been so bitter about his home.

Nothe let out an airy sort of laugh, the hundred or so years of his life now reflecting in his face. "You know, Rain and I, we didn't really get along when we first met. He was sooo obnoxiously positive. Even after his mother left him to the kyriki—"

"Wait—what? What are those?"

Nothe flinched. "They're these gigantic, ridiculously-soft, fluffy things that kind of look like cats with antlers—but, ya know, fluffy. Like, super poofy-fluffy. He, uh... he didn't tell you that, huh?"

I shook my head.

"Ooohhh... woops." He cleared his throat. "Well, uh. Don't tell him I told you." After a pause, he continued, "Um... well, anyway, his free spirit, um... it really irritated me," he chuckled. "But then, one day, our master came home. He'd lost a bunch of money on a bad deal or something—whatever sets those kind of people off. So he was drunk and pissed off at everything. He'd been looking at me for months, right? He'd purchased me. He'd approved of me. But that day... that day he took one long look at my eyes and decided they were the wrong color. So he and a couple of others," he shook his head and smiled, but not an amused sort of smile. It was the kind of smile that's left behind, struggling to hold the mind together after everything else inside of it is crushed. The nightmare shined in his eyes, as though the scene were playing on a screen behind them. "They dragged me out of my cage, chained me down, and cut out my eyes with a spoon."

He said it so easily, as if he were merely recalling a day when he'd had a particularly nasty disagreement with someone at work. My chest felt as though it'd been hollowed out like a jack-o-lantern, scraped and bleeding. Once again, I was at a complete loss of how, exactly, I should be responding, because I couldn't comprehend anything so horrible. I couldn't understand how anything like that could possibly be real. But there it was. I could see the truth, the reality of it, in his golden eyes.

He went on in the tone of someone discussing how they crashed their bike and scraped their elbow. "It was quite painful. I've... I've never experienced pain like that before or since, or that level of fear. It was terrifying." He snorted again. "When they were done, they threw me back in the cage, and I," he laughed a little, "ya know, curled into a ball. But then I felt Rain's hand on my shoulder. He... he grabbed me and just, held me, and let me be a mess. He helped me heal the sockets of my eyes. Didn't grow them back—yes, we can grow things back; it takes a lot of effort, but it can be done. Obviously, we *eventually* grew back my eyes and Rain's arm—"

"Rain's arm?"

"Yep. They ripped off his arm once. Can't remember why anymore. You've probably never noticed. It's kind of hard to tell, especially when he's always wearing those long sleeved shirts, but one arm is a slightly lighter color than the other. It's just something that's too hard to hide, like the resurrection scar.

"Anyway, we didn't grow my eyes back at that time because we were worried they'd just cut them out again. But Rain took the pain away." His expression changed to one of peace, and yet, was full of agony and sorrow. The mist of emotion pooled through cracks in the walls he was struggling to contain it in. "I don't know how long he held me for. It was until I calmed down, however long that took. Everything..." he rubbed his face, looking more solemn than ever, "everything changed after that. He helped me find my way around until we were free."

He shook his head. "When they broke him—it took them a long time, but they did, they broke him—I was devastated for him. I got my revenge, though." A cruel, satisfied grin curled his lips. "And I swore I would do everything in my power to put him back together again."

The mist of emotions vanished and he took a deep breath, breaking the surface of the dark pool he'd fallen into. He looked sheepish, like he'd said far too much.

More tears escaped from my eyes. Before he could feel any more embarrassed or upset for sharing this with me, I said the only thing I could think to say, "I'm so sorry, Nothe. I'm so sorry that happened to you and Rain. I don't even—I can't—those horrible things... they should never have happened. That kind of evil should not exist."

Nothe glanced over at me again. "No, it shouldn't."

My imagination ran wild, mixed with my own terrible memories, stirring something within me, something dark and ugly that crawled under my skin.

Nothe interrupted my downward spiral. "Well, we got away eventually. And now we're here. So there's that."

I smiled at the irony of Nothe trying to comfort me. I wiped away more tears. "At least there's that."

Nothe studied me as much as he could without running off the road. "You feel a lot, don't you?"

I furrowed my brow. "What do you mean?"

I could see him struggling to find the words. "You know... well, I don't want to say 'emotional' because that'll give the wrong impression, but, what I mean is, you're very... empathetic. Yes, that's it—I think, maybe—you know, you *feel* a lot. You don't just imagine yourself in other people's shoes, it's like you're actually walking in their disgusting, worn out shoes." He added quickly, "It's a compliment. A real one."

"Oh. Well, thank you, then."

"Most humans have a hard time doing that. They're very rigid. Selfish. Self-involved. So..." He looked like he was about to vomit, but then he looked resigned, like he had to admit he was wrong about the answer to a trivia question. "It's cool. It's... nice, that you're so... nice."

I had to laugh a little. "Well, I'm glad you feel that way." My spirits lifted and the crawling shadows were pushed aside. "You know, it's really nice to find that you're so nice, as well."

"Don't push it." Despite him saying this, I noticed the smallest of smiles creep into his expression. He cleared his throat. "Well, now that things are weird, how about we turn on the radio?"

As music broke the silence, conversation ensued more easily. Nothe gave me an overview of the evolution of music since the early 1900s, much of it going right over my head. I laughed as he made fun of ignorant people he encountered regularly, a tangent which came up after he was cut off by someone on the highway and said to them, "That's right, sir. The speed limit is whatever you want it to be." He spoke of how people always felt they were more wise and advanced than the previous generation, but how ultimately, they were all stupid in their own way, and each passing generation caused a whole slew of problems for the new one because of it. He went off on how the simplest solutions tend to be the right ones, yet they're always made a mockery of.

"Like love," he said. "It's like Rain always says—truly loving others would fix about 90% of the world's problems. Ever wonder why love stories sell so well? And I don't just mean romantic love stories, but friendship, family, *love* itself. It's because deep down inside, most everyone wants to be loved. Of course they do! Just imagine if the tables were turned. Imagine if people gave each other love as much as they desired it: in their marriage, in their friendships and families, when they greet strangers, and were just—genuinely kind? How many marital problems would be solved, eh? How many family disputes would end? How many friendships would be strengthened? How many strangers uplifted, maybe even changed forever? How many people would be *healed*? You know? Maybe it's a stretch, but then again... maybe world peace is just that simple."

I couldn't help but smile. I'd had such a similar conversation with Rain not long ago.

He went on, "People focus too much on what they can *get*, on what's missing, and not on what they already have, and can *give*. Then they wonder why they're so miserable, and why all the crap they buy and the things they take, don't fix it. But the solution is right in front of them. Give love, people!" He yelled at the dashboard. "The real kind of love, not the cheap crap that dumb songs talk about, that stuff's garbage. But the real stuff. It really is that simple." He pointed at the radio. "Like this song. This song is crap."

"We can change it—" I offered.

"No, listen to it. It's crap! Telling someone you're the only one that loves them *so much* is actually called 'manipulation.' Real love isn't manipulative, it's magic. And real romantic love is *knowing* you have something special, and to have the audacity to believe you're the only one who can see that is sick. Real love..." his eyes were alight with the truth of each word, "Real love is being able to give up what you want most, for the ones you love most."

I grinned. "Wow! Look at you, you little romantic, you."

"You never heard me say any of that."

"No! I mean—" I shrugged and looked around like I had no idea what he was talking about. "Say what? What'd you even say? I have no idea."

"Exactly."

I laughed and rubbed my face. My eyelids felt like they had small anvils chained to them, but I insisted on trying to stay awake.

Nothe gave me a look that reminded me of a parent finally caving in and giving their kid money for the candy machine. "There in the back, there's one of Rain's jackets. It's one of those ugly, super soft ones from Wal-Mart. It's got like, a Batman symbol on it or something. You can use it as a pillow, if you want."

I fumbled around until I felt plush fabric, then brought the jacket to the front. I balled it up and laid my head against it, hoping Nothe didn't notice me inhale the light fragrance of blossoms that it held—Rain's smell. I liked it a lot more than I probably should have.

"Thanks, Nothe. I promise I won't sleep for too long."

"Don't worry about it." He turned up the radio, drowning out any potential for silence with "Lean on Me" by Bill Withers, which he groaned at, but then never changed.

TRACK 4
THE SOUND OF SILENCE

The truck shuddered as we turned down a dirt road, waking me enough to hear that Nothe had switched on a talk show where they were discussing the science of wormholes. They might as well have been speaking Portuguese for all I could understand of it. I had neared complete unconsciousness again when Nothe turned off the engine, saying, "We're here." I pried my eyes open and sat up.

The first thing I noticed was the silence. It wasn't the sort of silence we'd had in our conversation on the drive there, where it wasn't really silence—there'd been the background noises of air rushing past us, of the fan, the engine. This... this was a different kind of silence. There were no crickets. There was no wind. It was the kind of silence I imagined falling over the funeral of a horrible person who'd died a horrible death, where the few in the audience were too shocked and disturbed to shed a single tear, and the pastor had no words of solace to give.

Then there was the darkness. I couldn't see anything beyond the still blades of grass and the figure of the farmhouse touched by the headlights. Off in the distance, I thought I could see the very first violet rays of morning, but other than that...

Nothe wrung his fingers a little. A faint, uneasy emotion radiated from him. "You know, maybe you should stay in the truck."

I remembered what had happened the last time I'd done that. I grabbed the notebook and pen, saying, "That's okay. I'm here to help and take notes, so yeah! Put me to work."

He looked as though he were about to argue against this, but then he brightened. "Well, okay then. If you insist." He popped open the door and got out. I did likewise, meeting him in the glow of the headlights. We stared up at the quaint, country style house. It had a porch lined with chipped, white columns that wrapped all the way around the eastern corner. It would've been a darling home that reminded me of my grandma's, if not for the darkened windows and the feeling of gloom that weeped from them, and the smell of dead, decaying things that permeated the air.

Nothe said cheerfully, "Let's start with the house."

My eyes widened. "Why? I thought we were trying to *avoid* the farmers."

"Well, I think if they were home, they'd have seen us pull up, don't you?"

"Yes. Let's make things worse by spying on them through their windows."

"Oh, no. That won't be necessary. The front door is wide open. See?"

He pointed to the wall where the porch ended. I wasn't sure how I'd missed it, but he was right. The door was wide open, leading into black emptiness. I swore, for the briefest moment, I saw two, glowing yellow orbs peering out from the edge of the doorway before disappearing from view.

I blinked. I rubbed my eyes, my face. That'd just been a trick of the light, right? I hadn't actually seen... what I thought I saw...

I looked up at Nothe. It might've been my imagination, but I thought he looked a little paler and slightly more serious than he had the last time I'd glanced at his face. I asked him, "Did you see that, too?"

Then I felt it. A whirlwind of terror, anger, and insatiable hunger, hunger so deep, it was as though nothing in the universe could possibly fill it. It erupted from the house and spread throughout my body, filling my veins with biting cold and turning my limbs to stone.

From Nothe, I felt a mostly-contained wave of fear and remorse, though this was not reflected in his voice at all. He whispered very matter-of-factly, "Did you write down that observation?"

It took me a moment to remember how to speak, "No."

Our gazes darted to the field at our right where two more sets of lights appeared over the grain then disappeared again beneath it, followed by more torrents of the hunger and fear.

Nothe asked, "What about that? Did you write that down?"

My fingers shook, my grip on the notebook bending it in different directions. "No."

"Good. Well, I think we've observed the house pretty thoroughly, don't you?"

"Yeah."

"And the fields."

"Uh, huh."

He backed up toward the driver's side door. "I think we've got plenty of information."

I hated that my door was next to the field. Why did it have to be next to the field? I peeled my trembling hand away from the notebook and armed myself with pepper spray as I made stiff, robotic movements toward my side of the car. "Okay."

"I think we're, uh, we're good to go."

Once around the front of the truck, I bolted for the door handle, dropping the notebook.

I heard it behind me. The off, high-pitched scream and the sound of feet fluttering through the grain, racing up to me faster than I could open the door.

I didn't have time to turn with my pepper spray. I didn't have time to cry out.

In the second it took to raise my arms over my head to shield myself, Nothe leapt over the truck and severed the top of the shamonster's head with a single swipe of a metallic-orange sword, showering us both in a spray of blood. The creature's body collided into him, knocking us both into the side of the truck. He shoved it to the ground where it twitched and convulsed, the top half of its head and face missing. The blood around the wound bubbled and little bits of wormy-like sinew tangled together, reconstructing the missing piece of brain and skull. Nothe raised his sword and hacked off its head completely, then kicked it into the field just for good measure.

This led to an eruption of screams from the field and house. The terror and anger that poured from them paralyzed me. I fought to separate these emotions from my own, but it was impossible to untangle. My heart thundered in my ears. I couldn't breathe. I couldn't move.

As if from underwater, I heard Nothe yell, "Get in the truck!"

But I couldn't breathe. I couldn't move.

His voice grew panicked, *"Get in the truck!"*

It was as though my very skin had become a one-hundred-pound suit. It took everything I had to reach for the door handle.

I took too long. Another shamonster leapt from the grain. Nothe swiped at it with his sword, nearly severing a wing, but it recovered with incredible speed. One was coming from the house and another from the southern part of the field.

I fought to push the crippling emotions away, gaining enough control over myself to attempt to open the door again. As I finally gripped the handle, the entire world around me flooded with white light. I raised an arm to shield my face from it. The shamonsters let out screams of shock and pain, fleeing back into the darkness. The terror subsided, the weight of my skin fading with it. I blinked as my eyes strained to adjust to the light surrounding me. I was being protected by something that shifted as grains of sand in an hourglass, and these tiny fragments emanated the light as they molded into a form.

I struggled to see. It was so bright.

As the grains of sand settled into place, I saw what they were becoming. I had to do a double take.

Wings.

They were wings.

Massive wings that stretched from Nothe's back.

Wings that had to be six feet long each.

His wings and arms were around me, covering me with light.

As the wings solidified, the light faded and the world returned to itself again, seeming darker than it had before, though the sun had risen a little more. The color of Nothe's wings very much resembled the light violet shade of the sky along the horizon. His shirt was in shreds on the ground, as his wings had torn through it. The rest of his skin remained its same pale color, but the tiny feathers that covered his wings were dark and shimmered like oil spilled on asphalt. Slowly, he looked around, then struggled to stand upright before falling to his knees. His eyes were drained of light and dark circles hung underneath them.

His voice trembled. "Get... in the car. Er, truck. It's a truck..." he trailed off as though he were fighting to not throw up, "I meant truck."

I couldn't stop staring at him. I was pretty sure my eyes, from then on, would be permanently frozen open. They were never going to close again. My face would be forever stuck in an expression of shock. Yes, *forever*.

I told myself that such a drastic reaction was unnecessary. Surely I had imagined the whole thing. I rubbed my eyes, then cradled my face as I forced myself to blink several times, only to find that, nope—the wings were still there.

I blinked once more for good measure and looked behind me as if looking to the past, consulting it. Nothe *hadn't* had wings before... no, no he hadn't. Because wings on people was not a normal thing. I was quite sure this was true and I was also quite sure they had not been on Nothe before.

I turned back to Nothe and resumed my wide-eyed staring contest with his wings. There was one wing *there*... and there was the other one. Yep. There they were.

To my reaction, Nothe patiently said, "Emily..."

I blinked again and looked at his face, remembering that he had one. "Huh?"

"Get. In. The truck."

I had to blink a few more times before I remembered we had nearly died a moment ago.

He continued, "If you don't, we will both die."

"Right." I opened the door. My knees buckled and I nearly fell over as I tried to climb in. I noticed that the majority of the hood of the truck was missing, which explained where Nothe's sword had come from. My fingers trembled as I slammed the door shut behind me. I realized then that I was still clinging to my pepper spray. I'd been holding it so tightly that, when I returned it to my pocket, it hurt my knuckles to let go of it. Outside my window, Nothe rose up on a knee and tried to stand before it gave out on him and he collapsed, face forward, onto the ground.

I felt it before I saw or heard it. It was distant, but it was there. The hunger and fear had returned.

They were coming back.

I panicked. My brain's first instinct was to jump into the driver's seat and speed away, and it was a strong one. I didn't want to die. Not right then. Not like that.

I was shocked when the realization hit me.

I actually didn't want to die.

I took deep breaths, trying to gain control of my terror. I opened the door and screamed down at Nothe. "Nothe! Nothe, they're coming back! Get in!"

He didn't move. He didn't even twitch.

I wanted to cry. The wild emotions of the shamonsters were growing stronger as they drew closer. I took several more breaths, closing my eyes, focusing on my own emotions—my own panic, my desire to live, the care I held for Nothe deep, *deep* down. I couldn't leave him there. I was ashamed the thought had even crossed my mind. I found the little light Rain had ignited within me and with everything I had, I seized it. I let it spread through my veins, pushing the darkness of the shamonsters out.

I threw open the door and jumped down to Nothe, landing in a puddle of shamonster blood. I fought through the stars that swarmed over my vision and the urge to vomit and knelt beside him, shaking him by the new shoulder blade that was attached to his wing. "Nothe! Nothe get up!"

He groaned. *A sign of life!* I took heart and shook him harder. "Get up and get in the truck!"

There was a small smirk on the edge of his lips. He mumbled something that sounded like, "Now you know how I feel," but it was so slurred and weak that I couldn't be sure.

There was a scream, and then another. They were getting closer.

"Nothe, c'mon! You've gotta help me out."

I threaded my arms under his and braced myself to try and lift him, certain I had no chance of getting him even a few inches off the ground. I let out a grunt as I exerted myself, and leapt upright with him in my arms with a surprised, "Oh!" He was absurdly light.

A wave of unspeakable sorrow and soul-crushing heartbreak consumed me. It felt as though someone were standing on my chest, splitting it in two. It was an agony with no end in sight yet refused to be soothed. Tears spurted to my eyes as I tried to push it away. It wasn't my pain. Nor was it coming from the shamonsters.

It was Nothe's.

His voice was solemn, broken. "Just go."

I knew my own emotion when it hit. It was rage. If Nothe wasn't about to be ripped to shreds by a bunch of people-eating, bottom-feeding space monsters, I would've wanted to stab him. "No. No you're not. You're *not* doing this right now. *You are not pulling that stupid stunt!*"

He lifted his head a little, half of his face and much of his body covered in shamonster blood. I swore he looked as though he'd aged ten years. "It doesn't matter. Nothing matters anymore."

"Stop it! *This is a really bad time to have an emotional crisis!*"

I glanced up at the field. Bright yellow lights appeared and disappeared through the blades of grain. There were more than before. How was that possible?

My heart thundered in my skull. I was going to kill Nothe. I was going to save him somehow, then seize control of the radio and make him listen to "She Thinks My Tractor's Sexy" by Kenny Chesney on repeat until he bled to death through his ears.

His eyes rolled back into his head as he lost consciousness. The heartbreak faded into a dull pain as I screamed at him in an attempt to wake him. I dragged his body the final few inches toward my door only to realize there was no way he could possibly fit inside with those wings. He needed to be put in the truck bed. I let out a cry of frustration. "Wake up! You need to get in the back."

I wished Rain were there. I prayed to God he'd magically appear. He'd know how to wake him up. He'd know what to say. He'd have some beautiful words of motivation that would get Nothe on his feet and in the truck.

I heard the rustling of grain. The sound of something racing through the field toward us.

I let Nothe fall onto the ground and shoved my hand into my pocket, grabbing my pepper spray. With shaking fingers, I turned the knob, and dropped it.

I cursed, falling to my knees, fumbling over the blood-soaked dirt. *Where is it? WHERE IS IT?*

I could hear the shamonster snorting. Its hunger was all-consuming.

It leapt out of the grain, its yellow eyes empty, its mouth full of teeth and its jaw unhinged.

I found it.

My fingers gripped the pepper spray and unleashed a stream of pain that stopped the monster in its tracks. Its shrieks rent the air, and the shamonsters surrounding us echoed its cries. Anger and fear filled everything around us like a fog. A shamonster leapt at me from the right and I sprayed its face, sending it screaming back into the field. Then I sprayed another.

We were going to die. I was going to run out of pepper spray, and then we were going to die.

There was the hum of an engine and the sound of wheels rumbling down the dirt road. The eyes in the field followed the sound, except for one pair that remained fixed on me. As it leapt out of the shadows, a figure appeared between us, wearing a shimmering, white dress and wielding a blue double-bladed axe.

Lipstick Rick.

With a single, well-aimed swing of his axe, he severed the shamonster's head from its shoulders. A new kind of rage tore through the air, emanating from Lipstick Rick. In pure fury, he hacked one shamonster after another into pieces. I looked to my right. Thipka was guarding us from the North, creating a pile of twitching, regenerating shamonster bodies with a thin white blade that must've been hiding in his walking stick.

Thipka and Rain were going to die, too.

I had no sooner thought this than Thipka let out a yell of frustration. He dropped his blade and held his hands out in front of him as his blue eye glowed. From the darkness, light pulled toward his fingertips, building into a bright ball of fire that could've competed with the radiance of the sun. With a final cry, he unleashed it. The light ripped through every shamonster around us, turning them into soupy puddles, and the world returned to its eerie silence.

I knew I had been right before. I'd never be able to close my eyes again. I was frozen with a sensory overload. There was so much to feel that I couldn't feel anything at all.

Lipstick Rick made his way over to Nothe and me, out of breath and furious. The sun was higher on the horizon now, chasing away the shadows. He said to me, "Well, I think you guys found the box."

Thipka hollered, "They won't be back, the shamonsters. The sun is out."

Among all the thoughts in my head scurrying around in a wild panic, one made it to the forefront of my mind, *Aww. Thipka calls them 'shamonsters,' too!*

Then he chased it away with, "They're still watching, though... still watching."

Lipstick Rick looked down at the unconscious Nothe, his expression mixed with concern and what I interpreted as a clear desire to make him listen to "She Thinks My Tractor's Sexy." "He shouldn't have lost consciousness over this."

That verbalized thought only added to the mess of queries and statements I had squirming around in a knot in my brain.

Lipstick Rick glanced between me and Nothe and let out a sigh, looking defeated. He said reluctantly, "I imagine you have some questions for me. Perhaps we can do an exchange of them."

Thipka limped over to us. "There isn't time for that. The sun is up." His gaze scanned over me and then fixed on Lipstick Rick. "We must get to the box."

TRACK 5

MAD WORLD

My heart punched my brain, shouting, *Don't let us do it!* I exclaimed, "What? Like, right *now?*"

Thipka didn't look at me. "I'm in a hurry."

My brain ran around in my skull with its hands in the air, screaming. I had narrowly avoided being ripped to shreds yet *again* and now Thipka expected us to just waltz into a den of shamonsters? Did he want us to jump into a pool of butter and spice first? Swim around and marinade for a while? Bring a side of rice?

I didn't know for sure that there was a den of shamonsters, but I imagined this was the reason why there were so many infesting the farm. There must've been a den here because of the box. It just made sense.

And I wasn't going to go! I wasn't doing it! I'd had it! I was done! I wanted to go home, get into my soft bed, pull the covers over my head, and pretend none of this had happened.

Lipstick Rick folded his arms across his blood-soaked dress, which was a sad sight. Like the poor green dress I was wearing, it was ruined forever. He said with a bright tone laced with irritation, "Well, it does seem like a great plan. We have an exhausted Emily—armed with her dwindling supply of pepper spray—an unconscious Nothe, and the two of us! Against a hoard of shamonsters. You're right. There's no way this could possibly fail."

Thipka nodded impatiently. "Yes. But the sun is out. We have the advantage."

"We have no idea what we're getting into. We are outnumbered and unprepared."

Thipka looked as though he were about to use his magical, I-will-destroy-everything power on Lipstick Rick. "Do you want the Therans to find this planet?"

Lipstick Rick's face paled.

Thipka went on, "Because that is what will happen if we do not act now. Time! Time is against us. We have nothing to spare. We have to seize what little is ours."

Lipstick Rick narrowed his gaze at Thipka, clearly hating everything he'd said. Yet, after a moment of consideration, he turned to me. "Someone must stay with Nothe."

Was he seriously considering this? The fire in my soul exploded. There was no room for me to pause and consider if what I was saying was polite or not. "No—no. This is stupid. *Stupid!* There is no plan! You're just going to go march after a bunch of monsters, all exhausted and-and with a sword and an axe? Are you kidding me right now? I mean, you're not actually considering this!"

When I looked over to scream at Thipka, I discovered he had somehow climbed onto the roof of the house and was pointing across the field at a thicket of trees. "It's over there. The tops of the trees are broken." He looked around and changed the direction of his pointing. "We'll take that road there."

My gaze followed his pointing to a road just south of us, cutting through the field toward the trees.

So, basically, I'd been right. It was in a den of shamonsters. A den made of trees.

Terror ripped through me. I turned to Lipstick Rick—my hero, my friend. "You can't do this! Sure, the sun is up, but it's in a bunch of trees! Where there's shade! I know Thipka's got that weird-fire-ball-thing-move and you can blow things up with your mind, but—"

"Hey," his eyes met mine. They were full of determination. I could feel the promise of his words emanating from him. "I will make it back."

The peace that filled me and his unwavering expression of confidence tried to toss my worries aside, but I wouldn't let them. Lipstick Rick studied me patiently, his bright eyes piercing my soul. He told me with words so deeply etched in truth that they could've been made of granite, "Emily, I always keep my promises. And I promise you —I will return."

TRACK 6
STARING AT THE SUN

I sat in a nervous ball in the bed of the truck next to Nothe's head, my arms wrapped around my knees like a child hiding in her closet. My eyes ached for want of sleep, but the dance my mind was having with the nightmares of the morning kept me awake. The sun rose until it was a full, shimmering circle in the sky, and the temperature rose with it. It baked shamonster blood into my skin and my dress, which made me sad. Yet, for all this misery, I didn't dare leave the bed of the truck to find shade. I wished I hadn't left my phone at Rain's the other day, or that I had a book, or anything at all to relieve me of my boredom and take my mind off of the merciless, burning sun. I wiped sweat from my brow and glared at the sky.

Stupid sun. The ultimate frenemy.

I'd definitely have to shower. Then clean the shower and shower again.

Nothe stirred beside me. He let out a groan of pain, reaching for his forehead as his eyes fluttered open. He looked around until he saw me, and then he cursed. "No, not you."

I couldn't help but be a little offended. "Wow. The words every girl dreams of hearing."

He backtracked, "No—I didn't mean... it's not that you have an ugly face, it's a fine face..." he gave up. "I'm too tired. No offense, but, your face is just not the one I wanted to see. And I have the worst headache."

"Well, I can't tell you how *thrilled* I am that you're waking up next to me. I should've left you here to get eaten." I felt horrible the second I said it. It was so awful and I didn't mean it at all. I yelled at myself, *That was so mean!*

"You should've. That would've been the smart thing to do."

Why was he being such a jerk? I fought back tears. I'd had enough. It'd been pretty much the worst morning ever, and if he said one more butthole thing, I knew the dam would break and I would cry. I really didn't want to cry in front of him. To make sure I didn't, I decided to not say another word.

He grunted, then whacked me with one of his wings as he flailed around with the extra limbs, trying to sit up. Looking at them closely, I noticed strange, muscular finger-like things lining the upper, inside part of the wing. I wondered what I should call them... flings? Thingers? Maybe thingers. Whatever they were, they grossed me out.

Once upright, he looked around. "What happened?"

Reluctantly, I told him the whole story, keeping it to as few words as possible. He only had insults for Thipka's plan, one of them being, "That's stupid." He tried to stand, desiring to go after them, but was too weak to stay on his feet for long. After throwing a little fit, he sat adjacent to me, facing the field and trees and giving his wings more room. He muttered, "Rain's smart. He'll be back." He rubbed his neck nervously. "He promised me."

I studied him, wanting to ask him what he meant by that—among a bajillion other things, like what those thingers were for—but decided to resume my commitment to silence. Then Nothe asked, "Did you really stay?"

I snorted, my hillbilly accent slipping through with my nerves. "You're still alive, ain't ya?"

He looked at me intently. "Why did you do that?"

What kind of question was that? "Why wouldn't I?"

He raised an eyebrow at me as if to say, 'Really? You can't think of any reason why you wouldn't stay?'

I looked away.

He asked with a grin, "Did we bond?" When I didn't answer, he pressed further with an over-exaggerated gasp, "Are you saying our quality bonding time was a success?"

I was ticked. And I was tired. I wasn't going to play his dumb game. I watched the grass sway in the breeze and did my best to pretend he wasn't there.

I could hear the smile in his voice. "I know. I felt it, too. No need to speak. Your silence says it all." After a few minutes of listening to an eerie amount of nothing, he told me in the sincerest, humblest tone I'd ever heard from him, "Thank you for staying with me."

My anger subsided considerably, as did all the other tumultuous waves of emotion that threatened to break the dam holding my tears back. I muttered, "You did the same for me."

There was a rustling in the field. Images from the *Jurassic Park* movies popped into my mind. At first, I couldn't see anything, but as the wind blew through the blades of grain, I saw them. They were lying low, near the very bottom—three pairs of glowing, yellow eyes, watching us. Terror and anger gripped me as I stared back at them, but it was all my own this time. I thought of all the pain they'd caused, of all they might do to Lipstick Rick, that I might never see him again.

My eyes burned with tears. "I hate them."

Nothe peered out at them, then studied me for a moment. He leaned back. "There's no point in hating them. They're the saddest, most pathetic, lost and miserable things in the universe. Except maybe for the Therans. Can't get worse than that. But your hatred won't make any difference, it'll just ruin your day."

"You've already ruined my day." I couldn't believe I'd said it. *Seriously, what's wrong with me?*

Nothe smiled wryly. "I was right though, wasn't I? This has been a morning you'll never forget."

"You're absolutely right. It'll haunt me forever."

He let out a mirthless chuckle. "You know, it was *way* too easy to get you here. You're too easy to push around. You've gotta stand up for yourself. Stand your ground. You deserve better from people. You should demand it."

This irritated me further, mostly because I knew he was right. It was the story of my life, really. I hated that.

He sighed, then said in a tone that suggested it was really painful for him to admit, "I... I'm really sorry that I brought you here."

That surprised me. A little more anger drifted away. I sighed, letting myself relax somewhat. "It's okay. I know you were just trying to help."

He let out a weird, snort-laugh. "Well, I *definitely* didn't bring you here to get eaten!" He snorted some more. I looked at him with suspicion and he squirmed a little. "I mean, I just, can see how it might look like that, but I mean—that'd just be rude."

"And a little hypocritical, given that whole *love-everyone* speech you gave me on the way over."

"Exactly! And why would I save you if I wanted you to get eaten? I mean... right?"

I thought he seemed to be trying a little too hard to convince me that he hadn't intentionally led me to a grisly doom, but then again, perhaps he was so defensive because he felt guilty about me nearly dying. Again.

After a moment of thinking about it, I was sure the latter was it. "Yep. Saving me would definitely be counter-productive."

He lit up. "Exactly! That's what I'm saying." He glanced away, then frowned. "Hey, I thought you said you had no idea what I was talking about with the love stuff."

"I still don't know what you were talking about." I smiled.

He smiled back, and I felt a very brief, tangled wave of sorrow, regret, and deep guilt rush over me from him. "I am truly sorry, Emily."

At this, I was almost completely anger-free. "I forgive you, Nothe." I hoped he could feel that I meant it.

He groaned. "Of course you do. Can't you be horrible, just once? It'd make my life so much easier."

I was confused. "I thought I *was* being horrible."

"When?"

"That stuff I said earlier..." I couldn't even repeat it for a demonstration.

"What stuff earlier?" A little lightbulb switched on. "Oh, that? About leaving me for dead? No, I completely agree! You should've left."

"I didn't mean it."

"Don't say that!"

"But I didn't! I'm so sorry."

He looked away. "Ugh. You're so righteous. It makes me sick."

I was far from that. "What? No I'm not. You gave a sincere apology and I forgave you."

"Well, I don't deserve it."

"Sure you do."

"No! Stop that! Every time you say something nice, it just... it's like daggers... in my brain..."

"Uh, would it help if I said something mean?"

"Not anymore. Because now you'd be saying something mean just to be nice."

How ironic. "What about this?" I asked him something I really wanted to know, but knew it'd make him really uncomfortable, "So, you were being really melodramatic at the worst possible time earlier. What was that all about?" I instantly felt terrible for asking it. It was such a nosy, rotten thing to say.

His eyes widened and he straightened defensively. I knew I'd struck a nerve and it made me feel worse. Why had I decided to go along with this? Was I trying to help? I thought so, but at that moment, I couldn't locate a logical train of thought. He fired back, "Why were *you* being so melodramatic?"

"I wasn't being melodramatic!"

"Yes, you were! You wouldn't get into the truck."

"I did eventually."

"So did I!"

"Yeah, after you were dragged into it."

There was a very uncomfortable pause of silence. I hated it. I asked him, "Do you feel better?"

"A tiny bit, yeah. Good job. Thank you."

After my stomach churned in guilt for a moment, I couldn't help myself. "I'm sorry. I shouldn't have—"

He cringed and held out a hand. "Stop. Just... stop. Let me have this one."

I nodded, raising my own hands in surrender. "Right. Okay." But I felt the need to say, "But seriously, if you ever want to talk about it—"

"No. Nope. Just..."

"Right. Sorry."

"...stop."

"'Kay."

We fell again into silence. I wiped more sweat from my brow and tried to absorb a swift breeze as it passed. I was magnetically drawn back to the eyes staring at us from the grain. They were just sitting there, waiting for a shadow to wash over us. I could sense their hunger, though it wasn't as strong as it had been before. It crossed my mind that the emotions they emitted might be part of a hunting tactic, something they did to debilitate their prey when they were about to pounce.

I needed something to take my mind off them. I turned to Nothe. "So... wings, huh?"

He lifted one and looked at it. "Yep." He added with the cheerfulness of a five-year-old showing off a toy dinosaur, "I have a tail, too. So does Rain." He froze, like he'd just dropped the dinosaur into a river. "He probably didn't want me to tell you that."

My stomach also dropped into the cold river. I knew Rain wasn't human, but that was a pretty big revelation. "What?" I couldn't help but try to look at Nothe's butt even though he was sitting on it. I hadn't noticed any tail earlier. "Where—? Where do you guys hide these things?"

"You can't see them when we look like this because... well, we're shapeshifters."

My eyes widened. "Oh."

"This isn't what I really look like. Our skin—well, it's the same color as my wings. Our feet are like claws—much more useful than these ones. You can actually grab things with them. It's very handy. Ha! Handy." He swatted me lightly with his wing. "Get it? Hand-y?"

"Ha! Yeah. That-that's great."

"I didn't even say that pun on purpose."

I struggled to picture what he was describing. I glanced over at the eyes in the field. It sounded unnervingly similar to what the shamonsters looked like.

I pointed to the thingers. "What do those do?"

"Oh, these?" He wigged them. "Well, we stretch our arms out really, really long, and these fingers fuse them to our wings. Our arms give our wings more strength and stability and all of that stuff. It's how we fly."

"Ah," I said, nodding as though I understood this perfectly. "How does it work? The shapeshifting part, I mean. How do you... shift?"

He was far more relaxed and happy to answer this question than I had expected. He was clearly proud of this ability. "Well, so, we can manipulate any matter that's within our reach. That's how I made that sword."

"Yeah, Rain mentioned you guys can do that."

"Well, this goes for our bodies, too. We can tear them apart and put them back together again any way we want. Of course, it's not like in the movies. It's not like changing clothes. You can't just change into a different form and then change right back, it's crazy painful and super exhausting. I could actually die if I were to try and switch from one form to another quickly. Once I'm in a form, I'm committed to that form until my body is all healed up and my energy recharged, which takes about a day, sometimes two or even three."

"Oh, wow. How does that not kill you? I mean, it's one thing to warp dead things or inanimate objects, but, your *body*...?"

"Because of our blood. It's basically the Fountain of Youth. It can heal any wound and disease. It can regrow limbs, organs. It's constantly healing everything. It keeps us from getting old."

"Whoa. So, you're basically immortal."

"Oh no. Definitely not immortal. If we bleed out, we die. Also, if we get deeply depressed—like, *very* deeply..." His lips thinned as he pondered the phenomena. "It's weird. No one's been able to figure out why, but something happens. The blood and our energy are somehow connected, so when it becomes darkened, our blood kind of... goes bad, I guess you could say. Everything catches up to us. We grow old really fast and we die."

I thought of how much Nothe had aged in less than an hour. Though a bit of his youth had returned, I could see that some of the lines were still there. I hurt for him as I wondered what was causing his pain.

But as I considered all of this, I connected some dots. "So it's not your energy that heals things..."

"Well, it does heal things, but on a deeper level."

I nodded, leaning forward. "Right. That makes sense. I totally get that." I thought of the atmosphere of the club and added the subsequent question about it to my growing list, but first I needed to clear this up. "But it's not what healed my arm, when Rain healed it. Or my body. Or made me look a hundred years younger."

Understanding illuminated his eyes. "Ooohhh... I'm not answering that question. You go right ahead and save that one for Rain. I wasn't there, so, you know, who's to say?" He went ahead and answered this, "Rain. Rain is the who, who's to say. Later. Not me."

I felt sick. How would he have used his blood to heal me? Hopefully he didn't. I couldn't even... no. I couldn't think about it. Each time I was tempted to, a swarm of nausea swept over me.

"Emily..."

I rubbed my face. "What?"

"You don't look too good."

"I'm fine."

"Well, good. Because if you puke in my truck, you're buying me a new one."

I thought of the metallic aftertaste of the hot chocolate Rain had given me back at the gas station. *"No. He didn't... did I...?"* I couldn't bring myself to finish the question. *"No..."*

"Uh, did you... what?"

I forced myself to finish it. "Did I... *drink his blood?"*

"Well, if you did—and I'm not saying that you did—"

"Oh my gosh," I was going to puke. I really was.

"Hey! No. I'm not saying you did. I wasn't there, I don't know, but if you did—if—don't puke in my truck!"

I stuck my head between my knees and took deep, steady breaths.

He went on. "If you did, it's really not a big deal. It's a very normal thing where we come from."

Another wave of nausea twisted my gut as I thought of how I'd chugged the hot chocolate he'd given me that night. I'd *chugged* it! My stomach lurched. I muttered, "I'm a vampire."

He rolled his eyes. "No, you're not."

"I am. It's official."

"You're a human. Vampires aren't human. They're... vampires!"

Anger tore through me. "He was so deceptive! I mean, hot chocolate?"

"Well it does mask the taste extremely well."

"I will never be able to drink it again!"

"That is cruel. But what was he supposed to do? Hand you a vial of his blood and say, 'Here, have some blood! It'll make you feel better!'"

"Why did it have to be hot chocolate? He could've picked *anything* else!"

Nothe reached over and tentatively patted my shoulder. "There, there. I'm sure he just wanted to help and couldn't see a better way. You know Rain. And seriously, the whole thing, it's not weird at all where we come from—"

"Well, it is here!"

"It is. Which is nice. But I bet it'd change really fast if people knew what our blood does."

I cringed at that thought and wanted to cry, because I knew he wasn't wrong. I remembered what Nothe had said earlier, *They needed a Hassune to bleed.* I felt like I'd been gutted. My heart bled for him—for both of them. "They can never find out."

"Psh. You're telling me. It was more than just slavery, really, for many of us. I don't even know how to say it. We were harvested. Like cattle. For our blood. The Therans would drink it. You guys drink milk, Therans drink blood. It cured everything. It kept them young for as long as they allowed each other to live. It was everyday life for us. That's the world I came from. And that's why, to Rain, using a few drops of blood to save someone who is an obnoxiously, painfully decent person, wasn't a big deal."

I was disgusted. I thought of Rain's little childhood home hidden in the trees in my dreams. I thought of the sadness and bitterness that had shown in his face as he'd spoken of it. It wasn't hard for me to imagine why he and his family had been in hiding and why he'd been left with the kyriki. Somehow, they'd escaped the terror in that little house and somehow, it had found them again. "I... I can't even... what kind of people would do that?"

Nothe's expression turned dark. "Humans."

My eyes darted to him in shock.

He glanced at me. "The Therans are human." He added off-handedly, "Well, I guess maybe people would call them 'humanoid', since they're not actually from Earth. I don't understand the difference between human and humanoid. Therans look a little different, but only a little. So you're all human to me. Thera is the only other planet I've seen that has other humans. Apparently, life evolved there much the same way as it has on Earth."

My anger was brewing into outright fury—for him, for his people. Of course those horrible things were human. The only thing that truly surprised me was the astronomical odds that life had evolved there so similarly—at least as far as I knew. I wasn't a scientist. But I couldn't understand how all of this pain had been allowed to happen. Was there nothing that could be done?

I asked him, "But what about shapeshifting? Can't you guys just— do, like, what you do now? Can't you guys hide?"

"Well," he explained patiently, "Those that know how to, *do*. They hide in plain sight. But most Hassune don't know how. Like I said, it's a very difficult thing to do. Lots of us have died trying, and most Hassune don't even know they *can*. Rain and I only know because, when Rain's brother rescued us, he showed us how."

"Rain's brother?"

"Yep. He'd infiltrated the mob, the army, teaching enslaved Hassune how to disappear. But transforming is the only defense we really have— or had, I don't know, things might've changed since then—so it has to be kept a secret from the Therans. The rebels are very outnumbered and any Hassune found with the slightest inclination to rebel..." The color drained from his face. "Well, I can tell you from experience, they have every reason to be terrified to try." He rubbed his forehead, as if trying to scrub away the memory he'd just fallen into. "But Rain's brother, he's a hero of mine. He went to extreme lengths—sacrificed his own well-being —to save as many of us as he could. More than anyone ever has."

Rain's brother. I felt a twist of pain for Rain at the mention of him, knowing he must miss him so much. Tears brimmed my eyes. I was so tired—so angry, frustrated, sad, tired, heartbroken, scared, hungry, and tired—I couldn't hold it in anymore. The dam finally broke and I started to cry.

"Uh, oh," said Nothe, "Uh... oh, no. You're crying. Why are you crying?"

"I'm just so sad for you guys..."

"Stop that."

I tried to stop the flood of tears, but it only made it worse. "Stop looking at me."

"I can't help it. Your eyes are leaking and you're making sniffy, crying sounds."

I sniffed. "Stop talking."

"I don't think I should. I think there's something comforting that I'm supposed to say."

I let out an annoyed groan and wiped my face. "Oh, my gosh. Just stop talking."

"Uh..." His hand returned to my shoulder. "There, there." He scooted closer and a wing wrapped comfortingly around me. I was in awe at how incredibly soft his feathers were, softer than a micro raschel blanket before being washed too many times and turning into cottage cheese.

Sweet sunlight radiated from Nothe, though it wasn't near as vivid and bright as when Rain comforted me. It felt restrained, as though sending me peace put him at risk of unleashing a tidal wave of other emotions at the same time. I couldn't help but appreciate the effort. I knew there must be a monstrous storm Nothe was trying to keep at bay. His small light was enough to help me gain control over my breathing and tears. I sniffed, wiping my face on the inside of my already-destroyed dress.

I could hear Nothe's grimace in his tone, but he didn't flinch or remove his wing, "Gross."

I ignored this and took a deep breath. "Thanks for helping me, Nothe."

He gave me the smallest-ever-hug with his wing. "Don't worry about it."

TRACK 7
BUTTERFLIES AND HURRICANES

"What is taking them so long?" Nothe was growing more and more antsy by the minute. It was killing him to be stuck there, feeling useless while Rain and Thipka were risking their necks to save the world. I knew this only because he'd told me about five or six times within the last half hour and he'd been losing control of his anxiety.

I understood how he felt. My blood was crawling. They were so far away and the trees were so thick that we couldn't see what was going on at all. Thirty minutes was beginning to feel like thirty years.

"Alright, that's it," Nothe said, rising shakily to his feet, "I'm going after them."

I felt a brief wave of fear and hunger from the field to my right and discovered that the three pairs of eyes were looking up at Nothe. Nothe's gaze fell on them, concern crossing his expression. He knew he was in no shape to fight and my pepper spray supply was low.

What help would either of us possibly be? Assuming they were alive, we would be a liability. He and I both knew it.

He let out cry of frustration and kicked down the tailgate, leaving a huge dent. His cry turned into a yell of agony. He bent over, his face going red as he took deep breaths and growled, "I really didn't think that through."

"Did you break your foot?" I asked.

He nodded vigorously, annoyed, and spoke as though he were being strangled. "I broke it good."

"I'm sorry."

"Stop saying sorry."

"Sorry—I mean..." My lips squished into a sheepish line.

He slowly turned and glared at me, then plopped down on the edge of the tailgate with his head in his hands.

I wanted to kick something, too. Or punch something, or throw something, or scream—or all of those things. I was totally freaking out, but anyone watching wouldn't know it, since I just sat there, doing nothing.

I didn't know what to do. It was a level of worry I hadn't felt since I was a little girl when my mother lay dying in the hospital. She'd been in surgery to fix her femur, which she'd broken when she slipped on a patch of ice on the front steps of our house. There'd been a complication with the anesthesia. It was stupid, like how Rain and Thipka's mission was stupid.

And just as that little girl had sat helpless in the waiting room while doctors rushed about, I sat with my arms wrapped around my knees, trying to think of anything else besides what was going on out there in the trees. But the only other thought my mind could focus on was the smell around us. It was getting bad. The sun was baking the corpses of the shamonsters. The air was heavy with blood, feces, and decay. It made my stomach bubble and squirm and my aching head spin.

I was desperate to think of something else—*anything* else.

I had to puke.

I only had enough warning to sit up and throw my head over the side of the truck, vomiting into a dried puddle of blood, which only made my gut lurch harder. There was nothing in there but stomach fluids, but it punished me as though I'd just eaten a hefty meal.

"Whoa, whoa, whoa!" said Nothe. "Where did that come from?"

Once my insides were satisfied with the beating they'd dealt me, I laid down in the sweltering heat and managed to mumble, "Anxiety... smell..."

Confusion took over Nothe's face. "What? Anxiety smell? Anxiety has a smell?"

I gestured to the death all around us. "Smell... blood smell... and I'm stressed."

"Ah. That makes much more sense." He looked me over. "I don't think the heat is doing you any favors, either."

"No. I hate the sun."

"It's a shame you need it to live."

I closed my eyes. "I hate the sun."

"You mentioned that."

"I hate it."

"You know what I think you hate more? Puking."

"I hate the sun more."

Nothe looked up at the sky and shouted, "She doesn't mean it! Don't go hide behind any rain clouds or anything!" He returned his attention to me. "Hey, thanks for not puking in my truck."

"Yeah, well, I can't afford to buy you a new one."

He laughed. I'd actually made Nothe laugh. I felt proud of myself in that miserable moment. It was my one ray of soothing—well, not sunshine, because I was getting plenty of that—but starlight, in my bleak, darkening despair.

I realized it wasn't just darkening despair. It was actually getting dark. My vision was cutting out.

Nothe said, "Uh, oh," just before my head gave an enthusiastic spin and stars took over my vision.

I woke up feeling like I'd been hit by a car. I'd never been hit by a car, but I imagined that this was what it would feel like. My insides twisted and constricted in pain and my head throbbed as if my brain were trying to hammer its way out of my skull. I didn't recognize where I was or remember where I was supposed to be. The soothing, cool air-conditioning brushed against my skin and I realized that it wasn't as sticky as it had been before. I glanced down and saw that, somehow, the blood was all gone, even from my dress, and it hurt my brain to try and think of how that was possible. I looked out the window to familiar billboards and buildings zooming past as we wove around cars along the freeway.

But that wasn't where I'd passed out.

I wanted to throw up again.

I heard Rain's voice, "It's alright, Emily. You're safe now."

The thrill I felt at the sound of his voice made me feel worse.

"Rain?" I looked over at him. He'd changed into a navy blue, long-sleeved shirt and jeans that'd probably been purchased last minute at Wal-Mart and his hair was a mess. Bits of dried blood remained on the back of his neck, but there he was, alive. Tears filled my eyes at his presence. It was a miracle I'd never had the fortune of experiencing before. He'd made it back. I still had him.

I tried to hold back the tears, but it was pretty much impossible. I threw my arms around him as best as I could, causing him to exclaim, "Whoa!" and swerve a little. I planted myself back in my seat, wiping my face. I was too overwhelmed with happiness to feel stupid for it and his smile assured me that I never should.

The tears and all the moving paralyzed me with pain and I slumped back into my seat and closed my eyes as I uttered, "I'm so glad you're okay." It was clear the only thing that had kept my body functioning at all was adrenaline, and now that I knew Rain was safe and we were out of danger, it was all gone.

Rain looked away, concerned. "Your brain needs rest. And you need to eat, even though you might not feel like it."

I was sure the thought of food would make me want to retch and for the most part, it did. Until I thought about fries. And a Coke. Those things sounded delightful.

I asked him what had happened out there as he exited the freeway. He was too frustrated with the outcome to be able to talk about it in more than brief sentences, which was really saying something for Rain. It had been what he had feared. "We were terribly outnumbered," he told me. "Thipka was drained, so his bizarre power was only strong enough to destroy a few of them. We were so close. We could see it, but then we were attacked by a dozen more. I couldn't get close enough to use my powers to destroy it." He grit his teeth and shook his head. "We need a new plan. Fast." A storm of terrible emotions emitted from him for a moment before he shoved them away, the look on his face clearly stating that he was done talking about it.

We pulled into the parking lot of an ancient gas station and he put the car into park. He reached out his hand for mine. "I can alleviate your pain."

Had my stomach not been occupied with feeling horrible, I was sure it would've done a little dance at the fact that Rain had just tried to take my hand. But then I thought of my conversation with Nothe and I knew that I absolutely did *not* want him fixing me. I pushed his hand away. "No!"

My insides twisted into a horrible knot of guilt at the fleeting, hurt expression that flashed across Rain's eyes. "I just want to help."

I was going to puke. I didn't want to puke. I took deep breaths and tried to keep my thoughts to as few words as possible. "I'm sorry. I just... Nothe told me about..." I closed my eyes, chanting in my head, *Don't puke. Don't puke. Don't puke.* I swallowed. "...the blood."

Rain's face paled a little. "Oh."

I nodded. "Mmmhmm." I had to ask. "Why hot chocolate?"

He looked deeply apologetic. "It hides the taste really well."

So I did drink his blood. I had hoped it wasn't true, but he'd just confirmed it. My stomach gave a nasty lurch and I panicked a little, my hand fumbling for the door handle.

Rain's jaw flexed, but he tried to sound cheerful. "I don't need blood to heal everything. When I healed you, I used my energy to pop the bone back into place and to take the pain away from you as I did it. It allowed me to absorb the pain into myself—"

I reflected on the moment, how he'd winced at setting my arm and yet I hadn't felt a thing. I was in awe. He'd actually *taken* my pain.

"—and to ease the pain you were feeling when I brushed your hair out of your face, and I used it to heal your heartbreak as best as I could. I don't need blood to ease your suffering now. You don't need to feel this way."

The worst part of my misery was that there was no end in sight to it. So, reluctantly, I surrendered. "Okay."

He took my hand. That light and warmth, as the early dawn, spread through me, soothing me. It spread throughout my abdomen and my head, replacing the terrible pain with comfort. I could think clearly and welcomed the ability to breathe normally again. Now, the only discomfort I felt was exhaustion. It was wonderful. The words poured from the bottom of my heart. "Thank you."

He gave me a small smile, but there was sadness in his eyes. "You're welcome."

Things continued to feel off as he pulled back onto the freeway. I noticed that I couldn't feel anything emanating from him at all. Rather, a chill went through me that had nothing to do with the air conditioner.

I had to ask him. "I didn't drink your blood when you healed my hip, did I?"

"No. It was applied directly."

I winced. Trying to think of something else to talk about, I said in a happy tone that was so forced, telemarketer robots would've been jealous of my skills, "So, my dress is clean. How in the world is that possible?"

"I used my energy to separate the blood particles from the fabric and skin particles to the best of my ability, and then tossed them in with the corpses. I know how much you love that dress. You've been going on about it all week."

"Wow!" I said, genuinely amazed. I joked, "Can I send you all of my dry cleaning?"

He smiled, but it was as forced as my chipper voice. He asked me, "So, what else did Nothe tell you?"

I was caught off guard a little and wondered if I dared say. "Well... he, um. He mentioned that you, uh... you don't really look like... you."

His knuckles went white against the steering wheel. "Did he tell you what we look like?"

I really didn't want to tell him. "He might've mentioned a few details. He said you're a—"

"I'm a shapeshifter." Rain continued with the sad tone of someone confessing to a horrible accident. "It.s why I'm so good at impressions. I am..." he took a deep breath, looking defeated. "I am a monster."

I was stunned. Baffled. My heart broke at those last few words. How could he possibly believe that about himself? Well, if he looked like the shamonsters... but that just made it even more heartbreaking. I wished I could borrow that brain of his for a moment, then I would know what to say to him to make him see differently.

But instead, all I could do was say, lamely, "I don't think you're a monster."

He snorted. His voice cracked ever-so-slightly as he blurted, "That's just because you haven't seen the real me."

I fired back—though gently, "It wouldn't matter. It wouldn't make any difference, Rain. It wouldn't change what you've done for me or the people around you. What you look like, that can't take those things away." I looked down at my hands, my heart sinking. "I'm the real monster, Rain. Me. And so many people out there." Tears burned my eyes as I shared what Nothe had told me of their history. "Why did you save me?"

"Because you're a good person, Emily." His demeanor softened as he glanced at me. "You are worth saving."

A tear escaped me and I brushed it away, shaking my head. "Rain, how do you not hate *all* of us?"

There was silence for a moment. "I did for a while. But it didn't do me a lot of good. It didn't do *any* good at all, in fact. There was no grace, no healing ointment in my hatred, only anger and pain that grew each day till it consumed me. But I didn't really know how to do anything else, until I finally realized there was something to hope for in humanity. That perhaps, what they needed was just to realize they could *choose* a better way.

"This is certainly not true for everyone. But it is true for many. And I refuse to place the sins of those who tortured me on those that are the good of humanity. It doesn't make sense and it doesn't fix anything. It only smothers the good. I'd rather nurture it, because that is what is needed to save it. It's a truth that's so painfully obvious when you think about it, but it's somehow regularly missed: You must nurture the good, in order to *save* the good. Because, see, you save one good person, and then that good person goes on to save a few more, and those people save a few more, and before you know it, there's light all over the darkened world, like stars in the night sky. It's so much better to destroy hate with love, and then use that love to save people, because all hate does is destroy what might've been."

In that moment, I was reminded of how he was such a better person—er, being—than me. Really, I knew he was wrong about me being a good person, about being worth saving. I wasn't any better than any other person around me. In fact, I was worse than most. I'd made such stupid, stupid choices, and they'd led to horrible things happening to me. I'd let myself get pushed around. I'd stolen my dad's money, broken his heart, ran away from home. I was the real monster in that car. And I had buried so much anger, so much hate, for what had been done to me. Though I did all that I could to ignore it, it was still there, festering inside of me—most of it toward myself, seeing as I was the one to blame. And yet nothing of what I had gone through compared to the things he'd suffered. But there he was, trying to save us human beings. Humans he had to hide from. Humans he knew would likely turn on him in an instant if they knew what he was.

The thought pulled at my heart, filling it with longing. I wanted to be everything he thought I was. I had no idea how I was possibly going to do it, but I was determined to figure it out.

He gave me a small smile, yet sorrow poured from him. "Now that you know all of this, you must be so..."

I immediately countered his thoughts. "What? Amazed? In awe? Astounded? Unworthy to be in your presence?"

He glanced over at me. "You're not frightened away by this?"

"Are you kidding? Of course not. It's quite the opposite, actually."

His smiled turned genuine as he gazed out at the road, and the terrible emotions that had been emanating from him faded away.

I asked him, "So do you ever just, go off someplace by yourself and fly?"

He nodded. "Sometimes. Most of the time Nothe goes with me."

I leaned against the armrest and sat my chin in my palm as I tried to imagine it. "Gosh, that must be so cool."

"I must admit, it really is."

"Any chance I'll ever see you in your real form?"

He was appalled. It was like I'd asked him to strip for me to the *X-Files* theme song. "*No!*" He quickly recovered. "I mean..." he said more calmly. "No. I... I'm terrifying. You don't want to see... no. So, no. Absolutely not. No. Never. That's not happening. That's a negative. Nope. No."

I wondered how long he'd go on like that if I didn't stop him. "Okay. That's cool. I get it. Sorry, I didn't mean—"

"No, no need to be sorry. I can understand how you'd be curious, but, no."

"I got it. That's a negatory."

"Very much so. A very big, N-O."

"Gotcha. You've made that very clear."

"I hope so."

I decided to move on to my next question, something that burned inside of me as I considered the injustice of his people. "So, like I said, Nothe talked a bit about your people, and about how your brother saved you, and I just wanted to ask... there's just one thing I don't understand." I had to really push myself to spit the question out, "You guys are so much more powerful than humans. *How* were you slaves?"

"*Are* slaves," he corrected. "I imagine my people are still enslaved." He pointed to his temple. "It's all in the mind. It doesn't matter how powerful you really are, if you *believe* you are powerless, then you're a prisoner from within. Those chains are the heaviest and the hardest to break, and those walls are far stronger than stone."

Scenes from the last few years of my life flashed across my mind. I thought about what my ex had done to me, how he'd manipulated me, how I had felt so powerless against him and how I had stayed even though the front door had always been there, unlocked. I could've left at any time, but I never did. I knew exactly what Rain was talking about. My prison had always been the one that had been built inside my head, and in some ways, those walls and chains were still there.

I told him, "Yeah, I know what you mean."

Rain went on. "Once you break through *those* walls and those chains, then you are truly free. Then, you can do anything."

I moved on to my next question. "What about the light that came from Nothe when he protected me? What was that?"

"That was his energy. He was amplifying it in order to change."

"Oh, wow. That's really cool." I was so disappointed in my own wuss energy.

"It is written that, the first shapeshifter learned of their ability under extreme duress, and the light that shone from her was so bright and powerful that her captors disintegrated on the spot."

"Oh!" I felt extra lucky to be alive.

Rain clarified, "I've never actually seen that happen. It's only legend."

"Ah. Well, that works out good for me—well, past-me—me-from-the-past." *Stop talking*, I told myself.

He smiled. "Indeed. And I'm glad for it." He glanced over at me with that beautiful affection in his eyes, making my heart flutter stupidly. Then he grew thoughtful. "Although, I do wonder if that's how Thipka does that—"

"—that terrifying, blow-everything-up move?"

"Yes, that one."

With my limited understanding of what he was talking about, I said as though I understood it all perfectly, "That's totally possible. It would make sense."

I leaned back in the seat and looked out the window, my eyelids heavy, thinking about that flutter. I felt like I should be weirded out after everything I'd learned about him and wondered how I wasn't. *There must be something wrong with me.*

There are SO many things wrong with you, my brain agreed, *but admit it, this makes sense. You hate people.*

I do. I really do, I replied.

He's not people.

I know. It's great. But I don't know what he looks like. He might be absolutely terrifying.

Sure, sure. But, does that really matter to you?

My first instinct was, *Well yeah, a little.* But then again, the more I thought about it, he was my friend, my hero. He was far better and kinder than any human I knew. And what made it so much more incredible was that, none of it was an act. It was just the way he was. The things I'd spoken earlier, they were absolutely true. His actions, his kind words—*that* was who he was. Nothing could change that.

Right then, I knew: he was everything to me.

Rain interrupted my introspection. "There's a Denny's down the road, here. I still owe you Denny's, I believe."

I'd completely forgotten about Denny's. "Oh wow, yeah! You totally do."

"Thipka and Nothe are following us in his Toyota, so they'll likely be joining us." He didn't sound thrilled at the thought. He moved on.

"Well, now that I've answered your questions, how about you answer some of mine?"

Turned out, he wanted to know how Nothe and I had ended up at the farm in the first place. It didn't take Rain long to get the whole story out of me. Rays of rage radiated from him, but only hit me in little bits, like sparks popping from a campfire. He was trying to control it but was clearly having a difficult time doing so.

"He was trying to help me," I told him, defending Nothe. "He..." I hesitated, feeling stupid. "He knew I wanted to, you know, contribute more to the group."

Rain cast me a confused glance that asked "Why?" without actually saying it. Thankfully, instead of prying into my psyche, he said, "It was stupid for you two to go alone." He shook his head. "What was Nothe thinking?"

"It worked out."

"Did it really, though?"

"We lived."

Fury-filled silence followed.

I tried to ease it. "We know the box is there now!"

Once again, Rain shook his head disapprovingly, muttering something that I couldn't understand but included the word, "unnecessary."

TRACK 8
AN HONEST MISTAKE

I looked for Nothe as I stepped out of the car, wondering how he even dared to go out in public with wings protruding from his back. I found that he'd shifted at some point and hidden them again—of course —but shifting back so soon had taken its toll on him. His face had been washed but was sickly and gaunt. His eyes were sunken and the skin of his eyelids was so red it looked like he'd cried blood on the way over. If I hadn't known better, I would've thought he was infected with some sort of horrible plague. The fact that he was hunched over in a The Smashing Pumpkins tour T-shirt that was too big for him, didn't help. A group of people leaving the restaurant stared him down and walked around him at a wide angle, looking worried they would catch whatever he had. Nothe didn't seem to notice. He saw me and brightened. "Hey! There's my new best friend!"

He made his way over to me, walking as if every little movement caused him agony. "How are you feeling?"

I had to admit, "Pretty good, just really tired. And hungry."

Nothe looked about nine times more tired than I felt, making me feel guilty for complaining, yet he smiled. "That's good to hear. Those are easy fixes."

Rain snapped, "What were you thinking, Nothe?"

Nothe looked shocked, but it was the kind of shock actors demonstrated in movies from the 1950s, "My, whatever do you mean?"

"Taking Emily out to a shamonster-infested farm in the middle of the night—"

"Psh... shhh... wshhh..." it seemed he could only make noises now.

"—were you *trying* to get her killed?"

"Psh! Nooo. I was trying to help her!"

"Right, by saving her from the despair of mortal existence."

"No! Nooo. I was making her a part of things! She wanted to be a part of things!" He turned to me. "Didn't you want to be a part of things?"

It was true. I wanted to be a part of things. "Yeah."

"She wanted to be a part of things! And bonding! We were bonding."

Rain wasn't buying it. "You tried to kill her! Admit it!"

"I didn't know monsters would be there! I just thought *maybe* monsters *might* be there. If I was trying to kill her, it was totally subconscious."

He might as well have punched me in the gut. "*Excuse* me?"

He turned to me. "I like you now!" Frustration erupted from him. "*Why* am I on trial? Why would I save her if I wanted her dead? There is no attempted murder here, Rain. And even if there was, it's not like it's that big of a deal. You don't even go to prison for that!"

Rain folded his arms. "Yes. You do."

"You do? Why?" He caught himself. "Wait—doesn't matter. It doesn't matter, because there was no attempted murder!" He looked at me to assure me. Waves of emotion emanated from him. I could feel how sorry he was and that he was telling the truth. "I didn't try to kill you. I didn't do anything wrong. Okay? I didn't *know* they were going to be there."

My shoulders relaxed. I believed him.

Thipka appeared. Or had he been there the whole time? I wasn't sure. His red hair was a mess. He was wearing a suit jacket with a button-up, white shirt that had several buttons undone, revealing much of his bare chest and more of the scar centered over his heart. He also wore a very long necklace chain that carried two rings. Leaning on his walking stick, he strode toward the entrance, his handsome features weary, almost hopeless. "Are you guys done?"

Nothe looked over at Rain. "Thipka's my friend now."

Rain grimaced. "Oh, Nothe. How could you sink so low?"

This made me cringe a little. It was a harsh thing to say, and I was shocked at Rain for saying it. Thipka smirked and looked Rain over like he'd just made an inside joke. "It's true. He couldn't do much worse." He opened the door and went in.

I really wanted to join him. I really, really wanted fries. And a Coke. I should've wanted a Dr. Pepper, but I wanted a Coke. It was weird. I was certain I'd never had such a craving.

A wave of hurt rushed from Nothe on behalf of Thipka. He cast Rain an angry glare. All humor was gone from his tone. "That was uncalled for. Seriously, what is your problem?"

"You're my problem."

"How old are you again?"

At this, I decided I was going to follow Thipka's example and ditch them to eat. I wasn't about to waste away listening to them argue. Eventually, they followed behind me.

The hostess led us through the nearly-empty restaurant to a booth at the back, next to another booth that had yet to be cleared of plates. Nothe graciously gestured for me to scoot in first. As he went to sit next to me, Rain jumped in between him and the booth and planted his butt in the seat, sitting half-way on top of Nothe. Nothe grabbed Rain by the shoulders and tried to shove him out of the way, whisper-shouting, "No! *I'm* sitting here!"

Rain grabbed hold of the table and refused to budge, whisper-growling, "No!"

"I was here first!"

Rain shifted his shoulder, freeing one hand and using it to shove Nothe away by the face. "Go sit by your best friend, Thipka! Emily's my only friend now."

I was starting to think this really had nothing to do with me at all.

Nothe finally surrendered. "FINE!" He jumped away from the booth, straightened his shirt and sat beside Thipka. "But it's just because I have so many friends and you're so sad."

After an awkward pause, the hostess handed us our menus and took off, likely to warn our future waitress about us ruffians.

Pretending that nothing had happened, Rain said in an overly cheerful voice, "Well, I daresay, French toast sounds absolutely delightful this morning."

Nothe chimed in with equal cheeriness, "When *doesn't* French toast sound delightful?"

"Indeed!"

They both let out pompous laughs and returned their attention to their menus.

I stared at them. I had no idea what was going on anymore. I raised an eyebrow and couldn't stop myself from asking Thipka, "Do you know what's happening?"

"Nothing, of course," explained Nothe. "This is how we always are! We are perfectly civilized people."

"Of course we are," agreed Rain.

Our waitress showed up with some apprehension in her eyes. My mind jumped to its deep longing for fries. And pickles. The waitress intended to just take drink orders, but I insisted on ordering immediately and, for the first time in my life, asked for a giant order of fries and a pile of pickles.

As she disappeared toward the kitchen, Thipka let out a sigh. "We don't have time for this. I'm in a hurry. Let's get to the important things."

"Yes," said Nothe, "because, of course, we're civilized people, concerned for the good citizens of Earth."

"Yes, of course you are," agreed Thipka.

"Of course I am."

"Of course" was apparently the phrase of the day.

Rain hesitated, then grumbled, "Alright. What's our next move?"

Had I been drinking water, I might've spat it out just for the effect of it. "We're talking about that here?"

"As much as it pains me to say it, Thipka's right. This really can't wait."

"But..." I gestured around. "Denny's!"

Nothe waved away my concerns. "No one's around. Besides," he went on very matter-of-factly, "if anybody were to overhear anything we say, they'd just think we're insane. Or in a book club."

"Or both," said Thipka.

Rain moved on. "Thipka and The Prophet went to the place where he had 'foreseen' the placement of the box and it wasn't there." He looked a bit smug. "So much for being able to predict the future."

Thipka slammed a fist on the table. "It was *supposed* to be there! That is where it was *before!*"

Rain and Nothe exchanged a look, and the three of us gazed around the restaurant to see if anyone had noticed the outburst. Thankfully, no one had. Thipka, who obviously couldn't have cared less, went on, "Before *this*. Before Time. Time, time, time... before Time was on to me —Time is on to me. Time..." he ran a hand through his hair, his gaze wild and somewhere else. "Time has its own version of what is right, even if it is wrong—because in its mind, what is right is what has already been written." He shook his head and pointed at nothing. "That—*that* is what The Prophet said. That was his great, helpful ti-P." He overemphasized the "P," expressing his intense displeasure with the situation all in one letter.

Nothe furrowed his brow. "As always, I'm dying to know—what do you mean by 'before?'"

Rain glanced over at Nothe, looking outright sick. He really didn't seem to want to know the answer to that question.

"Before!" Thipka shouted, like everyone should know what that meant. "As in before *now!*"

Nothe nodded as if this made sense and continued patiently, "Yeah, sure. I get that. But just to clarify, you're saying that, Time... Time somehow *moved* the box from where it was *before.*"

Thipka nodded once. "Right."

Nothe pointed at him. "Right, 'kay, but what does that *mean?*"

"It means it was there, and now it's gone."

"Yes, but..." he chose his words carefully, "how did you know where it was before Time moved it?"

Thipka rubbed his wrist, muttering, "Time, time, time, time, time..." until the words faded into the humming of a familiar song, though I couldn't quite place it.

Realizing he wasn't going to get an answer, Nothe switched gears. "All right. He's broken." He rubbed his forehead and muttered his own frustrated ramble, "It's like trying to reason with a manic butterfly holding a..." he briefly searched for a word, "a blowtorch." He took a deep breath and asked, "So, why would Time even move this box? Why would it do that? That would be like, rewriting *itself*, wouldn't it? Isn't that against its own rules?"

Thipka came out of his spiral with a wry smile. "Ah, but it's such a small thing, isn't it? A small move, a small change, to save the tapestry from being completely unraveled. A small sacrifice to save itself. It must rewrite a small part of itself, to save itself."

A strange panic gripped me. "So, wait. Are you saying that Time is like a... a living *thing?*"

Thipka looked at me, his eyes full of a strange longing, piercing me with a deep, growing sense of familiarity that I couldn't understand. Not the familiarity of getting to know someone, but as though I was realizing I knew him from somewhere else, somewhere far away. He quickly looked at the table, shaking his head. "Time. I don't know what Time is. I just know what it does, and that they need more. More time, more time."

"They?"

Rain cast me a sideways glance, looking gray now. "Save Them."

Thipka was repeating the word "Time" again, lost in his head as he scratched at the table with a butterknife. Nothe wrested it away with a reprimanding glare, as if Thipka were a toddler. "Stop that!" But Thipka simply continued scratching with his fingernail.

Nothe turned to me and said, as if Thipka wasn't there—and he really kinda wasn't anymore, "It doesn't matter what is going on. The world can literally be on the verge of ending and yet his mind always goes back to 'Them.'"

I considered this. "Well, maybe we're 'Them.' Ya know? The world —maybe everyone on it is 'them.'"

Nothe stared at Thipka, skeptical. "I dunno. Maybe."

Rain's voice was muted. "We need to destroy the box." He narrowed his gaze at Nothe. "How did you find it?"

Nothe brightened. "Well, I looked up reports of livestock getting eaten, people disappearing, that sort of thing, and that farm seemed to be very central to it all."

A wave of anger erupted from Rain. "And that's when you thought, 'hey, I'll take Emily to check it out.'"

Nothe repeatedly snort-laughed. "No! Not right *then*... I never said I thought it through."

The waitress finally brought our drinks. The silence that fell over us was heavy, something even the waitress could feel. She left as politely as possible and I inhaled my Coke.

Thipka broke the silence. "Back to other things. Weapons—need them, we will."

Nothe looked at him. "You're right, Master Yoda."

I couldn't help but let out an airy laugh. Thipka smiled at me, his eyes full of warmth. I was sure he'd set that up on purpose. However crazy he might've been, there was still an intelligent, thoughtful being lost somewhere in his mind. I had a pang of sorrow for him, thinking of his madness. Of how his eyes were kind, but there was always a glimmer of sadness in them. It was very faint, but no matter what the look on his face was, it was always there, deep, almost imbedded in his expression. Why? What terrible things had happened to him? I wanted to hug him.

Nothe was about to continue, but was silenced by the appearance of a familiar person at our table, who said in his always-shouting tone, "I'm sorry. I couldn't help overhearing—"

Nothe stared up at him in shock. "Oh my stars! It's Bill!"

He and Rain exchanged a what-is-he-doing-here look.

"I've been sitting in the booth behind you," Bill said. "I can't *believe* you didn't say hi. I'm insulted."

"We didn't see you," said Rain.

I squeaked out, "W-we thought the booth was empty."

Bill gave a small eyeroll. "I go to the bathroom for two seconds... well, whatever. It's fine. I guess."

Nothe asked, "Is anyone else with you?"

"No. You know what? Sometimes I just want someone to cook breakfast for me! But I've heard everything you've said, and I want in." He made a sweeping motion with his hands to Nothe. "Scoot!"

Nothe and Thipka scooted toward the window, making room for him. Bill sat down and his voice dropped to the kind of whisper children have when they think they're whispering but they're really not. "Listen. I have an AK-47—"

Nothe straightened in surprise. "What?"

"Actually, I have three. And a bunch of other stuff."

I had to ask. "How—?"

"Never you mind! But it's obvious I can help you. I want to avenge my sort-of-friend Devon!"

Thipka shook his head and resumed scratching the table, looking defeated. "It's happening again."

Bill looked at him. "Well, that's unsettling. I don't like it." He pointed at him like a two-year-old in a zoo. "Is that guy the one you were talking about—that was left behind in the portal?"

I wanted to tell him to keep his voice down, but Nothe and Rain were unphased. Rain admitted, "Yes."

Bill frowned. "So how did he get here?"

Thipka sighed. "The door opens then closes, opens then closes."

Bill gazed around the table, searching for a translation. I was right there with him. Rain could only glare at Thipka, so it was left to Nothe to explain. "The portal has been fixed somehow, but whoever is using it is being smarter about it this time. They leave it open just long enough to get to where they want to go, then close it to keep others from getting in. It's less likely to be discovered and destroyed that way."

Bill spoke my thoughts. "Well great. First monsters, and now this?"

Nothe shrugged. "Well, we all kinda figured that—"

"I know! But I was hoping none of it was true."

Rain finally spoke, "We can only take on one thing at a time. The most pressing matter is the box."

Bill said, "Well, I have an arsenal but I don't have extra vests."

Rain acknowledged this with a nod. "We'll take care of that."

With a sick twist, I muttered, "How?"

Nothe frowned at Rain. "Rain has his ways. Stupid ways."

What do you mean by that? I wanted to say, but then Bill said, "Well, whatever you do, make sure you get something for Chuck. I know he's going to want in on this, too. Steve will also want in, but he can't. He'll die for sure."

The waitress brought our food. Bill reached over to steal a few fries, but one wordless threat from me ended that. I ate until I thought my stomach might burst. It was so much better feeling like at any second I'd implode. The fullness made me sleepy. and I felt that if I died in that moment, I would die with a smile.

I glanced down at the table as we packed up to leave. Thipka had carved "Save Them" into the surface. Red splotches around the letters said he had scratched until his fingers bled. I thought of my suggestion, of how the world might've been the "Them" he was always talking about and was so determined to save. But looking at the blood surrounding those words, I understood Nothe's hesitation to agree.

TRACK 9
LITTLE TALKS

After a while of driving, my stomach felt funny again. Though we were close to home, I asked Rain to go through a drive-thru to get me another Coke. Rain eyed me with a curious suspicion at this request, as if I'd just asked him if Ronald Reagan were still president. "A Coke?"

"Yes."

"Really?"

"Yep."

"I thought Dr. Pepper was your preferred beverage."

Aww, I thought, *he knows me so well.* I explained, "I don't know. It's a weird day. I want a Coke. And ice. I want ice."

"Alright. Fair enough."

After the drive-thru, we stopped at a red light as a group of pedestrians crossed the street. I looked more *through* them than at them as I held my Coke, sipping it as if it were an oxygen tank giving me life-sustaining air. Rain pointed out a woman chatting with a friend as she pushed a baby in a stroller. He cleared his throat. "How do you feel about... children?"

I raised an eyebrow at this odd question. "They're okay. From a distance."

"A distance, eh?"

"Yeah." That wasn't true at all. I'd been spending increasing amounts of time daydreaming about adoption. "Well, actually I've always wanted a kid. I wasn't the little girl that played with dolls or anything, but I did have *one*—a little Cabbage Patch baby. It was really cute, and um, I was a teenager when I bought it." I grew defensive at his nonjudgmental silence. "It was so cute! I couldn't *not* buy it!"

He held up his hands with an amused smile. "I didn't say anything!"

"Anyway. You know, even when I was in that"—my tongue tripped over the ugly memory—"that horrible relationship with *that guy*, I'd actually hope to get pregnant. I just wanted a baby. It'd give me something to live for, ya know? Maybe give me the courage to run away. And I wouldn't feel so alone. I don't know. But it's a good thing it didn't happen. It was totally selfish."

He tapped his fingers on the steering wheel, his mouth twisting in thought, like he was throwing open drawers in his head, looking for something. "I used to think about having a family. I thought it might be nice, you know. I eventually let go of the idea, but, I still find it to be a pleasant thought."

"Why'd you let it go?" Then the answer seemed obvious. "Because you're stuck here with people and Nothe and not, ya know, lady Hassunes."

He shot me a sideways glance as the light finally turned green. "Well, uh, actually, our DNA—well, we're mostly human. And so, well, we're compatible with humans. My brother, for example—well, half-brother—his father was human."

My eyebrows shot up. "Really?"

He nodded. "My people, the Hassune..." his grip tightened on the steering wheel. "We were created in a lab."

"What?" I couldn't believe it.

He focused his gaze on the road ahead, full of bitterness. "It is written that it happened on the night of this infamous storm. It was so strange that it's in history books from different cultures across the world. And the lab results could never be replicated, because they had everything to do with that storm. There hasn't been one like it since.

"See, on our world, the southern countries wanted control of... well, basically the world, which sounds downright Dr. Evil, super-villain-esque, but it's true. And the Therans murdered each other the way humans on Earth slaughter imaginary people in video games. They had no remorse. They didn't fear the end of the human race, they feared *losing*. And as the northern people approached extinction, they gathered what remained of their scientists, and found that one of them had already begun development of the ultimate killing machine. Something that could be controlled, that could heal quickly on its own, and wouldn't cost much to produce. To have many of the qualities that they desired, it was created from other living things, including humans. There were some very ugly and awful creatures born from their many attempts."

I looked away, feeling sick as I put his words together. "The failed experiments. The shamonsters."

His expression was grim. "Precisely."

Rain pulled into the parking lot of my building and parked at the steps of my apartment. He looked down at his hands, his shoulders slumped and his expression downcast. "That is where my people came from. The Hassune won the North the war. Not long after, they stumbled upon—what you Earth humans would call—the Fountain of Youth. And when the scientists couldn't figure out what they'd done, exactly, to create this Fountain of Youth, and as they didn't need us as soldiers anymore... well, I'm sure it's not hard to imagine what we were used for. We were easily enslaved. We were loyal, and they used that against us. We became a beauty product to be harvested, a source of pleasure, lower than cattle. When you find yourself envying the animals they slaughter..." He shook his head and smiled, but it was hollow and broken. It ripped me apart, bringing tears of agony and anger to my eyes that I tried to swallow.

I didn't know what to say. I wished I did. I wished I had a deep well of comforting words I could use, like he did for me. I wanted to be the healer he needed. I wanted to hold him until all of these horrible things faded away. But I didn't have any words, and I couldn't hold him.

He went on. "They say that prophets came to them and prophesied that their creation would lead to the destruction of the planet, but of course, no one believed their superstitions."

My mind finally caught hold of something to say and blurted it a little too enthusiastically. "I hope they do. I hope your people wipe them out."

He smiled in an angry sort of way. "Well, my brother is working on that. When we were captured," I cringed inwardly, "well, since he wasn't born with wings, he looked very human—so much so that the nurse put him in a Theran orphanage to spare him from slavery. He eventually became a general in the army, and at this very moment, while you and I are here, he is leading an undercover rebellion against the Therans. He has Hassune teaching others how to shapeshift and is infiltrating the army in order to crush them from the inside out. My hope is," he sighed, rubbing his wrists, "if we somehow fail, and do not get to the box in time, that he will stop the Therans before they reach this planet. Any hope we have if we fail—any hope *my people* have in obtaining freedom—that hope is theirs because my mother saved him. Saved us both."

I leaned forward, waiting for him to tell me the rest of the story.

He took a deep breath. "So anyway. In theory, I suppose I could have a family."

"Oh! Is that what we were talking about?" I teased.

He laughed. "Yeah, I kind of went off on a small tangent, there."

"That's totally okay!"

"Sorry. Talk about too much information, eh?"

"That's alright. You can tell me anything you want to."

"If you haven't noticed, I already do. I feel very comfortable with you."

"And I feel very comfortable with you." The thought slipped into my head, *I could totally have a family with you.*

I was grateful I had the self-control to not blurt that one out loud.

"But yeah, for many, many reasons, the whole family thing—well, just before I met you, Nothe was trying to warm me up to the idea. Things are much better here than where we came from, so it seemed like more of a possibility, but," he grew uncomfortable, "I just can't."

I watched him carefully, part of me sad for him and the other part sad for myself. "Oh." I wanted to ask why he'd written off the idea so completely, but I didn't want to push him any farther. I could sense the storm brewing inside him, stirring underneath the pain—a kind of storm I knew all too well—and all I wanted to do now was help him calm it.

He added quickly, "And not because—like—it's just... emotionally, I guess. I... I don't know how to have a healthy relationship with anyone. Not the kind of relationship you need to have a family. The things that happened to me..." His gaze grew distant, weighted with torment, as if his mind were on the edge of a dark precipice and about to fall, but his voice was steady. "I guess I wasn't strong enough. It broke me." He ran a hand through his hair. "It broke a lot of Hassune, though. I'm not the only one. But then others had it much worse than I did and recovered. I don't know how they did it, but they did. And yet, here I am... and I can still feel those unseen wounds sometimes. Sometimes, when I breathe in deeply, they ache." He closed his eyes and swallowed tears, his expression full of pain.

Tears brimmed my eyes. I knew exactly what he meant, and I hated that he had those kinds of scars, too. They were surely so much worse than mine.

He took a deep breath. The shadows in his eyes passed. "But anyway, the end." He winced and a brief wave of embarrassment rushed over me from him. "I'm talking way too much. I don't know what I'm doing. What has come over me? I don't do this, ever. I—"

I stopped him, wanting to shove all of his pain and embarrassment away. I wanted him to feel safe. "It's okay. Please, you're fine. I get it."

"You do?"

"Yeah. I think I do. I'm pretty messed up. The only relationship I've ever been in was horrible. I mean, I know it's nothing compared to what you've been through, but, I think I can understand. It messes you up. I don't have any idea what a healthy relationship would be like. And I think, even if I were to have one, I'd have a hard time trusting it. And I'd have a hard time with..." I couldn't look at him as I said it, "with everything." I thought back to my past, to the nightmares I seemed to have constantly. I took a deep breath and looked out the window. "So I don't know if I'll have any of that family stuff, either." Then I confessed, "Maybe I'll adopt someday. Have a little family that way."

I looked over at him. He was watching me with a compassionate smile. "Well, perhaps this is why we get along so well. Our demons have so much in common." There was a light in his eyes that I couldn't say I'd really seen before, and a glow of hope radiating from him that I didn't quite understand. He looked at me with that affection that thrilled my heart every time I saw it. I allowed myself to bask in it for a moment, but only for a moment.

As we walked up the steps to my front door, I asked him, "Your brother, what was his name?"

He paused. I couldn't read his expression. "Rao." Then he said, "You know, I was wondering if you ever called your father."

This question knocked the wind out of me. For a second, I couldn't remember how to open the door.

Rain let out a slow, awkward, "Ah... sorry. I didn't mean to pry."

I regained my composure and forced a smile as I remembered how to use a lock, "No, no. It's fine. Um..." We stepped inside and I peeled off my coat—gladly—and tossed it onto the back of the couch before sitting down. "I did. I called him."

He closed the door and sat beside me. "Oh."

I debated telling him more. I didn't want to. But at the same time, he'd been so upfront with me. He'd made himself vulnerable, telling me huge secrets, how he felt like a monster. But what would he do when found out the real monster was me?

He read my silence. "It didn't go very well, I take it."

My hands trembled ever so slightly. "No. It didn't." I sighed. "Not at all."

I hung my head. He had a right to know. It was my turn to show my scars.

He asked me, "Do you want to talk about it?" I could sense that he wanted me to.

No, I immediately thought. But then again, some part of me ached for it to be out. It was a nasty knife in my soul that I'd been stabbed with just after dicing fish and onions, festering and unable to heal.

But what would he do? Would he regret being my friend? Would he regret trusting me?

Would he regret saving me?

I blinked away the urge to cry. I told him, "My sister answered and uh, yeah. She hates me. And apparently my dad does, too."

"Did he tell you that?"

"No."

"Then how do you know it's true?"

"I just... I don't know why he wouldn't." I took a deep breath. "You know that guy who pushed me down the stairs?"

His whole body went rigid, but he said calmly, "How could I forget?"

"Well," I felt the best way to get it out was to spill it as fast as possible, like dumping a jug of water down the drain with a spider in it. "So, I sort of stole my dad's savings and ran away with him."

I couldn't bring myself to look at Rain. There was nothing but the sound of our breathing for several seconds before he said nonchalantly, "Well, I know there's more to it than that."

His casualness toward the whole thing helped me breathe a little easier, but it didn't change the ugliness of the truth. "It doesn't get any better."

"I'm sure it doesn't, but probably not for the reasons you think."

I held my head in my hands. All of the shadows that had once been chased away crept underneath my skin, crawling and suffocating me. "I was so stupid. So stupid. I just... I met him and he seemed like a good guy. It seems so obvious looking back on it. I should've seen how bad he was. But I didn't. I just, I had this picture of him in my mind, ya know? He was... he was cute and seemed so generous. He-he always went to church. He participated in class, he was smart—actually he wasn't, but he was very good at acting like it and he always made me feel so stupid." I picked at a loose string in my skirt a little more violently than necessary and shook my head. "And I was. I was so stupid. He made me feel so small. And I am small. And I'm not smart. I know that. But I used to have goals, ya know? And I mean, I understood my weaknesses and shortcomings—it's not like I wasn't aware of them—but still, I had plans and I had... I had dumb confidence." I snorted a laugh at the image of young, dumb confident me. "I was ready to make the best of what I *did* have and conquer the world. Then I started dating him, and I just started to feel weak and pathetic. My dreams were pathetic, *I* was pathetic. And I was helpless without him. I had all of these ideas, and he made me feel stupid for all of them. But it was subtle, ya know? Like, if he'd been up front about it, I would've been like, 'Screw you!' and I wouldn't have given him the time of day, but it wasn't like that." I was baffled just thinking about it. "I don't even know how he did it. But he got into my head and made me feel so... so..."

"Powerless." Rain's voice was gentle, almost a whisper. There was profound understanding in his eyes.

I nodded. "Yeah. Exactly." I looked back at the string, weaving it through my fingers. "Powerless. Helpless. Believing all the horrible things he said I was. One second I was beautiful and amazing to him, but then the next....

"Like, one day, he went off about how gross potbellies are. And the next day, he was like, 'Wow! Look how beautiful you are!' but then later on, said, 'Aww, you have the cutest potbelly!' Then I got mad, and he said, 'What? I like potbellies!' and made me feel like I was the one that was crazy oversensitive and wrong. He'd tell me I'm smart, but then make fun of something I said—but not in a teasing way, but in a really *mean* way—then he'd say he was just teasing and that I had no sense of humor. He'd say my art was great, but then pick it apart until I didn't want to draw anymore, or sing, or play the piano. I used to be good at the piano. I used to write songs. Then I let slip my absurd dream of becoming a rockstar and he told me, 'don't get your hopes up.'"

I snorted another laugh, but was holding back sobs. I couldn't stop staring at the green piece of string that was now fraying. "My dad tried to get me to break up with him. He'd warned me about him from the very beginning, saying stuff like, 'You're friends. You should just *stay* friends.' Then it turned into, 'I really don't like that kid. He's not right for you. He gives me the willies.'" I laughed a little. "He really pressured me to break things off after we got serious. His tone changed from like, playful, to dead serious, 'He is not good for you, Emily. I don't like what he's doing to you.' But by then... it was too late." I shook my head, a broken smile taking over my expression. "My first *love*... it was all downhill from there. Once I slept with him, I started to feel horrible. He made me do stuff I didn't want to do... in... in bed... he'd trick me..." My voice cracked as my soul twisted in pain. "And then I didn't want to do it anymore... but I didn't feel like I could say no.

"Like, one night..." I knew I shouldn't tell this story, but the brakes had been cut and I couldn't stop. "I... I told him I didn't want to do it anymore. I was sitting at the edge of the bed, naked, and I started sobbing. I told him I didn't want to do it anymore—I didn't... He just waited until I stopped crying and then he just... laid me down and..." I pulled at my hair, "did it anyway. And I let him. I didn't fight him. Because... I didn't feel like I could. I didn't feel like I had a say. I didn't feel like my feelings mattered." Before I knew it, I was crying. "I've never told anyone this. Not anyone." I pulled my hair harder, ripping out a few strands. "Why didn't he stop?" I lamented, "Why didn't he just stop? I wanted him to stop! And he didn't stop!"

Rain pulled me into his arms. I pressed my head into his chest as he threaded his hand through my hair. Waves of comfort rushed through me at his touch, but he didn't say a word. He just listened, letting me get it all out. "I wasn't... I wasn't human anymore. My sister told me that I was as good as a thrown-away candy wrapper, all the good stuff was gone. I was worthless now and there was no way back. He used all the rumors, my sister hating me... he convinced me that they had a right to hate me, that what she said was true. But again, it was subtle. He just used it against me. He used it as an excuse to do whatever he wanted to me. And somehow, through all of that, I didn't blame my *boyfriend*. I blamed myself. But it *is* my fault! It is. And when he said he wanted to run away, I didn't see how I could say no. I mean, what would I be without him?"

I pulled away from Rain. I didn't deserve any comfort. I balled my hands in my hair again, unable to look at him, yet I went on like I was confessing my sins on my deathbed. "My dad had a bunch of money stashed under a floorboard in his room, for emergencies. It was 3,733 dollars. I stole it all, every last, wrinkled dollar. And we ran away."

The black pit in my gut had opened up again. It hurt. It hurt so much. I could feel myself drifting away, tears pouring down my face and onto my dress. "How could I be so stupid? *I am so stupid.*"

Rain's warm, calloused hands grabbed mine, pulling them away from my hair. "It's okay, Emily. It's okay."

"I'm the monster, Rain—"

He didn't let me finish the declaration. He brushed a strand of hair behind my ear and cradled my face in his palm, wiping away tears, his bright blue eyes burning as if a fire had been lit behind them. I could feel a distant fury radiating from him—biting anger that pierced my blood— but it was on my behalf, for what had happened to me. I could sense his hunger for vengeance. But at his touch, I felt a flood of serenity, of a calm that mirrored sitting on a mountaintop. There was a compassion and affection there, far deeper and more understanding than I ever could've imagined possible.

With the light that came from this, Rain showed me a glimpse of what he saw when he looked at me. It was so fleeting I almost missed it. I saw a beautiful young girl—far more beautiful than what I ever saw in the mirror—with a torn dress and covered with bleeding wounds, but still struggling to lift his broken soul with a smile. His voice seemed to thunder as the sound of rushing water, solidifying his vision, though his tone was only kind. "Listen to me. What happened to you, what he did —it is *not* your fault. You did absolutely nothing to deserve this. You are far from a monster, Emily. And far from stupid. You were a child. How could you have known? How could you possibly have seen the monster that *he* was?"

At his words, at the power behind his touch, the darkness lifted, changing the source of my tears from agony and sorrow to unspeakable hope and gratitude. Once again, he had pulled my drowning soul out of deep water and placed my feet on solid ground. He had placed a soothing balm on a wound I thought could never be healed. With those few words, that glimpse, I saw myself in a way I could forgive. Something shifted inside me, a broken piece of my soul fitting back into place. He was right. I had been a stupid kid. "I trusted him," I whispered, "I believed him. I believed him when he said he loved me."

Rain gently pulled me against him and held me tightly. For a long moment, he didn't say a word. When he finally spoke, his gentle voice resonated through the silence, through me. "Do you think that, for even one second, your father stopped loving you?"

"I don't know."

"I don't think he did. The past is over and done, but your life is not over. You can make it right. You can go home." He hesitated. "You *should* go home. I really don't want you to, but you should."

I could feel that he meant it. He wanted me to stay. The thought of me leaving hurt him somehow. My stomach fluttered. How could he feel that way after everything I'd just told him?

I shook my head, pushing him away. "I can't—"

"Yes, you can."

"No, I can't. Don't you get it? I broke his heart! I betrayed him. How could I look him in the face again?"

"Every second you spend away from him, you only break it more.

Emily, your father loves you. I saw it in your dream, I've heard it in everything you've told me about him. That's a kind of love that doesn't *ever* go away. I know, no matter what you've done, all he wants is for you to come back home."

I shook my head again. "I'm not ready."

I swore Rain looked relieved at this. "Well, whenever you are, know that's where you need to be. You should probably at least give him another call sometime. Have you talked to him since you ran away?"

I wiped away tears, gaining control over my breathing. "No. Well, I send him a music box and a letter on his birthday."

Rain said brightly, "Well, that's something! At least he knows you're alive."

"Yeah." I sniffed.

"Has he ever written you back?"

"I've sent it from a different post office each time. There's never a return address."

Rain frowned. I could feel that he was hurting for me and for my father. I gave him a small smile. "It's okay, Rain. I'm okay with where this story has ended up so far, because right now, I'm here." He returned my smile, though he didn't seem comforted. "Besides," I added, "I know it's nothing compared to," I gestured toward him, "well, you know. What you've been through."

He shook his head. "Don't do that. Don't invalidate your scars like that. What you've been through, that's your battleground. Maybe you weren't in physical chains, but the chains were in your mind. They were just as real, as are the deep scars. You still need to heal, even as I do."

He pulled me back into an embrace and I let him. I let the light and comfort he emanated push the guilt, the shame, and the darkness away. We leaned back against the couch and I closed my eyes as I listened to the beat of his heart. I thought about how much we understood each other, and just how strange that was. He was from another world. He wasn't even totally human. Yet there we were, comparing scars and understanding them in a very deep and profound way. I knew he understood me in a way no one else ever could. I reached out and took his hand, weaving my fingers through his. He flinched a little at first, but then let me, squeezing my hand in return. As he did, I felt a flurry of butterflies I swore weren't mine.

I turned my gaze toward the ceiling, to the sky I couldn't see, imagining the bright blue expanse and the stars that lay beyond it. "Seriously, what are the odds that we ever found each other?"

Rain hummed a little as he thought about it. "Really not great."

"Do you think God was just hanging out in the universe one day and saw us and thought, 'Wow, their lives really suck. You know who Emily needs? Rain. I'll just put them together.'"

"You know, I think that's *exactly* what happened." He chuckled. "And now I'm picturing God as Bob Ross." His voice turned into a perfect Bob Ross impression as he mimed painting. "'I think this little tree needs a friend. We'll give him a friend, right over here. There we go. Now he's a happy little tree.'"

I laughed, outright and genuine, feeling deep, impossible wounds begin to close. Rain kicked his feet up on the couch and laid back with me in his arms, and I fell asleep, content. How could I not be? Right there, with him, I was home.

I deeply resented waking when I did. I had no idea how long I'd been asleep, but the sunlight that spilled across the floor declared it was much later in the afternoon. For a moment, I got to relive all the happy, excited feelings I'd had as I fell asleep in his arms, because I was still there, my head resting on his chest and the echo of the slow, steady beat of his heart resounding in my ear. My body rose and fell with his breathing. He was still asleep. He was curled around me, one arm wrapped around my back, his hand knotted in my hair, the other draped over my waist. I was sure it wasn't just me that was perfectly happy to lay like this for eternity. I could sense his peace, like the rays of a sunset across the ocean. I closed my eyes and refused to be moved, determined to stay there for as long as time would allow.

TRACK 10
DEAD MAN'S PARTY

The phone rang. "Lady Marmalade" cut through the serenity like a chainsaw. Rain jumped awake and said in a daze, "Oh crap." He looked around like he'd forgotten where he was. "What time is it?"

He sat up, forcing me up as well. I was annoyed, but tried not to show it as I said, "I have no idea." I looked around for the clock I didn't have in my living room and thought, *I should really put a clock in here.*

Rain answered his phone, rubbing his face and sitting forward. "Yeah?"

It was Nothe. Rain was still struggling to wake up as he responded, "Yeah, fine. Give us fifteen minutes."

I heard Nothe ask, "What's the matter with you? Did you die?"

"Sort of."

"At least you can acknowledge it. That's the first step to recovery."

Rain sighed. "We'll be there in fifteen minutes." He hung up.

Silence fell between us. I tapped my fingers together as I wondered, *What happens next? Are we supposed to talk about our afternoon together? Will he think there's even anything worth talking about? What if talking about it ruins everything, the way sharing a wish makes it not come true?* I panicked at this last thought and decided to skip any possible discussion with, "So, uh, what was that about?"

Rain cleared his throat. "Nothe is hosting a meeting back at our house. Bill told everyone what we discussed at Denny's, and now the band wants to devise a plan of action."

"Alrighty, then. I'll just head to the bathroom, change my clothes, and we'll take off."

I thought I saw a flash of disappointment cross Rain's face, as though he maybe *had* hoped to discuss things—or perhaps that was my own wishful thinking. "Right," he said. "Yeah. I guess the sooner we get there, the better."

It took me longer to get ready than I had anticipated and, by the time we reached Rain's house, I was nauseated again. It was so bizarre for me to be so hungry so soon. I briefly wondered if I was dying.

The second we walked through the door, my gaze darted longingly past the group of guys in the living room to Rain's kitchen. The guys were laughing over some story Nothe was telling, which turned into an enthusiastic variety of the word "Hey!" once they saw us. Their cheeriness felt abnormal, given the purpose of our gathering. In fact, the whole room had a contagious air of optimism about it, which I soon realized was coming from Nothe. He did look infinitely better. Youth had returned to his features and his eyes were bright.

Steve glanced at his watch. "Hey Rain, that was way longer than fifteen minutes."

Rain apologized. "It took me a while to wake up."

I added, "And for me to get dressed."

Everyone's eyebrows soared skyward. Nothe's smile turned upside down.

I tried to clarify. "Because I'd been wearing my dress for almost two days."

Rain nodded. "Right. And she didn't change when we got to her apartment, because we fell asleep."

"Right, exactly."

"Just sleeping."

"Yeah."

"Together, but not like—"

"No."

"—*together*."

In the painfully long silence that followed, the air changed. Nothe's expression had turned to stone and whatever positive emotions he had been emanating were gone. I looked around to see if anyone else had noticed. Chuck, who had brought in a chair from the kitchen, studied

Nothe with a look of concern, as did Rain. Nothe refused to look at either of them. But no one else appeared to be the wiser.

I had to put a stop to this terrible awkwardness. "So! Do you guys have any food? I'm so hungry I'm going to puke. Like, literally."

Yeah, that didn't help anything.

Someone knocked on the door to the rhythm of *Jingle Bells*. Nothe brightened, and any sign that something was upsetting him, vanished. "That must be Thipka!"

Rain let out an annoyed groan and rubbed his forehead, as if the very thought of Thipka had given him a migraine.

Nothe opened the door and held his arms out in a warm greeting. "Thipka! Welcome! Welcome!" He threw an arm around Thipka's shoulders and escorted him in, kicking the door shut behind him. "We are just *so* glad to have you in our home."

Rain shot evil-laser-beams out of his eyes at Nothe, but said nothing. Thipka held a box of french fries.

Chuck inhaled the salty, potato-y scent. "Something smells good. Planning to share?"

Thipka said matter-of-factly, "Nope."

I was so disappointed by this, I wanted to cry—which I knew was absurd, but I couldn't help it. But before I could shed a tear, Thipka gestured to me. "They're for you."

Now I wanted to cry for the joy that filled my soul. "Really?"

"Yes."

"How did you know?"

Thipka shrugged.

I was far too happy to think about how weird this was. I almost hugged him. "Thank you!"

Rain was clearly unsettled and annoyed by this. Nothe took the fries from Thipka and handed them to me. As I thanked him, he smiled and spoke in a kind tone. "Yeah, well, I don't want you puking on my carpet."

I narrowed my gaze at him and gave him a fake smile. "Aww. Aren't you thoughtful."

Nothe gasped and beamed proudly at Rain. "Did you hear that? She called me 'thoughtful.'"

Rain shook his head. "Sarcasm, Nothe."

Nothe waved this away. "Eh, tomato, tomato." Only, he pronounced both examples as 'toe-may-toe', making Rain let out a suppressed snort of laughter. Nothe cast him a sideways smile and as he did, I thought I saw a light of pure adoration in his eyes. I looked over at Rain, who, of course, had noticed nothing. The look had been incredibly brief, like a mere flicker of thought that had slipped out of place and was quickly brushed back in line.

Nothe clapped his hands together. "Okay, let's get to it." He strode to the center of the room. "First of all, we have found the location of the box. It is surrounded by monsters—"

"Shamonsters," Rain corrected, probably more to annoy Nothe than anything.

Nothe's jaw clenched briefly. "*Monsters*. Emily and I found it. Mostly me. But Emily did help a little. And I really, *really* hate to admit it, but," he sighed, "I am still alive, because of her."

All attention fell on me, with Rain looking at me with pride and gratitude. My face flushed, and the flushing apparently flushed my brain down a toilet. I'd lost my ability to look anyone in the eye or speak. I hadn't really expected Nothe to follow through with what he'd proposed, and I felt terrible for doubting him.

He paused just long enough to give me an opportunity to say something, but when he saw that my brain had been flushed away, he went on, "Aaand I also saved her. She was being immature, and then I was being immature. I saved her life, and then she saved my life, and then Thipka and Rain saved *both* of our lives—but that part's boring. Anyway, the place is crawling with these things. Isn't it, Emily?"

My brain scrambled out of the toilet just enough to give me the ability to nod. "Yeah."

"We were totally outnumbered. We barely made it out alive. Well, except for Thipka and Rain. They were fine."

"Of course Rain was fine," mumbled Bill with a mixture of annoyance and admiration.

They weren't totally fine, but they'd been in better shape than us.

"Nextly, I feel you guys deserve all the good things life has to offer just for showing up here today. My friends, you are greater heroes than most people on this planet deserve. Most people suck, the rest are just okay, but then there's those few that really shine, and you guys are among them. So, many super points for showing up today."

I had to smile a little. Nothe definitely didn't share Rain's ability to give moving speeches.

"But," he continued, "you do not have to stay. No one will look down on you for bailing. Well, Bill might."

Bill nodded. "I will." He threatened everyone with a glare.

"But you guys need to know... you might not make it back." Nothe let his words hang in the air for a moment. "And if you die, it won't be pretty. I mean, think of Devon."

A different expression draped over each person's face at the mention of Devon. Thipka soundlessly muttered something under his breath, staring down at the carpet. Chuck, despite having mastered the beefy, lumberjack look, appeared to be considering an alternative route. Steve's jaw flexed, his eyes lost and angry, as if he were imagining taking down mountains of shamonsters with an AK-47 in each arm. Bill looked determined, his gaze fixed on Steve.

As for me, my legs lost their strength. I thought I might topple over as feelings of helplessness and terror overwhelmed me. For a moment, all I could see were those eyes. I felt like I was back there. Back in the alley. Back in the field.

Back in that bedroom.

I returned to the present with a touch of Rain's fingers against my hand, soothing me with warmth, chasing away the vicious memories. I took a deep breath and looked up at him, his gaze reassuring. I couldn't help but smile.

A fleeting mess of emotions erupted from Nothe. It was so quick, I didn't even have time to pinpoint what each one was, but the residue it left behind was painful and confusing, leaving me hollow. Rain looked over at him, concerned, but Nothe appeared to be perfectly fine. I glanced around to see if anyone else had felt it, but it seemed no one had. It had only reached Rain and me, who were standing closest to him.

As if he'd had no weird, mini outburst, he continued, "So... just, remember that. Know that Rain and I—"

"And me," said Thipka.

Nothe gestured to him. "And Thipka—will do everything we can to keep you safe, but these creatures... they're a lot, even for us."

Rain chimed in, "But I will make sure that we have as many weapons and as much protection as we will need."

Nothe glowered at him. "Through your stupid, stupid ways."

Rain gave an it's-just-the-way-it-is sort of shrug. "I wouldn't have to do it if people would learn to share."

I was lost. "Okay, what are these stupid, stupid ways?"

Nothe fired up. "Oh, I'll show you."

TRACK 11

MAGIC MAN

Nothe switched on the TV and used his high-tech devices to play a video he'd found on the internet. "While digging around for reports of people dying from bizarre animal attacks and all of that fun stuff, I found a website with some very interesting conspiracy theories... which led me to *this*."

Everyone leaned toward the TV, me still munching on fries. The video showed footage from different security cameras, each played on a loop—footage of celebrities making hefty withdrawals from their bank accounts. One of them was that one guy... what was his name?

Oh yeah. Harold Grossman. And in this video, he was the grossest of all the celebrities. I smirked.

Nothing seemed particularly out of the ordinary in any of the videos. The mannerisms of the individuals were spot on with how I'd always seen them act on TV—well, at least of the ones I recognized. But then, when the teller wasn't looking, each person looked up at the security camera, gave a small smile, and winked. Despite these mannerisms being featured on different faces, they were somehow all too familiar.

I looked over at Rain, who wasn't the least bit flustered. In fact, his eyes glowed a little brighter and a smug grin curled his lips.

Nothe continued, irritated, "I read the article, and they're claiming that all of these people are, in fact, shapeshifting aliens—possibly from a moon of Saturn."

Rain straightened himself. "Oh, you know those crazy conspiracy theorists. They'll believe anything."

"Hey!" yelled Bill, "I'm sitting right here!"

Nothe was not amused. "Really, Rain? That's all you have to say for yourself?"

Steve looked worried. "That's a little... I don't know. I don't like it."

Rain had told me he'd gotten rich by stealing from rich people, but I'd totally thought he'd been joking. I couldn't help laughing as I looked at him. "Wait. So when Harold Grossman said he didn't make those withdrawals... he was telling the truth? It was actually you?"

Rain smiled wryly. "I did say I was very good at impressions."

Nothe turned to me. "You don't make the kind of money Rain does by playing in a band in a club. You know, the kind of money where you can afford to give away small fortunes to random homeless people?"

Ignoring Nothe's playful dig at me, I looked at Rain and blurted, "Holy crap! You're Robin Hood!"

Chuck laughed. "He is!"

Rain waved away the compliment. "Oh, stop."

I pointed at Rain. "He's freakin' Robin Hood!"

Rain shrugged with the most bashful smile.

"Wait, how do you do it?" I asked. "I mean, to make those kind of withdrawals, it can't be as easy as just looking like those people."

"Well, sometimes it is. It depends on how smart they are and how hard they're trying to protect their money. The real trial is being stuck in the form of an obnoxious, awful person for so long."

A hum of understanding and empathy echoed through the room.

Chuck looked at Rain with subtle admiration. "Rain will study them for weeks, taking the form of people they trust and people that work in the banks until he has everything he needs to make those withdrawals. And there's nothing anyone can do. The details are so spot on, the celebrity can't prove it wasn't them."

Rain chuckled. "Some of them are such drunkards and drug addicts they end up believing that it was, indeed, them."

I laughed. What a fantastic idea. "This is amazing. I love it!"

Nothe shook his head. "No, it's stupid! What if he gets caught? What will happen then? Have you ever thought of that?"

Rain glowed with confidence. "I'm not going to get caught, Nothe."

Nothe gestured to the TV. "All it takes is the right person with the right amount of power and money, to believe this so-called," he made air quotation marks, "'nonsense.'"

"How would they ever track me down?"

Nothe didn't have an immediate answer to that, but it was obvious he hadn't given up on it.

I glanced around the room. "So you guys all knew about this?"

They looked at each other and gave their own version of the word, "Yeah."

I felt so special. I was officially part of the group.

Nothe shut off the TV. "Going back to what we were discussing before," it took me a moment to remember what we were discussing before, "there's no judgment if any of you want to back out."

Bill nodded. "Right. Of course not. It's just the fate of the world that's at stake. But if you're more concerned about yourself, there's no judgment. There'll just be constant harassment every time I see you till the day you die."

Chuck raised his eyebrows. "Well, in that case, I guess I'd rather get eaten by a monster."

Bill gestured toward him in a that's-what-I'm-saying sort of way. "Right, exactly."

"I'd also rather get eaten by a monster than go back home to my wife," Chuck said. "Can we start right now?"

There was a round of laughter from the guys.

Steve looked over at me. "She's so scary."

Nothe nodded. "She really is."

"She terrifies me!" said Bill.

Chuck's laughter quickly died. "But seriously, why aren't we calling, I don't know, the feds or something?"

Bill snapped, "Oh, right. Yeah. Let's bring the feds right to Nothe and Rain. *We can't trust the government, Chuck!*"

Chuck leaned away from Bill as though he had been pushed over by a strong wind. "I thought they were supposed to be monitoring stuff like this."

"This isn't the X-Files!"

Chuck surrendered. "Fine. I'm in."

Bill looked over at Steve. "Steve's not."

Steve was appalled. "Yes I am!"

"No. You'll die. Bless you for being here. Now go home."

"I won't die!"

"That's right. You won't. Because you're staying home."

"No, I'm not!"

I briefly wondered how old Steve was. He looked like he was in his late twenties, but his voice sometimes had a whine to it like he was eleven.

"Alright, alright," said Nothe. "Calm down, junior. You guys are all in."

Though no one was waiting for me to volunteer, the nightmare memories that surrounded the thought had my fingers shaking. I hated it. It made me feel so small. The storm they brought pressed upon me, expecting me to back down—and admittedly, I wanted to. Those monsters haunted me. If I were to go up against them, I'd die. I had no skills. I'd never shot a gun before in my life. I'd never wielded a sword or an axe. I was completely useless.

But I wasn't. I wasn't useless. I'd faced these things twice before and lived. I was sick of feeling helpless. I was done with letting my fears decide what I could do. I could do *something*. I could be a valuable member of the team. I could learn skills. I could learn how to use a gun. How hard could it be?

I balled my hands into fists. "I'm in."

Rain fired up immediately. "No!"

Nothe said gently, "Yeah, I don't think that's a good idea."

"I can learn how to use a gun or something. Let me help!"

Rain was not having it. "Absolutely not." He took my arm. "Emily, may I speak with you alone for a moment? Please?"

Rain led me outside, closing the door behind us. He said with pleading in his eyes, "Emily, you can't go."

"Why not?" I could think up a long list of why-nots but I was annoyed that he was equally aware of them.

He put a hand to his head. "Because I..."

My heart pounded, too afraid to hope at what he might say. "Because *what?* I can learn things! I can do stuff!"

He wouldn't look at me. "I know you can. You're very intelligent and so much stronger than you think. You've saved my life, and Nothe's."

Darn straight, I wanted to say, my insides filling with warm fuzzies that fought with my annoyance.

"But..." He looked at me, his expression full of worry. My frustrated heart softened a little at this, growing even more hopeful. He ran a hand through his hair, closing his eyes in defeat, muttering almost to himself, "I don't know what else to do." He held out his hand. "Take my hand. I'll show you a reason why."

I hesitated, taking a deep breath, then took his hand. I closed my eyes and, through Rain's energy, in a flurry of light, I could make out a small shape. Inside its tiny chest, I saw the quick pattering of a beating heart.

I froze, staring through my eyelids at the little form. The little arms and legs of a tiny human flapped happily.

I went numb. Completely and utterly numb. Tears brimmed my eyes. Slowly, I pushed his hand away. "That... that's inside of me?"

He nodded.

"That's growing... inside of my body..."

"Yes."

"And that... that's a..."

"A child." After a moment of silence where Rain studied me with intense concern, he forced himself to brighten. "Congratulations!"

VOLUME 4

"YOU CAN HAVE ANYTHING
YOU WANT, IF YOU'RE
WILLING TO PAY
THE PRICE."
~BOB ROSS

TRACK 1
UNDER PRESSURE

Once again, the lights went out over the dance floor. The usual panic thrilled me, only this time, my hands flew protectively over my abdomen. I breathed deeply, doing my best to convince myself we were safe while yelling in my mind, *C'mon, start the show already!* ... *TURN ON THE LIGHTS!*

A blue spotlight fell on the massive drum set at the back of the stage as Steve began a crisp drum solo that evolved into deep, rumbling booms to the flickering of multi-colored lights. Fog billowed out from the shadows, enveloping the floor. Then, in a musical twist I hadn't seen coming—as the drumming and atmosphere had me anticipating some sort of rock ballad—a white spotlight fell on Rain, who began to sing Stevie Winwood's "Higher Love." As *Screaming Riot and the City of Warning* always did with their songs, they had managed to weave a deliciously dark undertone throughout the song while still maintaining a clear 80s vibe. The crowd erupted with cheers.

It was 80s Night at Bob's Club Festivus and the band's attire matched the music. Nothe looked like an 80s bad boy with his blond hair combed back, wearing a white shirt and Levi jacket with a red and black flannel underneath. However, Rain's outfit took the award for "Most Committed." He wore a puffy, pirate-like shirt underneath a blue suit coat, his hair a well-tamed fro of curls, like a young Artist Formerly Known As Prince—or in one word: gorgeous. I didn't know how he managed to do that, as the outfit would've looked ridiculous on anyone else. Well, except for Prince. Even I went all out with my brightly colored leggings, a large, loose fitting shirt with a belt around it, glitter eyeshadow and a sideways ponytail, fully embracing my curly hair.

As the lights danced across the room, my fear of the dark wore off. I had to admit, I was glad that *Screaming Riot and the City of Warning* made an elaborate entrance with every performance. I allowed myself to get lost in the music and let go of everything for a while, like the fact that the world could be ending and my only friends might die trying to stop it —one of them being someone I cared for more than I was willing to admit.

Oh, and of the fact that I was pregnant. Couldn't forget that.

Rain had found out about my pregnancy when he'd healed me on the night we met, and had noticed it again after the shamonster attack, but he hadn't known if I'd end up losing it or not. He said it wasn't unusual to lose babies within the first few weeks of pregnancy, especially after what my body had gone through, even though he'd healed me. He didn't want to risk me slipping back into any level of depression over it, so he didn't tell me. When I passed out in the back of Nothe's truck, they both scanned me to see if there was anything seriously wrong, and discovered that the baby was still there.

I took the news less than heroically. I was *beyond* ticked off at Rain for never telling me about it. I'd given him a shocked, silent stare, then burst into tears when I attempted to say with fury, "Oh, and you didn't think that *maybe* I had a right to know that?" so my words came out pathetic and sad instead, with, "Oh, a-and you... you... didn't think that mmmah... *uh-ha-rahah-no-ah?*"

He said he had assumed I'd lost it and hadn't wanted to upset me over something I hadn't even known existed. Before I could hear another word, I took off, walking around the block and then hiding in Rain's Infiniti to cry for... I wasn't even sure how long.

It'd been, what? About three months? Maybe even more. I had always been so irregular with my cycles, I'd hardly thought anything of the months that had gone by without one. I'd taken pregnancy tests before and had always wound up disappointed, so I hadn't bothered this time. When I'd noticed the bump and my boobs getting bigger, I'd just thought it was all of the apple pie I was eating at the restaurant.

The only person I had ever been with was the maggot-infested pile of cat vomit that I had been running away from, and the last time we'd been together—the time where I'd decided I'd had enough—had been about three months ago.

If he ever found out, he would use the baby against me. He'd drag me back. He'd control our lives with a soulless grip that we could never escape from.

I'd thought I was rid of him. I'd thought I was free.

Once I'd calmed down, I saw that—I *was* free. He didn't know where I was. He had no idea this baby existed. And this baby was something I had wanted, a sincere wish that'd come true. I'd wished I wasn't alone. I'd wished I had someone to give me the courage to keep fighting—a little partner in crime. And I'd gotten away long before *that guy* could ever find out. We were safe.

I'm not alone anymore. I thought. *I have someone to live for. This baby is* mine.

I let Rain talk on the ride home. A lot. He scrambled over apologies and explanations very unpoetically, which wasn't like him. I could feel how genuinely upset he was.

How could I not forgive him?

Well, at least eventually (after many phone calls and a bouquet delivered to my apartment made of old black and white horror movies). I was too angry to let him completely off the hook right then. I let him know we were okay before I got out of the car, but in a growly sort of way.

As I lay in bed that night, I thought over my life and felt a familiar sense of numbness. I couldn't believe my past was mine and that my present was actually happening to *me*. It didn't feel real.

But then I caught myself fantasizing about a future. My mind opened up to a dream that had seemed almost impossible. I hadn't had a real goal or dream in years. They'd all been stolen from me. And now, there it was, in the form of my child, sure and bright, and within reach. Maybe the world would end, but whatever. I'd figure something out. Because I had my baby.

Maybe this was why I'd been saving all of that money.

The ending of the song snapped me back into the present moment. Rain smiled and spoke into the microphone in the tone he and Nothe saved for when they were being 'civilized people.' "My, that is a fantastic song."

Nothe nodded. "Indeed it is. It just makes you *feel* good."

"It's a feel-good song."

"Indeed. It gives me some hope for the human race."

"Indeed."

"Indeed" was apparently the word of the day.

Nothe said to Rain, "But I must say, nothing gives me hope for the human race quite like that outfit does."

Rain gestured to his clothes. "You mean, *this* outfit?"

"Yes, *that* outfit. I mean, look at you! You look like you're having fun." There was a whoop from someone in the audience who'd figured out where this was all going.

Rain gave a small shrug. "Well, I am having fun."

"And, with that outfit on, well, let's just say you absolutely..." Nothe looked dramatically out into the audience, "*spin me round*." Part of the crowd cheered. The rest of us were still lost.

Rain raised his eyebrows. "Right round?"

"Like a record."

There was more applause as more people caught on. Rain grabbed the bass while Nothe took over lead vocals and the band began to play Dead or Alive's "You Spin Me Round (Like a Record)." The dark, progressive metal undertones turned the song into something rich that sent chills through me and I had to admit, yet again, that Nothe was a pretty stellar singer.

When the song ended, Bill spoke into the microphone. "I hate to break it to you guys, but that outfit is sooo not in style."

Nothe threw up a hand. "Well, that's it. There goes my one thread of faith in humanity." He then confessed, "Actually, that's a lie. I never had any faith in humanity."

Rain contemplated this. "Perhaps we'd be better off in space."

Nothe leapt all over this idea. "That's what I've been saying!"

"We could follow in the footsteps of..." Rain tossed his hair and looked fixedly at the audience. "*Major Tom.*"

I cheered louder than anyone else.

Rain handed Nothe the bass and took over vocals and the band played Peter Schilling's answer to David Bowie, "Major Tom (Coming Home)."

At the end of the song, Nothe concluded, "You know, that's okay. I'll just stay here."

The entire show was like this. They'd turned the set list into a cheesy conversation, with each band member chiming in from time to time. Charlie got downright argumentative at one point. I was thoroughly amused.

When the show was over, I sat at a small table near the bar, waiting for the crowd to clear. As Rain emerged from backstage, he was bombarded by fans, one of whom had long black hair and big boobs and was wearing a homemade *Screaming Riot and the City of Warning* T-shirt. I felt a twist of annoyance at Rain's bright and very enthusiastic reaction to her shirt. As she closed in on him and brushed her big boobs against his chest, reaching out for his hand, my blood outright boiled over, making my stomach stew and squirm with horrible nausea. I wanted to vomit all over the front of her stupid shirt.

I should, I thought. *It wouldn't take much to make it happen, just a look at her stupid face and a whiff of the three-foot, nuclear cloud of stupid perfume she's probably wearing, because she's stupid...*

But before I could carry out my evil plan, Rain leaned away from her. With a look of disgust, he grabbed her hand with his thumb and forefinger the way someone would pick up an old, moldy banana peel and handed it back to her. He gently pushed her away and said rather loudly, "I need a solid three feet of space between you and me. Yes. Right about there. There we go. That's perfect."

I erupted with laughter. Both of their gazes fell on me, Rain's holding a small smile. She threw some bitter, curse-filled insults at him and stormed off.

Rain was unfazed. His eyes hadn't left mine since they'd found them. He strode away from the crowd and approached me tentatively. "Hello."

"Hey. No speech tonight?"

"I was feeling a little uninspired tonight. And," he shifted his feet, "I don't want to frighten people away with too many speeches."

"Nah," I told him, "that's impossible."

"Oh, I assure you, it isn't." We both laughed a little, though I could sense his very real concern and had the feeling that it had nothing to do with the audience. He muttered, "Not that I've ever cared before, but," he took a deep breath, "I hope you're still—you know, that you've continued to forgive me. That you haven't changed your mind."

I shrugged. "Yeeeah, when I thought about it, and saw where you were coming from... yeah, you're forgiven."

He looked beyond relieved. "I'm very grateful to hear that."

Nothe strode toward us. He glanced at Rain with a smile, though a worried, apprehensive look lingered in his countenance. The glare Rain gave him suggested that he had every reason to be concerned.

Nothe pushed past the glare, as if pretending Rain wasn't furious with him would magically make it so. "Hey! We're going to take off, keep the party going like it's the last night on Earth in 1989. What do you guys say?"

It sounded like a blast. But I was so tired and so nauseated. "Oh, man, that sounds like so much fun, but I'm dying." I meant every word and I hoped he could feel it.

Rain said, "I'm going to take Emily home."

Nothe asked, hopeful, "Then come find us?"

Rain cast him the coldest look I had ever seen from him. It was a merciless ice-storm in the bitterest winter. It chilled me to the bone and it wasn't even directed at me. "No."

If he'd sucker-punched Nothe in the gut, I was sure it would've hurt less. Nothe tried to hide it with a "Psh. Fine. Your loss, losers." His grin was indifferent as he walked away, but his eyes said it all. My heart hurt for him.

I turned to Rain. "Yikes. That was... wow. Kinda harsh there, Rain."

Rain appeared to be mentally shooting icy-darts-of-death at the back of Nothe's head. "He deserves it."

I chewed on my lip, debating what to say, the old-me being very certain that I shouldn't say anything at all. "Does he, though?"

Rain spoke in a tone that made me realize just what kind of enemy he would make. "Yes." Then the blizzard in his blue eyes disappeared into a warm, wonderful day at the beach. "Anyway, I would far rather spend my last-night-on-Earth-in-1989 with you."

That made my heart stop entirely for a solid three seconds. All concern was erased from my mind. "Oh. Okay then."

He quickly added, "If that's okay with you."

"Uh, yep. Yeah. I'm good with that." I only thought about the next words long enough to shove them out of my mouth before my brain could stop me. "Honestly, there's no one else I'd rather spend my last night on Earth with."

My brain cursed at me. *That sounded so stupid!*

But then a wave of fondness and joy washed over me from Rain. He smiled at me with that beautiful affection in his eyes—an affection that I swore had grown, in spite of our fight. My heart yelled at my brain, *Ha! Take that! You're not right all the time,* and went so far as to moon my brain, wiggling its heart-butt in its face. *Look who was wrong—YOU!*

My brain folded its arms and shook its head in a disgusted, tsk-tsk sort of way, saying, *Now, that's just childish and uncalled for.* But my heart disagreed, and proceeded to float away with a series of uncontrolled dance moves.

Rain glanced away, almost bashful—if it were possible that "bashful" could somehow also be cool, composed, and graceful. "Well, I guess it works out, then."

"I guess it does."

As we left Bob's Club Festivus, a bright, full moon greeted us from behind a soft haze of clouds. I inhaled the cool autumn breeze, and then beelined for the car, not wanting to be outside in the dark for longer than two seconds.

Rain took me home the longer, more popular way, stopping at a gas station to get me a Coke and shortbread cookies to calm my stomach. A moment later, we found ourselves stopped at a light next to a store window that was decked out with Christmas decorations. It was a lovely Christmas tree decorated with red ribbon and splashes of snowy white ornaments with a variety of Nativity scenes set up around it.

I groaned. "Geez. It's not even October yet! I swear I've never seen this stuff out so early. What the crap is happening to the world?"

To my surprise, Rain shrugged happily and said, "I don't mind it."

"Are you serious?"

"What? What's not to like?"

"Uh..." I could think of a few things. "It's not even October! Where's my Halloween stuff? They only have it out because it's commercial and they're greedy."

"Well of course you're going to hate it if you look at it that way, Scrooge.... Why are you looking at me like that?"

"Rain..."

"What?"

"It's September."

"It is."

"It's not even October."

"I know."

"This isn't just a few ornaments, it's a full Christmas *scene*."

"That it is."

"Yeah."

"I like it."

I continued to stare at him.

He laughed a little. "Why are you so surprised?"

"I don't know. I mean, you're a spaceman. I guess I kinda thought you'd think the whole Christmas thing was dumb." I looked up at him, curious. "How do you see it?" With my father being a preacher, I'd been brought up very Christian and part of me—especially after the events of the last several months—held on to those beliefs. I didn't go to bed at night without thanking God for hearing my prayers. But I didn't expect Rain to feel the same way. I grew concerned that he'd be offended by my assumptions.

He smiled, unoffended. "I see it as an opportunity. It's a chance for people to..." he considered his answer, "reevaluate their priorities." He gazed cheerfully over at the tree. "Honestly, I truly appreciate the whole idea, though I don't believe in any deity myself. The Son of God, out to free good people from eternal despair, willing to suffer unimaginable agony and die to make it happen. My people had a very similar diety in their religion. I don't find that dumb, I find it comforting, really. There's something different about this time of year. And I do. I like it quite a lot."

Just when I thought I couldn't possibly like Rain more. My heart floated higher than ever, officially well out of reach of reason.

I lookedat him and saw that he was looking at me with that

wonderful light and affection in his eyes again. I forgot how to breathe, but for once, it was in a very nice way.

The light turned green and he returned his attention to the road. "So, anyway. And that is why I like Christmas. The end."

I laughed a little. "Even in September."

"Precisely."

We parked and got out of the car. Rain offered me his arm as he walked me to my apartment. As we drew closer to the stairs, I saw a figure leaning against the wall. Rain stopped as if he were hit with a wave of something very unpleasant. The figure walked toward us. Once his face appeared in the streetlight, my stomach turned to stone and my happy heart was devoured by a cold, black pit.

It was him.

Tears burned my eyes. My hands shook, sloshing around what remained of my Coke.

It was him.

It was *that guy*. The pile of cat vomit. The one that didn't deserve a name. The one that didn't stop. The one who made me feel powerless, worthless, hopeless. The one who'd stolen years of my life away. The one who'd broken my heart into a thousand pieces and scrambled my brain into a dark, empty mess. The one who'd pushed me down the stairs.

It was Jesse.

TRACK 2
KILL AND RUN

Such a simple name. A biblical name. Yet it held a terrifying power over me. The face behind it was one that flooded my mind with pain, nightmares of a past that I now knew I'd never escape.

How? How did he find me?

The next thought that screamed into my mind was, *He can't know I'm pregnant.*

I was going to spill the beans. I'd slip up and tell him about the pregnancy and then he'd never let us go.

He can't know. He can never know.

A wave of comfort emanated from Rain, but this time it couldn't pierce through the storm I was caught in. He wrapped his arm protectively around my shoulders instead, pulling me tight against him, the safety and warmth of his body reaching me, consoling me.

Jesse winced as if he'd fallen off a chair and was pretending it hadn't hurt. His smile was broken. He was hurting. An exultant rush ran through me, filling my veins with the triumph of vengeance. For a fleeting moment, the only word that resonated through my mind was, *Good.*

His smile showed his nice teeth. He'd always had nice teeth. He'd also always had nice clothes, and tonight was no exception. Like a celebrity pretending to blend in at the grocery store, he embodied the phrase, "Oh, this old thing?"

"Hey! Wow, look at you!" he said with perfect charm. "You guys are all dressed up. That's so fun. You know it's not Halloween yet, right?" He chuckled to himself. The only thing missing was a laugh track.

We said nothing.

"Sheesh," Jesse said. "Why the cold shoulder? You're acting like we're strangers. Get in here! Give me a hug." He stepped toward me and my body lost all sense of place and time. I smiled robotically and let my arms fall over Jesse's shoulders in an embrace. I smelled his cologne, which always reminded me of a men's department store, of leather shoes, of his bedroom.

My smile faltered as I returned to the safety of Rain's arm around me. My arm gripped his waist as if he were the only thing keeping me from drowning—because he was. How did Jesse do it? How could I just look at him and doubt every move I'd made to get away? Why did I feel like I had to smile, after everything he'd put me through?

Panic tore through me. *He can't know I'm pregnant.*

Or... My brain countered, *should we tell him on purpose and get it over with?*

"Well," said Jesse, "aren't you going to introduce me?"

I blinked. "Of course. This is my boyfriend, Richard."

Rain magically resisted any temptation to react to this. Jesse raised his eyebrows and said, "Boyfriend?"

I blurted before my brain could stop me, "Yep. And we're pregnant."

Rain lost some composure at this and looked at me like he was certain he hadn't heard me right.

Jesse was clearly dumbfounded. "What?"

My head spun. I wanted to throw up. I was sure I was going to throw up. "Yep."

Jesse pressed his tongue against his cheek, an emotion overcoming his features that I couldn't read. "Huh."

I soon realized what the emotion was. I could see it in his eyes, in the flush of his cheeks. He was crushed. Humiliated. Angry. He looked to be truly holding back tears.

And I was not okay with it.

All the jubilation from seeing his pain was replaced with a hollow pang of guilt, then viciously laced with shame and regret. It sucked all the light from me, leaving me empty and cold. My heart was weary, bleeding from wounds that had only just begun to heal and with it, a shadow spread under my skin. If only it'd stop beating, I would stop hurting. I wanted to run, to hide. To die.

He asked me, "Can I, uh, can I talk to you alone for a minute?"

My arm tensed around Rain's waist and we both blurted, "No."

Jesse nodded, the hurt in his eyes growing, making him look around as though he suddenly didn't know where he was.

I blinked back tears. "How did you find me?"

He shifted his weight. "I had some help. Did a lot of asking around." He smiled. "I couldn't just let you go, you know. But it looks like I found you too late. I can't make you come back, but I just needed you to know that, you were my whole world. Still are." He didn't even flinch as he said it. There was no hint of a lie that I could see.

He was good. I told myself, *he must've watched a couple of chick flicks to come up with that line.* Yet I found myself aching, being torn away from the bitterness and anger I felt—because the idea that he'd do that for me was sweet.

I felt a strange disconnect from my body. Memories of the good times danced through my mind, of watching western movies together, laughing till we cried as we'd mute the sound and make up our own ridiculous dialogue. Those nights had been such fun. There were the times where he'd hold me so tenderly and tell me secrets, things he'd never shared with anyone. About how his father had beaten him, something I'd never have suspected of Mr. Evans. Sure, I'd overheard him tell Jesse that he was lazy and incapable of doing any real work, unlike his older brother, but I'd never thought he'd go that far. As Jesse described watching his blood drip from his eye and onto the cracked linoleum of their kitchen, I saw what had been hidden behind their oak front door. "That's why I need you, Emily," he'd said. "You're my escape."

He'd needed me.

And it had been so romantic running away together. I'd slept on his shoulder on the car ride to California as we listened to oldies on the radio. It had been us against the world.

Doubt fluttered more and more through my mind like passing shadows. I wondered, had I made a mistake? Had I given up on us too quickly?

Anger radiated from Rain ever so slightly. His voice was dark yet gentle, which was more terrifying than if he'd shouted the words. "You need to leave now."

There was silence. I realized Jesse was waiting for some sort of response from me, but I couldn't speak.

Jesse looked away, looking as though he might turn to leave. "Okay. I'll go." Then he whirled on me, his voice cracking as he spoke. "But how could you just leave like that?"

Guilt and shame consumed me, stabbing my veins. I'd hurt him. I'd hurt him so much. I was so wrong to cause him such pain. As he'd said the last time I'd tried to leave, I was just as cruel as his father.

Rain said with total, deadpan sarcasm, "Yes. How terrible of her to leave after you pushed her down the stairs."

Jesse looked betrayed. "You *told* him that? Who else did you tell?"

I couldn't see for the tears now. I shouldn't have told anybody. It wasn't anybody else's business. I quickly said, "Just Ra—" I caught myself, "Rick. I'm sorry. I'm really sorry."

Jesse's face was red now. Embarrassed. I felt so bad I'd embarrassed him and I was terrified at the thought that he might hate me. I didn't want him to hate me.

Fury now radiated from Rain like a fire, growing more intense as it drew nearer to the surface. His arm tightened around me as though he feared I might fall over the edge of a cliff.

Before either of them could say anything, I said, "I shouldn't have hurt you like that," I glanced at Rain, "like this. I'm so, *so* sorry. I didn't handle things right."

Rain looked at me in shock. "You don't owe him any apology."

Tears spilled down my cheeks. "I do. I do. I handled things wrong."

"*What* did you handle wrong?"

"I shouldn't have hurt him like that—like this," I moved to push Rain away, but he wouldn't let me. He could see a cliff that I couldn't, and he wasn't about to let me fall. I went on. "I've been cruel."

Jesse wiped his face with his sleeve. "You know, maybe a few months ago... ten minutes ago... I would've forgiven you. But this, now..." He shook his head.

My whole body turned to stone. I couldn't even cry anymore.

Rain's voice deepened into a tone I'd never heard before. "*What?*"

Jesse glanced at Rain as though he were nothing more than a statue.

"Just look at this! Look at what you're doing! After all I've done for you, after all the stuff I got you—"

Rage filled the air like a fog.

"—you just can't be pleased, can you? Nothing is good enough for you. You're just a spoiled, pampered, little—"

Hate now formed in the fog like dew drops, so much so that I actually turned my head toward Rain. His eyes were vivid, bright, cutting through the darkness like lightning.

"—after all I've gone through to find you. You're going to regret this when you realize that nobody—*nobody*—will ever love you like I did—"

Nothe's words flashed through my mind, *When you really love someone, you know you have something special, and to have the audacity to believe you're the only one who can see that is sick.*

"—because you're used up. People can see it. They all know the kind of girl you are. I've been looking for you for months. Who else would do that for you, huh? Who? Nobody. Not even your *dad*. You should've killed yoursel—"

Vengeance burst through the air, devouring it as though the hate-filled dew drops had set off a bomb. It was the only warning Jesse had before Rain had him pinned against the wall by his neck, his feet dangling above the ground. Rain's hand tightened around his throat, making Jesse's eyes bulge. Part of me almost rushed to make Rain stop— the part Jesse had so effortlessly romanced.

Almost.

But the other memories had come back. The memories that showed that those sweet, romantic moments were only the highlights. The rest of my time with him was spent feeling worthless, unless I was being used in the way he wanted. He made me feel stupid and empty. He made me feel as though I was broken beyond repair.

This kept me from moving, and this part of me found something satisfying in seeing sheer terror in his eyes, in watching him kick and squirm and feel helpless, his life out of his control—the way he had made me feel.

Jesse clawed at Rain's fist. He swung wildly at him, but to no avail. His eyes rolled around in his skull, and it became clear—

Rain had no intention of letting him go.

He was going to kill him.

I was not proud of how long it took me to finally say, "St-top it." And when Rain wouldn't listen to me, to finally yell, "Rain, stop it! Stop! *Put him down!*"

Rain looked over at me. Jesse dropped to the ground, coughing and spurting, gasping desperately for air. He tried to stand, but fell over.

He couldn't go anywhere. He couldn't speak.

I stepped toward him, my fists shaking. "It was you. *You* are the one who was cruel. You tore me apart. You stole years of my life away. I ran to get away from *you*. I wouldn't have, but you are just... a truly *terrible* person." I felt a surge of renewed strength—strength I had lost so long ago—and felt a deep, unreachable wound begin to truly heal. Seeing the truth with clarity, I finally declared, "*You* are a monster."

Jesse struggled to his feet and stumbled off, vanishing into the night without looking back. I wasn't sure if he'd even really heard me, but still, I felt better. As much as I could in that moment.

Rain breathed heavily, fighting to gain control over his emotions. I could feel how upset he was, ashamed. He pulled off his wig and ran a hand through his hair, refusing to look at me. "I'm sorry, Emily. I'm so sorry I put you through that. I shouldn't have..."

I was tormented by conflicting emotions. I wanted to comfort Rain, but part of me was horrified. I was afraid and disturbed by this side I had just seen of him, but even more, I was sickened by the little piece of darkness that had appeared in a small corner of my mind, the piece that had been fine with what Rain had done and regretted seeing Jesse walk away. It twisted my stomach into a horrible knot.

I pushed myself away from that place. I focused on Rain and the pain he was feeling, on what I knew and felt toward him. I knew death had been what his people were built for. I knew there was so much of his past I didn't know and could never understand. He'd had to overcome so much, and the fight continued every day.

And the moment he'd cracked, he'd been defending me.

No one had *ever* stood up for me. Ever. Not one person. In that moment, I knew. It wasn't just a suspicion or a rush of emotion. I knew it.

I loved him.

I went over to him. He flinched as I touched his shoulder. "Rain," gently, I turned him to face me. "Rain." I looked him in his eyes, my own filling with tears of gratitude. Gratitude that he'd found me. Gratitude that he'd stuck around. Gratitude that he was there, standing in front of me—that he was willing to fight for me. "Thank you. Thank you so much."

He looked shocked.

I went on. "No one has ever done that for me before."

"You mean," he raised an eyebrow, "no one has ever attempted to murder someone for you?"

I laughed a little through my tears. "Well, there's that. That's definitely a first. But, no. Seriously, no one has ever stood up for me before. I can't tell you... there aren't words... I can't tell you how much that means to me."

He brushed a loose strand of hair out of my face. "I will always stand up for you, whatever the monster may be. I'll always be here for you. I promise."

I threw my arms around him. He held me tightly, his arms strong and comforting. I breathed in the scent of him, orange blossoms with a tinge of sweat from his performance. I felt safe. Despite the fact that Jesse now knew where I lived and I would have to move somewhere else, I had Rain. I knew, as long as I had him in my life, I would be okay.

I never wanted to let go.

HIDDEN TRACK:

THE DEVIL AND DARKNESS

Meanwhile, waiting for Jesse

Within the dim glow of a street light, Thipka leaned against the cold brick of a cheap motel, where the pavement was stained with who-knew-what and the air smelled like stale cigarettes. His eyes glowed beneath the shadow made by his top hat and a vicious grin curled across his face. He watched as the black Ford truck pulled into a parking spot nearby. Jesse lumbered out of it. He sniffed and wiped his face. A bruise was appearing around his neck and he'd been crying. He'd actually been crying. Thipka found that pathetic and satisfying. He almost pitied him.

Ha! He thought to himself. As if he could pity him. There was no room for even the temptation of pity. He saw through Jesse—saw that his soul was rotten. It was like staring into a black hole, which was unsurprising. He was one of *those* people, the kind that drained people of their light without giving any back.

The man had tried to keep Emily in a little box, isolating her from her family, shattering her self-esteem till she thought he was all she could have, imprisoning her in her mind with walls of guilt and shame.

Now, Jesse had been slighted. She'd broken free, and he was about to carry out an ugly vengeance.

Thipka remembered it from before.

Time had thought to best him, but it had neglected this key piece. It had left Jesse vulnerable to his next move, one that he'd been planning so carefully for over a century.

And it was a delightfully wicked one.

Thipka's soul filled with an almost gleeful triumph as he stepped forward, the fire in his eyes burning through the night. He knew Jesse felt his presence before he saw him, for the thrill Thipka felt at this hunt, his rage, his thirst for vengeance—all of it swarmed around him like a hurricane. He could sense Jesse's growing unease, and when he finally looked up at him, his eyes widened in horror.

A dark giggle slipped from Thipka. *He should be afraid*, he thought. *He should suffer. He should regret that he lived through birth.*

Jesse's expression turned to one of feigned indifference, but with several glances at Thipka, he quickened his pace toward his room. Thipka followed him, his grin spreading unnaturally wide, showing far more teeth than any human smile could show. He felt Jesse's terror increase with each glance. He could almost hear the frantic beat of his heart—a heart crying out moments before it stopped.

Jesse fumbled for his wallet, pulling it out of his back pocket before dropping it. As he bent down to pick it up, Thipka stretched an arm across the doorway. Jesse nearly bumped into him as he stood and jumped back a step.

With a politeness stained with irritability, Jesse asked, "Can I help you?"

Thipka continued to stand in the doorway, his grin unflinching, his red eye burning and unblinking, not saying a word.

Jesse shifted his feet. "Is there a problem, sir?"

Thipka didn't move.

Jesse tapped the key card to his palm and then looked at it. "Whoops. It looks like I've got the wrong room." He gestured with his thumb toward the office. "I'd better get this worked out."

As he turned away, Thipka leapt upon the wall, scurrying over the bricks, his neck twisting at odd angles so his grinning face remained fixed on Jesse. Jesse cried out, letting out a stream of curses as he dashed toward his truck, dropping his keys as he struggled to open the door. Thipka leapt from the wall and slowly rose to his feet. Jesse panicked and bolted across the parking lot into the shadows.

Thipka followed. He crawled over the walls of buildings, guiding the vermin to the place he wanted him to go, remembering the news article from before. Now, an innocent person would be spared and an evil one would die.

Jesse tried to open locked doors to closed businesses, his eyes searched the empty streets for passing cars. He tripped over a trash can in an alleyway, clutching a stitch at his side. Thipka could feel Jesse's terror cutting through his mind, making him stupid like a hunted animal. Thipka dropped down from the building beside him. Jesse grabbed the lid of the trashcan and swung it at Thipka with everything he had. Thipka blocked it with his robotic arm, ripping it from him with ease and tossing it aside. Jesse stumbled backward, exhausted. He screamed at Thipka, "*What do you want from me?*"

Thipka wasn't masking his voice anymore. He wasn't pretending to be human, however much he might look like one. This night, he was embracing the monster. His true voice echoed through the night—deep, off-tone, like bubbling ink, his grin growing wider. "Vengeance."

Jesse's face turned a shade paler, his expression one of pure terror.

"Justice."

Jesse shook his head.

"For what you've done. And for what you were about to do."

Jesse turned to run again. Thipka caught him, threw him to the ground and stomped on his femur. A crack resounded off the alley walls and Jesse's scream for help choked out, his agony leaving him without a voice. Thipka could smell the blood. The bone had pierced his skin.

Thipka hissed, "Now you *really* can't get away."

Footsteps revealed the innocent person turning down the alleyway. Thipka twisted his head backward at them, their figure a silhouette in the shadows. Jesse tried to scream for help, but it was difficult to hear over Thipka's off-toned screech. The person fled.

A foreign feeling of terror, rage, and hunger filled the air.

It was there.

It'd found them, just as Thipka had known it would.

Thipka's face glowed and shimmered as he returned his focus to Jesse, shifting in small fragments like luminescent sand. "You tore her to shreds." The grains of sand settled, revealing a smiling face that was something born of the cruelest dream, the skin violet, torn and full of scars. The left half of it was gone, nothing but skull and metal. "Now you will know what that feels like. You will never hurt her again."

Thipka then, quite simply, walked away.

Behind him, he could feel the fear increase. The hunger closed in on the darkness, filling it with an insatiable emptiness.

He looked behind him. Eyes crawled down the side of the building, descending toward Jesse until his scream was cut short.

This sight gave Thipka comfort as he turned the corner—estimating that a brisk walk around the block should do it—because now, Jesse couldn't hurt her anymore. She would never have to see him again. He had received his overdue reminder of the meaning of helplessness, of despair. Of years of life stolen away.

Though the war with Time was not over, he had won this battle. He told himself with a level of confidence he hadn't felt in a while, *Time will not win.*

He stopped as he heard sirens shatter the stillness of the streets. He didn't have time for a whole walk around the block, this would have to do. He turned around and made his way back to the alley. Peering down, he could see that Jesse was very dead. It had been enough.

Thipka pulled light from the particles around him and sent it down the alleyway, turning the shamonster and Jesse's corpse into a cloud of blood and dust.

TRACK 3
IN BETWEEN DAYS

I was an absolute wreck all that day at work.

Rain and the gang had left early that morning and were out saving the world. My thoughts had become a garbled blob of stress that would occasionally burp out something coherent and then jump away from it, such as, *Rain better come back.*

He had to come back. That was all there was to it. I couldn't imagine —I couldn't *think*—of what would become of the world if he didn't.

On top of this, I was petrified for myself. I didn't want to return to my apartment at the end of the day because *that guy* knew where I lived. I needed to move. I needed to move somewhere far away. Spain, maybe? Maybe Rain would go with me. Nothe said he liked Barcelona. Maybe Nothe would go with us, too. Maybe we could all live in a haunted castle. That would be fun. We could adopt a dog. We could name him Scooberto and buy a van and solve mysteries.

Assuming Rain made it back. Which he would, because that was the way it was. I didn't make the rules.

The next day wasn't any better.

The day after that was even worse.

I hadn't heard from anyone at all. They shouldn't have been gone so long. It was only a six-hour, round-trip drive.

They were dead. I was sure of it. They were all dead and the world was going to end.

I threw up all day at work. Every time I darted to the bathroom, I spent a solid five minutes bawling hysterically. I tried to hide my swollen, bloodshot eyes and smeared mascara by plastering on a happy face, but apparently I couldn't hide anything. Marie finally sent me home, where I did nothing but sob through *Back to the Future* while eating a can of olives and a carton of chocolate ice cream.

My hysterics were eventually interrupted by a very loud knock at my door. The blood drained from my face and solidified in my gut.

I heard it again, louder this time.

It's him, I thought, my heart ready to burst out of my chest and flee through the back window, *It's that guy.*

Maybe if I stayed perfectly still, he'd go away.

The knocking threatened to break down my door. "C'mon, Emily!"

It was Nothe.

I jumped up, opened the door and froze. Nothe's hair was a mess. Dark bags hung under his eyes. A deep sadness emanated from him, though I could sense he was trying to control it.

I threw my arms around his neck, sobbing. I could only squeak out a whisper, "I'm so glad you're okay."

He tried to pry me off of him. "Don't—don't do that."

I gave him one last tight squeeze before letting go, wiping my gross face with the inside of my shirt.

Nothe grimaced. "Ew."

"Where's Rain? Is he okay?"

Nothe's expression darkened and my soul followed, but before I could say a word, Nothe said, "I need you to come with me."

I couldn't get my thoughts to align with his words. "Rain—"

"That's why I need you to come with me. Now." He took my arm, dragging me out the door.

"Wait—shoes—I don't—"

He threw me over his shoulder, closing the door behind him. "You don't need shoes."

He practically tossed me into the passenger seat of his truck. I demanded as we drove away, "Nothe, what's going on? Is Rain..." I couldn't bear the thought enough to even form the words, "Is he..."

"He's alive," answered Nothe, his voice dripping with irritation. "This wouldn't be so urgent if he wasn't." He swallowed, his eyes glued to the road. "The battle at the box... it didn't go very well. That's kind of an understatement. We, uh... we lost."

My heart sank. My body, the world, time itself—it all disappeared. I couldn't feel anything. "What?"

"We failed. The signal... it was sent. It'll take about seven years to get there," he snorted. "It'll take that long to get there, and yet there is nothing we can do about it. They're coming. As soon as they know this planet is habitable..." He shook his head, weariness and defeat etched deep in his eyes.

I searched my mind. "What about the portal? The one that brought you and Rain and Thipka here? Can't we use it to get to Thera? To beat the signal? Destroy the receptor or whatever? Or something? *Anything?*"

Nothe glanced over at me. "Maybe. But only Thipka knows where it's opening up and he's disappeared. We have no idea where he went."

I heard the words. I understood what they meant. But my brain had found them all so ugly and horrible that it decided to ignore them. It had to. A good look at those words might make it implode. So I blinked them away.

"But that's not what I'm worried about right now," Nothe continued. "The world can wait. I'm worried about Rain. I just—I need you to talk to him. The battle... it was bad. And he's not quite so optimistic about... well, anything. You need to talk to him."

I was baffled. I didn't have any words of wisdom, I was an idiot. What could I possibly say to help him? "Okay. But, uh, what do I say?"

"Anything."

"Good, good. That narrows it down. Will he even want to talk to me?"

Nothe's grip tightened on the steering wheel. "Just... do it. Please."

We rode the rest of the way in silence. I was terrified to ask Nothe for further information about what happened and spent the whole time mustering up the courage. My head spun with panic as Nothe parked the truck in the driveway, and I forced myself to say, "Nothe, what happened at the box?"

He shook his head and sighed. "If you really want to know, I'll just show you." He held out his hand.

I hesitated, remembering the last time I was with Nothe and curious about things. I braced myself for the worst, then took his hand.

TRACK 4

I WILL FOLLOW YOU INTO THE DARK

As Nothe downloaded his memories into my mind, I found myself sitting in the passenger seat of Rain's Infiniti. Only, I wasn't me, because I was much taller and in a foul-and-devastated mood. Nothe obviously wanted to hide his emotions from me as best he could—as usual—so, those feelings quickly vanished. However, I was sure they had stemmed from the stony look on Rain's face and how he refused to acknowledge that anyone was sitting beside him.

Bill, Chuck, and Steve were squished together in the back seat, riding in nervous silence and bulletproof gear. A glance through the side mirror showed Thipka following close behind them on his motorcycle. Nothe's focus was mostly on the road ahead of them, which cut through the fields toward the farmhouse that harbored the monsters. Its windows loomed ahead, dark and wreaking of tragedy, even in the daylight. Nothe blinked.

That was all it took. He blinked and there was a man standing in the middle of the road. He had not been there before, or at least, Nothe hadn't seen him there before. And judging by the startled yells and cursings that erupted from the back seat—and by how Rain slammed on the brakes, throwing everyone forward as the wheels skidded to a stop—neither had anyone else.

It was The Prophet.

Rain and Nothe exchanged a look—the first time Rain had acknowledged his existence the entire car ride there—then the two of them got out. Thipka was already on the march toward him, fists clenched, though his sad eyes held an unsettled look beneath their determination. The Prophet nodded a polite greeting to each of them, but then his brown, shimmering eyes fixed on Thipka. He shook his head. "What are you doing, Thipka? Didn't you hear a word I said?"

Thipka didn't reply.

The Prophet looked at the ground as if it were singing the saddest song. "You're messing with Time, Thipka. And Time is fighting back." The Prophet gazed back up at him, his eyes sorrowful and deep. It was as if one could see the entirety of the universe within them.

Thipka snapped. "Then *help* us! *Actually* help us!"

The Prophet shook his head solemnly. "You cannot win this." His voice drifted away, becoming an echo on the wind. *"You cannot stop them from coming."*

Nothe narrowed his gaze. "Whose side are you on?"

The Prophet's face melted away like water poured over a painting, and what was left in its place was a vast nothingness, a window into the dark void of space, a glimpse into eternity and the very fabric of Time itself. All Nothe could do was stare in awe as a deep seed of fear sprouted in his soul, tearing open a chasm in the pit of his stomach.

With an angry cry, Thipka unsheathed the sword in his walking stick and leapt at The Prophet, but as he struck him, The Prophet's form disappeared into a graceful cloud of winding smoke.

Thipka glared at the remains of the cloud, his expression faltering as he muttered, "I have to try... I have to try."

A cry of alarm erupted from the guys in the back seat of the Infiniti. The Prophet had somehow materialized beside the driver's side door, his face having returned to its rightful place. His eyes reflected the heartbreak that now emanated from Thipka as he said, "I know." He pointed toward the den of monsters and said in a voice loud enough for those in the car to hear, "Remember to stay in the sunlight."

At this, he was gone.

There was only silence in the Infiniti once everyone was back inside, staring off into nothing. After a few minutes, Bill broke it. "Okay. I don't even want to know what that was. I'm just going to say what we're all thinking.... Can I go home now?"

Nothe raised his eyebrows. "You're right. That's exactly what I was thinking." He turned to Rain. "Can Bill go home now?"

"You can just drop me off right here," Bill said. "I can walk the rest of the way back. I just follow this road until I get to As-Far-Away-From-Here-As-Possible, right?"

Chuck looked at him, appearing to be very tempted to punch him in the face. "After all the crap you gave everybody about bailing on this?"

"Oh. Did it sound like I was talking about myself? I meant Steve. Steve needs to go home or he'll die."

Steve gave Bill a look that clearly stated that if he said one more word, he *would* punch him in the face. "You know what, Bill? I really don't appreciate your butt-cracks right now."

Nothe furrowed his brow. "Did you just say, *butt-cracks?*"

"Yeah. You know, butt-cracks. Like *crack*-ing jokes, but they're bad jokes. It's something my girlfriend's kids say."

"Mmmkay, sure. I see it. But you're an *adult*, so—"

Steve put a hand to his forehead. "Oh my gosh..."

"—it's really hard to take you seriously when you talk like you're five."

"I hate you both so much."

Bill blurted, "Oh, I'm sorry. Did that offend you? Would you like to leave? There's the door. You're more than welcome to get out. Home is just *that* way."

Chuck rubbed his temple. "Just... stop. You two are worse than my kids. Look, if we're going to do this, we need everyone on board."

Rain said, "He's right. There is no room for division or hesitation." He glanced at Nothe, then gave a very soul-piercing look at Bill through the rearview mirror. "Or cutting down each others' confidence."

Bill hung his head a little and turned to Steve. "Sorry. I don't really think you can't do it. I just don't want you to die."

Steve raised a confused eyebrow.

Bill waved this away. "Forget it! I try to be nice..."

Nothe threw up his hands. "Alright! So what are we doing?"

Thipka drove around the car on his motorcycle, turning down the farm road toward the monsters and the box.

Steve watched him. "We should probably go."

Nothe agreed. "Yeah, let's go."

After their panicked conversation, Rain studied everyone. "Are we sure?"

"Let's go! Drive!" Bill said.

They sped off after Thipka, following the trail of dust into the trees. The only sound within the car was of branches scraping along the outside. All eyes were glued to the windows. The very planet seemed troubled and forelorn. Steve remarked, "Geez, it's like... it's like the trees *know*."

Normally, someone would've given him crap for that comment, but they couldn't. Each one of them knew exactly what he meant.

Nothe thought he could see eyes in the trees, appearing and disappearing as they followed them. He hoped it was his imagination, but he knew better.

A high-pitched, inhuman scream rent the air outside and fear filled the inside of the car like a fog. A shamonster dropped onto the roof with a thud, its claws tearing through the metal to torrents of startled cursing.

Bill busted out his shotgun. He gave a warning of, "Cover your ears!" but left no time for anyone to actually do so before he shot through the roof. Blood and brains spurted over the windshield of the Infiniti as the shamonster's body rolled away. Rain swore as he swerved over the trail—or at least, that was what Nothe thought he heard, he wasn't sure because he was hearing everything as though he were under water. This was followed by underwater-angry-shouts as everyone yelled at Bill.

"Fine!" Bill shouted over everyone. "You know what? Next time I'll just let you all get eaten!"

Their arguing died as they saw it.

A crater.

A few trees at one side had been obliterated, leaving a halo of sunlight draped across the center. Of course, as cruel fate would have it, everything else was in the shade.

Rain parked the car next to the eight-ish-foot deep hole. An unassuming, black, metallic box about the size of a coffee table rested in the center in the sunlight. There was really no rhyme or reason to its shape. It was almost square, but yet, it wasn't. It was like an uncommitted art student's final project, not something that held the fate of the world.

Thipka appeared at Rain's window and opened the door. "What are we waiting for?"

But what Nothe wanted to know was how he'd made it to the crater without a scratch. The shamonsters had taken on the Infiniti, how had none of them taken on Thipka and his motorcycle? Or had they, and Thipka was just such a Rockstar that he and his motorcycle had won the battle?

Before Rain got out of the car, he turned to the others. "Remember the plan. Keep the shamonsters—" Nothe cringed at the word, "—from Nothe, Thipka, and myself long enough for us to destroy it. Don't get distracted by anything else or think you have to do more than this. This is our only job. Once the box is destroyed, run back to the car and drive away."

The men nodded.

No pressure, Nothe thought. *Everyone's just counting on you to blow this thing up before they all die. No big deal.*

Nothe and Rain exchanged a quick nod before bolting out of the Infiniti. After distributing weapons from the back to the others, the men of *Screaming Riot and the City of Warning,* featuring Thipka, prepared to charge.

The trees around them moved. Eyes appeared and disappeared within the leaves and bushes. Terror and unquenchable hunger bled from the shadows and shrill screams filled the air, screams that grew closer. A pair of yellow eyes fluttered out of the shadows, its presence shattering the world with inexplicable terror and rage, only to quickly turn and vanish back into the trees. Then there was another. And another. The growing dread from the men was palpable.

Thipka glared at the trees. "They're toying with us."

"Well, they need to stop," Bill said in a very nagging sort of way, though his AK-47 shook in his hands.

Rain closed his eyes. A soft light emitted from his countenance and with it came a renewed sense of courage and hope, pressing against the darkness and triggering fury from the beasts. The men straightened, their hands shaking a little less and their eyes fixed on the forest around them with renewed determination.

Thipka shouted, "Let's go!"

As they descended into the crater, the shadows of the forest came to life, seeping from the trees and across the forest floor toward them, filled with pairs of hungry, yellow eyes. A monster leapt from the tops of the trees with the howling scream of a possessed, murderous woman as it flew at Steve. Steve didn't move, only watched as his end drew near, terror having rendered him immobile.

Bill unleashed a storm of bullets at its head till none of it remained. Steve finally ducked out of the way as the corpse fell toward him, colliding with the box and knocking it to the side.

"*Look alive, Steve!*" Bill yelled.

Anger flashed across Steve's face, followed by a twitch of shame and embarrassment, then more anger.

The men rushed toward the strip of light that covered the box, then did their best to stay in it. Chuck let out a startled yell as something flew at him and more bullets mindlessly tore through the air, some of them actually hitting the thing and sending it back into the trees. Steve and Bill shot at the floor of shadows, turning it into a sea of red, the screeches of pain growing so loud that Bill's maniacal laughter was barely audible.

As they reached the box, Thipka turned, summoning light into his hands, causing the hoard of monsters to pause before he released it, turning a large number of them into a mist of blood. Chuck hollered, "Thanks."

Rain, Thipka, and Nothe surrounded the box. Nothe's stomach dropped as he realized it was humming. "Was it doing that before?"

Rain shook his head.

"Oh, crap."

"How long do you think it's been doing that?"

Thipka reached a hand out toward the box, his expression cold, his voice unwavering. "What does it matter? Let's finish this!"

Rain and Nothe followed suit. Nothe fought to drown out the sporadic shooting around him and focus solely on the particles that made up the box. He could see each one. He allowed his energy to pour from him, to reach the box, cover each piece, and commanded them to separate.

But the box resisted.

How? It was almost like it was *magnetized*, or something stupid like that. He tried harder. The metallic smell of blood and gunpowder overwhelmed him, threatening to send his mind back into his cage on Thera, trapped in chains. Sweat poured from his brow as he struggled to concentrate and remain in the present.

The pieces of the box began to pull apart.

In the distance, there was a scream. A human scream. And a shout.

He had to ignore it. They needed to finish this.

This was really, much more difficult than he'd expected. Thipka was more powerful than Rain and himself combined. Was he having as hard of a time? He glanced over at him. He was gritting his teeth. Actually, he looked outright furious. Okay. As long as it wasn't just him. Still, Thipka was making a lot more progress than either he or Rain. A solid fifth of his side was nothing but dust.

He found himself chanting Thipka's mantra in his head, *Save them, save them, save them.*

With a glance at Rain, it shifted. *Save him. Save him. Save him.*

Nothe was making progress. The box was disintegrating.

Then little lights began to dance just underneath the surface.

No, thought Nothe helplessly, *NO!*

The entire box turned into one gigantic lightbulb. Nothe could hear the shamonsters scurrying back into the trees, screaming.

Thipka shouted, "NO!"

When the light faded, the box exploded into dust on the forest floor.

Nothe told himself it hadn't happened. It couldn't have happened.

He looked at Rain, whose face was frozen and pale. Nothe couldn't feel any emotion radiating from him at all, which was more terrifying than if he were throwing a tantrum.

Thipka shook his head. "No. We made it in time. We made it in time.... *This was supposed to fix it!*"

Bill and Chuck were covered in blood. Nothe couldn't tell what was theirs and what was from the monsters. Chuck turned to them. "They got Steve!"

The words pierced Nothe. "What?"

This was all it took for Rain to turn into a big ball of light, the sand-like particles settling into a dark form. In a violet-navy-blue-ish blur, Rain stretched his arms out to an unnatural length, combining them with the weird thingers found in his wings. He took flight with such speed that he was gone before the last of his torn clothing had hit the ground.

Nothe was officially on the verge of breaking. It was incredibly unhealthy to shapeshift and take off like that. Rain hadn't given his body any time to recover from the transformation.

The monsters crept back in from the trees, a few leaping into their path to the car. Thipka, in his fury, pulled light from the air, formed it into a ball and threw it at the creatures. One jumped out of the way, but the rest dissolved into puddles. Shooting at the remaining creature, the men of *Screaming Riot* climbed out of the crater toward the car, Nothe leading the way. A yawning, unhinged shamonster face greeted him as he crested the hill, and with a flick of Nothe's fingers and a splash of grossness, the face was no more.

Nothe was drained as he reached the vehicle, feeling as though he were carrying fifty-pound weights on each limb. He could taste blood in his throat and his eyes felt as though they'd been set on fire. To his great relief, he found Rain at the car, crouching low as he fought off monsters with an AK-47. But he wasn't the Rain that Nothe was used to seeing anymore, he was the version that'd so quickly taken flight.

The *real* Rain.

Nothe knew that, to the humans around them, Rain's body would've looked like a really awesome Halloween costume. His arms and chest were bare and quite muscular. His wings were massive on his back and shimmered in the light that filtered through the canopy of trees, and a long tail had torn through his jeans. At the end of it was a large, three-fingered hand-thing covered in feathers. On his head were more feathers where hair should've been. His ears were long and skinny and would've extended above his head were they not fallen backward in a threatening sort of way.

But his face was pretty much, exactly the same. Maybe his features were a bit softer, the lines not quite so carved from stone. His eyes were slightly larger and more prominent, but it was Rain's face.

Nothe could've collapsed for the amount of relief he felt. Maybe this world was ending, but in comparison to the way things could've been, it really wasn't such a big deal.

Rain yelled at everyone to get in the car, using his real voice, which sounded as though the black voids of space had learned to speak. Chuck and Bill startled a little at the sound of it, though they'd heard it before. It didn't bother Nothe at all, of course. It was as familiar to him as the sound of raindrops pattering against a window.

Nothe jumped in the driver's seat. Thipka sent one last ball of light behind them, obliterating all but a few of the remaining monsters with it. Most of them were very dead, and that was a comforting thought. Thipka then abandoned his motorcycle and hopped into the passenger seat while Rain clambered into the opened back next to the battered, bloodied body of Steve. As the car accelerated toward the sunlight, a very disturbing sound resounded from the shadows. It was empty, tin-like, high-pitched, and off.

It was laughter.

The monsters were *laughing*.

TRACK 5

SLEEPING BEAUTY

O nce they were back on the dying grass of the creepy house and surrounded by sunlight, Rain dragged Steve's body out of the back of the Infiniti. Rain's feathers were disheveled and his eyes were drained of light, like he'd flown across the Pacific Ocean and hit a hurricane on his way. Steve was covered in blood, both Rain's and his own, most of it clotting around his face and neck, indicating that this was where the major wound had been. Rain had healed him, but he'd been too late.

Steve was dead.

Rain fell to his knees beside him and repeatedly tried to start his heart, but to no avail. He was gone.

Steve. He'd been one of the few genuinely good people. Nothe's heart filled with an all-too-familiar ache, one that never got any easier to bear. But as he looked into Steve's face, he saw a serenity there. Peace overtook him then, soothing the pain like a balm over a burn. He knew that peace. He knew Steve was speaking to him, letting him know he was okay.

Unfortunately, Rain was not as in tune with the dead. He couldn't feel that peace, and all of his walls came crashing down with a shockwave of heartbreak and anger. He ran a hand through the feathers of his head as tears streamed down his face. "It was for nothing. It was all for nothing."

Rain's tears weren't just for the loss of his friend, nor for their failure. His tears were for the friends around him, the ones left behind. Their numbness, their horror, the madness that was beginning to take root in their minds. For Chuck, who was pacing with trembling hands, and Bill, whose expression was blank, his mind lost in the whirlwind of what lay before him. Bill muttered to himself, "I told him to get out of the car. If he'd just gotten out of the car... it should've been me."

Neither of them would ever be the same. Rain knew it just as Nothe did. He could feel it and it was destroying him. How could they tell them just how pointless their sacrifices were? How could they tell them that the signal had been sent, that the world as they knew it would end?

Perhaps Nothe would've been crippled with guilt and shame if he hadn't been so gripped with fear for Rain. It bit his veins, tensing the muscles in his back and arms. There wasn't room for anything else in his soul at the moment. He'd seen where these roads had taken his friend before.

Nothe closed his eyes, listening—his soul speaking through the veil between dimensions to the Dimension of Light, where he was sure Steve would be, asking if he'd be willing to return. If he could bring him back, maybe that would give Rain some peace. Steve shouldn't have been far. It was pretty typical for the deceased to linger around the scene of their death, especially if there were friends nearby. He could sense his light.

He sighed and opened his eyes. Steve didn't want to come back. Nothe rubbed his face, disappointed but not surprised.

Finally, Chuck stammered, "So... the signal..."

Nothe looked over at Rain, who couldn't seem to tear his empty gaze away from a small rock in the grass. Neither of them could bring themselves to answer. He hoped crazy Thipka would blurt out the ugly truth, but Thipka hadn't left the passenger seat. Judging by the way Chuck collapsed to the ground with his head in his hands, the silence was more than enough of an answer.

With tears brimming his eyes, Bill said in a cold, broken voice, "Bring him back."

Nothe raised his eyebrows. "What?"

Bill cast him an unfeeling look. "Bring. Him. Back."

Nothe glanced over at Rain for help, but he was obsessed with that tiny rock. Nothe scrambled through his brain. "I... I can't. I'm sorry."

Fire flashed across Bill's face. "You have to. You don't understand... it should've been *me!*"

There was nothing but silence. Nothe explained, "He doesn't want to come back, Bill. I already looked. His soul is at peace."

Rain's eyes closed. More tears poured down his face, giving Nothe a flicker of hope. Chuck's shoulders relaxed a little. But Bill wasn't accepting it. "No. No. Don't you tell me that. Don't you *dare* tell me that. You dragged us here. You two dragged us here, and for what? For nothing! He died for *nothing!*"

Rain hung his head, despair and shame radiating from him, though Nothe could sense he was trying to control it. This pissed him off.

Chuck's voice rose, "We volunteered, Bill. You started it. If anyone dragged us here, it was you!" Chuck winced immediately after he said it.

Bill looked at them wildly. "No. No!" He leapt to his feet. "I told him to get out of the car! *I told him to get out of the car!*" He pointed a finger at Rain and Nothe. "It's them! It's their fault this is happening! If they weren't here, those monsters wouldn't be here!"

Nothe was ready to strangle him. "Are you kidding me right now?" He knew this accusation was absurd. This was simply the closest planet to Thera with life on it. Yet some of his words struck a fear he hadn't realized he harbored.

Chuck straightened, looking outraged. "How are you making that stretch? What is the matter with you?" But Nothe sensed it. Chuck secretly held the same fear.

Nothe exclaimed, "They don't even know we're here!"

Bill wasn't listening. He was beyond reason. "This is your fault! You owe us this! Bring him back! *Bring him back!*"

All emotion vanished from Rain. Age lines had made their early appearances around his eyes and his face was stone.

This terrified Nothe.

He knew it was wrong. Never once had he ever heard of it ending well. When a soul didn't want to come back, they did *not* come back. But Rain was sinking fast. He didn't know what else to do. Maybe if he opened up the way, Steve would change his mind. If he could just get him to come back...

That was when Chuck punched Bill. Bill threw himself at Chuck with a fury that completely caught him off guard, throwing him to the ground.

Nothe made his decision. "Fine!"

All commotion stopped. Bill looked at Nothe, his lip cut. Chuck wiped blood onto his sleeve. Rain broke his trance with the rock to cast him a confused look. "What?"

Nothe commanded Rain, "Start his heart. I'll open the door."

Rain was about to argue, but Nothe silenced this with a sharp wave. He knelt at Steve's head, noting that it shouldn't have been so easy to shut Rain down.

He held his hands to Steve's temples while Rain held his hand over Steve's heart. They exchanged a nod before Nothe closed his weary eyes, his vision slipping into Steve's brain and heart, finding the cathedral-like doorway.

Only it wasn't really a doorway, it was more like falling into a pool of water.

Only, it wasn't like falling, it was more as if the water was something still and upright—hiding between a wardrobe and the wall—that could be stepped through. And it wasn't Nothe's body that was stepping through it, of course, it was a portion of his energy, his light, his living soul. As he slipped through the doorway, he fell into a world somewhere between dreaming and awake, and pushed. He pushed to widen the gap between the wardrobe and the wall, but the wardrobe and the wall did not want to be separated. They fought against his energy, exhausting him.

As the gap widened, a bright light fell through the door. It was more brilliant than anything he'd seen in his travels, brighter and whiter than the sun reflecting off the snow. But, as the light poured through, something gathered at the sides of the opening. Shadows with snarling, greedy faces that moved, fighting against an unseen barrier, struggling to get through the doorway of light.

He issued the call. It wasn't a voice, it was a feeling, a nudge, a silent alarm, letting Steve know the door was open. He could see the outline of figures standing in the light.

The shadows pressed harder. The invisible barrier bowed, the distorted, yawning faces becoming more clear, looking like extras in a horror movie. Nothe grew more and more weary. He let out one last pleading call. "C'mon, Steve..."

From outside of the water, Thipka roared, *"What are you doing?"*

The invisible barrier holding the shadows back, ripped.

Nothe was thrown from the vision, his back slamming against the dirt and dead grass, his face wet with sweat and staring at a blue sky. Thipka had given him a very hearty shove, knocking the air out of him.

He could hear Bill. "They were calling him back!"

Thipka's eyes, nose, ears and mouth were bleeding. His body was breaking down from all the energy he'd spent killing monsters with light-balls and destroying the box, and the sight made his roar outright terrifying. "He's not supposed to come back!"

Everyone fell silent. Not just everyone, *everything*. Even the air had grown still. Nothe knew, in that moment, that Thipka should've knocked him over about five seconds sooner.

Nothe pushed himself up onto his elbows. Steve was sitting upright, holding up his hand and looking at it. He turned it this way and that, then flexed his fingers. He listened to his own breathing as he inhaled deeply, then exhaled. He inhaled again, then exhaled. He chuckled and said in a voice that was Steve's, and yet so very not Steve's, "Air. Breathing. Such simple things. You don't realize how much you'll miss them."

Chuck grew pale. "That's not Steve."

Not-Steve reached up and touched his face, then looked at the fresh blood on his fingertips, tapping and playing with the sticky consistency. He chuckled again, then rose shakily to his feet.

Thipka didn't hesitate. In a flash of movement, he had Not-Steve by the throat. Steve's eyes looked as though they were going to pop right out of his skull. Thipka growled, "You don't belong here."

Bill launched at Thipka, knocking him to the ground. Thipka let go of Not-Steve in a knee-jerk attempt to catch his fall. Nothe forced himself to stand, stars blurring his vision and threatening to send him back to the dirt as Thipka pried Bill off of him and punched him in the face, dropping him like a sack of flour and rendering him unconscious. Nothe turned toward Not-Steve, taking a few steps before collapsing to the ground as he watched him race away, disappearing into the trees. One glance over the group showed him that not a single one of them, not even Thipka, had the strength to go after him. They were all broken.

Well, on the bright side, Not-Steve had fled into the shamonster den. There were only two or three left, but still, he was sure to be really disappointed in the duration of his second chance at life.

Thipka struggled up from the ground, turning on Rain. "What are you doing? How could you let this happen?"

Rain's eyes lit up with rage. "How could *I* let this happen? This—all of this—is on you. You are the one who is supposed to see the future!"

"You insisted on waiting!"

"I only waited to get supplies. Had we not done that, more of these men would be dead! And you—you are supposed to be stronger than all of us put together!"

Thipka answered this with a swift punch to Rain's face, a punch from his metallic hand. A crack resounded through the air. Both Nothe and Chuck winced. With a caved-in cheek bone, Rain rose to his feet and swung at Thipka, who expertly dodged it, returning with a blow to Rain's ribs. They were both so drained, it was like watching ninety-year-olds brawl in a senior citizen center. Thipka had gotten in one good swing, but surely he couldn't get in another. Nothe thought, *Maybe it's best for them to get this out.*

Rain caught Thipka in the ribs, but unfortunately it was nowhere near full power and hit the side that was mostly made of metal. Thipka then caved in the other side of Rain's face, and this time, Rain fell to the ground, bloodied and defeated.

Nothe felt a stab of panic. "Okay, children, that's enough."

But that wasn't enough for Thipka. To Nothe's horror, Thipka used what little strength he had left to hold his hands out in front of him. Blood poured from his eyes as he pulled light from the air, turning it into a ball of sizzling energy—a small one, but enough.

Nothe threw himself in between Rain and Thipka, and the ball vanished. Thipka's expression fell, all the fight disappearing with it and his profound sorrow in plain view. There was no smile, no anger, no other mask to hide it. Heartbreak as deep and unsettled as the storm-tossed ocean clouded around him like a mist. "Rain is a fool."

"Yeah, I know."

Thipka's next sentence struck a nerve. "He doesn't deserve you."

All of Nothe's emotions fell into deep hiding. He snorted. "I know that, too."

Thipka stood there for a moment, then, trembling, turned toward the Infiniti as Nothe rushed to the aid of Rain.

TRACK 6

BOYS DON'T CRY

I sat there in stunned silence as the vision faded.

"We took them all home shortly after that," Nothe said. "We never found Steve. Bill won't speak to us. Thipka is... who knows where. And Rain... he's a mess. He can't shift back because his blood has already started to change."

My brain wasn't equipped to fully grasp what I'd just seen or heard. It wasn't even trying to rummage through files anymore. It'd thrown its hands in the air and collapsed at the base of my skull, saying, *Yeah, I just don't even know. Is there a manual anywhere on this?*

Nothe stared at the steering wheel. "I probably showed you too much." His voice cracked a little with a forced smile. "But honestly, it feels better to show someone."

When I could finally remember how to speak, I said, "So... the world is... ending?"

Nothe gave a small shrug. "I honestly don't know what's going to happen. All I know is, the Therans will show up, and it's going to be terrible. So, I guess, pretty much, yeah. Unless Rain's brother miraculously gets to them first, or, you know, some other miracle happens."

I knew I should probably feel a certain way about that. Actually, I was pretty sure I *did* feel a certain way about it. I wanted to cry. But I couldn't. I couldn't cry. There was something there, I just... I couldn't quite reach it. Was I angry? I should've been... and I was. I was very angry. So angry that... well, I couldn't quite feel it yet.

And I was afraid. Beyond afraid. Afraid for Rain. For Nothe. For my dad. For Marie and Anthony at the diner. For the band. For me. And even somewhat for Jane. But it was such intense anger and fear, it was like being burned. Not just burned, but *really* burned—on the tongue after drinking something scalding hot. All the nerves had died. It was too hot. Too much fear. Too much anger.

But I wasn't angry at Rain or Nothe. Not at all. They'd tried. They'd tried so hard. Risked everything. They'd done more than anyone else had, yet they blamed themselves. It wasn't right. I wanted to comfort Nothe and Rain, to help them, but I had no idea how. What was I supposed to do?

Nothe let out a sigh that seemed to carry the weight of the ocean with it. "Do you remember that time when I was like, not moving, and monsters were like, trying to eat us and stuff?"

I let out an airy, heavy-hearted laugh. "And you wouldn't get in the truck? No. That's not seared into my memory at all."

"Well, so—this one time, you and I were like, surrounded by monsters..."

"Uh huh."

"And I kind of collapsed and wouldn't get in the truck so we could drive away together."

"Is that so?"

"But I was very heroic and said you should leave without me."

"Is that what that was?"

"But I... I..." His gaze drifted away. "So, once upon a time, I loved someone and I never told them."

"Oh." That took a turn I hadn't seen coming.

"I let all of the moments pass and never told him how I felt. And I regret it. Every day, I regret it." Tears brimmed his eyes as emotion slipped through. "I regret it so much." He quickly blinked them away.

I shifted a little. "Do you still have these feelings?"

"Always have, always will. I'm cursed. But that's what I get for letting all the moments pass. Maybe things wouldn't have worked out. At least I'd know. At least I'd have tried. But... maybe it *would've* worked out. Now, I'll never know. Now... I'm in love with the man, and all the things that might've been. And I always will be. There is a deep joy there in the universe that I'm starting to realize I will never know. I had hoped, but..."

My heart was pounding now. How had I not seen it before? I was terrified to ask, but I had to know. "Is it... is it Rain?"

The look he gave me said more than words ever could. It pierced through my heart, leaving it broken and bleeding. He quickly wiped away tears. "I wanted to tell him so many times. But when you've gone through what we've been through, there are some things you want, but you just... you don't know how to have. And then I got too content with what we *did* have. And now it's too late." He nodded to himself. "Now I just want to see him happy. Finally, really, truly *happy*. The real stuff, you know? The kind that's good, through and through. And I would do anything to see it happen. He deserves it. He spends so much time bringing peace and-and happiness to everyone else while he's dying inside. All I want is for him to stop dying. To just be happy. At peace. Even if it's not with me."

I swallowed my own tears, along with the sudden fear and ache that had appeared alongside the vicious jealousy that filled me. I forced myself to say, "You could tell him, you know. I know he loves you."

"I know he does." He smiled grimly. "But not like that. You have no idea how much I absolutely *hate* saying this but," he took a deep breath, "I have never seen him look at anyone the way he looks at you."

I stopped breathing. I knew less of what to think about that than I did about the world ending.

"Anyway," Nothe said, "we need to go inside."

TRACK 7

PRAYERS FOR RAIN

When Nothe entered the house, he went straight to Rain's bedroom and forced his way in. I was following a short distance behind him, completely unsure of myself. Nothe said something, and then...

The voice I heard from the bedroom was *not* Rain's voice—not the one I knew. Rain's deep, melodic tone had been replaced by something even deeper, something unnatural—the voice from Nothe's memories. It was viciously unhappy, chilling the marrow in my bones. The feeling that bit the air was not something I had ever felt from the loving and optimistic friend I had grown to adore. Instead, I was consumed by a torrent of anger, the kind that reduces a full-grown adult into a cowering child. I stopped in the middle of the hallway and stumbled backward into the living room where I sat on the couch, clutching my abdomen in a protective way.

An argument ensued between Nothe and Rain in a language I assumed was their native tongue, the dark voice turning into a threatening, yet panicked, hiss. Then the anger-whirlwind shifted, picking up cold feelings of terror and despair before vanishing at the slam of the bedroom door, somehow leaving the entire house feeling empty.

When Nothe appeared in the living room, his golden eyes were hollow. "Don't leave. Whatever he says, whatever he does, don't leave."

He marched through the front door, the slam an echo of the one that had come from the bedroom.

I sat there, baffled. I forced myself up from the couch and down the hallway, the silence in the air weighing on me, making me feel as though I were walking underwater.

As I pushed the door open, I was hit with the musty smell of sweat and scabs mixed with a hint of fabric softener. The heavy curtains were closed, shrouding the room in darkness. Only the faintest glimmer of light seeped through the window, giving the illusion it was early dawn outside though it was early afternoon. I let the door swing the rest of the way open, the light from the hallway spilling into the room, and was startled by the figure it fell upon, the one sitting on the floor by the opposite side of the bed.

Ee-yyah! Wings! Big wings!

I forced myself to stand still and did my best not to gasp—my *best*, which meant some strangled noise slipped out. I knew I should've expected to see them, given the memories I'd just experienced and having seen them on Nothe before, but I... I totally hadn't. The massive wings were nearly as tall as me. I would've thought they were part of some sort of life-sized, feathered-gargoyle-esque Halloween decoration, something that should've been sitting on someone's front porch, but instead they were peeking over the top of an unmade bed and wrapped protectively around the creature they were attached to.

I took a single, tentative step into the room, looking over every other dark corner. There was a desk off to one side, covered in piles of papers, books, cups, plates, and clothes. The chair that belonged to the desk had been flung across the room—or at least I assumed it had been flung, as it lay on its side beneath a chair-sized hole in the wall. The closet hung open, spilling out clothes as though it had been eviscerated. Blankets that had been on the bed were strewn across the floor. But in all of this mess, there was no sign of any other living thing, no familiar shadow, just the wings.

I was overcome with a wave of the most uncomfortable feeling, like I'd mistakenly walked into a funeral where I didn't know the deceased nor a single soul in the room. What was I doing there? *I should leave,* I found myself thinking, *I need to leave. Right now.*

A thread of despair wove its way into the emotion, gradually winding deeper and more powerfully into my veins until it was difficult to breathe. As I fought to reason with these sudden emotions, I soon realized they were coming from the wings—from Rain.

Of course he wanted me to go away. This was the part of him he had *never* wanted me to see, the part of him he'd become stuck in because he had lost all hope. My best friend, who had refused to leave me in my darkest moment, had fallen into one of his own.

I balled my hands into fists and fought to separate his emotions from mine. I carefully entered the room, stepping over mines of garbage as I made my way around the bed. The despair grew more panicked, tearing at my heart like a desperate animal and veiling me deeper in shadow the closer I got to him. Tears spilled down my cheeks and I wiped them away, pressing through until I was standing directly in front of him. Though I couldn't really see his body, I could tell by his posture that his knees were drawn toward his chest, his shoulders slumped and his head down, hiding behind his wings. His appearance was so very... intimidating. I couldn't help it. Fear of him rippled through me, fueling the urge to walk away.

But stronger than this was the love I felt for him. It was very much there, deep and unshaken underneath everything else, and more powerful and sure than anything else in my mind.

Rain's wings flinched, closing more tightly around him. That dark, terrifying voice spoke in a near whisper. "Please, go away."

His words pierced me as more of his emotions were released with them, filling me with anguish, making me realize that the fear I felt wasn't just my own. More tears poured down my face as remorse overtook me. How could I have possibly been afraid of him? He was my dearest friend. I fought even harder to push his emotions away as I asked, "Would you leave me?"

For a moment, the only answer I got was the flexing of his wings. Then finally, "I wish to be alone."

"You would never leave me like this."

His voice grew irritated. "I don't *want* you to do what I would do."

The anger he held rushed over me. The way his body flinched at his own words, I knew he hadn't meant to send it out, but he was at the point of breaking and had lost control. Fleeting though it was, it was powerful enough that I couldn't breathe, and vivid enough that it was as though I'd actually set foot into his mind. I studied it, realizing the complexity of it. I tried to separate and identify each particle, sensing the clear shame of the loss of the battle, and the fear... the fear was overwhelming. He was afraid of the Therans, of the torment they were sure to bring. He would rather die than experience it again. But there was more than just that fear. There were layers to it. Pieces that I couldn't quite put my finger on since the emotion had fled from me before I could adequately capture it all.

There was also very distinct *pain*. He was hurt, feeling as though my actions lacked sincerity. That being here, I was just giving him what I felt I owed.

I was tempted to be upset about this. After everything we'd been through, did he really think my feelings for him were that shallow? That I was simply driven by a sense of duty? Sure, maybe I had been a little frightened at his real form—er, maybe more than a little—but I didn't run. I would never run. I was there because I *wanted* to be. I would never abandon him.

I didn't know how to say that, but I tried. "Rain... I *want* to be here. I'm not here because I owe you. I'm here because I care about you. I'm here because..." *How do I put this?* "...because you're my best friend. And I want to help." My irritation slipped through. "And just because I want to help the way you do, it's not because I *owe* you—even though I do—it's just because... you're so..." Man, I was terrible at talking. "You're just, so genuinely *good*. And there's just not a better example—to me—of how a person should be." I rubbed my forehead.

This had the opposite effect on Rain than I was hoping for. The storm around him grew more intense, more depressed. Still, when he spoke, he didn't yell. His voice trembled. "Please, go away, Emily. Please."

I began to doubt myself. Was Nothe sure Rain liked me?

I could feel the whirlwind threatening to drag him away, locking him in endless darkness. I wouldn't let it. I had to do something. I would do anything—*anything*—to help him. I swallowed every flicker of self-doubt I had, every particle of fear, my resolution taking over as I closed the gap between us, kneeling in front of him and reaching out to place my hand on his wing as I said, "No, I won't—"

The second I touched him, I gasped and pulled my hand back. The emotions beneath his skin burned me as though I'd touched a hot stove. I sobbed as my whole body was consumed by what he was feeling.

He'd failed. He'd taken up his axe against Time—he'd fought, he'd bled, his friend had died—and it had been for nothing. Thera would receive the information and they wouldn't hesitate. Though it would take them many years, they were on their way. He might as well have sent for them himself. He'd brought the forces of Hell upon planet Earth and her inhabitants... upon *me*. Visions swept over my mind of what they'd done to him, the memories he had become lost in—being bound in chains, helpless against their brutality. They laughed at the pain, the humiliation, the shame, the violation, the loss of dignity, the horror and terror, the waves of agony. They thrived on it. It fed their souls.

I couldn't bear the scenes. They were flickers, lasting only fractions of seconds but stung like searing blades in my mind—in *his* mind. He was stuck in a perpetual nightmare that haunted him whether he was awake or asleep. There was no escape. There was no escaping Thera. They were coming... they were coming...

And it was all his fault. He'd failed. He'd failed us all.

To make matters worse, *I* was there, seeing him like this. Not just an emotional wreck in his disgusting room, but like *this*. I was seeing him for what he really was, what he'd never wanted to be: a monster. He was afraid of me. Of what I would think. Because what I thought mattered. It mattered a lot. He couldn't bear to know what I thought of him as a monster, as a complete and literally-Earth-shattering failure. He couldn't bear it. He just wanted me to go away. Why wouldn't I go away? He vowed to murder Nothe for bringing me here. How could he betray him so horribly, again and again? He was *dead* to him. *Dead.*

As the feelings faded, I had no idea how Rain wasn't weeping there behind his wings. I couldn't seem to stop. The pain was so deep, it was more than I could bear.

And why did my opinions matter so much to him? That was ridiculous. It was just me. But if it would make him feel better to know what I really thought, if it could ease his pain at all, I was determined to let him know. I fought to regain my composure.

"Rain, it's not your fault." I wiped my face. "I don't blame you." I looked at his wings, at the spot where his head would've been if he'd let me see it. "Rain..." With trembling hands, I reached out to touch him again. I needed to get through to him somehow, even if that meant my soul catching on fire. I placed my fingers carefully on the edges of his wings, expecting unbearable agony but feeling nothing. He'd gained enough control over his emotions that I could touch him without falling apart. I slid my hands over the ridiculously soft feathers and attempted to pry his wings open, but to no avail. "Rain, please don't hide from me. Please. I don't care—"

His wings split apart, revealing two very annoyed and very familiar blue eyes that glowed in the darkness, his very thin and very tall ears having fallen back in a very threatening way. The rest of his face was hidden by two human-looking arms that were resting upon human-ish-looking knees. Below the knees, however, his legs did not look so human. In fact, they reminded me more of the legs of a lion, only instead of paws for feet, he had something that looked like massive, hairless... well, paws, but with what looked like retractable thumbs, like he could absolutely grab something with them if he were so inclined. They were paw-claws. *Plaws,* I decided to call them. Woven around his feet was his tail, with the massive, three-fingered hand-thing at the end. "Emily, *leave!* I do not want you here! Don't you *understand?*"

I looked into his eyes and said with all the force I could muster. "No!"

He furrowed his brow.

"I mean—no, I'm not leaving. I'm not going anywhere. Not until *you* understand. I don't blame you for anything. No one does. You fought an impossible fight. You *knew* it was impossible. You knew it and you tried anyway. You tried because you care more about this planet than anyone who lives on it. You are our hero, Rain, and we need you." I prayed, searching desperately for the right words. "Maybe... maybe the world is going to end, ya know? And maybe the past sucks." I thought about that for a moment. "Which is a tremendous understatement. And maybe, no matter where we go, whether back or forward in time, there's just... an ugly... blah-thing."

He let out a snort that sounded like a repressed laugh.

I pressed on. "But you need to know, Rain, that you saved *my* world." I shook my head. "Wow, that sounded really cheesy—but it doesn't make it any less true! And whatever happens to the world we're actually on, we have a better chance with you in it. And whatever is in front of us or behind us, I know I can face it, as long as you're on my side. What matters is this moment, right now. This…" I reached out and touched his arm, hoping some of what I was feeling would come through. "This moment… it's real. And it's what matters. If you feel like you're slipping, just, hold on to me. Hold on to me and remember that the past is over. It's over! And the future is just… whatever! You know? It's an idea. That's all it is. An idea. A big 'maybe'. The *biggest* 'maybe'. But this moment, this is what's real."

He raised his head from his arms, finally allowing me to see his face. It was far more beautiful to me than the one I'd seen nearly every day since my first evening at Bob's Club Festivus, because it was *his* face. This was the one that was real.

I loved that face. I really, really loved that face.

Rain's gaze fell to his knees, looking embarrassed and uncomfortable. Though the touch of my hand against his skin caused me no distress, I could still sense the storm around him. I wanted it to stop. I wanted him to feel safe. I wanted him to know that I meant what I said. That I wasn't angry. That I was his friend forever and that I cared, that I thought he was beautiful.

So I did something stupid. Something that I blamed on pregnancy hormones.

I reached out, cradling his face in my hand, and kissed him.

His lips did not kiss me back. In fact, he didn't move at all. I would've thought the kiss had done the opposite of breaking any sort of spell and instead, had turned him into a statue—that is, if the storm around him hadn't disappeared almost immediately. The air turned into normal air that smelled like feet and fabric softener. The room turned back into a normal, gross room. His skin was warm, his lips soft and slightly dry—the lips of someone who'd locked themselves in their room for an extended period of time—and all of it was perfectly devoid of any overpowering emotion. I held the kiss long enough for his lips to twitch, but it was in a very confused and lost sort of way, like he'd thought about kissing me back, but changed his mind around three or four times afterward.

I pulled away, surprised at myself and not completely sure of what I'd just done. The inevitable ramifications of my actions were hanging well outside the atmosphere of my reality, but they were falling fast and sure to cause total annihilation once they hit. Rain's eyes were closed, but then they slowly opened. We looked at each other with shock. Finally, he said, "Th-thank you."

Thank you? Really? I blinked. "Uh... yeah!" I smiled sheepishly and playfully punched his shoulder like a moron. "You're welcome, buddy."

If there was any way I could've possibly made the situation worse, I'd just done it.

He took his turn to blink and ran a hand over his head, pulling on an ear. "I, uh. I should... I need to shower."

I snort-laughed. "Yeah. You kinda do." That would've been a fine thing for me to say to pre-kissed-Rain, but my stomach sank and I worried that perhaps post-kissed-Rain might not have the same sense of humor about himself.

Thankfully, he smiled—sort of—briefly revealing canine and bicuspid teeth that were much more pointy than the ones that had belonged to the more human version of himself. "I'll, uh, go do that, then."

I was overcome with a sudden urge to crawl under his bed and die among the socks, but smiled anyway. "Okay."

He gestured toward the door. "Some privacy, please?"

"Right." I bounced up and bolted toward the exit. The consequences were burning through my reality-atmosphere now, twisting my stomach into agonizing knots and setting my face on fire. I knew, from that moment on, nothing was ever going to be the same. In a matter of seconds, I'd ruined everything.

As I reached the doorway, Rain called to me from the floor. "But don't..."

I stopped, resting my hand on the door frame as I turned back to him.

He looked up at me, his eyes brighter than they had been earlier. "Don't go. I mean, leave. Don't do that. That is if... if you don't want to. You can go if you want to, but you're welcome to stay if... if you have nothing else going on."

I felt a small sliver of hope. "I don't. I'll, uh, just be in the living room."

He nodded. "Okay."

I robotically made my way to the couch and collapsed on it. The bad thing about waiting for Rain to shower at his house was the fact that I couldn't scream into a pillow. I couldn't pace frantically or yell out loud at myself about how I'd just destroyed our friendship, nor could I end the madness with me crying into a carton of cookie dough ice cream as I watched a marathon of *Parks and Recreation*.

But as I heard the shower turn on, I did, in fact, hear something that was better than cookie dough ice cream. It was Rain, shouting with audacity at the empty bathroom, *"Thank you?! Really?!"*

TRACK 8

TONIGHT, TONIGHT

Rain entered the living room shirtless and wearing jeans. He was perfectly sculpted, just as he had been in his human form. However, his muscles were significantly larger, especially his chest—his chest was ginormous, putting Mr. Universe to shame. The scent of fresh orange blossoms on a springtime morning followed him like a heavenly, cloud-like cape. For the first time ever, I noticed what Nothe had told me about one of Rain's arms being a lighter color than the rest of his body. It was almost indistinguishable. It was a hint of difference, a suggestion. Had he not mentioned it, I probably never would've noticed it.

Rain was clearly more aware of it than necessary. His left hand rested over his shoulder as if trying to hide it. It was such a strange thing for me to see a strong, elegant creature, who was the living embodiment of self-confidence, look so truly vulnerable. Though he tried to stick out his massive chest and stand tall, his head was slightly bowed, and his wings draped around him as if he had to restrain himself from hiding behind them.

I wanted to leap up and hug him, but after the scene I'd just made in the bedroom, I knew better.

He looked at me, surprised. "You're still here."

"Of course I am." *I'm so stupid,* I thought. *I made things weird. Why did I make things weird?*

He made his way over to the couch and sat awkwardly, his massive wings not really fitting against the cushions. The most terrible, horrible silence fell between us.

I wanted to die.

Stirring in my thoughts was the knowledge that the world was ending, but that didn't feel real. In fact, it felt more like a *maybe*. It was so far away—so beyond my ability to comprehend. But if I couldn't make things right with Rain, then my world would truly and completely, absolutely and perfectly, totally and definitely *end*. For sure. No doubt about it. That was something sitting right in front of me, something that ripped at my heart, something that I could feel.

Rain smiled a little and shook his head. "How?"

That wasn't at all what I had been expecting him to say. "How what?"

"How can you even stand to look at me? Let alone *like* me, at all."

I also wasn't expecting that. "Are you serious?"

"I mean, just look at me! Or don't. Or, well, you already are. Looking at me. Still. For some reason. And I'm, well, *this*."

"You're a spaceman. I've known that for a while."

He raised an eyebrow. "Admit it. You thought I was going to be a Doctor Who sort of spaceman, where the oddest physical difference between the two of us was that I had two hearts."

Alright, he had me there. "Well, okay, sure, yeah, sort of. But you totally led me to think—"

"Yes I did." His ears fell and his head hung a little lower. "You should hate me."

I understood why he'd want to hide this from me. I probably would've done the same thing. How could I hate him for something I would've done? "But I don't."

"You have no idea what I've brought upon this planet. Upon you."

Alright. I'd had it with all the self-blaming. "It is *not* your fault, Rain." I looked away, gaining control over myself. "It's not your fault. It's not Nothe's fault, it's not Thipka's fault, it's not any of the guys' fault, it's just something that happened. You tried, but Time was literally *not* on your side. The Theran's sent the stupid box, they sent the monsters, they're the ones that are making all the horrible choices, not you. You can't control them. This is not on you."

He shook his head and rubbed his mouth. I realized just how much he'd needed to hear this—really *hear* it. I scooted closer to him, taking his hand. He flinched at first, but then let me.

"Hey." I held his gaze, his eyes full of all the emotion he was struggling to hide. "It's not your fault."

He looked down at my hand in his, then squeezed it, saying softly, "Thank you."

"It's just the truth."

He smiled, his words pained and sincere. "It's so much more." He looked up at me, and, hesitantly at first, he reached up with his free hand and brushed a strand of hair behind my ear, his fingertips lingering at my cheek. My heart beat too fast, my lungs forgot how to expand.

I loved that face.

Nothe burst through the door, and Rain and I let go of each other's hands. There was clear relief in the slump of Nothe's shoulders. "Oh, good," he said. "You got him out of his room." He glanced Rain over. "And to shower! You truly are a miracle worker. That's wonderful. Thank you. You're free to go."

There was a rush of annoyance and anger from Rain—the first emotion I'd felt from him since I'd kissed him. "No, she can stay. However, *you* are more than welcome to leave."

Nothe winced. I had a mind to gently call Rain out on his insensitivity, but then Nothe sighed, annoyed. "Fine. I guess she can join us in a round or two of the Oregon Trail Card Game."

This was a surprise, but I was good with it. "Oh, fun!"

Rain protested. "No! No—we're not playing that."

Nothe clapped his hands together and exclaimed as he crossed the room into the hallway. "Well, that's two against one! You lose, Rain. We're playing The Oregon Trail. Besides, you need to rest and recover and all that stuff."

"We clearly have different ideas of what 'rest' is."

Nothe chuckled, appearing with the card game. "No, we don't!"

I died of dysentery on my first draw, three rounds in a row. I couldn't prove it, but the way Nothe found it more and more funny each time, made me sure he somehow had something to do with it. Nevertheless, it was clear that Rain's spirits were lifting. Nothe was on to something. He'd just needed to get Rain out of his room.

NOTHE PULLED into the parking lot of my apartment and put his truck into park. We'd ridden the entire way in silence. I'd debated whether or not to ask how he was doing and see if he wanted to talk, but I was sure I was the last person he wanted to open up to. I unbuckled my seat belt and reached for the door handle, but the look on Nothe's face stopped me. His eyes were downcast, the hundred or so years of his life reflecting in the dark circles beneath them.

He took a deep breath, pushing away all of the bad feelings that had been so clear in his expression. "Well, have a good night."

I raised my eyebrows. "Oh! Uh, okay. Thanks. And thanks for the ride."

"Yep."

I hesitated before I opened the door.

"Don't worry about being in a rush," he said. "I know that particular door can be intimidating. Gotta work up the courage. Take your time."

I glared at him and got out.

"Wow! Look at you go! You're living proof that when you really put your mind to it, you can accomplish anything."

I continued my glare as I said, "Bye, Nothe."

He sped away as I walked up the steps to my apartment in my bare feet, his wheels squealing a little as he made the turn.

I felt horrible. I was causing Nothe pain. Did Rain see it? No. No, I was sure Rain was clueless. Whatever their problems were, Rain would not be so cold if he knew. And if he knew...

If he knew, he might choose Nothe.

My insides froze over at the thought.

That night, I brushed my teeth with a little more vigor than necessary, and later dreamed of Rain marrying a tree who had better hair than me. After their wedding, the world was obliterated by an angry Bruce Willis riding on the asteroid from the movie Armageddon. He drove the asteroid into the Earth on purpose. No one knew why.

●

I WAS at work two mornings later when I saw Rain again. Marie alerted me to his presence. "That guy you're obsessed with is sitting at table five."

My heart leapt into my head. I scanned the booths by the windows until I found him. He was back in his human form, his dark skin flawless, his black hair curling around his ears. He wore a long-sleeved, black shirt with the buttons undone near the top. Part of me missed what he would've considered imperfections. At the same time, I just really loved that face, however he chose to wear it.

Marie said, "I guess I'd better wait on him."

"Nah. I've got this one."

"But you've been working so hard, I can give you a break." She grabbed a menu and stepped toward him.

I caught her shoulder and seized the menu, which she refused to let go of. "I must insist."

"No, *I* must insist."

"No, really. *I* insist." I pulled on the menu until it slowly slipped out of her fingers.

I approached his table more breathless than I should've been after dashing across less-than-twenty-feet of flat tile. "Hi."

He smiled at me and my legs turned into blobs. When had I become so stupid? Oh, right. When I kissed him. This was all my fault.

He fidgeted with his fingers. "Hi."

"Hi."

"Hello."

I grinned stupidly. "Howdy."

He chuckled and gestured to the seat across from him. "Want to sit?" He answered his own question. "Right. You can't. You're working. Never mind." He ran a hand through his hair and muttered to himself, "Wow."

"Well, you know I totally would if I could."

"Yeah."

I gestured behind me. "Y'know, if Alejandro wouldn't yell at me."

"Right. Well, it makes sense that you'd want to sit, being on your feet all day."

I couldn't help but give him a curious look and wonder if he was feeling well. I was usually the awkward one. I nodded. "Sure. Yeah. It's nice to sit after... after a long, uh, day... but I haven't been here for very long yet, so..."

"Ah."

"Just an hour-ish. But that's still, you know... I guess, you'd still want to sit after that, ya know." Yep. There I was. I had regained the title of Most Awkward.

Silence followed. Terrible, terrible silence. It was only a few seconds, but it felt like a solid half an hour.

I remembered that I had a menu. "Well, here's your menu." He didn't take it. "If you want a menu."

He hesitated, reaching up for it and then deciding against it. "I... no. I don't think I can eat anything, honestly. Um..." He ran a hand through his hair. He looked so tired. And anxious. I swore I could feel his gut twisting and I could see sweat lining his brow. Maybe he really wasn't feeling well.

"Are you okay?"

He forced a smile. "I am. I'm okay. Just tired. Um," He took a deep breath. "I... I'm mostly here because I wanted to ask you something." His fingers shook.

"Okay. Anything."

"Right." He rubbed his wrist. "I was just wondering if... if you would care to go with me to the pier tonight. Or just... sometime. Tonight, maybe. Tonight would be preferable. There's this theme park there, with this Ferris Wheel that looks out over the ocean. I've never really been there, but I remember you saying that you like theme parks, so, I thought you might enjoy it, and be willing to go... with me... on a... on a..." I barely heard the word. He wasn't looking up at me anymore, he was fixated on his hands. Had he not so overemphasized the 'T', I wouldn't have known what he said at all and would've had to make him repeat it. "on a... daTe."

My eyes widened. My heart asked my brain, *Did I hear that right?* And my brain replied, *Yes, yes I believe you did.* They both proceeded to join hands, jump up and down, and squeal in a very girly way. But I managed to keep this contained so it only came out in an overenthusiastic, "Yes!"

He looked up at me in shock. "What?"

"Yes. I would love to go with you to the pier, on a date."

His face brightened, illuminated by that beautiful affection in his eyes and a genuine grin. "That's great!"

"That sounds like a lot of fun."

I could feel his relief, and even a brief rush of joy before he managed to contain it, which only added to my giddiness. Was he really that happy I had said yes? Really? About *me?*

He rose from the booth. "Okay, then!"

I couldn't stop smiling. "Great! I get off work at four, just, give me a bit to get home and get ready."

"Okay. Six o'clock, then?"

"Sounds great!"

As he went out the door, I swore I caught a glimpse of him skipping a little. I floated back into the kitchen where, from another world, Alejandro said, "About time!" followed by Marie taunting me with a cryptic, "Marriage leads to murder," but she was smiling. She was happy for me.

I couldn't stop thinking of that word—marriage. It wouldn't go away. It demanded attention. It stood front and center in my brain and danced around stupidly. It was stupid. I knew it was stupid. But still...

I pictured our own house. Just a small one. Elegant, yet nice and cozy. I imagined painting a room together. A nursery. What color would it be? Pastel blue? Maybe white with light pink decorations? Or would we go for classic, old-school *Winnie-the-Pooh* colors? Those could work for a boy or a girl.

I continued floating for an hour. Then another. I watched the clock religiously. It was 12:55 when the pervs came in for lunch. No rude comments from them could ruin my day. It was 2:34 when a little kid threw up in the booth. It was all good. I hummed as I wiped up the vomit his flustered mother had missed. I'd probably get sick in a couple of days, but that was alright, because it wasn't tonight.

The world was ending. But it was alright, because it wasn't ending tonight.

I had tonight.

It was 3:11 PM when Alejandro asked me to toss some boxes into the dumpster. I lifted the lid and dropped the boxes in when a foul-smelling hand covered my face.

The last thing I saw were clouds in the blue sky, happily swimming in the haze overhead.

TRACK 9

BURN

My eyes blinked open to fluorescent lights lining the ceiling of a sterile-smelling room. I was lying on my back with a screaming headache, aching joints, an absurdly dry mouth and an overwhelming urge to vomit. To my right were tables with computers and high-tech-looking equipment, tubes, and screens. None of the stuff was familiar to me, though it reminded me of Mr. Staker's science lab from my sophomore year in high school.

What was I doing there? Hadn't I just been throwing boxes away?

I looked down over my body and my heart seized up in panic. An IV was plugged into my arm, and an older woman with glasses and brown hair stood over my abdomen. My shirt was lifted over my stomach as she pressed a cool, slimy, metal wand against it. My brain scrambled to make sense of my situation as she said, "There is nothing abnormal about this fetus that I can see. She looks," she hesitated, "completely human."

She? I thought, my heart thundering in my head. *What is that lady talking about? She's not talking about...*

There was an image on a screen. An ultrasound. She was conducting an ultrasound. The little body and heartbeat on the screen was my child.

A stern, cold-yet-familiar voice said, "Hmm. Well, we'll see. We'll see."

I'd heard that voice before. I'd heard it everywhere and yet, somehow, *nowhere* all at the same time. Where had I heard that voice?

It clicked then. It was that guy from TV. I couldn't think of his name, but I could picture his insanely huge, yellow eyebrows, and very large belly. His hair was like a sad, used cotton ball on top of his small head. He'd claimed he'd twice been robbed of millions of dollars, though the security systems set in place showed it had been him who had made the withdrawals. But of course, it wasn't him. It was Rain. Rain had stolen his money and given it to the poor, like Robin Hood.

My panic turned to terror. Why was he looking at my baby?

All I could do was whimper. I tried to move, to bolt from the table, but my hands were stopped by the wrist. I was strapped down to the table like an unruly patient in a movie. I tried to wiggle my hands through the straps of the restraints.

Footsteps scurried across the floor and a man with white hair emerged from behind me. I watched, struggling against the restraints, fighting the fog of confusion and crying out, "Wait," as he pulled out a syringe full of a clear fluid that reminded me of tears.

My brain screamed, *NO! What is he doing?*

He injected the tears into my IV.

●

I WOKE AGAIN in horrible pain. My hips and shoulder blades were numb and stiff, like I'd been asleep on the floor for a very long time, and my skin was worn and sore, but none of this compared to the feeling of my body trying to split itself in two. I couldn't breathe to scream. Sweat beaded my brow and tears poured down my cheeks as I tried to grip my abdomen, but my hands were still bound to the table. I could hear people talking—the woman and the guy from TV. The guy sounded furious, but my brain was so shattered with agony that I couldn't focus on what he was saying.

The white-haired man appeared again, injecting more tears into my IV.

●

I AWOKE AGAIN, but I wasn't in a well-lit room anymore. I was stashed out of the way in what looked like a dimly lit storage closet that smelled like bleach, plastic, urine and blood. I was still strapped to the table, wearing loose-fitting scrubs that had been haphazardly put on. My insides twisted with echoes of the intense pain from before. My stomach was in angry knots with the worst hunger and nausea I'd ever felt. Tears had dried against my face. My back ached like it'd been kicked several times. I could feel sores where my body touched the table, which was pretty much all over.

After what felt like hours, I realized I'd been discarded. Thrown out with all the other used things. I was shattered and empty, though I didn't fully understand why. I just knew—it resounded through the broken remnants of my heart—that something terrible had happened, and I would never be the same. New tears streamed down my face, tears I couldn't wipe away. Maybe I wouldn't have even if I could. Because I knew it. I could feel it. I couldn't quite explain how, but I knew.

My baby was gone.

Why? Why had they taken my baby? What had I done?

I knew what I had done. This was the universe getting revenge for my mistakes. I hadn't suffered enough. No, I had to lose everything. Just when happiness was within reach, it had to be stolen from me.

It didn't feel real. It didn't feel like it was happening to me. I couldn't believe it, though my head ached like I'd been hit with a baseball bat and from the waist down, my body felt like it'd been crushed. But none of this pain compared to what I felt in my chest.

My baby had been taken from me. She was gone. Staring at the speckled ceiling, I slipped into despair, reaching depths I hadn't felt since that first night I'd met Rain. I was trapped in this room, a prisoner once again, robbed of every good thing that had bloomed from the ashes of my life. I thought of Rain, of all the beautiful things he'd brought into my world, of the hope he'd given me, of the date that I was sure would've been amazing had I made it home.

But if I were to let myself die now, *they'd win.*

That guy who'd shattered me, that celebrity who had stolen my baby, these horrible people... they'd win.

I couldn't let that happen.

Rage burned in my veins, spreading through me like fire. That light —the one that Rain had set alive within me—grew brighter with purpose. I couldn't give in to this. I couldn't let them win. I couldn't let myself die here, because the memory of my baby would die with me. I couldn't let Rain go. I couldn't let go of the hope he'd given me. Though my heart was broken and the pain of it weighed heavy on my chest, and though I had no idea what the future held, I was not going to die here, discarded like garbage under that stupid, speckled ceiling.

I pulled on the straps around my wrists. I focused on my right, straining against it. My skin turned purple, stretching and twisting until it tore. Blood seeped through the leather and I worked the blood over my wrist and hand.

There was a commotion outside the door. The sounds escalated from shattering bottles and things falling over to gunshots and screams. I pulled on my wrist harder, blood dripping onto the table and then the floor. A very masculine voice erupted in a cry of horror that ripped through my mind like a thousand dead hands before it was silenced in a gurgle.

My hand slipped through.

Beads of sweat poured down the sides of my brow as I started on the strap around my left wrist. My fingers were numb and kept slipping in the blood.

The door burst open. Light spilled into the room. I let out a scream and fought off my attacker the best I could, knowing it wouldn't do any good.

"Emily. Emily!" The stranger grabbed my arm with gentle force, holding me. "It's me. It's me."

I blinked, focusing on his face, his eyes vivid and blue. Something broke as relief overwhelmed me and I started sobbing.

It was Rain.

He undid the straps on my ankles and my other wrist, then pulled me into the tightest embrace I'd ever received in my life. His entire body trembled. He kissed my head, my cheek, and held me tighter still. I returned his embrace, knotting my hand in his hair, promising myself that I would never let him go. Ever.

Words tumbled from Rain's mouth. "I'm so sorry, Emily. I'm so sorry."

I wanted to ask what he could possibly be sorry for, but couldn't shove any words past my sobs.

Rain pulled away from me, cradling my face. "You're safe. You're safe now. I'm going to get you out of here."

He looked as though he'd aged twenty years. His hair was even turning gray. How long had I been out?

My brain was in a fog, but I managed to nod. "Okay."

Rain helped me down from the table. My knees gave out and I nearly fell over, prompting him to carry me. His shirt was stained with blood. In fact, he was covered in it. Upon closer inspection, I could see deep wounds in his shoulder and chest.

He'd been shot, and he wasn't healing.

"Rain—what happened?" My voice cracked. It was sore and hoarse.

"I'll explain later." His face paled. He was not okay.

"Why aren't you healing?"

He ignored my question as he rushed through the door and down a bleak hallway. I started to look over his shoulder to the end of the hall when he said, "Don't look that way."

I took his word for it. "Where are we?"

"In a rich man's private lab."

My heart ached, torn apart by rage and sorrow. I blurted the question that had been plaguing my mind since I had the sense to ask it, "Why?"

His expression was full of pain. "Because he thought your child was mine."

I could only stare at him.

It was my fault. It was all my fault. It was my lie.

But what else was I supposed to do? If I'd told *that guy* the truth... but at least maybe my baby would be...

Although deep down I knew I hadn't been far enough along for her to be alive, in a last-ditch grasp at hope, I asked, "My baby, is she...?"

Rain wouldn't look at me as he crossed the lab toward a door at the corner of the room. "I'm so sorry, Emily."

Fresh tears spurted to my eyes and I looked away. Rain exclaimed, "Don't look over there."

I glimpsed what he was talking about. There was blood all over the wall and at the base of it was the celebrity, his head twisted in a way that heads were not supposed to twist. That image brought back his name. Harold Grossman.

As Rain reached the doorway, three gunshots resounded through the room. Rain fell to a knee. His breathing stopped, his eyes wide with pain. I cradled his neck, my voice a screech, "Rain... *Rain!*"

A voice spoke, a familiar voice that was devoid of the kindness it once held, "Funny. I thought you were supposed to be immortal."

It was Not-Steve. Rain whispered to me, his tone pleading, "Run."

I couldn't do that. I would not abandon him. I would never let him go again. "I'm not going anywhere."

"Stop that," Rain wheezed. Panic that was not mine rushed through me. Panic, terror, despair, affection, and a glimpse of something bright and beautiful and warm in the midst of it all—a whirlwind of a thousand heartbreaking emotions burst from Rain like a supernova. "I will not let you die!"

There really wasn't time to argue.

Shakily, I rose to my feet, ready to fight the gunman to the death. Rain forced himself to stand and gave me a gentle shove, my unstable body plopping right onto the ground. He stepped in front of me and turned to face Not-Steve. I could see the three wounds in Rain's back. He was bleeding profusely, and again, the wounds weren't healing. I felt like I was falling through the floor in a very bad way. Why weren't they healing?

Glancing down at me, Not-Steve addressed Rain, "Looks like it's just you and me." He added brightly, "You probably have a better chance at winning without her—quote-unquote—'help.'"

Rain pulled out a knife. Was that all he had?

"Ooo," taunted Not-Steve, "I guess I'd better put my gun down."

He moved as though he were about to put his gun on a table. He smiled. "Just kidding."

Rain wobbled a little as he stepped forward, not saying a word.

I had to do something. I looked around for anything that might help and saw a gun laying beside Harold Grossman's gross body.

Not-Steve smirked. "The great speech-maker is speechless."

I dragged myself toward Grossman, just a little at a time. He was about eight feet away. I just had to make it eight feet.

Rain said something I didn't hear, but it made Not-Steve laugh. "That was good! Thank you. Laughing is so nice. That's one of those things I really missed. You really take laughter for granted when you're alive. There's something so satisfying in the way your stomach muscles tighten up, and the air moves through your lungs, and that feeling you get in your chest." He took a deep breath. "It's magical."

I slid a little closer. I'd moved about a foot.

Rain took another step forward, the color draining even more from his face. He already looked dead. I moved faster.

Not-Steve continued. "That fat guy—he'd make all of these jokes. They weren't funny."

I'd made it another foot.

The wall in front of me exploded with a boom. I let out a scream and cradled my head in my arms. Not-Steve said, "Nuh, uh, uh! I'm watching you, Emily."

Another gunshot went off as Rain lunged, knocking Not-Steve to the ground. Shaking all over, I forced myself to recover from the shock. *Get the gun! GET THE GUN!*

Rain let out a cry of agony as Not-Steve hit him in one of his many open wounds.

My hand slipped on blood as I seized Grossman's gun with the other.

A weakened Rain grabbed Not-Steve's wrist, but a knee to another wound loosened his grip.

Leaning heavily against the wall, I climbed to my feet.

It happened with the speed of a glance.

I heard it before I saw it. I heard the air rush from his lungs. I heard myself scream his name, but I felt like someone else, someone watching from somewhere far away.

Time had slowed to a crawl. *Don't look,* I told myself, tears spilling down my face and my eyes unable to look away, *It won't be real if you don't look.*

I had a brief flashback of Mr. Staker standing by a skeleton in my human biology class. He spoke about the major vein and artery that connect to the heart, how they run along the spine and are so full of blood that to nick one would be like cutting open a garden hose full of water. A person would bleed to death in a matter of seconds. "So, don't do that," he'd said.

He had been right.

Blood gushed like a fountain around the blade that stuck out from Rain's abdomen.

With a heart full of rage, in the midst of my scream, I turned the gun on Not-Steve. His eyes met mine, his expression of victory turning to one of surprise.

I pulled the trigger. Again and again, and one more time just for good measure. He staggered backward before falling to a knee, then to the floor. His legs and fingers twitched for a moment, then stopped. The surprise was frozen in his cold, brown eyes.

I just killed somebody.

I dropped the gun and collapsed to the ground, vomiting bile, my head a torrent of misery. I missed my couch. I missed my TV. I missed eating ice cream and laughing with Rain over the original *Gremlins* movie. That was what I wanted right then. That was the only thing I could bear to think of.

I just killed somebody.

I wanted to go to sleep. I wanted to sleep and wake up on my couch, with Rain, and my baby, and be watching *Gremlins.*

He wasn't really human, though, right? He was a monster... a monster from another dimension...

My baby was a she. I could've named her a beautiful name. Maybe Grace. I'd always liked the name Grace.

I had to move. I had to save him.

I had to save him.

I blinked and was at Rain's side, not sure how I got there and mindlessly repeating his name. "Rain... Rain!" The light in his eyes was fading. I cradled his face. What was I supposed to do? "Rain! Rain, hang on! Hang on!" Blood pooled around him. He was dying. My hands trembled. Stars fizzled in my vision. "Why aren't you healing? *Why aren't you healing?*"

I didn't know what to do. I removed my shirt and used it to apply pressure around the knife. I remembered hearing somewhere that you should never remove knives, that it could make the bleeding worse. I didn't know if it was true, but I thought it made sense and didn't dare test otherwise. I helplessly pressed my shirt around the wound, trying to stop the bleeding. It turned red. "Hang on," I kept saying. "It'll be okay. It'll be okay."

Towels. I needed towels. This was a laboratory. They had to have towels somewhere.

His warm, calloused hand rested on my shoulder, sticky with blood. "Emily..."

"No."

"Emily..."

"Where's your phone? I need your phone. I'll call Nothe. *I'm calling Nothe!*"

I finally looked at him. The world around me shattered at the sight. His face held no color. The light in his eyes had dimmed, barely holding a flame. A look of peace and immense sadness fell across his expression as he brushed hair behind my ear, that beautiful affection deeper than I had ever seen it. "Our first date would've been really fun, I think," he whispered.

I was out of time. I didn't want to admit it. It wasn't possible. *It wasn't possible.*

I had so much regret, more than I could bear. I couldn't let this moment become another one. The words poured from me. "I love you."

The smile on his face vanished. His eyes widened, the sorrow in them opening up into the darkest abyss. It flooded through, consuming me, twisting me in his uncontrolled heartbreak and regret. He opened his mouth to speak, but before any words could leave his lips, the light in his eyes disappeared. His hand became lifeless in mine, and the room slipped into an empty silence.

My world ended.

This wasn't happening to me. This wasn't happening at all. This wasn't real.

My trembling fingers squeezed his hand. If I refused to let go, he'd come back to me.

The strangest sound rended the air like wind howling through a broken window. I didn't realize it was coming from me.

I was dreaming, wasn't I? I'd just gone to work this morning, I was sure of it, and I must've fallen asleep. I just needed to wake up. Why couldn't I wake up?

He was gone. Rain was gone.

No. No, he wasn't. I couldn't accept it. I couldn't. I was dreaming. I could feel myself floating, so it wasn't real. None of it was real.

Still holding his hand, I fumbled through his pockets until I found his phone and scrolled through the names until I found Nothe's number. I was maniacal, nonsensical, spilling words from a broken mind. Nothe struggled to understand. "Wait—slow down. Where are you?"

"I don't know."

"Emily—"

"*I don't know!* He's not healing, Nothe!" There was a disconnect that wouldn't allow me to say he was dead. "He's not healing. *He's not healing!*"

"Okay, okay. Just—have you left the facility?"

How did he know to even ask that? "No. I don't know. I don't know where I am. I haven't left where I *was*..."

"Okay. Stay there. I'm on my way."

"Don't hang up." I wasn't sure why I said it. I was dreaming. It shouldn't have mattered if he hung up or not. But I said it anyway. Because this was a nightmare. I was alone, half naked in a room full of dead bodies and no baby, with my hero looking up at me with no light in his eyes.

"I won't—"

"Please."

"I promise."

He stayed on the phone with me, saying things I didn't really hear, but the sound of his voice comforted me. I was barely aware that Nothe had arrived when he appeared beside me. I kept trying to express thoughts, but all that came out was, "He's not healing. He's not healing."

Nothe grabbed my shoulders and tried to pry me away from Rain. My grip tightened on his hand and I cried, "No! *No!* I promised I wouldn't leave him!"

Nothe pulled me away more forcefully and shook me. "Emily, stop!" When I did, he went on. "I need you to calm down. Okay? I need to see him, so I can help him."

I managed a nod.

"Okay." He held my face in his hands, his bright, sunset eyes piercing mine. "It's going to be okay."

I nodded again and clung to those words. They were the only things keeping me from slipping further into madness.

Nothe looked over Rain's body, the wound in his abdomen, the wounds in his chest. He reached out and gently cradled Rain's neck and caressed his face, and then all of his walls fell. He laid his head against Rain's shoulder, his breathing shallow. The room was engulfed by agony like a fog. I breathed it in. It filled my lungs. It drowned my shattered soul in crushing blackness and sorrow. The deepest waves of the ocean were not equivalent to the weight of this pain. For a moment, it awoke me from my own grief, gripping me with fear—fear that he was really dead. That there was nothing to be done.

I repeated in my mind, *It's going to be okay. It's going to be okay.*

Tears streamed down Nothe's face as he sat back, resting an arm on his knee. I watched him close his eyes.

I pulled at my hair. I couldn't breathe... I couldn't breathe...

I'd lost everything. How could such stupid choices make me lose everything?

It's going to be okay. It's going to be okay.

More pain erupted from Nothe—pain that I felt distinctly. It was as though his heart had been seized by cold, decaying hands and ripped asunder. But this was washed away with a firm resolve. He didn't look at me as he said, "I know what to do."

In the closet Rain had rescued me from an eternity ago, Nothe found a box and blanket. He wrapped the blanket around me, and then scoured the lab, filling the box with things before handing it to me. Nothe removed the knife from Rain's abdomen, then lifted his body over his shoulder and commanded, "Follow me."

TRACK 10

GONE AWAY

O n the drive to Rain and Nothe's home, I asked, "Why didn't he heal?"

"You've been through enough. I don't—"

"Why didn't he heal?" This was the only phrase I could say.

Nothe hesitated. "Harold Grossman... he had all sorts of connections. He hunted Rain down. Thipka tried to stop him by killing Jesse. I guess Jesse had been hired as part of his crew, that's how he found you. He probably decided that, if you took him back, he wouldn't turn you over to Grossman. But if you didn't... well, yeah. But there must've been other people working for him that got into the club. Probably someone we trusted—that Steve trusted. Steve was very naïve and trusting. And well, before Steve became Not-Steve—we were loading up the truck with the stuff we'd need for the Battle of the Box, and Rain told Chuck about the baby and your er... well, the whole thing with Jesse. I'd overheard, and Steve must've overheard parts of it, too, but just parts, and so he thought the baby was Rain's. It was part of his memories. It was in his head when Not-Steve took over." Tears filled his eyes. "I guess Time found another way."

I felt a twinge of something almost like sorrow at the knowledge that Jesse was dead, but that was quickly overwhelmed by relief. Really, this was the closest thing to good news I'd had since Rain asked me out. I wondered how long ago that was.

Nothe continued, "So, like I was saying, I think one of Grossman's informants must've warmed up to Trusting-Steve before he became Not-Steve. Maybe it was that girlfriend of his, I don't know. And Not-Steve must've told this person—I'm assuming—that you were pregnant with Rain's baby. And Grossman decided he wanted the baby. I have no idea *why*, except he must've wanted to experiment on..." He glanced over at me and stopped.

I meant to say nothing—what was there to say?—but instead, I asked, "Why didn't he heal?"

Nothe eyed me patiently for a moment. It was clear this was not the first time he'd seen someone fall apart. He pulled into his driveway and put the car into park as he explained, "About eleven days ago, someone burned down the diner after they abducted you, trying to keep Rain off their scent. They didn't want him looking for you, so they made it look like an accident."

I wanted to ask about Marie and Alejandro, but I couldn't get the words out. I couldn't deal with more people dying. If I didn't ask, maybe it didn't happen.

Nothe continued, "There was a body found there that the coroner said was yours. It was so burned up that there was no way anyone could tell, but he said the dental records matched. She was even pregnant. They called your dad and he came to get you. So Rain thought you were dead. Everyone did. And Rain... he didn't handle it very well. His grief, it poisoned his blood.

"So I did some investigating. I went straight to the coroner and his guilty conscience was so bad, he spilled everything after, like, two questions. He'd been paid a lot of money to forge the reports. So, obviously, the dead girl wasn't you. The man who had bribed him worked for the government, a section run by a guy who was close to Harold Grossman. Then Thipka showed up—said something about how he'd been looking for the portal but the entrance had moved—I didn't really care at the time. He went all crazy when I told him about you and said over and over, 'I tried to stop it.'

"In Thipka's weird way, he knew exactly where you were. And I made the stupid mistake of telling Rain. I just, he was such a mess... I thought it'd help. I'm so stupid. We were supposed to rescue you together, but, apparently, he had to make it a suicide mission." He shook his head, heartbroken and furious, muttering, "He did it again."

The words raced through my mind. *It's going to be okay. Everything is going to be okay.*

Nothe carried Rain into his home and laid him on his bed. He gave me one of his The Offspring T-shirts to wear. I followed him everywhere like a lost and starving animal, stupid and desperate and unaware of what else to do.

Nothe looked down at Rain, his eyes full of sorrow, yet there was a profound adoration in them—the same sort of affection Rain's gaze had held for me. I'd never seen it so clearly in Nothe's face before.

Nothe said, his voice hoarse, "You know, Rain took care of me for years after I lost my sight. He helped me get around and helped me learn to see in other ways. And when we were rescued, the first thing Rain asked for—it wasn't to regrow his missing arm, or for food, or anything—it was to grow back my eyes. So that's what they did.

"Everything was blurry at first, but hey! It was something, ya know? Then I blinked and, I just... stopped breathing. Because for the first time in *years*, I could see the stars. Each one, just, scattered across the sky.

"But then I saw Rhaenmeinnah sitting beside me with this look of perfect contentment, and I knew. *There* was my light. My safety... my home." His eyes filled with tears. "The stars held nothing in comparison."

The room filled with pain, twisting my heart until I thought my chest would collapse. I thought of how Nothe had kept all of these emotions in a pen, holding them there for a hundred years while he felt them so deeply. I wondered how he'd done it, and how he could live with the hole they had left behind.

Nothe began removing Rain's blood-soaked shirt. He didn't look at me as he told me, "You left your phone here a while back. It's on the counter, plugged in. Rain had some weird thing about... about not letting it die. You should check your voicemail." When I didn't move, he bossed me like a parent reminding their kid for the seventh time to go find their shoes. "I mean it. Go check your voicemail."

I obeyed. What else was I supposed to do? I went into the kitchen and found my phone. My voicemail box was full. There were a couple of telemarketer-bots mixed in with several hang-ups. Then my heart stopped as I heard Rain's voice. He was singing Bastille, "Good Grief." Another spammer later, he spoke. "So, um... I don't know if you've noticed—apparently everyone else has—but I... I am in love with you." I froze at the words. The world stopped spinning. My eyes brimmed with tears again.

He let out a deep breath. "I never told you that. I never dared say it once I realized it. And believe it or not, despite what Chuck has said, I've known for some time, I just—I couldn't say it, because I treasured what we had and I didn't want to ruin it by saying... *that*. I couldn't see how you could ever really love me in return and I didn't want to put you in that position. Believe it or not—I've said 'believe it or not' twice now—three times—but I never saw what you saw in me. But the fact that you saw it, it made me believe something good might be there, and that was both a fantastic and terrifying thing to hope for.

"Emily, for so long I felt alone. I was surrounded by people whom I considered friends, yes, but still felt alone. I was so... strange. So broken beyond any sort of repair. But the moment you took my hand, as we sat upon your couch, comparing battle scars—I remember that moment perfectly—I felt my whole world shift. Like, broken bones set back into place. I no longer felt quite so broken, and certainly not beyond repair. I suddenly knew that I wasn't alone. I will always cherish that moment... cherish you. You were more virtuous than any creature I've ever met. No one could shine with such great light, with such love and genuine kindness, and see such beauty in broken things. No one could do that, heal deep wounds in someone like me with a mere touch and a few compassionate words, and not be a creature of purity—"

The voicemail robot cut off his sentence. "To delete this message, press one..."

Tears stained my jeans. I wanted to Hulk-smash my phone as I quickly moved on to the next message. Rain's voice said with frustration, "I wasn't done! There're so many things that I never got to say, so just, bear with me this one last time, and you will..." His voice cracked a little. "You will never have to hear from me again. Emily, one last thing, please. I just want you to know, it doesn't matter where we are... *were*. Where we were or could ever be... whether gazing at the sky in a dream or drinking chocolate milk at the club while everyone else was getting drunk," a laugh broke through his words at the memory, "or... or alone on the couch with just the walls and the TV..." His tone grew heavy, like speaking of it all in the past tense was adding weight to each word.

He took another deep breath. "It doesn't matter, Emily. It doesn't matter. When I am with you, I'm home. We could go to the other side of the world, backpacking across China with nowhere to lay our heads for the night, and I'd still be home, because I would be with you. That is what I wanted to say to you. I was going to say it. I was. I thought about being brave and telling you on the Ferris Wheel at the pier. But now you're gone. And now that you're gone, I feel truly and completely... lost. I'm without a home. And I know that, in the grand scheme of things, we've only known each other for a short time, but I really can't seem to bear the thought of my life without you in it."

His voice wavered, "Isn't it strange how that can happen? You've completely changed my world, like sunlight on a cold earth. Like I was just some, icy rock floating in space until I stumbled upon your warmth and light and suddenly, I found new life. I didn't know what I was missing, and now, to be without it... to go back into the cold, dark void... it's killing me.

"But my dear friend, I can't bring myself to ask you to come back to me. You must be so much happier where you are. You are free. No longer do you have to put up with other humans and their awfulness. I can just picture you and your little one laughing at something ridiculous, in a world rich with colors that are far brighter than the ones here. I know you must be such a good mother. Your compassion is unmatched. And I imagine that your light is shining brighter than ever, because you're free. So I can do this." He let out a heavy sigh and said, more to himself than anything, "I can do this. As long as I know you're finally happy. I'll admire your light from afar as a distant star..."

"To delete this message, press one..."

I nearly pushed the wrong button as I moved on to the next voicemail. "I realized at the end of that one that I made a rhyme. A very ridiculous rhyme. Which makes me think that I should write poetry. I really believe, at this point in my life, that I could be the next Edgar Allan Poe. Well, a ridiculous version of Edgar Allan Poe, which is something I feel the world really needs. Also, I'm quite surprised that your voicemail didn't kick me off sooner with that last one. I swear it was much longer than the one before."

There were a few more hang ups. I realized these were Rain listening to my voice in the recording and then hanging up. Finally, I reached the last voicemail. "I love you. I just had to say it again, since I never got to say it a first time. Okay. Until we meet again, Emily."

I curled up in the kitchen chair, my hands pulling on my hair. I rocked back and forth, trying to breathe, muttering, "It's going to be okay. It's going to be okay. It's going to be okay."

I had nothing. My world was gone. My home... he was my home, and now he was gone. *We should've left after Jesse showed up. We should've run away. We should've moved to a haunted castle in Spain.*

"It's going to be okay. It's going to be okay. It's going to be okay."

I shouldn't have gone to work. We should've just packed up and left right then. Then I'd have Rain, and I'd have my baby, and none of this would've happened.

Nothe had said he knew how to fix things. Weakly, I dragged myself out of the kitchen and into Rain's bedroom.

I had to catch myself on the doorframe as I nearly collapsed, my knees giving out on me, but this time, it was for all-consuming joy.

Rain was breathing.

He was shirtless and unconscious, but his wounds were healed and he was breathing.

I rushed to him, ignoring the form sitting on a chair in the corner of the room. I leapt onto the bed, kneeling beside him, touching his face, making sure that what I saw was real. There was a sunburst scar over his heart, signifying his return from the dead.

From the chair in the corner of the room came a heavy wheezing. Nothe sat there, his mouth hanging open at an odd angle, looking as though he'd come down with some dreadful, parasitic disease. His skin was like paper and patchy. Blood seeped from his ears, eyes, nose, and mouth. He didn't even look like the same man, but the zombie alternative.

"Nothe!" I went to him. A bloody tube hung out of his arm.

He'd given Rain his blood.

No, it wasn't just that. He'd expended energy—energy meant to be given by two Hassune—to call Rain back from the dead.

I reached out to him. "Tell me what to do." I thought quickly. "Thipka! I'm getting Thipka!"

Nothe grabbed my arm. "There isn't time." My senses were overcome with a feeling of desperation, the last wish of a dying man. His eyes were full of bloody tears, pleading. "Please, I just..." Nothe swallowed blood. He said in a whisper, "If you are the sun and Rain is the Earth... then I am the moon." Tears streamed down my face, mirroring the tears of blood that poured down his. He smirked. "Dumbest thing I've ever said..." More tears spilled down his cheeks, the light in his eyes dimmed further. "Truest thing... tell him. Please tell him. Tell him what I never got to say. Tell him to keep his promise."

I looked at him and nodded, hoping he could feel my sincerity. "I promise."

Peace softened his face. There wasn't another breath. His body stilled and the light faded from his eyes.

Nothe was gone.

He had followed Rain across the stars. He'd fought so hard to save him, to see him happy.

He had given Rain everything.

My whole body trembled. I wanted to cry. I knew I should be crying. But I couldn't feel anymore. This was happening to someone else. I was sure it was happening to someone else, and I was simply watching it from another world.

I rose to my feet. My knees shook and I swallowed bile as I found Nothe's phone and made my way to the living room. I searched for the number. I was hardly aware of the ringing. My brain almost missed the hello and took a moment to respond, "Th-thipka? Help... please. I think... I think Nothe is dead. We're at Rain's house. Please..."

I collapsed onto the couch and stared off into nothingness, not listening to his replies, wishing I could disappear, or at least go to sleep for a century or two. I didn't notice the front door open. Thipka's presence didn't register till his hand touched my shoulder with the lament, "No... none of this was supposed to happen. I stopped it. *I stopped it.*"

He knelt in front of me with tears in his eyes. Heartbreak and discouragement radiated from him. "I will heal your mind as best as I can, but not your body. Not this time." His tone turned dark "They must see what they did to you."

As a wave of light rushed through me, I lost consciousness.

TRACK 11

ASHES

I awoke to Rain's fingertips caressing my face.

Unconscious me didn't know they were his fingertips, however, and swatted them away as if they were a bothersome fly.

I opened my eyes and saw his face, that face I loved so much.

I threw myself from the couch, falling into his lap with my arms around his neck, sending stars spinning in my vision and leaving me lightheaded. I'd started sobbing before I'd even realized it. He returned my embrace tightly, threading his hand through my hair. We held each other, crying stupidly. Relief, joy, and the comfort of sharing pain and hope with someone that was trusted so completely—for a moment, these feelings were the only ones that filled the room, surrounding us, enveloping us.

Then I remembered Not-Steve.

Rain had declared he would never come back from the Dimension of Light.

Then, just to make things worse, I thought of Nothe. I fought more tears at his memory, at the rush of guilt that consumed me for all the pain I'd caused him. Rain must've seen him there, his body bloody and still, curled up in the chair at the corner of the room. I could hear Nothe's voice in my head, *"Tell him. Tell him the things I never got to say."* I couldn't. Not yet. Not right now.

And then my mind returned to the haunting thought that Rain might not be Rain.

I pulled away from him. With an arm still wrapped around me, he reached out and lovingly took my hand. Warmth spread through me at his touch, filling my soul with that familiar, soothing light. I looked at his eyes, a brilliant blue that reminded me of winter, but the good part of it

—curled up with a blanket, reading books, and telling stories in front of a fire in the living room.

In that moment, I knew it was him. He'd come back. He'd really come back.

Why? Not that I was complaining *at all*, but seriously, why?

His eyes searched mine before he finally said, "I know this might be the wrong time to bring this up, but I am absolutely famished. I suddenly understand zombies," I laughed as I wiped away tears, though I felt the joke was too soon. He continued, "Shall we eat something? And then I shall brush my teeth, because I feel like I have zombie-breath since, you know, I am one. Wait—maybe I should do that first. I'll do that first."

And he did. I couldn't believe how nonchalantly he made his way to the bathroom, passing the bedroom where Nothe's body lay. It was like it wasn't a big deal. I couldn't help staring at the room as if it held a doorway to the starless part of the night sky, simply because, I felt like it did.

How could Rain not feel it?

I crossed the hallway entrance to the kitchen, hurrying as though I were darting out of the way of a speeding truck. I sat at the table, trying to ignore the pit that lay in the house. It seemed to stretch down the hall, reaching right into my chest, wrapping my heart in a vice.

Nothe's voice was in my head again, *Tell him. Please tell him.*

The moment Rain walked into the kitchen, the words burst from me, "I'm so sorry about Nothe, Rain. I'm so sorry."

Rain froze. "What about Nothe?"

I looked up at him, shocked. "Isn't... isn't he in there? He's in there."

"In where?"

"In... in the bedroom. On the chair."

Rain looked quite confused. I could feel his worry. "No. No one's on the chair."

"But he is. I saw him. I..." I couldn't say it. All the heartbreak and horror overwhelmed me and I couldn't say it.

Rain went back into the bedroom for another look and returned shaking his head. Despite how badly I wanted to see for myself, I couldn't go in there. "Thipka must've taken him."

Rain's worry filled the room. "What happened to Nothe?"

I told him everything as best as I could, telling him all that Nothe had done. "He said to tell you to keep your promise." I wanted to ask what that promise was, but it didn't feel like the right time. I was trying to get to the hardest part, the part that tore my heart into a thousand little pieces for so many reasons. "Everything he did, he did because... because he loved you. He was in love with you, Rain."

I couldn't look at him as I said it. I was afraid of what I'd see on his face. I stared at his hands, which were balled together. He sat across from me now, leaning forward with his elbows on his knees. I continued, "He'd loved you ever since you got him through... through losing his eyes. He'd wanted to tell you, but never dared. So he asked me to tell you. That was his final wish, and to see you happy. He just wanted you to be happy." At that, I let out another sob. Rain handed me another paper towel. I'd already gone through two.

Rain held his head in his hands. All the emotion that had surrounded him disappeared, leaving the room feeling horribly empty. He ran a hand through his hair, pulling on it a little. When I finally looked at him, his eyes were full of tears. "All these years..." He shook his head.

Then one feeling slipped through. A very profound one.

He wanted me to leave.

I couldn't feel any explanation behind it. Just the nudge that I needed to not be there. That he wanted to be alone. I wasn't sure if it was something he was letting out intentionally or if it was something he'd lost control of, but either way, it stung.

I'd told Rain someone else had loved him. And now he wanted me to go away.

I held back the tears. I was sure the second I left the house, I would never stop crying.

I didn't want to leave. I'd just gotten him back.

I tried to be understanding, to not make a scene. I knew this was a lot for him to hear. I didn't look at him. "I should go."

He made a half-hearted attempt to stop me. "Emily..."

That bugged me. "No, no. I, um... I need to go to the police station." *Good job, Emily.* I told myself. *That's a good excuse, even though you don't need one. He wants you to leave. But it should stop him from any polite attempt to get you to stay when he clearly doesn't want you here.* "They need to know the truth about..." *Grossman,* I almost said, but couldn't bring myself to speak his name, "that other guy."

Rain nodded. He didn't even offer me a ride. Instead, he gave me money for a cab, which was as good as lemon juice and salt dumped over the wound.

TRACK 12

WELCOME HOME

There was a bit of a shock among the investigators of the burned down restaurant. A lot of hubbub happened after that. I was lost in a whirlwind. I went through the necessary motions, getting the exams that proved my story, answering their questions and lying when they wanted to know who rescued me, claiming that someone had killed everyone before I'd gotten away—minus the guy who'd attacked me as I tried to flee, whom I'd shot in self-defense. I had managed to escape because no one had bothered to look in the closet they'd stored me in. My wrists looked like hamburger and my blood was on the shackles, giving validity to my story. I was so devoid of any life that everything I said sounded the same, whether truth or lie. So they believed me. They believed what I'd said about Grossman's paranoia, as it had been well documented. But they never found the remains of my baby. In honor of her, I bought a ring with little flowers carved into the band. I would never take it off my finger.

No one could explain the strange blood they found all over Grossman's laboratory. And when the coroner who'd helped Grossman was found dead, it was eventually decided that Grossman must've dug too deep, finding himself involved in something that came back to bite him, though no one knew what that possibly could've been.

I couldn't sleep at my apartment anymore. When I told my landlady I would be moving, she wished me all the luck and love the universe had to offer, since I'd brought such good fortune to her family. She explained that shortly after I'd moved in, her son had miraculously been cured. After nearly two years of suffering, he was completely whole. The doctors had no explanation, but I knew what had happened.

Rain had healed him.

Leaving my furniture at the apartment for the time being, I took the money I'd saved and stayed at a different hotel each night until I could find a new place, though nothing I did made me feel safe. I couldn't sleep. And any sleep I did get was restless and full of nightmares. I had to leave the lights on. There were only two nights of this, however. On day three, I was summoned to return to the police station and found someone there waiting for me. It was a face I hadn't seen in ages, but one I had missed most desperately.

It was my dad.

He sat on a chair in Reece's office, looking very gray. His shoulders, once full of strength, were now slumped and weary. His brown eyes were weighed down with shadows, though I thought they lit up at the sight of me. He rose to his feet.

My sister's words flooded into my mind. I knew he hated me. How could he not? He looked so different, so awful. What had I done to him? I wanted to turn and bolt, but my feet wouldn't move. The only clear thought I had slipped from me with tears and a whisper, "I'm sorry. I'm so sorry."

His eyes also filled with tears. That proved it. He hated me. My sister was right. What was I doing there? I needed to leave.

I turned toward the door, but he grabbed my arm and then hugged me, holding me tight, the way he had when I was a child and woke up in the middle of the night from a bad dream. He smelled like homemade chicken soup and old books—like home. Ignoring the audience of detectives, I clung to him, unable to stop sobbing. "I'm sorry. I'm so stupid. I'm sorry."

"It's okay," he said, "It's okay."

"It's not. It's not. I ruined everything."

"It's not your fault. None of it is your fault. It was that disgusting, toilet-stain-licking—"

In spite of my self-loathing-meltdown, I giggled like I was eight-years-old again.

"—fungus-at-the-bottom-of-the-bowl."

"How can you say that?"

"Because it's true. That's what he is."

"No, but..."

He pried me away and cradled my face in his aging hands. My gaze reluctantly met his kind eyes. He shook his head. "You are my daughter. Your first laugh, your first smile," emotion overcame him as he pointed to his heart, "it was magic. The light in your sweet face... I look at you now, and I know you've been through hell. You're battle worn, but that light is still in your face. You're my little daughter. My dear, long lost friend. And I love you. All the time. No matter what. Always, always. And there is *nothing* you could ever do to change that. Nothing.

"But you listen to me. *None* of this is your fault. None of it. Okay?"

I couldn't help it. I fell apart. I laid my head against his shoulder, hugging him more tightly, more grateful for those words than I would ever know how to say. Shadows fled my mind at them. A heavy weight lifted from my shoulders, something I hadn't even realized I carried. I could breathe with an ease I hadn't felt in years.

"You're okay now," Dad promised. "You're going home. I'm taking you home."

TRACK 13

WHAT IS LOVE

At the hotel that evening, my phone rang.

It had taken everything I had not to call him. What had it been—three days? It'd felt like three weeks. No, weeks didn't cover it. It was more like three months, and I was sure I hadn't slept in all that time. There was no escape from the images that haunted me and the pain I had felt. And Rain...

Rain had been my comfort. My rock. My home. If he were with me —it wasn't like it'd all magically go away, but it would be easier to bear. In his absence, the black hole in my heart was opening back up.

But how could I call him? I could see now why he'd wanted me to leave that day. How on Earth could he have wanted me to stay after everything I'd done? All the pain I'd caused? I was so stupid. I'd made a wreck of everything. He and Nothe had had a good life until I wandered into it. There was no way I could ever make up for that. What could I say? How could I even *try* to apologize for it? The words would be meaningless.

That's probably what he's calling to tell me, I thought. *He's calling to make sure I know it's over. That he...* I couldn't stop the tears from burning my eyes. *That he regrets saving me.*

I didn't answer the phone. I couldn't. I was sure I would never recover from what he had to say to me.

He left a voicemail. I considered listening to it, but I was sure I wouldn't live through anymore heartbreak. I deleted it.

He called me twice the next morning and twice more while I was at lunch with my dad. And each time, I let it go to voicemail. On the last ring, I turned my phone face down and sat it off to the side, my heart hammering at the mere sight of Rain's name popping up on the screen.

I'd told my dad about Rain, how he'd saved my life and helped me throughout my difficult situation and how we'd become friends—leaving out his magical powers and fantastic origins, of course. I'd also told him how we were no longer talking, but without any real explanation.

My dad stared thoughtfully at the phone I'd just put in time-out. "Why didn't you answer it?"

I told him as nonchalantly as possible, "Because I'm at lunch with you."

He raised a skeptical eyebrow and let out a skeptical hum. "I don't think that's it."

I hesitated. "It's part of it." That was true. I hadn't been to lunch with my dad in years. I wasn't about to interrupt it by answering a phone call. Though I might've, under different circumstances.

"What's the other part?"

"He hates me. That's all. I really don't want to talk about it." I realized how rude that probably sounded and added, "Sorry. Just. Maybe I can sometime. I just can't right now."

He glanced over at my phone. "He's pretty persistent for someone that hates you."

That was a good point. The thought had crossed my mind, but I still didn't dare answer, or listen to the voicemails he'd just left. I shrugged. "People do that."

Dad nodded. "Sure, sure. People like Jane. But, from what you've told me, he really doesn't seem like that type of person."

He was as perceptive as ever. I knew he was right. Rain wouldn't be calling like this just to tell me how much he hated me. I grew dizzy for a moment as a flutter of hope rushed through me—cruel, cruel hope.

Dad leaned forward, clasping his hands together in a very, I-have-something-important-to-tell-you sort of way. "You don't have to tell me why you think he's calling over and over to tell you how much he hates you—"

My phone started buzzing with text messages. All I could do was look at it. I didn't want to read any of them.

"—aaaand, texting you—"

There was another buzz.

"—a lot. For the same reason, I'm sure." He paused to gather his thoughts. "Do you know why your mom and I were so awesome together?"

I looked at him. "Well, that's a no brainer. You were both awesome people."

He pointed at my words. "True. Especially your mother. She made me a better person. And that's why I've never remarried. There is just absolutely no one more awesome than your mom. She's worth the wait."

I couldn't help smiling, feeling all warm and fuzzy before another buzz from my phone sent me back into a panic.

Dad went on, "But that's not because we never fought. I mean, I could *really* be a butt, and your mom was, well, stubborn. We'd knock heads and yell." He started laughing. "Your mom even threw a pan at the wall once—put a big ol' hole in it."

"No way! For real?"

He was still chuckling. "Yep. True story. She immediately felt bad, though. And I was mad, but mostly glad she hadn't thrown it at me! That was only once, though. It wasn't like that all the time. I don't even remember what we were fighting about anymore. I really can't. Life's funny like that. Something can seem so big at the moment, but once you forgive and let it go, it's just gone. And you realize just how not-worth-it those dumb things are. I'm just saying, these things happen to everybody. But you want to know what we did different from everybody else?"

"Yeah. Let's hear it."

"We did what all best friends do. We calmed down, gave it some time, and then we talked about it. And we didn't stop talking until we could see each other's point of view. We apologized where necessary— and most of the time, we both had some apologizing to do, but ya know, sometimes it was just me—and then we did the most important thing of all, and forgave each other. Because that's what friends do. She forgave me for..." He let out a slow breath and shook his head. "A lot. And not just that forgive-long-enough-to-bring-it-up-again-later-and-win-a-fight kind of forgiveness. She *really* forgave." His eyes grew watery. "It was gone. And that just made me love her all the more."

I knew he was trying to make me feel better, but he wasn't. "Right.

But he's the one that needs to forgive *me*. And I just don't know how…" I couldn't finish the sentence.

Dad looked me in the eyes. "Emily, does he make you happy?"

I blinked back tears. "He does. He really does."

"Then give him a chance to forgive ya. Don't push him away. You two need to talk. You've gotta fight for him. Go out on a limb. *Break* the limb. Go through all the difficult and the boring and all the good and, all of it. Don't expect things to be perfect. They never are, because people aren't perfect. They can't be perfect. Not in this life. But you *can* be perfectly happy. Things don't need to be perfect for you to be perfectly happy. And you can have absolutely perfect moments. And the perfect moments, in the good or bad or boring—that's a good life, my dear. And that's worth going out on a limb for. So," he gestured to my phone, "now's as good a time as any."

I stared at my phone. Glared at it. How could such a small, scratched up, make-up covered thing hold my fate so coldly, with such a lack of compassion?

Before I lost my nerve, I snatched the phone up from the table and looked at the text messages.

They weren't at all what I was expecting.

Hey. I hope I'm not disturbing you. I just wanted to check in and see if you're okay.

Basically, how are you?

Sorry. Those texts were dumb.

I'm so sorry that I haven't checked in sooner. I haven't meant to be distant. I've been a bit stuck in my head. And an idiot. I was hoping we could talk.

Just if you want to.

I'm going to stop texting now. Sorry to bombard you.

I don't know why I just texted you to tell you I was going to stop texting you. I could've just stopped and it would've got the point across.

But it's not because I don't want to text you. Or talk. I would really like to talk.

I don't know why I let myself send that last text. Or any of them. Will you please put me out of my misery?

If you're willing to put me out of my misery, please meet me at Bob's Club Festivus at 7 PM.

Or don't. It's up to you. I hope you do, though.

Okay, I'm really done texting now.

When I looked up from my phone, my dad held a small, knowing smile. "Well..." he picked up a fry from my plate and ate it. "Does he hate you?"

I smiled. "No. I don't think he does."

TRACK 14

JOURNEY FROM A TO B

My stomach twisted in burning knots as I stepped through the black curtain into the cheerful lights of Bob's Club Festivus and was beyond unnerved to see the place so bright and so completely empty.

But as I walked onto the dancefloor in my teal dress, one last light flipped on. The stage was illuminated with a single spotlight, shining on a man playing an all-too-familiar riff with an acoustic guitar. He wore a black, leather jacket with a button up, dark gray shirt. His hair was in perfect, messy waves that curled up around his ears.

It was Rain. And at the words he sang, all doubt, all despair and all of my fears, fled away.

It was my song.

"I'm Gonna Be (500 Miles)" by The Proclaimers.

My song.

His rendition was sweet, rich, and melodic, carrying my soul away to a beach to watch the sunrise on a springtime morning. And in that moment, I was quite certain there wasn't a greater song in all the universe.

When the song ended, he set his guitar in its stand and hopped down from the stage. I blinked back tears and applauded, swept away by a whirlwind of his nerves—of fear, trepidation, joy, hope, doubt, despair, grief—all of which he quickly wrangled up with a deep and angelic, "Hello, Emily."

It took everything I had not to throw my arms around him. I composed myself as I said, "Hey! That's a pretty good song you sang. Best love song in the world."

He smiled. He smelled very strongly of orange blossoms—more

potently than usual, as though he were particularly nervous about this get together and was sure that the better he smelled, the better it would go. This gave me even more hope.

He glanced down at his black shoes, which looked brand new. "Yes. Well, I decided I wanted to go all in. I hope you don't mind. I just—I decided that, if I'm going to live, then I'm going to make my life meaningful. And it is far more meaningful with you in it."

I blinked, my mind floating away. I caught it before it'd gone too far. "But you wanted me to leave. I felt it."

He ran a hand through his hair. "I didn't know what I wanted. I haven't left my house. At all. Or really slept or ate or, anything. I haven't been great, honestly. I... I was lost. But I know these last few days must have been a nightmare for you, and I am so profoundly sorry that I haven't been here for you. I've been an awful wreck with... with it all."

That was so very understandable. He had no need to apologize. My heart ached for him. "I'm so sorry, Rain." Guilt consumed me. It was all my fault, wasn't it?

Rain didn't look up. "I've really needed you, Emily. I kept hoping you'd walk through my front door."

Now I felt bad for leaving him alone for so long. But why on Earth would he want me there? "I don't know why you would want me there. I..." My head spun as I forced myself to say it, "I know it's all my fault."

He furrowed his brow. "What?"

"Nothe—"

"You did everything you could to help him. Calling Thipka was the right move."

I shook my head. There was so much more I was guilty of than just failing Nothe. "Have you heard from him at all?"

"Thipka? No. I haven't any idea where he has taken Nothe. I know he had plans to continue his search for the portal entrance, but I don't know what's become of that, either."

"I'm so sorry, Rain. I'm so..." The words were empty, I knew it, but I had to say it. "I'm so sorry that I caused Nothe pain and you pain, and for not saving him, and just..."

"Are you kidding me right now?"

"No."

His eyes were bright. "You're serious?"

"Yes. I know what I did."

"I don't think you do. Emily, all of this would've happened whether or not I'd have met you. Nothe likely would've gone on not telling me how he felt, as he had for over a hundred years. I still would've set off the madman and been caught in some way. Nothe probably would've died trying to save me. Rather, without you, Nothe wouldn't have been able to tell anyone the truth. And I... well, I would've likely died and stayed dead. Because I wouldn't have had anything to come back for. Never, in my life, would I have imagined that I'd want to return from the Dimension of Light, especially with the prospect of the Therans coming to Earth, and yet... I did. I don't remember much of being there, but I do remember this—" His bright blue eyes burned with radiant light. "I returned because of you."

My heart stopped beating for several seconds. I was sure of it.

"You are the reason I came back, Emily. The moment you told me you loved me, I knew I could never be happy anywhere but at your side."

"And you still feel that way?"

Rain's eyes filled with that affection I'd loved since I first saw it in my dreams. He caressed my face. His arm wrapped around my waist, pulling my body against him.

As his lips touched mine, I was consumed with light. I could feel it within me and I could distinguish it from my own. It was his light, and I watched it as my lips parted his. It rushed over me at his touch and burned, sweetly and brilliantly, so much so that it made my heart dance. It glowed brighter the more passionate he became as he kissed me. It showed in the movement of his lips, in the way he cradled my face, in the way he closed his eyes, and suddenly—I knew. It stole my breath as I realized that, he loved me. And not just "loved" me, but it was something as deep and alive as the heart's blood, pure and almost innocent, something I thought had been as likely to exist as unicorns. It was more clear and true than if he had spoken the words. Because anyone could say those words and it could be nothing more than a cold, cruel lie. But this sprang from the light in the very core of his heart, with no trace of guile. And it grew brighter with each passing moment, as if his heart were singing. I returned his feelings with feverish intensity, curling my fingers in his hair and pulling him closer against me.

He stopped and looked at me, his eyes not leaving mine. "I love you, Emily."

I tried not to cry like a stupid person, but I'd never felt anything like what I felt then. It was a level of happiness that was as deep, rich, and wonderful as had been my despair. "I love you."

He smiled, genuine and beautiful. His joy overflowed, adding to my own. Tears brimmed his eyes as he told me, "I know I said that I don't know how to have a relationship—and I don't, it's true. I'm... I'm so broken and the world is ending and everything around us is horrible and wrong. But, with you, I want to try. Even though everything outside of us is a mess, I... I really want to try."

I couldn't stop smiling. I was numb, in shock, but finally—for once in my life—it was because I was overwhelmed with joy. I placed a hand to my cheek, as if to make sure my face was still there, that this moment was indeed really happening. I told him, "Me too. I would really like to try, with you." I shrugged. "You're my best friend. And we'll move as slow as you need to, Rain. I just want to be with you. You're worth waiting for."

That wonderful love and affection lit up his eyes, brighter than it had ever been before, and his joy radiated from him like brilliant sunlight.

We were absolutely ridiculous, standing there together. Had we been cartoon characters, tiny, red hearts would've been floating around us and popping like bubbles. But I definitely didn't care. Not at all. I was happy. I had something I didn't think I could ever have—a cheesy, heartfelt moment with someone I absolutely adored.

It was a perfect moment.

One that was worth living for.

B-SIDE

THE DREAMING MOON

A year or so later

Nothe stood on top of the giant flower on the strange moon-planet of Lolaar. It was a world of less-intense gravity, full of giants and worms that could reason. It was one of the more interesting planets they'd been to, but it certainly wasn't where he had expected to find Rain when he had slipped into his dreams. He smiled at the surprise. *Perhaps he does miss me after all.*

Rain was in his human form—the one he was most comfortable in—wearing a long-sleeved, button up shirt and jeans, and his very nice, black shoes. Other than these details, everything looked as it had the evening Nothe had yelled at him all those years ago. The sun was setting along the horizon, unfamiliar constellations were making their appearances, and the giant eye in the center of the flower was squinting, not very comfortable with having someone standing on it.

Dream Nothe morphed into his human form as he walked across the flower, making its eye close completely with a clear expression of annoyance. He wore a light brown coat and a The Cure tour T-shirt, with jeans and sneakers. He stood beside Rain, looking out into the distance.

He could feel Rain's emotions at the sight of him—surprise, confusion, regret, remorse, anger; these were all present, yes, but they were all overwhelmed by joy. Nothe let out a breath of relief he hadn't known he was holding.

Rain's blue eyes filled with tears. "You're actually here."

Nothe nodded. "Yep."

"How? Are you..." He hesitated, "Are you alive?"

Nothe looked away. He was alive, and really not happy about it. Though he couldn't remember everything about the Dimension of Light, he remembered feeling greater peace than he'd ever had, *ever*, in all of his life, and seeing his mother—her full self, happy, sane, the mother he'd always imagined. It hadn't at all been his choice to come back. There had been a voice—Thipka's voice—as though whispered in his ear, "You deserve a happy ending." Then he'd been yanked out of the Dimension of Light and thrown back into his body. It was all a very traumatic and painful experience. He'd *been* happy there. He'd died for a good cause. Was he really expected to die all over again?

And how in the universe had Thipka ripped him out of the Dimension of Light? He swore that no living thing had that kind of power. Frankly, it was a bit disturbing.

And now he had to suffer. There was a constant tightness in his chest where his heart sat, gripped in a dead hand and bleeding from the piece that had been torn from it. And he was alone. He had to be, because he couldn't witness seeing Emily in Rain's arms every day. The pain would be more than he could bear.

Well, okay. *Technically* he wasn't totally alone. He had spent every day with Thipka hunting for the entrance to the portal until they'd found it, which was why he was here. But he was more like hanging out with a butterfly holding a blowtorch.

He glanced away from Rain, choosing not to answer his question. Yet he knew Rain needed peace, so he said, "I'm okay, Rain. I'm okay."

Rain closed his eyes, tears running down his face with an expression of relief and sorrow. "Nothe, I'm so sorry. I didn't know—"

Nothe raised a hand to stop him. "I know, Rain. It's all right."

"And I'm so sorry for how I left things."

"I get it, Rain. I do." He moved on. "So you and Emily are married now, huh? Went with that tradition?"

Rain nodded cheerfully, but was clearly uncomfortable, afraid of causing him pain. "Yep. Been married for nearly a year. Our officiator was Paul—you know, from the club? Truly a saintly man. It's a good thing he's so saintly, too. Since he's such a *massive*, muscle man, no one would ever dare challenge his philosophies. He'd say, 'This is how things are,' and everyone would be like, 'Okay.'"

Rain was doing that thing where he felt awkward and didn't know what to say, so he just rambled. Nothe smiled. Man, he missed him.

After a moment, Rain said, "You know, I swore I saw you there. It was only a moment, but I just... I thought I saw you."

He had. But Nothe didn't tell him so.

Rain went on, "We uh, just found out she's expecting."

"Oh, yeah?"

"Yeah." He couldn't contain his joy, though he tried. "She's only about eight weeks along."

"Congratulations!"

"Thank you."

Nothe sensed an intense stab of nerves and fear there, underneath Rain's joy. He smiled and told him reassuringly, "I always knew you'd be a good dad."

Rain let out a slow breath. "I hope you're right. I hope that..." He stopped himself as more fear rose to the surface. Nothe knew he must've been worried about the future of the world, of his child. He wished he could tell Rain he was on it and not to worry, but he didn't want to make him any promises he wasn't sure he could keep, or give him the opportunity to sabotage his happiness over some sense of duty.

A sadness overcame Rain's demeanor. "I wish I could share all of this with you."

That meant more to Nothe than he dared say.

They stood there for a moment, watching the gas planet rise on the horizon, a silhouette in the atmosphere. Rain broke the silence. "I keep trying to think of the right words..."

Nothe's heart picked up the pace for a moment, a sudden rush of hope running through him that he expertly kept to himself.

"...but I am at a loss." A few more tears filled his eyes. "Nothe, everything I am, all that I have and have become... it is because of you. You kept my head above water, and I never once thanked you." He shook his head, upset at himself. "And now, you've given your life.... How do you thank someone who has given their life for yours? What words can you possibly say?"

Nothe really should've known better and shouldn't have felt disappointment at this, but he didn't know better, and did. At the same time, it was a very kind sentiment. He could feel the pure depth of Rain's sincerity and how unworthy he felt. It was ridiculous that he felt unworthy, but that was Rain for you.

"Stop it," Nothe said. "I made the choice. You deserve to be happy for once. You know, you spent your whole life trying to lift everybody else. You made so many people feel safe and happy, now it's your turn. That's what I decided. Actually, that's kind of why I'm here. I wanted to ask you..."

Rain waited patiently, perfectly. He truly was as close to perfection as any creature could get, especially without this human form he wore. Nothe wished he could've made him see it, that his perfection wasn't this. It was simply who he was. The real Rhaenmeinnah.

And for a moment, he considered changing his question. He desperately wanted to ask, *If I had told you how I felt back then, right here, on this ridiculously huge flower, would it have made a difference?*

But he didn't. Instead, Nothe asked what he'd always intended, "Are you happy?"

Rain didn't hesitate. "I am. I am, Nothe. Because of you. I didn't know such happiness existed."

Nothe's eyes filled with tears, over the joy at his dearest friend's happiness, and the pain of knowing it wasn't with him. He kept all of this perfectly hidden. "That is all I needed to know."

Nothe allowed himself to drift away, leaving Rain alone with his dreams.

ACKNOWLEDGMENTS

Let me just tell you—there is no way this book would've happened without these people. I would've given up a long time ago. Way back in my junior college days, in fact, if it wasn't for my professor, Jeff Carney, whose kind words gave me the courage to try. And again in my university days when, at a crucial time, my professor, Jason Olsen, gave me the courage to keep going. So did many of my fellow students in his class. I will never forget their kindness.

I have to thank Karen McKinney for introducing me to Kaci Morgan, my amazing partner-in-writing who put up with the terrible first drafts of this book. Kaci's thoughtful insight was absolutely *essential* in making this book everything I wanted it to be. I don't even want to think of what it might've turned into without it. Just... ew. Yikes.

I also have to thank Amanda Mills for her hard work, catching plot holes and helping me spell words that I really should've known how to spell. And Melissa Meibos for her hard work in helping me trim it down to a more reasonable size and for her encouragement. And thank you to Diana Rose, for reading and editing a scary, early draft and being so kind about it. And to Amanda Clement, for reading some the worst stuff I've ever written and remaining my friend, and for standing by me through the best and worst of times, whether living nearby or far away.

And thank heaven for Holli Anderson, for hearing out my pitch and for seeing potential in this story, and for never giving up on it. For her final edits and catching one last, glaring plot hole that I should've caught way back in like, the third or fourth draft. Man, she is awesome. Without her and Jason King, this book absolutely wouldn't exist. Thank you so much for giving it a chance. Seriously. *Thank you.*

And a mighty thank you to KrisAnn, Kenny, Jeff, Corey, Brook, Katie, Scott, Mom and Dad. These guys... seriously, they're so amazing. I have the best family in the whole wide world. Thank you so much for supporting me and for helping me keep my head above water. For the lessons that changed my life. For the laughs and stories told around the dinner table. And to the Rose family. I will never forget the 2019 family reunion. And to the Cox family. I will never forget all of their kind words. The support of these families has changed my life. I don't know how I got so lucky. And thank you to Anna Anderson, for believing in my storytelling abilities from the start.

And thank you to my dear friend, Rachael Pedersen Christensen, for letting me consult her repeatedly throughout the writing of this book, and for all the days spent at Barnes and Noble, judging books by their covers, discussing story ideas and life. For supporting me through the good and the very bad, and for helping me find light and hope through all the dark. I'd be lost without you.

Thank you to my little boys, Canon, Dexter and Oliver, for being wonderful and giving me reasons to keep trying. And of course, a mighty thank you to Paul, my teammate, my best friend, for putting up with me. For cheering me on through this whole thing. For standing up for me. For staying up late into the night to read and edit an early draft so I could send it into the publisher, and then telling everyone that they should read it. For giving me the best writing advice, ever, which was, "Hey, why don't you, like, stop editing the first chapter and write another one?" For his beautiful artwork on this cover. For just, being an incredible human. I have no idea how I got so lucky. And I'm so grateful to God for filling my broken heart with light, for guiding my feet and my words, for rushing to my rescue and never giving up on me. This book—and myself—would not be here without Him, and that's just the way it is.

So, basically, this journey has been made possible through the love and kindness of those around me. Never underestimate the power of kindness. It can absolutely change a person's life. It's certainly changed mine.

The end.

ABOUT THE AUTHOR

 Samantha J. Rose is a forever-student at Utah State University, who will one day have her Masters Degree in Psychology. She wrote her first novel in permanent marker on her sister's vanity chair when she was three-years-old. It wasn't well received.

She currently resides in the mountains, in a little house full of toys, where she's enjoying her happily ever after with her Prince Charming and three adorable, little bears.

This has been an
Immortal Production

CPSIA information can be obtained
at www.ICGtesting.com
Printed in the USA
FSHW010854300720
72028FS